ESCAPING TRANQUIL

ESCAPING TRANQUIL

A Story of Intrigue and Redemption

Book One of the Escaping Series

Deanna Hansen-Doying

This is a work of fiction. Names, characters, organizations, places, events, and incidents are either products of the author's imagination or are used fictitiously.

© 2020 by Deanna Hansen-Doying

ISBN: 978-1530509393 (paperback)
Library of Congress Control Number

Printed in the United States of America

For Jack

Dedicated to every person who has suffered at the hands of another
and found redemption in the grace of Jesus Christ.

PART ONE

Happiness is entirely a matter of choice.
—Jane Austen

THE BEGINNING
TRANQUIL TANDY

First shards of sunlight fractured the sky behind the Smoky Mountains as I turned onto Deer Spring Road. I ran hard, but my body, strong and willing, responded to the pace; sweat dripped from my temples, and my shirt felt damp.

The last half mile was the true test of endurance. Though running was my passion, the last sprint for home took discipline. It was my habit to push hard at the end of my usual five-mile run. Turning down the dirt road for home, I poured coal to the fire.

I leaned into the pace, arms pumping, palms open and relaxed, legs engaged, moving faster, harder, carried by momentum and exhilaration. My thighs stung with a familiar burn as I left the road and shot up the trail for home.

Running along the customary forest path, I watched morning sun flicker through autumn leaves, splashing dappled light across my face and chest. Before me lay the steep uphill charge toward the top of West Hill, where the path turned to a narrow corridor and the trees felt as close as a hug. Evergreens and hardwoods blended together here, and first light was nearly blocked by changing foliage.

September's nip in the air gave the forest's last bright leaves a kaleidoscope of color. Leaves still stubbornly clinging to branches made crackling noises in the breeze, while those that had fallen lay sodden on the path.

The air, cooler in the deep shade, nudged me to pick up the pace. My breath chugged plumes of steam as I leaned into the terrain, running on my toes, feet pushing away the path, hands reaching and pulling air past myself as if I were climbing a rope to the top. It made me feel powerful, every part of me engaged—invincible.

The path ended abruptly at the top of West Hill, where the descent into the valley zigzagged through boulders pushed down from a massive rockslide some fifty years before. I paused on the edge of the high embankment to catch my breath and brace for the downward run. A forty-foot drop at a 30 percent grade was nothing to be taken lightly. It seemed more like controlled falling than running.

I tucked my mother's necklace inside my T-shirt and looked out over the meadow, the river, and the big white house standing sentry over it all—a view that hadn't changed much in more than a hundred years.

On this side of the hill, sunlight edged into the valley later in the morning, the sky still a dark blue; a single star twinkled over the river.

This land had been homesteaded in the mid-1840s by my paternal great-grandparents—Cajun French from Louisiana. The homestead passed from generation to generation until it landed on my dad's shoulders, me being next in line. It felt like both a blessing and a curse—as heavy on my back as the boulders that lay before me.

Sweat dripped from my neck and trickled down my chest. I reached to wipe it away, my palm brushing across the thick, gnarled scar just below my right collarbone, the scar I made sure no one ever saw, not even my family. A wave of panic pinched somewhere in my brain then, and I felt my heart rate ramp up. Sickening memories gripped my gut like a vice as fear trumped reason. *Don't think, Quil. Run!*

I lurched forward, and in an instant, I was hopping through boulders in a familiar dry slalom pattern, heading for home. No time to think about anything other than staying upright. I landed in a two-footed, bone-jarring thud at the bottom of the hill, falling forward onto all fours. *Ugh!*

The meadow lay before me now like a thick carpet of green, and the grass felt soft under my palms. There had yet to be a killing frost, and the grass, still long and lush, moved gently with the softest breeze. *Get up. Don't stop.*

In the meadow, I ran toward the narrow, covered bridge that was once traveled by Civil War soldiers and wagons but was now limited to foot traffic. The river ran this way, and I raced it to the bridge. I often wondered how many more winters it would take before the bridge broke apart and the river claimed it.

In the distance, I could see the cove and the dock and my dad standing in his faithful, old bass boat. His arms were loaded with gear, but he still managed a wave. I waved back as I glanced at my watch. *Thirty seconds over, Quil. You're slipping, girl!*

My lungs felt it now. I leaned into the turn as the path connected to the gravel driveway, my heart pounding, lungs aching, muscles burning, pushing the last few yards for the front yard. *Just a hundred more feet! Move!*

At the lawn, I slowed abruptly from full speed to sloppy lope, arms and legs flapping as though I were tied together with loose string. Gasping, hands on hips, I walked around the yard, breathing deeply and shaking out my muscles. *Why do I do this?*

I glanced over at Daddy's boat, but I didn't see him now. It was seven o'clock, and we had a date to fish. *Probably getting coffee.*

"Paddy! Up and at 'em, buddy. *Allons attraper!* Let's go catching!" I called as I took the front stairs two at a time to the second floor, pulling off my sweatshirt on the fly.

"Patrick Henry, are you awake? *Mon petit homme?*" I called again as I pulled back the shower curtain and turned on the tap.

"Yes, ma'am," came a sleepy reply from the hallway.

"Okay, get dressed and have some cereal. I'll shower and meet you at the boat. Papa's waiting. *Depechez-vous!* Get a move on!"

CHAPTER 1

HENRY

Hackberry, Tennessee
September 1961

Henry had seen his daughter running for home, her smile, her vigorous wave, her dark brown hair tied into a thick ponytail and pulled through the back of a ball cap flapping in time with each stride. He loved to watch her run. Still a bit of a tomboy at twenty-five, she was a beauty nonetheless: round face, high cheekbones glowing with health, large hazel-green eyes with dark lashes, and full lips that could set firm when she was angry. She was stubborn and willful, but though he would never admit it, these traits were what Henry loved most about his daughter. *A woman needs to be strong to get by in a tough world—rèsiliente.* A crooked smile curved one side of his face as he remembered saying more than once how his daughter had a steel rod for a backbone.

Watching her run was almost lyrical—like a bird in flight or summer rain, fresh as a spring filly. He knew her life in New Orleans had somehow been a struggle. She had left Tulane, giving up a graduate studies internship, saying she was coming home to help Henry with the business. Henry knew better. Tranquil was *barachois*—calm on the surface yet teeming with life beneath. She held her cards close to the vest, but for Henry, the subtle signals of trouble others might not notice flashed long rays like a lighthouse beacon. He knew the signs: periods of silence, far-off gazes, and running. Always running. Something was very wrong, but he would have to wait for her to open up. There was no use pressing her. His hope was that she would land with both feet on the ground, because the truth was he did indeed need her and so did Paddy.

Henry watched her disappear inside the covered bridge and was turning to set down the fishing gear when the first twinge of pain nudged him. It caught him off guard, though it did not completely surprise him. He had been expecting it, knew it was hovering, but he had thought, or at least hoped, that it would come at night in his sleep like a silent thief.

He let go of the gear, and it clattered loudly against the bottom of the boat as he fumbled in his pocket for the small bottle of nitro tablets he carried with him nowadays.

His neck felt tight. Another sharp, penetrating pain seized his chest and caused him to gasp. He stood still, knees locked, right fist pressed tightly against the center of his chest, eyes blinking, throat contracting, trying to catch his breath. *Get out of the boat, Henry. Don't let them find you face down in the water.*

He reached for the edge of the dock, but before his hand touched cedar, another greater, more searing pain rocketed through his chest. Now both hands clutched the front of his woolen jacket as if the fabric were responsible for the assault on his heart. His jaws clenched tightly, eyes wide, face taut in a silent grimace, and he realized that he wasn't breathing. Sinking to his knees seemed like an act in slow motion. *This would have been better in bed, you old fool.* He slumped from his knees to his side and finally rolled onto his back. His arms relaxed. He ran a thumb across the back of his wedding band, and it turned easily on his finger, an involuntary comforting habit for nearly forty years.

Henry looked up at the indigo blue of the early morning sky. High above, a single star lingered stubbornly, unwilling to give in to dawn. Mourning doves cooed softly in the trees that rimmed the cove. *I love that sound.* Through his eyes, the sky turned pale, then velvety gray, then silvery white. The pulse echoing in his ears quieted, and an indescribable peace washed over him. *Is Glee there with you?* A passive smile slowly replaced the grimace, and his body conceded. Air escaped quietly from his lips. He closed his eyes. Henry Patrick Tandy had stepped into eternity a day before his fifty-eighth birthday.

I trotted down the back stairs into the kitchen and found Paddy dawdling over breakfast.

"You are such a poky," I teased, ruffling his hair and planting a wet kiss on his cheek.

"Yuck!" Paddy complained, wiping his cheek with his sleeve.

"I'm starved!" I shoved a banana and a blueberry bagel into my jacket pockets.

"*Affeme*," Paddy said, rubbing his tummy for effect.

"That's right, starved! You get another gold star!" I pulled a sheet of stickers from a kitchen drawer and pressed a gold star next to the day's date on the wall calendar. "Good job! *Bon travail!*"

I reached for the coffee pot. It was still full, untouched. *That's odd. Dad always has coffee first thing.* I poured two mugs of coffee, a dollop of heavy cream into one.

The phone rang its familiar two long rings and one short. I considered letting it ring. *It's only seven thirty.* But on the third set, I put down the mugs and picked up the receiver.

"Tandy Fish Camp. Oh, hi, Libby."

"Hi, Mrs. Dawson. Hi, Mrs. Watson," Libby sang out in a sugary voice.

There were two distinct clicks.

"I hate it when you do that, Libby."

"Hey, what's the fun having a party line if you can't torment the parties? It's not my fault you live in the weeds. Got a minute?"

"I am headed out to fish with Dad and Paddy. What's up?"

"Well, aren't we a bit short this morning?" Libby huffed.

"Just hungry. I'll call you later. I promise."

"Okay. I want to tell you about my new guy."

"What happened to the old guy?"

"Married. Wouldn't you just know it?"

"Gee, Libby. Maybe you should come up for air."

"And be a recluse like you?"

"Where are you? I'll call you later. Oh, and by the way. Did I leave my fiddle in the trunk of your car Saturday night?"

"I'll check. I'm at the diner. Call me after the lunch rush. Ta-ta."

Libby and I had been best friends since grammar school. As different as two girls could be in looks and personality, somehow we meshed like one hand laced into the other. Libby was fine boned with girly curves. She had pale blonde curly hair and lively blue eyes. If she had been born in California, Libby would have been a classic beach bunny. She, unlike me, had always been an effortless flirt—a natural guy magnet. She played the dumb blonde role to its limit—dumb like a fox—but as far as I knew, Libby had no aspirations to do anything with her life other than run her parent's diner and collect suitors, whereas I had dreamed of a life on the coast. Becoming a marine biologist had been my only focus, and I followed it with laser beam aim. A scholarship to Tulane had fallen right in line with my plans.

"I'm going to the boat, Paddy. You better get a move on or we'll leave without you, okay?"

"Got it." Paddy grinned through a mouthful of cereal, milk dripping from his bottom lip.

I gave my brother an eye roll, pushed the kitchen door open with my hip, and stepped out into the wakening day. I looked out at the cove, my eyes drinking in the early morning as I listened to the doves cooing. I could see the boat at the dock but still did not see Daddy's familiar outline.

"Papa!" I called as I sauntered toward the river. There wasn't a breath of wind now. *The fishing will be good.*

"Papa!" I called again, scanning the shoreline. "*Ou` estes-vous?*" *Where is he anyway? He was just out here twenty minutes ago.* I stepped up onto the dock.

"Papa, where are…Oh, there you are!" I could see him lying in the boat. "Get up, you old goldbricker! Let's get a move on!" I teased, strolling toward the boat. He didn't move.

"*Papa, ce n'est pas drole?* Not funny at all." Not a sound. No movement. The moment felt breathless.

"Papa!" I cried, dropping the mugs and stumbling down into the boat, my heart in my throat. *No, not yet. Please, not yet.*

I knelt, lifted my father's head and shoulders onto my lap, pulled off my gloves, and pushed two fingers against the side of his neck. His skin felt damp and cool. His lips were blue. There was no pulse, no breath. I pulled open his jacket and shoved my ear to his chest. There was only the sound of my own rapid breathing. I shook him and begged him not to be dead even though I knew he was.

I laid a hand against his cheek and looked at his peaceful face, the curve of his bushy brows, the long, dark lashes, the deep laugh lines that grooved the corners of his mouth. I held his hand and traced the scars and calluses that spoke of hard work. *This isn't real. I'll wake up, and it will only be another bad dream.*

I held him, listening to the coffee from the spilled mugs drip through the slats of the dock and into the river.

I had known for more than a year that my father's heart was failing, and though I tried to prepare myself, I could not. I had hopefully imagined when this moment came he would look asleep, peacefully asleep, but he didn't look asleep now—he looked gone. *Oh, Papa, I'm so sorry you had to do this alone.*

When Mama had been killed in a car accident five years earlier, I had never seen her body. In my mind's eye, she looked the same as my last memory of her cooking breakfast the morning of the crash, happy and laughing and kidding Daddy about a bad haircut.

Slowly, I felt the numbing reality saturate the edges of my mind. Daddy was really gone. Tears clouded my eyes as I held him close. I just wanted to hold him, keep him with me, but I knew he was no longer there in his tired body. He had shrugged it off like an old coat.

The smack of the screen door slapping closed shook me to my senses. Paddy was galloping toward me on his pretend horse, his honey-blond hair flopping up and down as he raced along. My little brother wore a perpetual grin, his brown eyes bright and excited about every detail of life, but his flat face and slanted eyes betrayed Down syndrome, and at ten, Paddy still played like a six-year-old.

I laid Daddy's hand across his chest and, wiping my eyes with the heels of my hands, quickly scrambled out of the boat, hurrying to intercept Paddy.

CHAPTER 2

FLETCHER

Key West, Florida
August 1961

The remains of the Key West evening sun made their descent as if slipping silently into the ocean, and the gentle lapping of waves against the beach made a sound like hissing. It was hot, a typical August evening with a hint of hurricane in the air, tropical sky ablaze with sunset and distant angry clouds. The air tasted of salt, and the water smelled of seaweed.

Pickford Cottage had been in Fletcher's family since the 1880s—a solid limestone block structure, whitewashed and stubbornly facing the sea as if daring the elements to an argument. Large for a beach getaway, it sprawled along a wide covered porch. The ceilings were tall, with walls of double door windows on all sides of the cottage to let the sea breeze wander through. The rooms were open and spacious, each with a huge wicker fan slowly turning—quintessential Key West living.

The cottage had taken a beating in the 1935 Labor Day hurricane that had killed hundreds and demolished Flagler's railroad yet remained like a defiant child refusing to budge. It was the one place Fletcher felt completely comfortable, able to be himself. He had often considered moving here permanently—maybe changing his looks or his name to something innocuous—start over.

He pushed back in the teak armchair and balanced his bare feet on the bungalow's whitewashed deck railing, tossing bits of shrimp to the stray cat that lived under the porch.

When he was a boy, there had been a calico cat living in the same place. She had had a litter of kittens, and Fletcher had crawled under the porch every day to leave tender morsels of food for first the mother and then the babies. Only two kittens had survived infancy: a solid black one he named Louis and an orange tabby he called Cheese. He had begged to take them home to Miami when the mama cat weaned them, but his stepmother was adamant, and in the end, his father had drowned them in the same place that now held Fletcher's gaze. A renewed wave of acrid loathing washed over him as the memory flashed before him.

Fletcher looked away to change the subject. He considered his drink, holding it up, turning it slowly, watching the sunset's changing colors through ice and amber liquid, colors flickering like firelight. The ice rolling in his glass made a tinkling noise like crystal wind chimes, and Fletcher let out a throaty, satisfied sigh.

In the background, Fletcher's weekend date, a woman he had met recently in Miami and invited to go scuba diving, was packing angrily.

"You're crazy!" she shouted from the bedroom as she tossed a suitcase onto the bed, stuffing it with clothes. "What was the one food I told you I disliked? Oysters, that's right, oysters! So where did we go for lunch? Unbelievable! Are you listening to me?" She slammed the closet door for punctuation and waited for a response, fists jammed into hips.

Fletcher calmly sipped his drink and said, "You know, if you look straight out past that spit of land on the right, Cuba is a mere eighty-two miles away."

The woman threw her cosmetic bag and a wet swimsuit into the suitcase.

"Oh, and what about all that *playing* in the pool?" She made a couple of air quotation marks with her fingers. "Perhaps you forgot I couldn't breathe underwater!"

Fletcher said nothing, closed his eyes, and forced his teeth together, being conscious not to grind them. Her voice reminded him of a screeching train sliding on metal tracks, and his palm went automatically to the scar at his temple, pressing hard. *She sounds like Clarice.* Involuntary images of Clarice pushed to the front of his brain, and old hatreds oozed into the back of his throat. He filled his mouth with liquor and swallowed, but the acid taste remained.

"Are you *actually* going to sit there and pretend that you didn't nearly *drown* me today?" The woman's voice was shrill and incredulous. "And, oh, by the way, there's a hurricane coming! Stay if you like, but I am getting out of here while I still can," she snarled at Fletcher's back. "Don't jump up and offer to take me to the airport. I've called a cab."

"Hemingway did his best work here." Fletcher's voice was flat. A mosquito buzzed past his ear and landed on his wrist, the business end driving home. He did not flinch, patiently letting the mosquito fill his belly before the slap flattened it, smearing bug and blood across his hand.

The woman railed on. "Oh, shut up. What was I thinking coming all the way down here with some guy I hardly knew?" she barked, zipping the suitcase closed and yanking it to the floor. "I'm gone." She slid into her sandals, quickly fashioning her damp hair into a careless twist. Picking up her bag, she muttered, "What a jerk!"

Fletcher set his drink down on the glass side table so quietly it hardly made a sound and stood. "For whom the bell tolls," he whispered.

His left eye involuntarily winked at the setting sun now disappearing quickly into the Gulf. He smoothed his pale blue linen shirt with his palms and combed back his sun-streaked hair with his fingers in a controlled, deliberate motion.

"I am out of here," she repeated as she stomped toward the door and reached for the latch.

"I think not." His voice was menacing and must have seemed startlingly close.

Fletcher lunged as she turned to face him. His hands were instantly around her throat as he slammed her body against the door.

He could see she wanted to scream but could not. His thumbs pressed expertly against her windpipe, and her eyes bulged with terror.

The power of the moment felt intoxicating to Fletcher. A rush of desire rose up from somewhere deeply hidden, and his eyes closed slowly as his thumbs pressed harder against her throat.

His cheek was against hers now, and he whispered, "A jerk, did you say? I think you're going to want to find another definition for me."

She struggled, grasping at his hands, sliding toward the floor. Her mouth filled with saliva, and her knees gave way.

Fletcher suddenly let go and stepped back, watching her fall. She was choking and gasping for breath, rubbing her neck, fear wide across her face, one hand outstretched as if it might protect her.

"No more?" Fletcher asked, his voice sugary, his gray eyes dark, pupils round with pleasure. His left eye winked several times, and then he kicked her hard in the belly as she tried to get up.

He grabbed the front of her dress as she fell backward and pulled her onto her feet. His hand squeezed her face, and he kissed her hard on the mouth. She struggled, but one hard blow to her face and she collapsed unconscious into a heap.

He stood back and took a deep quieting breath. "Now that's better."

Out on the deck, Fletcher finished his drink and said good night to the sun as the sea swallowed it in one last gulp. The breeze had turned gusty, the coming hurricane becoming evident. He picked up the phone and called the caretaker to close up the house.

As he was packing his bag, the woman moaned, pushing herself onto an elbow, her expression frightened and confused.

Fletcher squatted in front of her to get a good look at her face. Her eye and lip were beginning to swell, and the red fingerprints on her neck were vivid. There were sticky trickles of blood at her nose and mouth.

He pulled out his handkerchief and dabbed at the bloody spots. She recoiled.

"Don't worry. We're done here," Fletcher said evenly, folding the handkerchief and sliding it into the back pocket of his khaki slacks as he stood.

He picked up his bag and car keys. "Oh, and by the way, I wouldn't talk with anyone about our weekend together. I don't think you ever want to see me again."

Fletcher quietly closed the door behind him and left the bungalow without a backward glance.

CHAPTER 3
THE LETTER

Hackberry, Tennessee
September 1961

I was born the much-loved only child of only children.
My mother was of Nova Scotian Acadian descent, and my father had deep Cajun Acadian roots. They both spoke French at home, but it was not the perfect Parisian French I learned in school. It was a kind of musical language that rolled and swayed with humor and emotion. Both Acadian and Cajun dialects blended into one easily understood song in our home, and I learned to speak their French, flipping between Tennessee English and Acadian/Cajun French without missing a beat.

I said that I was an only child, because for my first sixteen years I *was* before Paddy came along. Mama's pregnancy was such a surprise to everyone, and there were the usual number of jabs about spacing her children out.

I was more than a little ashamed to say that at the first sight of my baby brother, I thought he was some sort of freak, but even as an infant, Paddy had an infectious smile and sweet giggle, and soon I, along with everyone else, was smitten. Now it was only the two of us, Paddy and me, with this great house and considerable homestead acreage.

This place—the fish camp and the land—was essentially timeless. Political unrest and erratic changes in cultural thinking or economic upheavals all seemed to pass Hackberry by like distant thunder. Even the current rumblings in Southeast Asia or the Cold War with the Russians weren't often press worthy. Nothing much affected this tiny dot on the global map. It was more spectator than participant to history in the making, and I liked it that way.

A chilly wind came in from the northwest at around noon, and I trotted up to close all the rooms I did not need to heat.

At the top of the main staircase, I hesitated and looked out the huge paned window at the giant oak in the front yard, the rope swing swaying in the wind.

Walking down the wide hallway, I paused at each room and closed the door—Grand-mère and Grand-père's room, Good-daddy and Gigi's room, Mama and Daddy's room.

The large sitting room at the end of the hall looked out over the river. I slowly circled the room, running a palm over the fireplace mantle, the ancient upright piano, the bookshelves, the plush fabric sofas. This big old house had voices resonating everywhere, in every room, at every time of day. It smelled of Good-daddy's cherry pipe tobacco, lemon-waxed floors, and Daddy's leather boot soap. Even empty, our home was filled with bygone days: music and singing and dancing and laughter—lots of laughter. I learned to play the fiddle in this room, and Paddy had learned to step dance.

Standing at the window watching the river roll by was like watching time move along its course to a destination yet to be decided. As Grand-père would often say, *"Temps sans fin, Amen."* Time without end.

But I stopped believing in time without end long ago, the truth being I never really believed in the first place, though I pretended to. I was not a confused child or a rebellious teenager. I just didn't get religion on any level.

I would often think, *There simply can't be anything more than this life. Why would there be? What proof do we have that we are made up of anything more than the here and now?*

I wished I could have Paddy's childlike beliefs in God and life eternal—unquestioning belief, deeply cemented in some sort of spiritual knowing far beyond what he should be able to comprehend. I couldn't, or wouldn't, believe without solid evidence. Facts, I was all about facts. I was a scientist, after all. *Indication without verification is not substance.*

Though my mother used to tell me, "*La foi est la substance des choses qu'on espère, la preuve des réalités qu'on ne voit pas...*faith is the substance of things hoped for, the evidence of things not seen..." I wasn't buying it in French *or* English.

The teapot screeched urgently from downstairs, and it made me jump. "All right, all right already!" I shouted back.

I left the room and hurried down the back stairs to the kitchen for the comfort of a steaming cup of Earl Grey and a fistful of freshly baked macaroons. *Less thinking and more eating.*

As I poured boiling water over fragrant tea, I remembered with a laugh how I once complained about how noisy the teapot was, and Good Daddy had said wryly, "Well, Quil, you would scream too if somebody poured boiling water up *your* nose."

With Paddy gone to Bobby Brently's house for the night, I had the rest of the afternoon to myself to sort through some of Daddy's papers and make decisions that could not be put off.

Sitting at Daddy's desk in the den, the place my father and grandfathers sometimes gathered to talk about business or trade stories, I sipped my tea and munched on cookies. I swiveled from side to side in the large leather chair and absently slid the gold charm on Mama's necklace in the same motion—back and forth—lost again in memories.

"What are they doing in there?" I had once asked Grand-mère.

"*Ces sont les hommes parlent. Ne faites pas l'esprit,*" was her reply. It is only men talk. Pay them no mind.

"But what do they talk about?"

"Nothing mostly." Grand-mère had chuckled.

I leaned back and gazed out the bay window overlooking the vast apple orchards healthy with varieties Grand-père had perfected through years of cross-pollination and grafts. Pears, peaches, and plums had come later, but they, too, flourished under his skillful hand.

In spring, beautiful fragrant blossoms stretched for nearly a half mile wide and a mile long; in summer, the lush foliage bore shade and sheltered birds; fall brought luscious fruit and the busy harvest. Now, with winter coming on, the trees stood nearly bare, ready for sleep.

The phone jingled loudly from the kitchen—two long rings and one short. *That's us.*

"Tandys, Quil speaking."

"Hey, girl."

"Hi, Danny."

"Mom wants to know if you'll come by for dinner tonight. She thinks you shouldn't be alone. I don't either, and besides, I'm pretty sure she's got chicken and dumplings on the stove."

"She's sweet. Tell her thanks for the invitation, but I'm not good company right now."

"Good enough company for us. How about I pick you up?"

There was a long pause. The thought of Betty Owens's cooking and the warmth of a loving family on a chilly night was tempting, but I had things to do.

"No, Danny, really, I can't, I've got stuff to do."

"Okay, but call me if you need to talk. I'm here…you know that."

"I do. Good night, Danny-boy."

Yes, Danny had always been there for me, even when it was difficult. Back in the den I pulled out the file Daddy had made with all the information and documents I would need. I opened it and had good intentions but couldn't stay focused. Instead, I poured another cup of tea and sat on the edge of the desk to drink it. My eyes traveled from the orchards to the cabins laid out like little log soldiers along the river near the cove and marina. Life had been good—the best.

Before I knew it, a fiery sunset seared the river ablaze in waves of gold and magenta and put an end to my daydreaming. I touched the scar on my chest for morbid inspiration, and sucking in a deep breath, I took a sheet of writing paper from the cubby on the desk and began to write…

September 30, 1961

Cher' Papa,
I have tried my best to hide my past, but you and I both know that all is not right with me…

Between fits and starts, I poured out angry pain onto paper until I felt familiar panic closing in again and left the desk for a brisk turn around the wraparound porch. *Pull yourself together, Quil. It doesn't own you. Just say it and let go of it. You should have told him. Now bury it deep in the ground.*

I remembered thinking then about the oddity of violence in an upbringing devoid of it. Having never experienced brutality on any level beyond the childhood single swat on the behind to get my attention, I couldn't recognize it fully even when it was staring me in the face. It was as if I felt something, a natural instinct. But looking at it close up was a curious glance at something hidden behind a milky curtain rather than a fight-or-flight sensation. I should have known better, but I hadn't.

More than an hour later I folded the letter and slid it into an envelope. I'd said it all on paper—all I could not say out loud.

That night I went alone to the funeral home. One last look, one last touch—the final goodbye had come.

"Papa, please forgive me."

I placed the letter in the casket and closed the lid. *No tears, not now, not ever again.*

Something shut in me at that moment. I felt it—a toughness, a shield, a veneer of steel covered my spirit.

CHAPTER 4
DICKIE BLEVINS

Baton Rouge, Louisiana
September 1961

Henry Tandy had been well known and well loved, and his obituary ran in several newspapers, including one in St. Bernard Parish, Louisiana, from where his family hailed, as well as the papers in Lafayette and Baton Rouge.

It was in the Baton Rouge newspaper that a private investigator by the name of Dickie Blevins happened to take notice over his morning coffee. *Henry Tandy. Why does that ring a bell?*

Dickie Blevins had an uncanny memory for detail, and something about the name nagged at him. *Tandy is not an uncommon name. What's special?* The name ate away at him until finally it drove him to the storeroom. He spent most of the morning in his basement digging through old files but found nothing.

Later at lunch it hit him. *Tandy! That's right! Baton Rouge, 1935, no, '36! Tandy was attached to that admitting clerk, no, the nurse. Yes, the nurse!*

Dickie hurried back to the storeroom where boxes of old case files were stored, many of them still unsolved. "Nineteen thirty-four, thirty-five, thirty-six," Dickie counted out loud as he thumbed through dead case files—Rawley, Stanley, Tandy. "There you are," he breathed. Of course, that hush-hush adoption case! Arsenault was the delivery nurse, and Tandy was related.

Back at his desk Blevins pushed his lunch aside and flopped open the dusty file. "Oh, Dickie, you've finally hit the jackpot, buddy! There's going to be some big money in this one!" he said aloud, taking a long gulp of his RC.

Dickie had taken money on this case for years—regular money, though never doing much to earn his fees. Month after month he had sent padded invoices along with bogus leads and search information and, in turn, received a check until his disgruntled client had either given up or moved on. He was an expert at working both sides of the fence.

In Clarice Pickford's case, it was also a roulette game. She was paying to have him find the baby she had left behind in Baton Rouge, while her husband, Charles Pickford, was paying for the information to stay hidden, and he was paying a lot more than she. No matter to Dickie. Ethics weren't his strong suit; money was money no matter where it came from.

It had been more than fifteen years since he had spoken to Clarice Pickford, but she had been one of his more profitable clients—so eager to find her child and, as far as Dickie knew, had never succeeded.

Dickie knew Charles Pickford had died of a self-inflicted gunshot to the heart in 1951, and therefore the money had dried up, but now this case might just get solved, and it could mean some big bucks. *Just think how grateful she is going to be!*

He surveyed the contents of the file, the hospital records, the employee statements, and the administrator's interview.

Since Clarice Pickford had been admitted to the hospital under an assumed name to protect her privacy, and since she had abandoned her baby at the hospital without signing a single document, technically neither she nor her child had ever been at Mercy General Hospital in Baton Rouge. It was a dead-end case from the beginning, but Dickie had cleverly insisted there was always hope and therefore strung Clarice along. For five years, she paid invoice after invoice without result, and Dickie often wondered why she hadn't hired another investigator.

He leaned back in his chair, plopped his feet onto the desk like the big shot he wasn't, and with the phone resting on his chest dialed Clarice Pickford's number. He got a disconnect recording. He called information and was told that Clarice Pickford's calls were being taken at another number in Miami.

Miami, Florida
September 1961

The phone rang in Fletcher Pickford's offices, and his assistant, Emily Wallace, answered.

"Pickford Financial Group, Emily speaking."

"I'd like to speak with Clarice Pickford?"

"Who's calling, please?"

"Her attorney."

"One moment."

Emily buzzed Fletcher's phone. "There is someone on line two asking for Mrs. Pickford. He says he is her attorney."

"Did you get his name?"

"No, sir, I'm sorry, I didn't. I supposed it was a family matter."

The line on hold was blinking red, and Fletcher contemplated whether to answer it. Clarice was dead, and she no longer had an attorney who wouldn't call him directly. This call was either a prank or trouble. *Better take this head-on.*

"Yes." Fletcher's voice had an edge.

"I was calling for Clarice Pickford."

"This is Fletcher Pickford. Clarice was my stepmother."

"Was?"

"Yes. She passed away this summer. Who's calling?" His voice was stiff.

"Oh…well…just an old friend trying to get in touch," Dickie stammered.

"I thought you said you were her attorney. And your name is?"

The line went dead.

Suspicious by nature, especially when it came to his stepmother, Fletcher mulled the short conversation over before buzzing his assistant.

"Emily, can you see if the system can recall that last number?"

"I can try, but I'm almost certain I can't. I'll only be able to get the area code."

Just the mention of Clarice's name made Fletcher angry; his neck felt hot, and as usual when he was annoyed, his facial tic flared up. It wasn't quite a twitch, more like an uncontrolled winking when he was stressed.

Fletcher set his jaw and grimaced. He hated his father, and he hated Clarice, but his animosity for Clarice was deeper; it had history and longevity. Though she had never directly abused him, she had allowed it, and to Fletcher, her indifference was worse than his father's cruelty.

He sat for a moment contemplating the phone call, tracing a circle over and over in his palm with an index finger.

The tone of the call troubled him, but then, Fletcher had been on edge ever since the reading of Clarice's will two months prior. *"...and to the child, Baby Jane Doe, born to me on October 12, 1936, I leave the entirety of my estate."*

Certainly, Fletcher had not been surprised that Clarice kept secrets, but he had never guessed that during her marriage to his father, his stepmother had given birth to and then given up a baby girl. That Clarice would will her estate to a child she had never known was at first outrageous, then infuriating. Fortunately for Fletcher, there had been no provision outlined in the will to search out or notify Baby Jane Doe of her windfall. According to Dade County law, the named heir would only receive the money if she stepped forward to claim it and could prove she was indeed Clarice's daughter beyond a reasonable doubt. Fletcher knew all he had to do was let the seven-year waiting period tick by, at the end of which he would be named the only surviving heir by default.

His eye was beginning to bother him. Sometimes rubbing his forehead was soothing, but not even that was helping this time. Fletcher felt the smolder of well-fostered hatred churn in his belly.

Pushing back from his desk, he walked over to the window and stared absently over downtown Miami. This had been his father's office and his grandfather's office before him. The Pickford wealth was old money, wealth established in the banking business almost a century ago, one so stable it had survived the October 1929 stock market crash. But thanks to Fletcher's father, Charles, most of it had been squandered during the military contract boom of WWII and then the recession following.

Fletcher, too, had fumbled the ball. The truth was Fletcher lacked the people skills to succeed in a business that required a client's complete trust, and even in a good economy, Pickford Financial showed little growth. In fact, he was secretly in personal financial trouble. Thank goodness the other associates working under him were productive. He needed control of Clarice's money, but all the legal juggling he had performed to date had failed to achieve results in his favor.

"Emily, cancel all my appointments for the rest of today," he growled as he passed her desk and left the building.

Emily acknowledged with a nod. She knew better than to speak when her boss barked orders this way. She both feared and was fascinated by him.

Certainly, Fletcher could be considered attractive in the same way any other predator, like a sleek panther or a powerful bird of prey, might be admired. A tanned, firm body and sun-streaked hair in contrast to cool gray eyes gave Fletcher a beautiful yet dangerous appeal.

He was a well-bred, well-educated Southern man with impeccable manners, but there were icy edges around his personality, and he could easily be described as unpredictable.

Women were drawn to Fletcher, but no relationship ever lasted. To him, frilly girls were a waste of time. He was attracted to strong, smart women and in many ways liked the challenge a confident woman presented. He liked their ability to take risks, ask for what they wanted, but they were no match for his vicious temper. Let any woman be the slightest bit contrary or display a glimmer of independence not in line with his own opinions, and they were in for trouble.

Emily knew all this and a lot more. She knew because she made it her business to know. It might be useful someday.

Fletcher had left a trail of brutalized women, all of whom were kept silent by money or other influences. He had never paid a personal price for his actions. He did what, and how, he pleased.

There had been the girl in high school, his prom date, who laughed at him when he tried to kiss her. He had shoved her, torn her dress, ripped the corsage he had given her from her wrist, and crushed it under his heel. Then he had kissed her hard, bruising her lip. Her father had complained to Clarice, but no further action was taken.

There had been the woman in the Bahamas whom he had met on a holiday while he was in college. They had spent several days together, entertaining one another, but in the end had argued, and he had beaten her badly. It had taken eleven stitches to close the gash on her forehead, but she told the emergency room doctor she had fallen. Fletcher had threatened to kill her if she pressed charges, and she had believed him.

The woman from Miami had been a messier affair, too close to home. It had taken money to silence her.

Fletcher's rage was deep seeded and had begun to manifest itself in his early teens. Never one to directly confront those who hurt him, he was more apt to get even through more indirect ways. He became adept at stealth, malicious vandalism, and eventually clever breaking and entering just to see if he could get away with it, in the process often stealing items that had no value to anyone other than the owner—family photos, one expensive shoe, eye glasses. But as he matured, his rage took another course—one far more dangerous.

Though he sometimes fantasized about a lasting relationship with the perfect woman, the truth was women made him feel weak and vulnerable, and every attempt at establishing some sort of connection ended badly. The pattern was always the same. In the beginning, he masked his true character with charm and good manners, but this shallow camouflage wore through quickly. To him, being with a woman was all about control.

Fletcher's life, in every way a lie, had marched along unchecked for all his thirty-one years. Since he was never challenged, it never occurred to him that he ever would be. He got what he wanted when and how he wanted it. Rules and laws, right and wrong, they were made for others and had nothing to do with him. He felt invincible.

CHAPTER 5

THE FUNERAL

Hackberry, Tennessee
October 1961

As I fastened the delicate pearl buttons on the pale pink cashmere cardigan that had been Mama's favorite, I caught the faintest hint of my mother's perfume and pressed the sleeve to my face, breathing in deeply. It smelled like comfort.

My mother, Christmas Glee Bouchier, had been the long-awaited child born on the day for which she was named. Though she was always called Glee, "Christmas" still hovered like a poor pun, and she hated it. Yet she and Daddy had done the same to their own daughter. I supposed they may have chosen the name Tranquil hoping for a girl who would live up to the moniker, not the tomboy I turned out to be. At least my name had been shortened to Quil, for which I was grateful.

I slid the zipper closed on a light gray straight skirt and slipped into a pair of dark gray pumps. *No black for me. I'm sick of burying everybody I love, and I will not respect death today or any other.*

"Paddy, are you getting ready? *Mon petit ami.* Do you hear me?" I called down the hall while fashioning my hair into a neat chignon.

"*Oui soeur.*"

"Yes, that's right! Good job, Paddy. Give yourself another star."

"*Oui chère sœur!*"

29

"Now you're showing off. Get dressed!"

I put on the pearl earrings that Daddy had given me on my eighteenth birthday and closed my eyes, thinking of Dad on that day lighting the candles on my cake and singing in his rich baritone voice. *Don't think so much, Quil.*

A hard look in the mirror showed the stress of the week, but I decided on no makeup other than the slightest sheen of pink on my lips. *Don't fuss. Not today.*

I waited in the kitchen for Paddy to dress and Danny to arrive, arms pressed across my chest in a self-embrace, looking out the kitchen window at the river rushing toward the reservoir thirty miles downstream. It was a glorious red apple–crisp morning, and overhead geese honked loudly as they passed, moving south for the winter. *I wish I were going with you.* The thought of my first Tennessee mountain winter in six years sent a little shiver up my spine.

The house was filled with flowers, the air thick with their fragrance, and quiet except for the sounds of Paddy upstairs in his room, the consistent ticking of the kitchen clock, and the persistent drip at the sink faucet. Home without my dad felt as hollow as an empty well—as if life itself had been removed.

I glanced around the new kitchen we had painstakingly refinished over the summer: the cabinet doors painted a glossy vanilla white, decorated with pulls made from river stone collected along the shallows of the upper river. It made me smile thinking of the three of us searching for and choosing each stone, none alike in shape or color. *What fun that day had been.*

The kitchen walls were painted a creamy butter yellow, warm as yeast bread rising in a covered bowl; the battered kitchen table was marred with decades of memories; and the doorjamb had been left unpainted, which marked every year of growth for me and Paddy. They spoke of all the good years. I ran my hand over the cool sea-blue ceramic tiles on the countertop, absently tracing the grout with a pinkie.

The past week had been a flurry of details and conversation. Visits and phone calls had filled every moment of every day, and then there was Paddy, who looked for Henry everywhere, unable to grasp the idea of death.

When Mama was killed, he was barely four years of age, and he missed her, but he still had Papa and Grand-mère Bouchier and Good-daddy Tandy. Now there was nobody left but me, and he seemed on the verge of breakdown. It was Danny who had finally put it all into language and an example Paddy understood.

There had been discussion about an open casket, and for Paddy's sake, it would remain closed. *Thank goodness for Danny.*

The nighttime, the silence and the knowing how life would be, the sleeplessness and the choking grief that wore through the thin veneer of strength I held up like a shield. I was exhausted.

I had never believed in a heaven or hell or life beyond the grave. There was no silver lining to life's passing, no promise of reunion. My mother, father, and beloved grandparents all gone in ten years' time; what remained of one hundred years of Tandys and Bouchiers lay deep underground. *Dead. Gone. Terminé.*

I heard the sound of hard shoes on wood floors and then a moment of silence before Paddy squealed, "Here I come to save the day!" sliding bottom first down the banister, landing with a thud on the kitchen floor, and collapsing in laughter. He had on his Mighty Mouse costume, the one he had insisted on having for Halloween last year.

"Did I miss something? Are we early or late?" I smiled.

"I'm all dressed up for Daddy. He said I was the best Mighty Mouse there ever was." Paddy spun around, his cape unfurling as he turned, his mop of blond hair, pulled by gravity, standing straight out from his head. He was a blur of blond hair and bright red, blue, and yellow nylon fabric.

Paddy's body had the classic lines of a Down child. To some, he might appear odd looking, but to me, he was beautiful, and I could not imagine life without him. Who could help but find his ability to enjoy every little bit of each day irresistible?

High-functioning Down syndrome—a mild case, the doctors had told us. Indeed, Paddy seemed to grasp concepts easily, but we had been warned that these abilities would be stunted as he aged. His childlike joy might turn to frustration.

"Well, carpe diem, buddy," I said when he stopped spinning.

"Carp's a fish!"

I squatted to eye level in front of him. "Listen, I know you love Mighty Mouse and you want Daddy to be proud of you, but maybe it would be more respectful to wear something you would wear to church."

"It's Tuesday." He raised his hands palms up as if to say, "What's the deal?"

"I know, but we are going to church. Remember? Today's the day we are going to talk about all the good things Daddy did." My throat suddenly felt tight, and my eyes burned.

"If it's about good things, then why are you sad?"

"I miss Daddy, is all. You miss him too, right? Well, I'll just be sad for a moment or two while you run upstairs and change. Go on. Danny will be here any minute to pick us up."

There was still so much I didn't know about raising a boy like my brother. Every day was a learning experience. "Just be consistent and he will be too," Daddy had told me time and again. I squeezed the bridge of my nose, pushing back the tears that threaten to overtake me. *Don't cry.*

Gravel popped under tires out in the driveway.

"Danny es ici!" I called up the staircase. "Danny's here! Let's go. Do you hear me?" I said, picking up my fiddle case. *"Vous m'entendez?"*

Paddy and I walked into the church we had attended all our lives, now packed with people who had loved and admired my father. People stood along the sides and back of the church and in the balcony. It sounded busy with whispers, but as we entered, the crowd fell silent.

I stiffened and looked straight ahead as we moved down the center aisle. Paddy, dressed in a white shirt and blue slacks, smiled and waved to all his neighbors and friends already seated for the funeral. Most smiled back; some discreetly waved. A pleasant murmur rolled through the gathering as Paddy breezed past.

It felt unbearably conspicuous to me—Paddy and I sitting in the front row alone. *The word "grief" might as well be tattooed on the back of my neck.* But I was an expert at keeping my feelings to myself. I checked my posture, got my breathing under control, and looked straight ahead.

The service dragged along as people spoke about Henry's kindness and goodness but in the saddest of words. To me, it all seemed a blur—the music and words. In the years to come, the only part of the service I would vividly remember would be the casket rolling past me to a waiting hearse and the feel of polished mahogany sliding under my outstretched palm as it passed.

Finally, it was up to me to bring the service to a close. I stood and walked forward with my fiddle. I took several moments to gather my thoughts, then lowered myself slowly onto the chair waiting there. I looked at my brother. Mama was written all over him. *Quil, how are you going to live an example for him?*

There was a long, uncomfortable pause before I could speak. The room seemed to move, and for the tiniest instant, I lost focus. I could feel myself lean forward, and I thought I might faint. Danny stood and took a step toward me, but I motioned I was all right. I took a deep breath and swallowed hard.

"I know I was supposed to play a favorite hymn of Dad's today, but I think I should play his favorite song instead. Y'all know my dad was all about living and making the most of every moment. I think we should end this service today with joy rather than sadness. I am going to play the song that Paddy and I learned to step dance to." I paused. "Though Paddy was always better at it."

Knowing chuckles moved through the crowd like a rolling wave.

"Paddy, vous danser pe ndant que je joue?" I nodded to my brother, and he eagerly stepped forward. Paddy loved to step dance, and though he had little dexterity in his hands, his feet had wings.

"Ready?"

Paddy nodded.

"I'm going to play the reel Grand-mère and Grand-père Bouchier wrote for Papa's birthday years ago. Here is 'Papa's Reel.'"

I tapped out a beat with my foot and gave my brother a wink as my bow touched strings, and lively music suddenly filled the church.

Paddy's feet flew into action, hopping and stepping like a barefoot boy on hot coals. Clickety, click, click, stomp, stomp, clickety, click, hop, turn. The beat was infectious and the tune so engaging that soon the packed church began clapping along, tentatively at first and then full bodied, some even keeping time with their feet.

My fingers and bow scampered along the strings as expertly as my brother's feet danced around the floor. He was grinning and hamming it up. And I felt a strange kind of euphoria rush over me, as if all my family were right there in the front row clapping and stomping as usual. It felt more like a harvest dance than an autumn funeral.

And then, as fast as it had begun, the music and dancing were done. For a moment, there was silence, and then applause and people standing, some with tears, and a great roar of appreciation replaced the music. Paddy was grinning and bowing, turning around and bowing again. It was a magical moment, and I was lost in it.

At my request, only Paddy and I went to the graveside, and there was no reception following.

At the cemetery, Paddy seemed confused. He leaned against me and turned his face into my coat.

We watched silently as the casket was lowered into the ground. It was a bright, colorful fall day, the kind Daddy would have loved, but I knew I would never see a day like this again without thinking about the weight of this moment.

I looked around me—Tandy headstones were everywhere, along with those who married them. My beloved grandparents had, one by one, passed away, my Acadian grand-mère being the last to go when I was twenty-three. Mama was here, and now Daddy joined her. I felt like an orphan and would like nothing more than to run away. Just run and keep running until I disappeared into vapor.

Paddy looked up at me, his sweet face strained. I took his hand and squatted next to him. "If Daddy could see you today, he would be so proud of you," I whispered. *"Donc très fiers,* so very proud." I squeezed his hand.

Paddy stared down at the coffin. He did not whisper. "Daddy can always see me. He's not in that box."

CHAPTER 6
EXTORTION

Miami, Florida
October 1961

Dickie Blevins waited only ten days before he called Fletcher again. He was eager and greedy and had hurriedly formulated a cunning plan to extort money. To him, Mrs. Pickford's death was an enormous windfall, and blackmail seemed like easy money.

Dickie guessed that Fletcher probably knew nothing of the baby for whom Clarice had been searching. Perhaps Mr. Pickford would like to keep an illegitimate child out of his snooty family tree—enough so that he would be willing to pay big money to keep the missing baby missing.

"Mr. Pickford?"

"Speaking."

"My name is Dickie Blevins. I knew your mother—"

"Stepmother," Fletcher corrected.

"All right, stepmother." Dickie hesitated.

"What do you want?" Fletcher's voice sounded flat and measured.

Dickie hesitated again and then said tentatively, "Money."

"Excuse me?"

"Money," Dickie said more clearly.

"And why would I give you money?" Fletcher was tense but controlled.

"Because I have information you might like to own."

"Really? And what would that be?"

Dickie could hear the anger in Fletcher's voice now. It was a reaction Dickie felt to be positive, since he believed where there was anger there was fear. Dickie sensed he was on the right track. To his way of thinking, Fletcher had exposed a small portion of soft underbelly, and he felt bravado creep in.

"Well, Mr. Pickford, I don't believe I am ready to tell it all just yet, but I will say that it concerns your stepmother's daughter." Dickie paused to let his words sink in. "Perhaps you might encourage me to say more."

"Encouragement in the way of currency, I suppose?"

"Now, don't you catch on fast?" Dickie let his words roll off his tongue like butter in a warm pan.

"And if I give you money, what do I get?" Fletcher said without inflection.

"You get to look at the file I have here on my desk."

There was silence on both sides. Dickie figured Fletcher was connecting the dots.

"Where did you say you are calling from?"

"You don't need to know that yet." Dickie was feeling cocky. "Here's the deal. You send me ten thousand dollars in cash—we'll call it earnest money—and when I receive it, I will tell you what I have here in this file. In return, you may own the only copy of the file for an additional fifty thousand dollars. If you don't agree to these terms, I could always sell the file to the *Miami Herald*. You Pickfords don't care for the media much, I'm guessing. It's your choice. Either way, I win."

"All right, Mr. Blevins. Give me the address of your office, and I will have a ten thousand dollar check sent by messenger. You and I could speak again tomorrow and complete our business."

Fletcher's condescending tone made Dickie laugh out loud.

"What kind of an idiot do you think I am, Mr. Pickford? Let's handle our transaction this way instead. You overnight the money, in one hundred-dollar bills, to post office box 921, Lafayette, Louisiana. When I receive the package, I'll call you."

"Well, all right, then. Have it your way. I'll send it off today."

Dickie heard what he thought was a change in Fletcher's tone—from anger to acquiescence—and it made him feel like a winner.

"Nice doing business with you, Mr. Pickford." He hung up the phone and slapped both palms down on his desk in delight.

Fletcher stood and shoved the files neatly stacked on the edge of his desk onto the floor. He did not tolerate ultimatums well.

"Emily!" he barked into the intercom. "Get me the address of the post office in Lafayette, Louisiana."

Fletcher sat at his desk conjuring a plan, subconsciously arranging the paper clips on his desk in an exact line, like little silver bullets. If Blevins had any substantial information about Clarice's child and indeed sold it to the media, the child, or rather woman, could easily get wind of the money and come claiming. On the other hand, Blevins might not know anything of substance at all, in which case Fletcher would not be willing to invest. In fact, how dare this nasty pimple of a man threaten him?

Fletcher left his office early and drove across town to the house where he had grown up. It was for sale now, and Fletcher would be happy to have it out of his life. The palm tree–lined circular drive set off the magnificent old Florida colonial. The structure, which had withstood fifty years of tropical heat and a dozen hurricanes, still looked as substantial and stately as the day it was built.

As Fletcher walked up the front steps, the late afternoon was alive with musical birdcalls and the salty smell of the sea. He stopped to listen and then spit on the porch.

The house was virtually empty except for a few furniture pieces and several boxes of old documents, photos, and memorabilia awaiting disposal piled in the foyer at the foot of the grand staircase.

Since Clarice's death, Fletcher had been through this house a dozen times looking for clues about Baby Jane Doe. He had dug through every closet, every drawer, but had found nothing.

There must be something here that links Clarice to Blevins. Fletcher began pulling boxes open and carelessly dumping them onto the tiled floor, pawing indifferently through the contents. One box contained nothing but old photographs. Fletcher's jaw tightened as he thumbed through photos of the grand parties that were held in this house, smiling faces of impeccably groomed people exuding wealth and privilege, the facade of happiness etched in their expressions—pictures of people dancing, playing tennis, croquet matches, and bridge, and enjoying pool parties.

Fletcher remembered all too well the comings and goings of this fancy life. He had watched it from a distance. He dragged a box over to the staircase and sat down on the first step. He flipped through photos of his father and Clarice and, one by one, discarded them into a growing pile on the floor.

In the bottom of one box, Fletcher found a small photo album, but as he tossed it aside, a loose picture fluttered to the floor. It was a black-and-white close-up, a snapshot of Clarice. Fletcher figured she must have been about twenty-five at the time. She was at the beach, sand and surf in the background, lounging in a beach chair, her impossibly blonde hair—shoulder length and glossy—blown by the breeze. She was smiling and waving a perfectly manicured hand at the camera. Her swimsuit was strapless, and her necklace seemed to sparkle in the bright sunlight.

It was the necklace that caught Fletcher's eye. A small gold, diamond-encrusted heart with the initial C elegantly embossed in the center dangled from a thin gold chain. Though it looked exquisitely expensive, Fletcher could not recall ever seeing his stepmother wear it, nor had he found such a necklace in her personal effects after her death.

He could feel a headache coming on; just being in this house was stressful. He groaned as he leaned against the curved banister. He closed his eyes and rubbed his forehead and tried to relax but only felt more agitated. He bent forward, putting his face in his hands. *There is nothing worth finding here.*

Fletcher was ready to leave, but when he looked up, his vision blurred, eyes coming to rest on the broad front double doors standing wide open. His mind saw his father there, staring back with clenched fists, his drunken expression menacing. His father's slurred shouting seemed to echo off the walls.

Anger and fear welled up in Fletcher's throat like vomit. He held his arms up as a shield and cried out in fear, but when he looked back, his father was not there.

Fletcher jumped to his feet, eyes darting around the foyer, searching, frantic to find his enemy.

He spun around. "Get away from me! I hope you are burning in hell!" he screamed.

Fletcher kicked a nearby box with all his might, breaking it open, sending its contents exploding into the air. Over and over he kicked at the boxes filled with the remnants of his parents' world, all the while screaming and cursing with rage. He kicked and screamed. Boxes flew apart, their guts spilling out everywhere.

He stormed into the dining room, picked up a chair, and smashed it to the floor again and again until it splintered. One small wooden shard punctured Fletcher's hand as he tossed the shattered chair aside.

Blood oozed from the wound, and Fletcher suddenly became as still as stone, watching blood dribble down his fingers and drip onto the floor. He was overheated from the exertion of his rage, yet a cold silence swept through him.

That same afternoon, as she sat on the back porch of her tiny house shucking corn and praying, LilaJune Walker sensed her Lord's gentle nudge, like butterfly wings fluttering against her heart. She sensed something was wrong.

To her church and her rural Savannah, Georgia, neighborhood, LilaJune Walker was known as a prayer warrior for good reason. People believed this tiny, aging woman had a clear link to heaven when it came to intercessory prayer.

Who is it, Lord? LilaJune closed her eyes and waited on God's answer.

She was troubled, and her spirit ached as she became acutely aware of what she believed to be the Holy Spirit's presence settling in around her.

She carried the bucket of corn into the kitchen and set it in the sink. Standing at the window, wrinkled face pressed into wrinkled hands, she asked again, *Father, who is it?*

Only a few steps away, LilaJune's bedroom was the first room off the kitchen, and she thought perhaps she might need to lie down. *You an ole woman, LilaJune. You need a nap.*

As she shuffled into the bedroom, a photo of a young blond child stared back at her from its perch on her dresser. This same photo had been on this same dresser for more than twenty years. *Lord, is it the boy?* She picked up the photo and studied the child's face again. His eyes held no happiness. *You got the eyes of a caged animal, you do.*

"I was the only person who ever loved you, I know," she whispered. "I held you and rocked you. I read you Bible stories and taught you bed-time prayers. We sang songs about Jesus, didn't we? And I told you every day that Jesus loved you."

LilaJune pressed the photo close to her cheek and remembered the last time she had seen this child as she began to pray. "Lord, you know this boy. Let your hand be upon him…"

She lay down on the bed still holding the photo, thinking about the last time she saw the little blond child.

CHAPTER 7

TRANQUIL

.Hackberry, Tennessee
October 1961

The morning after the funeral broke clear and bright, but the days were getting shorter, as if time were running out. I could see clouds creeping in over the mountains.

I lazed in bed with the goose down comforter pulled up to my chin, studying the wallpaper in my childhood bedroom for the thousandth time, unwilling to get up.

Mama had chosen this paper when I was ten—cascading cream-colored lilies of the valley against a background of watery blue. I remembered the day she, Grand-mère, and Gigi had painted the opposing walls a pale mossy green and the trim a delicious French vanilla white. The ceiling was painted sky blue, and I had spent hours lying on the bedroom floor gazing at it, pretending I was flying. Paned windows banked the eastern side of the room where the morning sun often streamed in early and kissed my face awake. A small cherrywood desk lived there under the windows, and next to it rested an overstuffed green and white plaid chair, perfect for curled-up reading and dreaming.

There was a bay window on the south wall near my bed. Outside a huge, ancient oak threatened the three large double-hung windows, small branches brushing against the glass. *I need to get that trimmed.*

41

In summer, the fluttering leaves threw flickering light onto the four-poster bed my granddads had made. Good-daddy was a master wood-craftsman, and Grand-père had painstakingly rubbed coat after coat of linseed oil into the wood until it was smooth and rich with color. The lily of the valley quilt at the foot of the bed had been a gift from my grand-mothers. The tapestry of my childhood was everywhere.

While I was lying there, one memory led to another and then another until the good faded into bad, and I threw back the bedcovers as if to change the subject on an uncomfortable conversation.

I brushed my teeth, drank a huge glass of warm water, pulled on run-ning clothes and sneakers, and hurried down the front stairway and out onto the porch. A quick stretch and I was off.

Paddy hollered from his bedroom window, "Ready, set, go! *Quelle heure?*"

"Eight twenty-seven," I called back, looking at my watch without turning.

I ran down the driveway and onto Deer Spring Road, feeling the familiar rush of relief as my body reacted to each step like scratching an itch. With every stride, I listened to my body hum as blood pushed through big vessels, and muscles contracted and released in a compli-cated dance. Within a few minutes, I reached that sweet spot that all serious runners achieved, the moment where the body and brain meet in an *I-can-run-forever* euphoria.

My cheeks flushed, and sweat formed on my brow and at the base of my neck.

At the end of Deer Spring, I turned onto the main road just as Betty Owens pulled out of her driveway. We waved. Betty had been like a mother to me in the past few years, and I loved her.

The Owens had owned the land next to the Tandys from homestead beginnings. Like us, their land had been in the Owens family for gen-erations. Danny would be expected to keep and manage the land when Warren and Betty were gone. But unlike me, Danny was completely com-fortable with that reality.

He had had several opportunities to live bigger but chose not to do so. After high school, he had joined the marines and served six years as an MP. Later he had been offered a job with the FBI in Atlanta, had finished schooling and training and nearly taken a post, but in the end returned to Hackberry, taking the sheriff's spot from a retiring Louie Voss, making him the youngest sheriff in Tennessee history at the age of twenty-five. He was smart and good looking in a rugged way—dark hair and eyes, tall, and strong, though a bit doughy nowadays from too much desk time.

Moving up the hilly grade to the halfway point, I paced myself for the long, slow climb. Brisk pace turned deliberate, and my body's attitude automatically adjusted. My breathing became measured—in through the nose, out through the mouth.

My family and Danny's, and everybody else for that matter, had expected us to marry, join the two properties, and raise a family. Even if Danny and I might not be the perfect match, the land would be.

Tandy land had more than a mile of river frontage, a hundred acres of orchards, and a thousand acres of timber. The Owens' land had hundreds of rich grazing acres for the Red Angus they raised, along with good soil for hay and grain crops and first water rights from the river.

I supposed Danny had expected that we would end up together, but when he came home from the military, I was off to college in New Orleans, and our relationship had become lukewarm. Libby wanted him, I was fairly certain, and Danny might even want *her*, but the unspoken childhood bond between Danny and me stood in front of us like a heavy door—one nobody was willing to open. *Danny is too good for you, Quil. You would only disappoint him.*

I reached the red maple at the top of Four Mile Hill and, like always, tapped the tree before heading for home. Moving downhill now, I found my breath came easier. I relaxed a little and found another pace, now more on the heels and less on the toes. The sky turned cloudy.

I began a list of all that needed to be done before winter set in. That oak tree outside my bedroom window was one for sure. The apple harvest was finished and off to market. That was a relief. Fishing season was done, but all the equipment and boats would need attention.

Hunting season would open in less than two weeks, and all the cabins were booked for the entire six-week season. Everything would need to be cleaned and freshened. Tandy hunters liked to come back to comfortable digs and good food after a day in the woods. There would be meals to plan and prepare for the hungry lot of them.

Besides that, all the boats and motors needed to be winterized, along with the fishing gear. The boathouse roof needed a small bit of repair, and the dock was going to need to be completely replaced before the spring run. It all felt overwhelming—like a gigantic beast with sharp teeth hungrily glaring at me.

A light mist turned to gentle rain and then to big soaking drops as I made the turn for home, pounding onto the covered bridge, frightening a sparrow from its sleeping place. By the time I reached the other side of the bridge, it was pouring buckets. Lightning cracked close by, and thunder boomed overhead. I automatically covered my head with both arms and shrieked, high-stepping onto the back porch.

Paddy poked his head out the back door. "It's eight twenty-three, and it's raining."

"You are a brilliant boy."

CHAPTER 8

LILAJUNE

Miami, Florida
Summer 1937

Charles Pickford staggered through the front door one Saturday afternoon as LilaJune was passing through the foyer on her way to the kitchen.

She could tell by his attire he had been golfing, and by his demeanor, he'd had more than a few happy hour cocktails under his belt. *Oh, this ain't gonna be good for nobody.*

There was a slight commotion in the hallway, and LilaJune watched as a ball bounced into the foyer. She knew the boy would not be far behind, and she moved to intercept him but was too late.

She was helpless to stop stocking-footed four-year-old Fletcher from colliding with Charles. She watched as he slipped on the highly polished tiles and slammed hard into his father, knocking Charles to the floor. A vicious backhand to the face literally lifted Fletcher off his feet and smashed him into the banister. LilaJune could see the child was too stunned to cry, and she was reaching for him as he crawled across the floor to hide behind her.

"Fletcher, don't be such a sissy!" Charles unleashed an inebriated sneer. "Get out from behind her. She's only hired help. She can't protect you."

Fletcher was shaking with great gulping sobs, his hand pressed over his swelling eye.

LilaJune hesitated. She was not in the custom of speaking back to authority, but at that moment, she felt brave, if not wise. Having turned a blind eye to Charles's abusive behavior in the past, she could no longer ignore the obvious: her love for the boy was stronger than her fear of her employer.

"Yes, I can," LilaJune whispered.

"You said what?" Charles slurred.

"I said I could protect him. I may not always be able to protect him, but right here, right now, right this moment, I can, and you bettah not think about layin' another hand on this child." LilaJune straightened her back, pushing Fletcher behind her as she did so.

"Is that so? Who let *you* get so uppity?"

She stared at Charles as he stared at her. *He can't believe what them big ole ears is hearin'.*

Charles rose slowly to his feet, straightening his clothing and brushing back his hair with his fingers. Nanny and employer faced off. Charles spoke first.

"Well, LilaJune, let me finish what you have begun."

She knew what was coming. How could this confrontation end in any other way?

"Your services are no longer needed here, and I don't think you ought to bother seeking employment anywhere else in Miami either. You will be gone by morning if you know what's good for you."

"No!" Fletcher cried out and began to whimper, burying his face in LilaJune's skirt.

Word traveled fast in Charles's world, LilaJune knew. Nobody would hire a nanny who was openly confrontational and insubordinate, but LilaJune leveled a glare at Charles that told him in no uncertain terms that she meant what she had said. Lifting Fletcher into her arms, she left the room.

Up in the nursery, LilaJune doctored the boy's swollen face and dried his tears. There was a deep purple crease over Fletcher's left eye where he had connected with the banister, and the eye itself was swollen shut. *This child needs a doctor.*

Lila June laid him in his bed with an ice bag across his face and went to find Clarice. She was by the pool, drinking a gin and tonic and reading. *Oh, now, Mrs., please…Somebody needs to be sober.*

"Miss Clarice, Fletcher's been hurt. He's…uh…fallen and hurt his eye. He's gonna need a doctor."

"Tell his father." Clarice did not look up from her book.

"Miss Clarice. Please look my way, ma'am. He's hurt real bad."

"He'll get over it, LilaJune. Put some ice on it, or a Band-Aid, or whatever. Is that all?"

LilaJune knew by Clarice's dismissive tone their conversation was over. *Horrid woman.*

Lila June sat in the rocker by the window that overlooked the garden, Fletcher on her lap, his face in her shoulder, weak and too spent to cry.

"Now, Fletcher, my little man, you gonna have to be a big boy. Hear? I know you are afraid, Lord knows. But life ain't always fair, and you might as well understand that. The only thing you're ever gonna be able to count on in this world is Jesus. Hear me? I know you're young, but you need to hear LilaJune. When you are afraid, you just ask Jesus to make you brave, when you are sad, you ask him to make you happy, and when you are happy, you tell Jesus thank you. When you are lonely, Jesus gonna be your friend." She wrapped her arms tightly around Fletcher and kissed his blond hair. "And you know when you miss LilaJune, she'll be here." She laid a palm against his chest over his heart. "I'm gonna be right here."

She held him through the night. He slept fitfully, but in the morning when he woke, LilaJune was gone.

She hated to leave him and for a moment entertained the folly of taking him with her, but of course, she couldn't. There was one, last brave act in her, however.

As she left, LilaJune stopped in the foyer, set down her bag, and picked up the phone on the entry table. "Yes, could you please send an ambulance to number six Sea Island Drive? Yes, come right to the front.

Don't bother to knock, come right on in. A boy has been hurt, and you can find him in the third bedroom, right side, at the top of the stairs."

LilaJune left Miami and moved back to Savannah to live with a sister, and though she was no longer in touch with Fletcher, she still prayed for the child every day. *I might be helpless to save your body, child, but I'm not gonna never let go of your soul, and neither is Jesus.*

She prayed, hoped, that somehow Fletcher would choose to let Jesus love him and that he would survive through childlike faith.

CHAPTER 9
FLETCHER

Baton Rouge, Louisiana
November 1961

Fletcher was waiting in his rental car outside the Lafayette post office with a clear view of box number 921.

Around two o'clock, a small, sweaty man who looked as untidy as an unmade bed walked into the post office and headed directly for the box Fletcher was watching. The man opened the box and pulled out a package that Fletcher recognized immediately.

He started his car as Dickie hurried out of the post office and watched Dickie rush through the parking lot toward his car, a grin stretched across his face.

Without so much as a cautious sideways glance, Dickie got into his car and drove straight to his office in Baton Rouge. Following him was incredibly simple.

Fletcher waited at the curb while Dickie trotted up the stairs to his office and unlocked the door.

Dickie was at his desk prying open the package with a pair of scissors when Fletcher opened the door without knocking.

"Uh...sorry. I'm not open for business today," a startled-looking Dickie stammered, sliding the package under a pile of papers on the desk.

"Oh, I think you are."

Dickie stifled a little gasp, and Fletcher sensed he had recognized his voice.

"I can explain," Dickie said, getting to his feet.

"No doubt." Fletcher closed the office door behind him with a quiet click and locked it. "Explain what—that you are an extortionist?" His perfectly rich Southern diction sounded civilized, but his demeanor was menacing.

Fletcher leveled a composed glare at Dickie. He knew how threatening he must appear. Intimidation was what he did best, and Dickie's obvious cowardice was appalling yet appealing.

He advanced slowly toward the desk, and Dickie backed away, bumping into the file cabinet, knocking over a huge stack of files that was piled carelessly on top. The files hit the floor and scattered everywhere, but Fletcher did not lose eye contact with Dickie. He was enjoying Dickie's obvious discomfort and was in no hurry to alleviate Mr. Blevins's anxiety. *Let's get our money's worth.*

It was an unusually warm fall day in Louisiana. The broad window was wide open, and a large fan turned lazily overhead. In the silence, Fletcher noticed the sound of an off-balance fan blade as it ticked along in sync with the wall clock located directly above Dickie's head.

Fletcher moved closer, and Dickie continued to back up, sliding around the file cabinet and against the wall.

"Okay, Mr. Pickford. You win," Dickie said, raising his hands in a predictable act. "There's your money back. It's right there on the desk."

"And what was it that you thought you knew about me?" Fletcher asked, picking up the package from the desk and slipping it into his jacket pocket. He covered the scissors with his palm and watched with pleasure as near panic became evident on Dickie's face, his lips quivering slightly.

Dickie held his hands out in a pleading gesture. His back was against the wall in more ways than one as he inched along toward the office door. Fletcher watched him with amused interest—like a cat with a mouse. He was savoring Dickie's fear, and the thinnest smile pulled at the corners of his mouth. *Who does this slimy man think he is threatening someone like me?*

"It's there in the desk drawer, lower left, in the back," Dickie croaked, sweating so profusely he left a damp smear behind as he slid along the wall.

"Come here and get it out of the desk for me." Fletcher's voice was low and controlled.

"I'd rather not." Dickie shot a glance at the scissors under Fletcher's hand.

Fletcher looked down at the scissors and laughed. "Don't be ridiculous, Blevins. You're not worth killing, though the thought is admittedly tempting. Just give me the file."

Dickie swallowed hard and stepped cautiously toward the desk, never taking his eyes off Fletcher. He opened the desk drawer and dug out the file.

"Here. Just take it and go. All right? Just go."

"Back up, Blevins. You're so good at backing up," Fletcher said quietly, taking a couple of quick steps toward the now terrified man.

"Just go!" Dickie cried, stepping back hastily, slipping on the files strewn across the floor. He stumbled, then slid backward, catching himself on the wide sill of the open window. "I'm sorry, all right? I'm sorry. You will never hear from me again!"

"That would be correct. Watch yourself, you almost fell." Fletcher closed the small gap between himself and Dickie with a single step.

Dickie glanced over his shoulder toward the alley below. "You can't do this," he whimpered.

"Do what?" Fletcher said, stepping closer, his face now only inches from Blevins's.

Dickie leaned away from Fletcher, his palms gripping the sill. Fletcher studied his face with interest, the sweat trickling down Dickie's cheeks, flushed red with fear.

Below, rush hour traffic moved along swiftly and noisily in contrast to the slow-moving fan overhead that cast flickering shadows across Dickie's face.

Fletcher felt the first twinges of familiar expectation. Dickie's fear was palpable, and for a moment, Fletcher thought he might beg for his life; the power of the moment was intoxicating. Never before had Fletcher experienced such delicious power. Power over women had felt completely different: sexual and angry. This dominance burned deeply visceral: man dominating man. His body tingled with excitement and anticipation.

Fletcher leaned into Dickie, forcing him to shift his weight.

Dickie sucked in his breath and attempted a sideways move, but Fletcher held his ground.

Fletcher's eyes narrowed, his smile broadened, and his heart rate quickened.

Dickie swallowed hard. The moment seemed suspended, weightless. It was surreal: Dickie sweat soaked, leaning backward out the window, horrified and trembling; Fletcher calm and expectant, uncertain of his desire, only certain he wanted more. Somehow Dickie's fear felt electric and explosive.

"Jump!" Fletcher suddenly barked into Blevins's face.

Dickie gasped and lurched in alarm. His sweaty hands slipped on the sill, and he lost his footing, but his legs caught firmly against Fletcher's body. Utter terror was now etched on his face as he balanced precariously, too petrified to make a sound.

Fletcher could easily reach out and pull the man to safety; he had no real reason to kill Dickie. He was in possession of both the money and the blackmail information. After all, Fletcher was not as yet a murderer, though he had often wondered how it would feel to take a life. Now, with the possibility dangling helplessly before him, he felt empowered, exquisitely primal, with a churning undercurrent of revenge.

Fletcher hesitated while Dickie flailed, desperate to grab onto anything solid. *How perfectly convenient that Blevins would offer to kill himself.*

Fletcher fingered the incriminating file in his right hand and touched the packet of money with his left. He smiled broadly at Dickie and for an instant thought he saw a glimmer of hope on poor Dickie's face. But instead of reaching out to save him, Fletcher took a single step to the side.

Dickie's feet flew up in a contorted jackknife, and with a shriek, he disappeared out the window. He tumbled a full story and did so head-first, landing on the garbage cans below, his neck presumably snapping on impact.

The fan turned, the clock ticked, and the traffic moved along as if nothing significant had occurred.

As Fletcher stepped away from the window, an unexpected sense of gratification rushed through him like an electric current. He shivered, turned his face toward the ceiling, and released a deep-throated groan, like a lion roaring over a kill. His body felt satiated, but his mind was alight with hunger, and Fletcher was acutely aware of both—a sensation like warm water over cool flesh washed over him. A cocoon had opened, and something fully evil had been released.

He carefully wiped clean all the surfaces he had touched and casually left the building.

Fletcher clicked on the television in his hotel room and tossed the file onto the bed. He took a shower, ordered dinner from room service, and, while he waited, turned through the local channels looking for the six o'clock news. It wasn't the lead story, but it was there.

"In what is being called a freak accident, a local man died today, apparently falling from an office window sometime this afternoon. He was dead on arrival at Mercy General. There were no witnesses to the accident. His name is being withheld pending family notification."

Fletcher felt neither fear of discovery, nor remorse, nor a single flicker of conscience. In fact, he was as much alive as poor Dickie was dead.

He ran the image of Dickie's last moments around and around in his brain like a continuous film loop: Dickie flailing and falling, screaming with terror as he plummeted, and the immediate silence after impact.

Fletcher had undergone some sort of change, as if somehow his hatred had appetite instead of just pain. Dickie Blevins had threatened Fletcher, and Fletcher had eradicated him. He had taken control, and control always felt satisfying, and he realized it was what he craved.

Fletcher reached for Clarice's file. It was thin and included very little information, and he wondered how long that slimy little man had been swindling his stepmother.

Inside, Fletcher found two lists. The first was an accounting of births at Mercy General for October 12, 1936. Three babies were born on that day: a boy to Lindsey, a girl to Wilson, and a girl to Henderson. The second list was a copy of the hospital log for women admitted to the hospital on the same date. None of the names rang a bell for Fletcher. Clarice Pickford's name was certainly not there.

In addition, there were scribbled notes from an interview with the hospital administrator, Jacob Waters, who claimed he knew nothing about any person by the name of Clarice Pickford or a baby that might have been born to her on October 12. And there were more notes from conversations with an admitting clerk, Doris Lawson; an emergency room orderly, Walter Summers; and a maternity nurse, Naomi Arsenault, all with the same answers as the administrator. In fact, Fletcher couldn't help noticing how similar the statements were in content and phrasing.

Fletcher tossed the file back on the bed in disgust, but he was relieved that Dickie Blevins had apparently been bluffing. Clearly, Clarice had hired him to find her baby, that was obvious, but there did not seem to be anything incriminating in the file. *Hardly worth dying over, Blevins.*

Dinner arrived, and Fletcher flipped the file over, out of sight of the waiter. The pleasing smell of steaming shrimp étouffée wafted into the room. The waiter laid out the table. He opened a chilled bottle of chardonnay, pouring a glass that Fletcher took immediately, who then tipped the waiter and watched him leave. Sipping the wine, thinking about the day, Fletcher ran the facts of the file again through his mind.

He was about to chuck the file into his suitcase and call it a day when he noticed a name, Lyle Henderson, scrawled on the back of the file, the ink well worn. Wait a minute. Wasn't there a Henderson baby born on the twelfth?

He opened the file again. Yes, a baby Henderson, but why was this name on the back of the file? And why wasn't there a corresponding name for the mother of baby Henderson?

Fletcher sat for a moment, pondering the possibilities, tapping the file absently with a pen. He opened the phone book and searched for a Lyle Henderson. He found lots of Hendersons but not one Lyle.

Then Fletcher noticed a listing for Henderson, Hathaway, and Jenkins, attorneys-at-law.

Fletcher finished dinner and poured a third glass of wine, standing at the hotel window rolling the wine gently around in the glass, thinking. He should have just let it go, walked away, and left well enough alone, but there was too much at stake.

He attempted to piece all the possibilities together. If an incompetent nitwit like Blevins could blackmail him, the field was wide open, and Fletcher did not like the prospect of an attorney being involved. What if Dickie and Henderson were working together? What if Henderson was actually behind it all? Fletcher decided he had to work the problem to a conclusion.

The next morning, instead of flying back to Miami as planned, Fletcher drove by the offices of Henderson, Hathaway, and Jenkins. It wasn't substantial looking but was large enough to have a good-sized clientele.

Back at the hotel he picked up the phone and dialed.

"Good morning. Henderson, Hathaway, and Jenkins, Janet speaking."

"Good morning, Janet. I was hoping to speak with Lyle for just a moment."

"Lyle?"

"Yes, Lyle Henderson."

"Well, you must not know Mr. Henderson very well, sir."

"And why is that?"

"Because Mr. Henderson retired four years ago and now lives in Virginia."

"My name is Richard Blevins. I am a private investigator working on a case, an old case, one I thought Mr. Henderson might help me with. It actually concerns his daughter."

Perhaps dropping Blevins's name would spark something in Janet. If Blevins had been involved with Henderson, the name might ring true. It did not.

"Daughter? Sir, Mr. Henderson has no children." Janet's voice had a suspicious edge.

"Perhaps my information is incorrect. Perhaps it is his wife."

"Mr. Henderson was never married." Janet was curt. "I think Mr. Hathaway might be more useful to you," she said. "I'll ring him."

"No need. I obviously have the wrong Henderson. Thank you for your time."

Janet scribbled the name *Richard Blevins* on her desk calendar.

That evening Janet read a small article in the newspaper describing Richard Blevins's death. She remembered the name instantly and thought what a coincidence it was that Mr. Blevins would call the office the same day he died. If she had noticed the date of the accident instead of assuming it to be the same as the date of the paper, she would have realized the discrepancy but instead dismissed it.

Fletcher's mind was working overtime now. Baby Jane Doe had become a big problem, and he was in too deep to back off. There was indeed a Lyle Henderson, an attorney no less. Henderson had no children, but he could have represented an adopting couple in 1936. It all had a cat-out-of-the-bag feeling, and with so much money at stake, nothing could be left to chance. *Think, Fletcher.*

Fletcher rubbed his forehead as he paced around his hotel room. Henderson could have any number of links to Clarice. He might be the biological father of Clarice's child, or Dickie's accomplice, or just a family friend running interference, or maybe he was simply a hired attorney, in which case there would have to be evidence somewhere. It was all conjecture at this point, but Fletcher was not leaving until he got to the bottom of it. In truth, this sort of intrigue ignited Fletcher's predisposition for risk taking.

At around midnight, Fletcher stepped into the alley behind Henderson, Hathaway, and Jenkins and inspected the back door for any wires that might trigger an alarm system. None were obvious. Further inspection revealed the door had no dead bolt.

As a teenager, Fletcher had become adept at breaking-and-entering techniques, mostly pranks. Though he never needed what he stole, it was the thrill of deception he enjoyed.

Fletcher pulled his driver's license from his wallet and slipped it between door and jamb at the strike plate, wiggling the card into place. The lock jimmied, the knob turned, and the door cracked open. Fletcher hesitated, but no alarm sounded. He took from his pocket the penlight he had purchased that day and stepped inside.

He walked directly to the desk with the "Janet Evans" nameplate and pawed through the file cabinet but found nothing under the headings of adoptions, Blevins, or Clarice Pickford. He searched the file cabinets in the other three offices and the supply room but still found nothing. Back at Janet's desk he rummaged through the contents of the drawers. Nothing. He flipped through the Rolodex near the phone and under the heading "storage" found the name Sanford Storage. An address and a phone number were listed. At the bottom of the card in parenthesis was the word "archives." *Bingo!* In Janet's top drawer, he found a set of keys. One of the keys was labeled "Sanford." *This couldn't be better.*

Fletcher let himself into the storage unit a few minutes after three o'clock in the morning and got to work. The boxes were arranged according to years, and he quickly found the boxes labeled "1936." It only took minutes to find what he was looking for—a box labeled "adoptions." A file named "Arsenault" stood out, though at the moment Fletcher was not sure why. Inside the file were adoption papers prepared by Lyle J. Henderson chronicling the adoption of Baby Jane Doe. Clarice's name was not mentioned anywhere in the documents. Naomi Arsenault was the adopting parent. Though it seemed odd that there was no Mr. Arsenault mentioned, Fletcher considered it all a dead end.

He looked at his watch. It was almost four o'clock. The sun would be up in a little more than an hour. He replaced the box, taking care that nothing seemed disturbed, folded the file in half, and tucked it under his arm. He carefully relocked the storage door as he left the building.

Back at Henderson, Hathaway, and Jenkins, Fletcher hurried to replace the keys in Janet's desk, barking his shin on a file cabinet drawer he had left ajar. He fell against the desk, cursing from the pain. A bud vase tipped, dribbling water onto the desk calendar. Fletcher mopped the water up as best he could with his handkerchief, noticing Richard Blevins's name written at the top. *I hope Janet isn't going to be a problem.*

Tossing the keys back in the top drawer, Fletcher hurried out, rubbing his shin.

At his hotel room, Fletcher opened Blevins's file once again and arranged the contents neatly on the bed: the list of babies, the list of mothers, and the employee interviews. It was then that a newspaper clipping that had been stuck to the back of one of the other papers fell loose. It was Henry Tandy's obituary.

For a moment, Fletcher looked at the clipping lying there as if it were a gold nugget sparkling in a stream. *Henry Tandy, fifty-eight...died September 21 ...born in St. Mary's Bernard Parrish, Louisiana...had lived in Tennessee for the past forty-five years...survived by a daughter and a son.*

Fletcher smoothed the obituary next to the lists and studied everything carefully. He opened the lawyer's file and skimmed the papers for names. The only common denominators were Henderson and Arsenault. Maybe the nurse and Henderson were romantically involved.

Fletcher struggled to tie it all together. A birth certificate had been issued to Henderson. What was Henderson's real connection to Arsenault? Perhaps this was all a wild-goose chase. It was beginning to look like the baby in question was actually Henderson and Aresenault's and had nothing to do with Clarice. Or maybe it was an elaborate ruse set up by his shrewd father to cover Clarice's misdeeds and protect the Pickford "good name."

The only piece of the puzzle that did not fit was Henry Tandy. Was he connected to someone at the hospital?

Later that morning Fletcher walked into the administration offices of Mercy General Hospital.

"Hello. I was wondering if you could help me?" Fletcher smiled at the clerk. "I'm looking for my aunt, Naomi Arsenault. Does she still work here?"

The young woman behind the counter was about nineteen with frizzy red hair pulled into an explosive ponytail on the side of her head.

"Oh, gee, I've only worked here for a couple of weeks, and my supervisor is on break, but let me just check the employee roster." She pulled the roster off a hook on the wall and flipped through it. "Nope, no Arsenault. Sorry," the girl said, reaching into her pocket and pulling out a stick of gum.

"Well, perhaps she has retired," Fletcher pressed.

"Oh, well, that could be. I'll just check the dead files cabinet, then." Fletcher waited while she looked through files.

"Okay, yes, here's something. What did you say her first name was?"

"Naomi."

"Well, here's a past employee list with her name on it, but it's against the rules to show these files to anyone other than authorized personnel." She smiled apologetically, holding the file against her chest.

"Maybe you could just give me a phone number or an address." Fletcher leaned in and whispered, "I have a gift for her, money a relative left for her."

"Oh, gee, that's nice. Sure wish somebody would leave me some money. I had an uncle who was really rich, and he didn't leave anything to my family. In fact, he left it all to some charity and—"

"Miss!" Fletcher said impatiently, forcing a smile.

"Oh, sorry. Well, I am really not supposed to give out any information, but hey, wow, an inheritance. Well, don't tell anybody I did this, okay? I could get really fired."

"It's our secret." He tried to whisper, but it sounded more like a hiss.

"Let's see, now. There's no phone number, and, um, no address either. How about next of kin?"

"Sure." Fletcher was trying not to look eager.

"Elizabeth Bouchier in Hackberry, Tennessee. Wow, that's pretty cool. Imagine living in a town named Hackberry. Wonder where that is? I bet it's one of those cute country places where—"

"Thanks. You have been a great help." Fletcher turned abruptly and headed for the door. One more second with that fuzzy-headed ninny, and he would have come undone.

He was muttering as he headed for the car. "Well, at least Arsenault connects to Tennessee. Does Arsenault equal Tandy?"

Fletcher's plane landed in Miami late that afternoon. His BMW was all that welcomed him. He shoved his luggage into the trunk and threw his briefcase onto the passenger seat as he slid onto the cool leather of the driver's seat. A push of a button engaged the electric convertible top release, and Fletcher let the late afternoon sun warm his face as the BMW's top rolled back and folded neatly into its cradle. He drove directly to Clarice's house.

He pushed open the front door and stood for a moment in the foyer. He was exhausted and at his wits' end. *There has to be an explanation somewhere in this house. Where would she hide things?* He had tenacity and desperation driving him, and he would find an answer.

He trotted up the stairs and pushed open the door to Clarice's bedroom. Glancing around the room, he decided to completely disassemble it if need be. He felt sure her secrets must be hidden there.

Fletcher started with the bed, stripping it, pushing it off its frame, examining the mattress and box spring for hiding places. He pulled all the drawers from the bureau, yanked the mirror off the wall. He looked behind every picture, under every rug, through every drawer.

It was Clarice's desk that finally gave up its prize: a neatly wrapped package was taped securely under the bottom drawer.

"Bingo," Fletcher whispered as he peeled the package free.

He sat down at the desk and laid out the contents of the package. There were three love letters addressed to Clarice at a post office box in Miami, and Fletcher read each one with interest. There was no return address on any of the envelopes, and the letters were signed only with the initial "A." The postage dates on the envelopes ranged from February 1935 to April 1936. Fletcher knew that Clarice and his father had married in the spring of 1933 when Fletcher was only eighteen months old.

Under the letters was a thin address book, and Fletcher found Richard Blevins's address and phone number printed inside. At least this one clue had been validated.

There were lots of other names and addresses in the little book, and Fletcher thumbed through for a clue to the identity of the mysterious "Mr. A" but found nothing conclusive. There was a phone number, and Fletcher dialed it, but it had long since been disconnected.

In the very back of the address book, Fletcher found a copy of a photo, the one of Clarice at the seaside. That felt odd to Fletcher. *Why would she save a copy of this particular photo? Maybe the photographer was Mr. A, and maybe the necklace was a gift from him.*

There was one last envelope, which revealed a notarized document between Charles and Clarice dated June 8, 1936. It was an agreement Fletcher had never known existed but immediately realized made perfect sense. The document clearly stated that Clarice agreed to give up her baby and keep it secret, and he agreed to give her seven hundred and fifty thousand dollars as compensation.

That his father would be willing to pay big dollars to keep another child out of his life did not surprise Fletcher. After all, Charles had never hidden the fact that Fletcher was the biggest mistake he had ever made and having more children was out of the question. Certainly, if Clarice was having an affair and became pregnant by another man, Charles would have been heartless. The thought of how brutally Charles might have punished his stepmother made Fletcher smile.

As he read through the document, Fletcher was amused by how both Clarice and Charles had attempted to outsmart one another. Clarice had indeed been pregnant with another man's baby. She had agreed to be sequestered in Baton Rouge, Louisiana, for the duration of her pregnancy, then give up the child in return for money of her own. Charles had agreed to the deal but had put the money in a trust with irrevocable stipulations. Though he could never touch the money, neither could she; she owned the money but could never spend a penny. She was free to manage and invest the funds but could only pass it to an heir. *Fiscal limbo.*

Charles must have thought he was safe. She supposedly had no other family. To whom would she will her money? To Charles, it was a win-win arrangement, but he had not planned on Clarice outliving him. The trust, worth seven hundred and fifty thousand dollars in 1936, was now worth four and a quarter million in 1961 and growing in value at an incredible rate.

Fletcher hastily stuffed the letters, the agreement, and the address book into his briefcase and called it a day. But let go of this poisonous snake's tail? Not a chance. He had to know who Clarice's daughter was and what she knew.

CHAPTER 10
TRANQUIL

Hackberry, Tennessee
November 1961

It was the same dream. It was twilight, and angry waves crashed against cliffs. Roaring from deep water to shallow, the waves collided with the cliffs, and the cliffs began to crumble. Great boulders broke away one after another and fell into a black sea, but the hollow left behind was bright with illumination. The light was not comforting; it had an alarming quality, yet it felt strangely alluring. The waves grew bigger and closer together. They were relentless and merciless in their assault, and the shoreline was torn apart one huge chunk after another. I felt terrified and wanted to run but could not move. My feet were stuck as if they were molded into the rocky cliffs. I struggled and screamed out in fear as gigantic waves advanced.

Suddenly awake, soaked in sweat, the covers kicked off the bed, I was panting in short, quick breaths, one hand on my throat, the other touching the scar on my chest. I could see the broken bottle and hear my own screaming. Rain was slapping hard against the bedroom window, and I remembered where I was. *You were supposed to have buried all this with Daddy.*

It had seemed the magical cure—writing the whole story on paper and sending it to the grave with my dad. For more than a month, I had not a single panic attack, and though I still flinched at the sight of the scar,

I thought I was becoming an expert at containing the past. I was obviously wrong. Unresolved mental pain had a way of seeping through tiny cracks until the dam in the mind could not hold it back and a flood rushes in.

My feet hit the floor with purpose. *I have to get out of here.*

I pulled a mismatched hodgepodge of clothing from the dresser and was still wriggling into clothes and shoes as I yanked open the front door. A blast of wind and rain greeted me, but I needed to run. It was what felt real—tangible. It was the metaphor for my life. *Run, run away from the pain.*

Rain beat at my face, and I had to squint to see where I was running. My shoes were already soaked, and they slapped and squished with every footfall. I ran into the meadow toward the rockslide. I felt smothered by the storm, suffocating, like a heavy, wet blanket was over my face.

I remembered Paddy standing next to Daddy's grave saying, "Daddy is not in that box."

"Okay, God, I wish I could believe that!" I raised my fists in the air. "But you take everything and leave nothing!" I screamed into the wind. "I hate you! If you love me so dang much, then you are going to have to save me from myself!"

I clawed my way up the rockslide. Torrents of water rushed down the hillside on both sides of the path, running downhill with the same urgency as I climbed. All around me the vivid colors of autumn had turned gray and brown, leaves decaying on the ground, the trees nearly bare.

At the crest of the slide, I slipped and stumbled to a stop, bent at the waist, gasping for air. Wind whipped against the cliff and slapped my wet hair across my face. Far below, the house that had stood like a sentry for a hundred years was being battered by the storm, yet it held strong and solid, its lights burning yellow through its windows, smoke billowing from its chimney. It beckoned me home, safe and warm, yet I ran from it into the forest.

I was beginning to feel the chill, drenched through every layer and starting to shiver as I turned away from the cliff and raced on. Though the storm was less forceful on this side of the mountain and the path not as steep, it was dark in the woods, and suddenly, all I wanted was home. *This was pretty stupid, Quil.*

The path turned downhill and was slippery. I knew I should slow down, but the wind was behind me now, pushing. I was running and sliding, catching my balance, then losing it. There were a few near misses and several acrobatic recoveries. I desperately wanted to slow down, but momentum had me in its grip, and I was riding it to the end.

At the bottom of the hill, I managed an unbalanced, uncontrolled leap and almost cleared the swelling ditch between the path and Deer Spring Road, but my feet slid in the mud on the opposite bank, and I skidded backward, arms cartwheeling, grasping at air. I landed hard, bottom first, in the ditch.

The muddy water was shockingly icy and surprisingly deep. Struggling to my feet, I fell again and then again. It would be comical to watch but not so to experience. The water was rising quickly, swirling dangerously around me, rising fast, pulling me. The ditch was filling, and a broken limb pushed past me, hitting me hard in the back of the head. My teeth began to chatter, and suddenly, the peril of it all hit home. Getting out of the water easily was no longer optional.

With the help of a protruding root, I manage to pull myself up the bank and onto the road. For a moment, I stood in the driving rain, shivering, dripping, staring down at the debris-filled water rushing by in the ditch. It seemed metaphorical that the ditch seemed to be cleansing itself of all that was old and useless. When the rain stopped, the ditch would dry and be free of refuse as though nothing ever happened. *The ditch is cleansing itself. That's what you need to do, Quil. Don't expect your parents' God to do it—you do it!*

I turned for home, running to warm myself, exchanging the little fuel I had left into energy before hypothermia took hold.

The ditch and my life had a lot in common, I decided as I ran. "You have the power to change," I shouted into the wind. *"Contrôlez votre propre destin.* Nobody has the right to rule you. *Dieu ne vous appartient pas!* Nobody knows the truth. Get a backbone! Throw the past away. In fact, make a new past, Quil. If you speak it, it becomes truth—the new truth. *La nouvelle vérité. "* Yes, the new truth.

Paddy was waving to me from his bedroom window, and the next moment he appeared on the porch.

"Run, Quil. Run!" he shouted.

Yes. Run, Quil, run. I stumbled up the lawn toward the house, up the steps, and onto the back porch.

"Wow, you were really fast today." Paddy had happiness written all over him.

"I was racing the rain!"

"That's silly. Rain doesn't race."

"Brr, I'm freezing and famished." I pulled off sodden clothing in layers: shoes, socks, nylon slicker, and T-shirt dropped into a soppy pile on the porch. I was down to a bra and running shorts, skin blue and body shivering. "I am going to the bathtub, and then let's have some hot cocoa."

"And cinnamon buns!" Paddy clapped.

I looked into his sweet face, his lips rimmed with icing.

"I see you already found them," I said, wiping his mouth with my wet shirt. "*Vous ne pouvez pas me tromper.* You scamp."

"My nose found them."

The familiar clickety-clack of tires on the bridge interrupted us, and I hopped into the house, hiding my half-naked body behind the door.

"Danny!" Paddy yelled, running down the steps.

"Patrick Henry! Get back in here right now. It's pouring rain."

"You run in the rain," he called over his shoulder.

"Well, who can argue with that logic," I muttered.

I filled the bathtub with water and sank up to my neck in bubbles and steam and a bit of lavender oil. My skin tingled, frigid nerve endings on fire in reaction to the warm water. It hurt and was soothing all at the same time. Wind and rain battered the window above the bathtub, and I sank deeper, groaning with pleasure.

From downstairs, I heard the happy voices of Danny and Paddy scuffling and teasing each other. *A new truth. What will it be?*

I could have soaked for an hour if I weren't so unbelievably hungry. When I hoisted myself from the tub with a groan, my muscles felt used up.

Warm from my bath, I pulled on fat woolen socks, a pair of

tired-looking jeans, and a bulky, pale yellow sweater, followed by a wide-toothed comb through my hair, a brush for my teeth, and a coat of menthol for my weather-burned lips.

I trotted down the front stairs into the living room and noticed the fire had been stoked and the woodbox filled.

I loved this room: the massive rock fireplace with an ancient hardwood mantle and slate hearth. Comfy blue and white plaid chairs and a sofa in dark red leather hugged the hearth, and substantial wooden bookcases filled with books lined the walls. In the foyer, I brushed my fingers along the frames of family photos as I passed.

Paddy and Danny were making cocoa and heating the leftover cinnamon buns.

"Figures you would show up in time to eat, Owens," I said, braiding my wet hair into a thick cord and rummaging around in a kitchen drawer for an elastic band. "Thanks for bringing in dry firewood."

"Well, somebody needs to come around and protect you from yourself. Good grief, Quil. It's raining sideways out there. What were you doing out in this weather? I heard on the news it's the tail end of a tropical storm in the gulf."

"It feels good to run in the rain. A little running wouldn't hurt *you*." I patted his belly, reaching past him for cups and plates.

"You really know how to hurt a guy."

"Crushed, are you? What a pity. Get the marshmallows. They're in the cupboard, right side, bottom shelf."

"What's the magic word?" he whispered into the back of my head.

"Now!" My teeth gritted, but my eyes smiled.

"Grumpy, grumpy," Danny said, leaning over me to open the cupboard. "You smell good."

"Never mind how I smell." I turned to carry the cinnamon rolls into the living room, and he smacked me on the fanny with a dish towel.

"Grow up, Owens." I laughed.

I liked having Danny around. I knew he would like to be around a lot more, but I wouldn't encourage him. It would be so easy to settle for Danny. He adored Paddy, and Paddy adored him. He loved me. I knew he loved me, but there was no electricity, no fire. *And face it, Quil, he's too good for you.*

The three of us sat on the living room floor in front of a blazing fire while the storm raged outside.

"Boy, now that feels good," I said, stretching my feet toward the fire, taking a long slurp of cocoa, followed by a too-big bite of a buttery cinnamon bun.

"You're such a delicate little thing."

"Oh, hush, Danny. When are you going to get out of my life?"

"Never."

"Yeah, never," Paddy piped up.

"Thanks, buddy. Us men have to stick together, right?" Danny put an arm around my brother.

"Right!" They exchanged a predictable high five.

"What's this?" Danny asked, pulling out a thick book he had found on the floor near the sofa.

"Old photos—old memories," I said, finishing off a cinnamon bun and reaching for another. "Want more cocoa?"

Paddy grabbed the book and flipped it open.

"No thanks. I need to get going." Danny gave Paddy a friendly jostle and headed for the door. Pulling on his boots and reaching for his coat, he added, "Mom says to remind you about Thanksgiving dinner. Come early and stay late."

"We'll be there. Thanks for checking on us," I said, giving his arm an affectionate rub.

Paddy pressed his face to the kitchen window and watched Danny's truck disappear into the storm. I couldn't help but feel a deep aching. I knew my brother was going to need a strong male figure in his life. In three years, he would be a teenager, and I wondered if I would be prepared to handle the inevitable changes. I wondered what his future would hold. What would he remember about his family, having lost all but his sister at such a young age?

"Paddy, come back in the living room. I want to show you something."

He scooted up close to me on the floor by the fire, our backs against the sofa, and I deposited the big photo album onto his lap, flipping it open to the first page.

"There is a picture of Daddy and Gigi in Louisiana when Daddy was a baby. And over here is one of Mama and Grand-mère. I think Mama was about your age when this was taken."

My mother was looking into the camera. Her smile was toothy, her arms cradling a skirt filled with apples. Grand-mère was turning the crank on an apple press. I traced the edges of the picture. "That's how they made cider back then."

"Who's that?" Paddy pointed at an old black and white.

"That's Daddy when he was about your age."

"I don't look like him."

"No. You look like Mama. I look like Daddy."

"I don't remember her."

"You were just a little guy when she died, honey."

"How little?"

"Four. Look, here she is with you and Daddy in the bass boat." I ran my fingers through his thick hair as we talked.

"She's pretty."

"Very, and oh, look! There she is playing in the leaves with you."

I leaned against the sofa and stared at the fire as Paddy studied the picture. I had been home from college the Thanksgiving that photo was taken. I remembered feeling all grown up and self-important.

"Hey! Here's a picture with you in it." Paddy laughed.

"It's all of us at the swimming hole. There's Gigi and Good-daddy, Grand-père, and Daddy." I looked closely at the picture and for a moment was transported. *That had been such a fun day. We all seemed so carefree, not a worry in the world.*

"Wow, look at that bucket of chicken, Paddy. Your mama knew how to fry a chicken."

"There's Mrs. Betty and Mr. Warren," Paddy said, pointing to Danny's parents, waist deep in water, waving at the camera. "Where am I?"

"You weren't born yet, buddy. Look at Mama and Daddy stuffed into that old tire swing kissing!" I laughed, making smooching noises into Paddy's ear.

"Yuck! Kissing." Paddy pretended to gag.

"Oh, come on, Paddy. You like kissing. Maybe I should slobber some kisses all over your face right now!"

"No! Yuck!" Paddy covered his head with his arms.

Paddy was giggling and covering his face with his hands when the phone rang with two long jingles and a short.

"That's us!" Paddy was on his feet running for the phone.

CHAPTER 11

TRANQUIL

Hackberry, Tennessee
November 1961

Three days before the start of deer season, Frank Phelps called.
"Hey, Quil. I really hate to do this to you, but Ernie is down with the flu, and I can't find anybody else to travel with me at this late date."

I groaned inwardly but said, "Don't worry, Frank. We will miss you, but I understand. We'll see you next year, right?"

"Absolutely. Thanks, Quil. Oh, and I was so sorry to hear about your dad. Henry was a great man."

"Yes, he was. Thank you for remembering him, Frank."

I set the phone in its cradle. *Great. How am I going to fill Frank's slot at this late date?*

The phone rang again, and when I picked up, I heard the two soft clicks I knew to be Lois Dawson and Sharon Wallace hanging up. When the phone rang, no matter whose ring it was, these two picked up unless they were already talking to each other. Listening to people's conversations was their not-so-surreptitious secret.

"Hi, Libby. No, I'm okay. I just had a pair of regulars cancel for the hunting season, and I was counting on the income to get us through the winter. Disappointed, is all."

"Well, girl, I may be your hero, because I just had a guy in here who

71

was asking me about hunting and accommodations. I've got his number here somewhere."

"Why do *you* have his number?"

"Quil, you know I never let a good-looking guy escape without at least getting a phone number."

"Well, thank goodness for your active libido."

I could hear her rifling through scraps of paper. "Okay, here it is. Steven Lewis. He is staying at the Horton Inn over in Knoxville."

"La-di-da."

"Hey, you know what I always say…never judge a wallet by the leather."

"Huh?"

"Just call him."

Steven Lewis arrived a day before all the other hunters, walked up to the office, and casually glanced in a side window before he tried the door.

"Hi!" Paddy said loudly from behind him.

Steven whirled around and clonked his head against the dinner bell hanging above the porch railing.

"Ouch. I've done that before. I'm Paddy. Are you Mr. Lewis? Let's go down to number five cabin. You can follow me."

Paddy, wearing the Davy Crockett raccoon hat Danny had given him, raised his arms in the air as if he had made a grand announcement.

"Where is Quil Tandy?" Steven was rubbing his forehead and looking Paddy over.

"She's running."

"Well, when will she be back? Who are *you* anyway?"

"I'm her brother." Paddy patted his chest proudly. "She'll be back in sixteen minutes," he said, looking at the boldfaced wristwatch his dad had given him.

"Really," Steven said with a sarcastic edge, which Paddy recognized but politely ignored.

"Really." He looked at his watch again. "Now it's only fifteen minutes."

"I'll wait here for her to get back." Steven slid onto a porch stair.

"I'll wait with you." Paddy pulled a chair close to Steven. "Want to play a game? We could play dominos." Paddy got up and hurried into the office.

"Let's not. Just go off and play somewhere."

Paddy sat down in the office to wait. For Steven's benefit, he loudly counted down the minutes before Quil would return.

"Only one minute left! There she is on the bridge!" he shouted, dashing from the office, bumping Steven's chair as he skipped down the steps. "Run, Quil, run! Nineteen, eighteen, seventeen," he counted seconds loudly, jumping up and down. "Hurry, hurry, hurry!"

I thundered across the bridge and up the gravel drive, straining to beat yesterday's time. I could hear Paddy urging me on.

"Nine, eight, seven…!"

I charged onto the lawn in front of the office and heaved to a thunderous stop, shaking out, noticing our guest, arms folded with an annoyed expression.

"Yippee! You did it! You did it! Two seconds under!" Paddy danced around the lawn, throwing his arms in the air in joyful abandon, the tail of his raccoon hat swinging wildly.

"Where did you get that shirt, Paddy?" He was wearing a lime-green shirt with the words "Rock 'n' Roll" printed boldly across the chest.

"Bobby gave it to me."

I was still catching my breath, Paddy was still dancing, and Steven's scowl was deepening. He stood and walked down the steps, obviously waiting to be spoken to. Now Paddy was dancing, singing some foolish ditty.

I didn't like Steven already. Handsome, icy, and sure of himself, he was just the kind of guy that would have turned my head once upon a time.

"Welcome to Tandy's," I finally said.

"I'm Lewis and I'd like to check in."

"You didn't have to wait. Paddy had the key."

"He doesn't like me," Paddy called as he twirled by.

"Don't be rude, please. *Dites que vous êtes désolé, Paddy.*"

Paddy stopped dancing, reacting to the sternness in my voice, and came to my side.

"Je suis…" He hesitated, searching for the word.

"Désolé," I whispered, putting an arm around his shoulders.

"Désolé," Paddy repeated.

"Now in English, please."

"Don't bother, I understand French." Steven's response was more comment than conversation.

"Eh bien, Paddy, escorte notre invité dans sa cabine."

I waited as Paddy skipped down the path toward number five, leaving Steven to carry his rifle and luggage.

The "kick-off" dinner was served at seven o'clock to nine mildly boisterous men: rib eye steaks off the grill, garlic-roasted potatoes, sliced tomatoes sprinkled with blue cheese, green beans topped with crispy bacon, fresh yeast rolls with butter and honey, and hot apple pie with vanilla ice cream for dessert.

The praise was abundant as usual. "Quil, you have outdone yourself…delicious…the best ever."

Paddy cleared the plates and did the dishes while I served coffee and tea, and the men traded lies about hunting trips past. I had asked Paddy to only speak English in the presence of our guests.

"I'll have a beer," Steven said matter-of-factly.

"Sorry, no drinking in the main house—my dad's rule. You'll have to do that in your cabin," I said just as matter-of-factly, bending to gather the salt and pepper shakers from the table.

"That's pretty narrow thinking for this day and age."

"Narrow, maybe, but it's the rule, like it or not," Bud Lacey commented from across the table. The others got quiet.

"Well, what would hunting be without rules?" A smiling Steven lifted his coffee cup to all present, and the men resumed conversation.

I watched Bud lean toward Steven and say quietly, "Give her a break. She's been through a lot. Her dad just died."

"Got it." Steven leaned back and watched me as I refilled cups and finished clearing the table.

I could feel his eyes on me, and it sent an uncomfortable flutter through me, a sensation I had had a dozen times before with a dozen other guys, but the last thing I wanted in my life was romance on any level.

I leaned past Bud and nudged him. "Thanks for sticking up for me," I whispered as I lifted the cream and sugar from in front of him.

"That's a pretty necklace," Steven remarked, his eyes looking up at me through dark lashes.

I closed a hand around the gold charm.

"Thank you. It was my mother's," I said, tucking the necklace back inside my shirt and turning toward the kitchen. I could feel his eyes follow me.

"Okay, guys, let's call it a night," I said from the kitchen. "See y'all at five o'clock for breakfast. Your guide will be here at six o'clock to gather you up."

I bid them all a good night from the porch as they headed toward their cabins.

The dishes were done, the kitchen cleaned, and breakfast prepped. Paddy was in bed, and I stepped out onto the back porch with a steaming mug of peppermint tea.

Wrapped in one of Daddy's thick cardigans, I stretched out in the porch swing. I listened to the river gurgling and the laughter of my guests congregated around the firepit behind the cabins.

Down at cabin number five, a figure stepped out onto the porch. Steven's outline was silhouetted against the lighted window. He lit a cigarette, and I watched him. I knew he was watching me, too, though in the darkness it was more sense than sight. Long minutes passed as he smoked and I watched him. He stepped off the cabin porch and crushed the cigarette butt under a heel. No longer illuminated by the cabin light, I could not see him, but I knew he was moving my way. I could hear him walking slowly along the gravel path toward the main house.

I felt uneasy but tried to shake it off. *He's just a hunter. Don't get jumpy.* I was indeed jumpy, and the closer he got, the more uncomfortable I became. My throat got tight. *You are flirting with danger.* I stood suddenly, more a reflex than a decision, spilling my tea.

I nearly fell through the kitchen door as I pushed it open. I locked it behind me, stepped back, and stared at it for a few seconds, rattled by what I was feeling. I ran to the front door and locked it, too, then all the windows.

I dashed upstairs and locked myself in Paddy's room. I looked at my brother sleeping peacefully and realized what jeopardy I might have brought into our home. I slid down the door, face against bent knees. *What's the matter with you?*

The next morning Steven Lewis was gone.

CHAPTER 12

REMEMBERING

New Orleans, Louisiana
June 1960

I t began while we prepared dinner at Pruitt's apartment a block off Tulane's campus. A prime location for a graduate student, but then, Pruitt, or Pit, as he was known, had lots of money—or at least his parents did.

I lived in economy housing on the other side of the campus.

We both had the same goals for our master's degrees and met during field research. My attraction to him was undeniably electric, but then, I had always been attracted to dangerous men. Odd, since all the men in my life before I came to Louisiana had been safe and emotionally healthy. Nevertheless, I seemed to choose men who demanded too much, were controlling, and selfish. Why I would gravitate to more than one of these was the million-dollar question.

Over the past couple of weeks, I *had* noticed that Pit's allure was fading, and more than once I wondered if our relationship had reached the end.

We were cooking dinner together. I had made a huge pot of boiled crawfish, chilling in a big bucket of ice out on the deck. Pit opened a bottle of wine—I had one glass, and he finished the bottle.

Pruitt was annoyed over the attention my lab professor had shown me the day before.

"That's ridiculous. He's twice my age," I said, waving off his accusations and attempting to slice the sourdough loaf with a very dull bread knife. Pit took the knife and pulled the sharpener from the drawer, shutting the drawer a little too hard.

"I think you like to flirt with him. I think you like the way he looks at you." He expertly slid the blade along the steel, but his eyes were fixed on me.

"Come on, Pit. You know how I hate it when you start this jealous thing." I was breaking romaine into a large wooden bowl.

"This jealous *thing*?" He put the knife on the counter.

"That's what I said." I squeezed a lemon into a bowl and was reaching for the olive oil when he grabbed my arm. I leveled a searing glare at him. The attraction for him melted like the butter melting in the pan behind me and was replaced with repulsion.

"Look, you don't own me, and you sure as heck aren't going to tell me what to do." Through clenched teeth I said, "Let go of my arm. You're hurting me."

We were face to face, eyes fierce, each daring the other to move. I jerked my arm from his grasp.

"That's it! You know what, Pit? I think I have had all the *Pruitt* I can stand. I'm done, gone, out of here. Enjoy your dinner." I turned to go, grabbing my house keys off the counter.

"You're not going anywhere."

"Oh, really. Watch this!" I shouted over my shoulder. I reached for the door, but as I did so, I saw him snatch the empty wine bottle by the neck and smash it against the counter's edge. A sudden fear I had never felt before shot through me like a bullet. *Just get away from him. Let him calm down.*

I knew I should have seen this before, but I hadn't. Of course there had been obvious signs that I either ignored or wouldn't recognize. It was a numbing sense that I denied until, like a beautiful snake, it struck without clear provocation. In that moment, fear and knowledge fought an instantaneous battle, and the winner would determine the difference between safety and disaster. *Run, don't talk. Run, this is serious.*

I was out the door and racing down the stairs before he could reach me, but I could hear him behind me. It was a warm June night, and I was wearing only a light summer dress and sandals. I slipped and skidded and stumbled down two flights of stairs. When I hit the grass, I kicked off my shoes and ran. I caught a glance of him as I turned onto the campus park lawn and realized, to my horror, that he still had the bottle.

"Pit, stop this! You're scaring me!" I screamed. Was this the same guy I had been dating for the past three months? I was terrified and confused. I picked up the pace. *He can't last. I can outrun him.*

Halfway across the park, my bare foot caught the edge of a partially buried sprinkler head, and I went down face-first onto the grass. I couldn't recover fast enough before he was on me. I saw the bottle bounce off the grass near my face. Then his hands were around my neck squeezing hard. I was winded from exertion and fear, and now he was choking the rest of the air out of me.

"You think you are such a virginal prize, but you're really just a country bumpkin…a hick. Nobody talks to me the way you just did…nobody!" He let go of my throat and grabbed my arm. I heard a loud crack as he jerked me onto my back.

"Stop. Please stop," I begged.

He ripped open the front of my dress. I tried to scream but could not.

"How about I take a little of what you have been offering up in the lab?"

He shoved a forearm over my throat and in a single motion ripped off my panties.

It was odd now when all the violence rushed back in flashes of panic that my one thought at that moment was, *He's done this before.*

I struggled and cried and tried to scream, but I was no match for him. He was bigger and stronger, filled with adrenaline-charged rage, and when he was done, he calmly picked up the bottle, yanked my head back by my hair, and slashed me from armpit to sternum. *Was my throat the target and he changed his mind?*

Blood was everywhere. He left me there—walking away like he hadn't just ruined my life.

I used my dress to try to stop the bleeding and stumbled naked onto Saint Charles Street. A campus security guard found me, called police and an ambulance, and applied pressure to the wound with his shirt. I remember hearing sirens and the guard telling me it would be okay.

I lost consciousness somewhere along the way and woke in a hospital room. The gash had been stitched and a thick bandage applied. My left arm was in a cast. I had a black eye and split lip with cuts and bruises everywhere. The police came the next morning, and I gave them a detailed report of the attack, naming my attacker.

"Yes, I want to file charges. I want him locked up forever!"

But in the end, Pruitt's affluent parents swore on all that was holy their son had been right there in Lafayette having dinner with the family the night before. The bottle was gone, and no evidence of the rape remained other than my bloody clothing and battered body.

I could tell by the expression on the detectives' faces that the case was about to be closed. They had that good-girls-don't-get-raped expression.

I didn't call home. I didn't tell anyone. I asked to have my name withheld from the newspapers.

At first, I felt inexplicably ashamed and guilty, which I knew was irrational but could not escape. I felt as though in some ways I *had* asked for it. After all, I had been the one to invite a monster into my life. I had encouraged him and enraged him. On one hand, I felt culpable, but on the other, I only wanted revenge.

I informed the university that "due to an accident" I was unable to continue with my graduate studies and withdrew. I spent a week in the hospital, then took a taxi to my apartment. My physical scars were beginning to heal but were soon replaced by a deep-seated anger, which took root like a cancer. Fiery hatred dug in so deeply I could actually feel it grab hold—long tendrils of loathing wrapping themselves around my guts, a vivid, permanent rage tattooed across my spirit that clearly read, "The next man who tries to hurt me had better kill me."

For the next two weeks, I didn't speak to anyone or leave the apartment. I ate what was in the cupboard: boxed macaroni and cheese, canned fruits and vegetables, soup and crackers, tuna, Vienna sausages.

I anxiously paced most of the day, sobbing or plotting vengeance, but at sunset, the fear seemed to creep in along with the darkness. I went to bed at dusk and trembled until the pain pills and sleeping pills took hold and I slept, waking again each morning anxious and angry.

Then when my broken arm was the only obvious wound, I ventured out to the grocery store for fresh food. I kept my doors and windows locked and never went out at night.

I went to the hospital to have the stitches removed. The scar was astonishingly clean on both ends. Only the center six inches below my collarbone were wide, red and frayed looking.

"You were lucky," the doctor said as he removed the stitches. "The muscle wasn't severed. This center part may be permanently numb," he said, touching the center of the wound, "but other than that, it's healing well." *Lucky. Did he really say lucky?*

Somewhere around the six-week mark, I returned to the hospital to have my cast removed and have a routine pregnancy test. Though the odds for a pregnancy resulting from rape were slim, I was not surprised when the hospital called to tell me my test was positive.

Looking back, I realized so many decisions I made then were askew. I was damaged in every possible way and suffering from such emotional upheaval I was in no condition to be making life-and-death decisions—but I did.

In my near psychotic state, I decided there was no possibility I wanted a baby, especially one fathered by my rapist. I couldn't tell my family. I couldn't tell anyone. I thought I knew what I needed to do and through a sympathetic nurse found a doctor in the French Quarter that would do what I wanted. At the time, I thought nothing of this decision, it was simply something that needed to be done, like taking out the trash or crossing off items on a grocery list. I had no feelings of loss or remorse. I was numb, and I wanted to stay that way.

A resulting serious infection ensured that any pregnancy, wanted or otherwise, would never happen again, and after another brief hospital stay, I packed my car and left New Orleans in the rearview mirror. I headed for Hackberry—my life course irrevocably altered.

PART TWO

Just as hope rings through laughter, it can also shine through tears.
—Maya Angelou

CHAPTER 13

LIBBY

Hackberry, Tennessee
November 8, 1961

Libby's Volkswagen Beetle rumbled across the bridge and slid to a stop in front of the house. She squealed her usual "yoo-hoo" at the top of her best soprano screech as she exited the car. By the time she hit the porch steps, I could see she was wearing a hot pink tie-dyed shirt, sweatpants, and high heels.

"What, no pearls?" I said, opening the kitchen door.

"One of us needs to look like a girl."

I rolled my eyes. "You're so crazy."

"Okay, well, we can't all look like Miss Exotic America in grubby jeans and a torn T-shirt."

I wiped my hands on my shirt for effect and grinned. "Coffee?"

"Got any tea?"

"Top drawer on the left next to the boxed matches."

"Yum. What smells so good?"

"Sugar cookies. Gigi's recipe."

"What's the occasion?"

"Just felt like baking."

"You must be thinking hard about something. You only bake when you're anxious." Libby was digging through the drawer. "Don't you have any plain old Lipton?"

"In the back," I said, shaking a fistful of sugary sparkles over two dozen huge, warm cookies.

"Bit of a nip out there today." Libby reached for a cookie. "Frank Watson says it's going to be an early and *hard* winter. Something about the woolly worms and the chestnuts, or maybe it was the woolly chestnuts. Beats me," Libby mumbled through a mouthful of cookie.

"Oh, great, just what I need—cold and snow." I groaned.

"Listen, girlfriend, you might want to put some of that sugar in your coffee. You're a little tangy."

"Sorry. I guess I am feeling a bit overwhelmed. I've been making a list of all the things that have to be fixed and winterized before all those woolly chestnuts turn into worms."

Libby's disarming laughter made me laugh too. It felt good. In fact, it felt better than good. I couldn't remember the last time I'd laughed, really laughed.

"You're a stitch and a half," Libby said, putting the kettle back on the stove while I checked the oven. "Where's the Paddy man?"

"He's staying over at Jessie's tonight. Milk or lemon?"

"Lemon. So what are you going to do?"

"Actually, Libby, I have been considering taking on a hired hand for a few weeks, but I'm not sure if I am going to keep the fish camp running. I might take Paddy and go back to the coast." I lifted a pan of cookies out of the oven and put in another without looking up. "I'd probably be able to get another internship somewhere around the panhandle, maybe even south Florida, maybe even Key West. I could put Paddy in a good school with the money from an equipment sale and Dad's life insurance money. A good school for Paddy, a manageable home at the beach, and an easier life all sound pretty good to me right about now."

I looked up to see my friend standing with hands on hips, staring at me.

"Tell me you're not selling the land!" Libby's tone was incredulous.

"No, not selling the land, just not running the business anymore."

"But Tandy's has been open for about a million years. You can't close it down."

"Okay, brainiac, you tell me how I am supposed to do it all." I shoved my fists into my hips too.

"Well, hire somebody just like you said. As a matter of fact, my new fella is looking for work…nice Southern boy from Georgia."

"Honestly? The last guy you sent my way was a problem."

"Can't win them all." Libby shrugged, sliding into a chair at the kitchen table. "Besides, he *did* pay for the whole week. Sounds like you won on that deal."

"What's the *new fella* doing up here?"

"I don't know, really. We don't do a lot of talking, if you know what I mean."

"I do know what you mean, and don't give me any of the details."

"His name is Ted. Want to talk to him?"

"Let me think about it."

"Sure, think all you want, but he's looking for work, and somebody else might snag him."

"Okay, Okay. Send him by, and I'll talk to him," I said, sliding a plate of cookies onto the table.

"Problem solved, let's have a cookie or ten," Libby said. "Oh, yum, these are good. Maybe you should open a bakery in some exotic place like Paris and bring me along to entertain the clientele, sort of a Parisian diner." Libby was already on her third cookie.

"Libby, how can you eat like that and never smear your lipstick?"

"Told you, one of us needs to look like a girl."

The next day a green pickup truck, presumably Ted Fisher's, drove up the driveway and parked in front of the office.

Paddy and I were down at the dock winterizing boat motors, and I watched a man walk slowly and confidently toward the office door, looking the place over as he did.

"We're down here!" I called, and he turned my way. I sized him up as he headed toward the dock—medium height and build, blond hair, glasses. *Perfect, not my type.*

"Hi, I'm Tranquil, but everybody calls me Quil, and this is my brother, Paddy."

"Ted Fisher." He extended his hand.

"Libby says you're looking for work. What kind of work do you do?" His handshake was firm, but I couldn't help noticing how smooth his hands were and how well cared for his nails appeared.

"Well, until about a month ago I was working for an oil rig supply company outside New Orleans but got laid off."

"And why was that?" His face was pleasant and his smile friendly enough.

"Too much bad weather this year—lots of losses."

"What kind of work?"

"Yeah, do you do work, because Quil really needs help," Paddy chimed in.

"Paddy, *n'interrompez pas, s'il vous plait.*"

Paddy turned back to coiling landing lines. He smiled at Ted but got no reaction.

I noticed Ted's mild surprise at the use of French. He seemed to understand what had been said, though he made no remark.

"*Parlez-vous francais, Monsieur Fisher?*"

He did not respond. "I was in management mostly."

"So why do you want a handyman job?"

"Work is work, and I like the area. I might want to stay."

"No offense, Ted, but fish-camp work is hard and dirty, and you don't really seem the type."

"Not now maybe, but I grew up on a farm in central Georgia, and I know all about hard, messy work. Want some help with that motor?" he said, pointing to the Evinrude on the engine stand.

His accent was as smooth as his hands, not country sounding, but could have been polished by big-city living. A New Orleans accent had more of a northern inflection than a Southern twang.

"Sure. Go ahead and drain the gas into that can by the door."

"What about the oil?"

"Change that too. There's a case of oil on the floor in the corner. The old oil goes in that barrel," I said, pointing to the rusted metal tub strapped on the tractor. "We use it to oil the road—keeps the dust down in the summer."

I busied myself with fishing gear and watched Ted work. He seemed surprisingly skilled, but something about him didn't ring true. *Probably just your general mistrust of men, Quil.*

"Come on up to the house, and we can talk about hours and pay, and I'll need references."

"Of course."

The sound of a car door closing sent Paddy squealing, "Danny's here!"

Sheriff Danny Owens stepped into the kitchen and took off his jacket as Ted put his on.

"Sheriff Owens, meet Mr. Fisher," I said, crossing the kitchen to get the coffee pot.

Ted nodded an acknowledgment and stepped past Danny and out the door.

"See you tomorrow, then," I called after him.

"Yes, ma'am, eight o'clock."

"Sounds good," I said, watching Danny watch Ted.

"Hey, Danny, can I go sit in your car?" Paddy asked.

"Yeah, sure, buddy—back seat only." Danny and Paddy traded pretend punches as my brother rushed for the door.

"Hey, Paddy. Don't forget to put that gas can away," I called after him. "This is the second time I've asked. Please don't make me ask again. *Vas bien?*"

"Yes, ma'am." Paddy was already halfway down the back steps before he answered.

I regarded Danny as he stepped to the window and pretended to be looking at Paddy, knowing he was really watching Ted head for his truck.

He hung his jacket on the coat-tree by the door, walked over to the cupboard, pulled out a mug, and held it out for me to fill with coffee.

"Who's the dude, Quilly?" Danny asked, pulling a chair out from a kitchen table as familiar as his own.

"Danny, could we please get past the nicknames?"

"Doubt it."

"Is this an official visit, or are you just looking for a place to get a free cup of coffee?"

"Coffee's good. How about breakfast?"

"How about not?"

"Harvey down at The Pump said a green pickup he had never seen before stopped for gas this morning and got directions to Deer Spring Road. Said the guy looked weird and I should come out here to check him out."

"And as usual, Owens, your suspicious nature got the better of you. You just had to come out here and meddle, didn't you? Well, you can rest easy. He's just a guy looking for work, not some sort of ax murderer. He's dating Libby."

"Work? I thought you were closing down for the year after hunting season?" Danny stirred both cream and sugar into his coffee. "Bet he's running from something. What's his first name again?" he asked, lifting three fat sugar cookies from the sweets jar.

"You know what, Mr. Sheriff-Big-Britches, that's really none of your business."

"Just looking out for you. Where's he from?"

"He didn't say," I lied without thinking.

"Didn't say? I think that is a violation of some sort of innkeeper's law—not getting address verification from an employee at a licensed facility. Don't make me arrest you."

"That'll be the day." I laughed. "You'd have to catch me first, and we both know that will never happen."

"You know what your problem is, Quil? You need somebody to teach you some manners."

"Like you?" I flicked the extra drops of coffee that had pooled in my spoon in his general direction.

"Hey, this was clean," Danny complained, dabbing at the spot on his shirt. "I'm being serious, Quil. You can't trust everybody so blindly. The world is not as safe as it used to be. Good grief, there's hippies everywhere, drug- and sex-crazed idiots if you ask me. And race riots, and now we've got a Democrat in the White House who thinks we're going to the moon." He bit into a cookie.

"Since when are you so political?"

He gave me a serious and knowing look.

"Okay, okay," I said. "His first name is Ted, you already know that. Ted Fisher, and his truck has Georgia plates. Satisfied?"

"For now, but, Quil, all kidding aside, you are out here with Paddy alone now. You may not think or feel that you are vulnerable, but you are."

"Okay, doomsayer." I patted his hand. "I promise to be careful. He gave me references."

"Can I see those?" he asked, pointing at the paper lying in plain sight.

"Sure." I shoved it across the table and watched Danny's keen eye scan the page for details.

"Are you memorizing everything?"

"Yep."

"Oh, and by the way, I am giving him room and board as part of his employment. He'll be staying down in number five."

"You're kidding, right?"

"Nope."

CHAPTER 14
TED

Hackberry, Tennessee
November 9, 1961

"Patrick Henry Tandy," I said to my brother. "That gas can is still on the porch, next to the woodpile of all places. Don't make me ask you again. I mean it."

"Yes, ma'am," he said softly.

I could tell I had hurt his feelings. Speaking sharply to him never resulted in positive results.

"Good," I said, ruffling his hair.

Paddy headed out to the porch, picked up the gas can, and yelled, "Mr. Ted is here," setting the can back on the porch again next to the woodpile and running down the steps to greet our new hired hand. *Honestly, that kid.* I considered removing it myself but resisted. *That won't teach him anything.*

"Breakfast, Ted?" I said as he stepped through the door.

"No, thanks. I had breakfast at the diner."

"And how is Miss Sparks this morning? Coffee?" I asked, holding the pot up.

"Sure, and she is pretty sparky." He smiled.

"Cream? Sugar?"

"Just black."

"All right. Let's lay the day out," I began. "Paddy, you are on lawn mower. Clean it really well, okay. I will help you drain the gas and oil for the winter."

"I can do that," Ted offered.

"Good. Thanks for that. Paddy, Mr. Ted is going to help you. Got it?"

"Got it!" Paddy raised a hand and pretended to catch something.

"My brother is taking the day off from school to help us. Friday is Veterans Day, so we will have his excellent help for four whole days. Right, buddy? *Quatre jours!*"

"Yeah, four days in a row!"

"And, Patrick Henry, if that gas can is still on the porch at the end of the day, you are going to be grounded for a week. *Comprendre?*"

Paddy put his forehead on the table and said, "Yes, ma'am."

"Okay, Ted. You and I need to get both bass boats and the rowboats out of the water, pressure washed, and stored on the lifts in the boathouse. That should take most of the day, but if there is time, we can winterize the Mercury motor."

"Maybe I *should* have an extra breakfast," Ted quipped.

"Yeah! Let's have another breakfast. Pancakes!" Paddy was instantly on board.

"Forget it, both of you. Let's get to work. Oh, and Paddy, don't forget to wear your life jacket if you get near the river."

"Yes, ma'am."

"*Rappelez-vous la limite?* Limits, Paddy." "*La première étape sur le quai.* Yes, ma'am. The first step on the platform."

"Good boy," I said with a gentle smile. How I loved him, and how I wished I could be like him, so easygoing and happy.

The three of us headed for the boathouse; Paddy ran ahead.

"Why the life jacket?" Ted asked as we walked.

"Can't swim. Sinks like a stone. Something about bone density, and he got very frightened once when he was little. He likes being on the water, but *in* it terrifies him."

"What's wrong with him?"

"Nothing besides Down syndrome, otherwise he is more perfect than any of the rest of us."

"Seriously?"

"Yes, seriously, and you would do well to remember it." My voice had a no-nonsense edge to it.

"Got it!" Ted said, raising a hand as if catching a ball.

Was it acquiescence I heard in his voice or sarcasm? Or maybe just a quirky sense of humor. Whatever it was, it made me feel defensive. *Shake it off.*

By day's end, we had completed our list, including the Mercury engine. Ted was an excellent worker—fast and efficient—and the morning's minor dustup was put aside. Though Ted was not friendly with Paddy, his ambiguity was tolerable. After all, he was only temporary help.

I had put a pot roast piled with onions in the oven at lunchtime, and the aroma of slow-cooking beef greeted us as we entered the house.

Paddy snapped beans while I peeled potatoes and carrots.

Ted built a fire in the living room and put on the kettle for tea.

"I'm going down to wash up," Ted said.

"Dinner in an hour," I said as he closed the kitchen door and trotted down the steps.

"Feel like a pie?" I whispered to Paddy.

"Nope."

"What? You're kidding?"

"Yep." He was grinning. "Let's have cobbler. Peach." He was rubbing his tummy and licking his lips.

"Okay, cobbler. Run down to the cellar and get two jars of peaches, please."

"It's dark," he said, shaking his head.

"I'll turn on the light and sing while you go so you can hear me. Remember? Like Gigi used to do?"

He turned to go. "Start now, okay? Sing 'Great Is Thy Faithfulness.' That's my favorite."

I began to sing, and he left for the cellar. "Louder!" he called.

I amped up the volume, peeling and singing. I was on the third verse when I realized Paddy had been gone a long time.

"Paddy!" I called.

"Ma'am." His voice was so close I jumped. He was sitting at the kitchen table with the peaches.

"Why didn't you tell me you were back upstairs?"

"Because I like to hear you sing."

"You scared me."

He dissolved into laughter as Ted came back into the house. Ted watched him, smiling. Nobody could resist Paddy's laughter, not even Ted.

"Set the table, Mr. Smarty," I told my brother. "There will be four of us. Danny is coming."

"Oh, sorry," Ted said. "I am having supper at the diner with Sparky. I should have said so earlier, but I didn't know you would be going to so much trouble. I'll just go on into town, then," he said, reaching for his jacket.

"See you at eight o'clock tomorrow, and we will get started on the dock. Good night."

From the kitchen window, I could see his headlights disappear around the bend of Deer Spring Road at about the same time Danny's appeared.

CHAPTER 15

DANNY

Hackberry, Tennessee
November 9, 1961

"What a surprise," I replied, setting the roast on the table.

"Yeah, well, I ran his plates, and they are registered to a George Brewer in Augusta." Danny sat down at the table.

"Maybe he just bought the truck and hasn't registered it yet. Paddy, bring the butter and the green beans, please." I carried the mashed potatoes and the steamed carrots to the table.

"I have a call in to the Augusta Police Department. I'm checking on his record."

"George Brewer's?" I gave Danny's arm a playful pinch as I set the gravy bowl down beside him.

"Don't get smart, Quilly."

Paddy poured milk for himself and Danny while I pulled a pan of buttermilk biscuits from the oven.

"I don't like him," Danny said as he hung his jacket on the coat-tree.

We gathered around the kitchen table.

"Paddy, you can say grace if you like." I patted my brother's hand.

"Dear Jesus, thank you for the food, and help Danny and Quil be nice. Amen."

"Amen," Danny and I repeated.

"Okay, truce," I said, reaching for the potatoes. "If you find something derogatory concerning our resident ax murderer, do let me know, otherwise mind your own business, please. He's an incredible help, and we should be ready for winter by the end of next week, which, in case you haven't guessed, has been weighing heavily on me." I reached for the beans. "Are you going to cut the roast or just stare at me?"

Danny and Paddy plunged into friendly banter about football teams and players. I said little, concentrating more on feeding my face. As usual, I was famished by mealtime.

After supper, I dished peach cobbler and poured tea, and we all went to the living room to sit by the fire. Nothing more was said about Ted, though I knew Danny was dying to dig for information.

As I walked him to the door, I slipped a waxed paper package of gingersnaps into his jacket pocket. "I know they're your favorite." I hugged him. "Thanks for being concerned for us. I appreciate it even if I don't show it."

He looked hard into my eyes and said, "Watch yourself, Quil."

I followed the illumination of the cruiser's headlights bounce over the bridge and was reaching for the porch light switch when I saw the gas can still by the woodpile.

"Paddy, get ready for bed, please. And by the way, you're grounded."

CHAPTER 16

THE DOCK

Hackberry, Tennessee
November 10, 1961

Ted arrived promptly at eight o'clock, passed on breakfast again, but took coffee. We got right to business.

"Today we are going to start replacing the planking on the dock. Ted, you can start pulling planks, every third one to start so we have safe places to walk until we can start laying new boards. Paddy, you can carry the old boards up near the house and start a *neat* pile. We can use them for kindling this winter. Meanwhile, I will go to town to get the galvanized nails I ordered and the new planking before all the stores close for the holiday." I looked at Ted. "How are you at figuring board feet?"

"Fair."

"Good, then let's do that first," I said, pushing back from the table.

We all got our coats and boots on and headed out the door.

"Can I go to Bobby's on Friday?" Paddy asked.

"No, sir," I said, picking up the gas can.

I stopped at Nelson's Hardware for the nails and was headed for the lumber yard when Libby passed me going too fast in the opposite direction in her VW Beetle. I waved her over.

"Hey, girl. How are things going with you and Ted?" Libby wanted to know.

"He's a great worker but not very friendly."

"Oh, he's just a bit introverted. I keep trying to get him to talk about himself, but not much luck."

"Let me know if he spills anything juicy, will you? Danny is worried about him."

"Sure." She shrugged and added, "That's quite the groovy outfit you're wearing. Do *all* your clothes come from the feedstore these days?"

"Like it, do you? I have coveralls to match. Borrow them anytime."

"Later." She laughed as she threw the VW into gear and roared off.

"Later," I called after her.

The truck was loaded, heavy with cedar, and I headed home. I saw Danny's cruiser parked in front of the courthouse as I passed through town. *What's he up to now?*

Hackberry might as well have been called Mayberry, and I could imagine Danny as Andy Griffith. I smiled at the thought of Danny dressed like Sheriff Taylor with a deputy like Barney. *Paddy could be Opie.* I laughed out loud as I turned down Main Street.

Hackberry had always felt warmhearted and safe. The storefronts were old but not tired—open nine to five on weekdays, until noon on Saturdays, and absolutely never on Sundays. There were no parking meters. It had a town square with tall oaks and a bandstand with benches for spectators on summer nights for bands and dancing.

The Stars and Stripes were waiving on light poles for Veterans Day. Paddy had marched in the parade dressed as Uncle Sam when he was eight, high-stepping to "Seventy-Six Trombones" played by the entire Hackberry High School marching band—a cast of eleven. *What a ham he had been.*

As Main Street became County Road 31A, I could see the patrol cruiser lights flashing wildly behind me. "Come on, Danny," I groaned, lumbering my old truck to a stop on the shoulder. I was out of the truck by the time Danny pulled in behind me.

"What is your problem, Owens?"

"I don't have a problem, but you might," he said, ushering me off the road. He leaned against the cruiser. "Listen, Quil, I ran a check on Ted Fisher, and though I didn't find a criminal record, I didn't find anything else."

"Meaning?"

"Meaning I don't think Mr. Fisher exists—at least not in Georgia or Louisiana. Did you check his references?"

"No, he started work the next day, and we have been hard at it ever since."

"Not very smart, girl. What are you thinking?"

"I'm thinking I need a new dock. When that's finished, I'll dig a little deeper."

"You make me crazy, you know that?" Danny barked, slapping the cruiser's hood.

"And you drive me nuts. Just back off, Danny. Just back off!" I shouted.

He stared at me for a long moment, jaw locked, veins in his neck pulsing, then wordlessly got back in the cruiser, made a U-turn, and drove back toward town.

Ted was busy ripping up boards and Paddy was industriously dragging them onto a pile when I got home.

"Okay, guys. We've got lumber," I called from the truck. "Let's unload. Good job on the used board pile, buddy," I said as Paddy approached the truck. "*Très bon mon petit homme.*"

Paddy bent at the waist in a dramatic bow and said, "*Je suis votre homme moyen.*"

"Oh, you are more than medium." I hugged him as I got out of the truck. "Okay, Ted, could you back the truck down to the dock? I'll guide you," I said, reaching for my gloves. "Paddy, you will need gloves too. There's a pair in the shed."

I guided Ted to a level spot near the boathouse where we could set up and cut the planking. Ted and I gathered the tools we would need:

circular saw, sawhorses, hammers, measuring tapes, a level, square, and straightedge.

"Paddy, grab a couple of carpenter pencils from Daddy's workbench. Oh, and bring nail aprons too."

Ted and I measured the dock for width, both ends and center, and found the measurements to be exactly true. Good-daddy had built the original dock in 1921; not even time could change what he made. It did not surprise me in the least that it was perfectly square. Replacing planks would be a snap.

"All right, let's cut a template board, and the rest will be easy. You do the cutting, Paddy can haul, and I'll set them," I said to Ted. "Just make sure your cuts are straight."

"I always cut straight," I heard him mutter.

"You don't like being bossed around by a woman, do you?"

"Not used to it, is all."

"Well, if you see this project running amok, speak up. I can take criticism—kind of."

We both laughed, and I felt the tension between us soften. We worked along steadily, and a third of the dock was laid by lunchtime.

"Let's break," I told them. "Lunch in fifteen minutes."

I had made two loaves of sourdough bread before my run that morning, letting them rise while I was gone and baking them while I showered and dressed.

I fried bacon, sliced tomatoes, and put the kettle on for tea while Paddy set the table. Ted arrived as I was cutting thick slices of fresh bread.

"Mayo? We're having BLTs."

"No, thanks, just mustard."

"Mustard? Who eats mustard with bacon and tomato?"

"Me," he said flatly.

"All righty, then. Mustard it is."

Paddy pulled a bag of potato chips from the pantry and tore open the package, shoved his hand in the bag, and stuffed a fistful of chips into his mouth.

"Patrick Henry, où sont tes manières?"

"I'm really hungry."

"Offer our guest some first."

"I'll pass," Ted said.

We ate hungrily, not saying much until we began to feel satiated. I served the rest of the peach cobbler, and we finished it off without comment.

I stretched back in my chair, thinking about my confrontation with Danny that morning, and picked up my mug of Earl Grey. "So tell me about life in New Orleans, Ted."

"Not much to tell. I didn't like it there."

He sounded evasive, so I pressed on, throwing out facts and destinations that any New Orleans resident would know and a few that were fictional. He didn't test well, knew very little about the culturally rich city he said he had lived in for five years.

After lunch, I sent Ted and Paddy back to the dock project while I cleaned up the lunch dishes and got dinner ready for the oven. I thought hard about Ted's responses to my questions as I stuffed and seasoned a large chicken. He was more than vague. I knew he was lying.

In the den, I pulled out the single sheet of references Ted had provided and picked up the phone. As usual, Mrs. Dawson and Mrs. Wallace were on the line. I could try again later, and then I realized it was Veterans Day and a holiday weekend. I would have to wait until Monday.

CHAPTER 17

ALEX

Hackberry, Tennessee
November 10, 1961

Danny called his friend Alex Bennett with whom he had served in the marines. Both men had been military police, but unlike Danny, Alex had moved on to a field job with the FBI. He was married with a family, located in Atlanta.

"Hey, buddy," Danny began. "How's it feel to be a big shot?"

"Tired. And how is the youngest sheriff in Tennessee?"

"Rested."

"There must be something on your mind for you to call me at home. What's up?"

"There is a guy in my district that seems a bit shady, and I don't have access to the resources you do to check him out."

"Okay, tell me what you know."

"Name's Ted Fisher. Says he's from New Orleans, raised in Georgia. He's driving a 1957 green Ford truck that is last registered to a man by the name of George Brewster. I can't find anything on him in either Georgia or Louisiana. He's about thirty years old, I'm guessing, and has taken a job here as a handyman. I don't like him."

"Well, I would trust your instincts any day. Did you run his license?"

"I haven't had a reason to stop him. In Tennessee, you better have a reason."

"Come on, Owens." Alex laughed. "You never were a by-the-book kind of guy."

"Just help me out here, would you? It's personal."

"How personal?"

"He's working at a fish camp owned by a friend."

"Okay, enough said. I'll get on it on Monday."

"Thanks. Oh, and Alex, while you're at it, run a scan on Tranquil Elizabeth Tandy—New Orleans, 1957 to 1960."

"I'm not even going to ask what *that's* about."

"Thanks for that too."

Danny knew something had changed his girl. She had lost her carefree attitude and replaced it with a defensive edge. He had hoped to rekindle the affection they had once had for one another, but her soft edges had become prickly. He wanted to know why.

We finished laying the rest of the dock planking as the sun set in a blaze of splendor.

We were all tired, grubby, and famished. Ted went to his cabin to wash up, and Paddy and I went to the house to do the same.

The chicken was nearly ready, and I had only to make the rice and gravy and toss a salad.

I filled the bathtub and evaporated into the steam and bubbles. I had soaked for at least a half hour when Paddy knocked on the door.

"Quil, when are you coming out? I'm groovy hungry."

I wonder what that means. "Me too. Go set the table, and when Mr. Ted gets here, help him start a fire. I'll be down shortly."

I groaned as I lifted myself from the comfort of the bathtub. I dressed in relaxed jeans, thick socks, and a navy sweatshirt imprinted with Tulane University. I towel dried my hair, creamed my face and hands, brushed my teeth, and twisted my wet hair into a casual knot.

We all fell on dinner like starving dogs, too tired for much conversation. I put gingersnaps on a plate and invited Ted to join Paddy and me in the living room for cookies and hot chocolate, but he declined and headed back to his cabin.

I turned on the television to watch the national news. We had just settled in on the sofa when there was a knock on the door. It was Danny.

"You could smell gingersnaps all the way over at your place, couldn't you?" I quipped.

"Nope. Just missing my two favorite people."

"Pour yourself some hot chocolate and come join us."

"What's on the box?" he said.

"Just catching up on the news."

Danny scooted me to the center of the sofa and set his cup on the coffee table.

"Hey, you've got some nerve. I just warmed that spot."

"That's why I took it." He pinched my earlobe, then threw an arm around my shoulders and pulled me close. "I'm sorry about this morning," he whispered.

"Me too," I said.

"Hey, I want to cuddle too," Paddy chimed in.

I motioned for him to snuggle in, and he did. The news came on, and Walter Cronkite's familiar voice related news of race riots and the race to space, the latest on the escalating Vietnam conflict, and President Kennedy's trip to France. I snuggled deeper into Danny, tucked up under his arm like a chick burrowed under a hen's wing.

He was warm and smelled of soap, and I couldn't help but feel comfortably safe. My stomach was full and my body clean. I was tired and was having a bit of trouble keeping my eyes open when I heard Cronkite say, "There was a gruesome murder today in New Orleans. Pruitt Ingram Penn, known to his friends as Pit, was killed in his apartment..."

I sat up straight and stared at the TV. Cronkite continued, "Michelle Conners, age twenty, was taken into custody at the scene, as was the knife admittedly used to stab Penn to death. Miss Conners said Penn had raped her, and the police have declined to prosecute, stating lack of evidence. Penn was twenty-seven, the son of prominent businessman Edward Penn and his wife, Marilyn."

Danny touched my back, but I shied away.

"Good grief, Quil. What's the matter? Do you know that woman?"

"No."

"Did you know that *guy*?"

"No, I didn't. I just don't like to hear about that kind of violence." I began removing cups and cookies and tidying up. "I've had enough news. Paddy, turn off the TV, please."

"But *Truth or Consequences* comes on next, and we always watch it on Friday."

"Not tonight, buddy. We're both tired, and tomorrow is another big day."

"Yeah, *Truth or Consequences*, Quil. What is going on with you?" Danny pressed.

Danny tried to hold me, but I squirmed away from him.

"I need to get some sleep. I'm tired, is all. Say hi to your mom and dad for me," I said, walking toward the back door.

"Have it your way." Danny held his hands up in submission. "But I know something is up with you, and sooner or later you are going to tell me."

"Good night, Danny," I said, handing him his coat.

I waited until he was in his car before I locked the kitchen door. I locked the front door and the side door as well, turned off the lights, and hurried upstairs. Paddy was already in his room.

"Bonne nuit, mon pote," I said as I passed his room.

"Bonne nuit," was his short reply.

I closed the drapes in my bedroom, changed into warm flannel pajamas, and fell exhausted into bed. My body was ready for sleep, but my emotions were on fire. I felt irrationally afraid—anxious. My heart began pounding. I was short of breath. I started to sweat. *Perfect timing, God. Let me have a heart attack like Dad and leave Paddy completely alone.*

I got out of bed and paced. I thought about Pit's well-deserved death and hoped it had been excruciatingly painful—that he had died slowly—that he had felt terrifying fear and not even the darkness of death would ever release him. I hoped he was in hell, if there was one.

I thought about Michelle Conners, locked up in a cell charged with murder, who would, of course, be convicted. Whether she got life in prison or the death penalty, her life was over—over at only twenty. She should get a medal, not incarceration or electrocution. At that moment, I felt a deep kinship with a woman unknown to me by relationship but closely connected by violence. We, and how many others, had suffered at the hands of Pruitt Ingram Penn. We had been failed by the legal system—the "Good Ole Boys Club"—and left to lick our physical and emotional wounds on our own. I should have done what Michelle had. She was courageous, and I was a coward. I had to help her. I knew I had to help her.

After a while, my heart rate slowed, as did my breathing. The fear subsided, and I felt a gradual return to physical normalcy. Eventually, exhaustion took over.

I finally fell asleep sometime after midnight.

CHAPTER 18
PADDY

The next morning I was too tired to run but not too tired to eat.

"*Paddy, que diriez-vous des crêpes pour le petit déjeuner*," I called up the kitchen stairs.

"Oui, oui, oui! Yes, pancakes," he called back.

"Get dressed and go tell Ted that breakfast will be ready at seven o'clock." I looked toward number five, but there were no lights on, and his truck was gone. "Never mind, Paddy. Ted's not here." *Sparking with Miss Sparky, I bet.*

I whisked buttermilk and eggs together in the brown crockery bowl that had been used for this purpose for at least two generations. I was adding the vegetable oil, vanilla, and a little brown sugar when Paddy made his customary entrance, sliding down the bannister and landing in a heap on the kitchen floor.

I rolled my eyes at him as he lay there giggling. "Do you want orange juice or milk?"

"Both."

"Set the table, and pour a big glass of milk for me," I said, reaching for the canister of buckwheat flour. "Don't forget the maple syrup and the butter."

"They eat margarine at Bobby's house. Yuck!"

"Yuck is right, but I hope you don't say that at Bobby's. Do you?"

"Only once."

"What happened?"

"His mama scowled at me."

"Learned your lesson?"

"Yep."

I poured silver dollar–sized batter onto a sizzling cast iron griddle.

"Bring your plate over and you can have the first batch," I said as I flipped each perfectly golden pancake onto his plate. "You go ahead and say grace, and I will be there in a minute."

"Dear Jesus, help Ted to like me, and thanks for the pancakes."

I filled the griddle with more batter. "Ted doesn't like you?"

"No, ma'am." Paddy already had a mouthful.

I flipped the cakes and didn't ask him if he knew why. I *knew* why. The more I was around Ted Fisher, the more I disliked him.

Finally at the table, I slathered my pancakes with butter and smothered them with maple syrup. I took a big bite and washed it down with ice-cold milk. *Yum, yum, yum.*

Breakfast was finished, the dishes done, and Paddy and I were hard at work by the time Ted arrived at nine-thirty.

"I overslept. You don't mind, do you? It *is* Saturday, after all."

"I do mind," I said, my voice edgy. He said nothing.

We started at the far end of the dock, working backward, side by side, finishing the nailing on each board, three nails into each support to prevent warping. Ted and I nailed while Paddy carried nails for our nail bags.

Ted and I did not speak, just worked. At about noon, Ted hollered, "I'm out of nails, Paddy!" His voice was sharp.

"I'm coming!" Paddy sang back as he ran down the dock with a box of nails, awkward in his life jacket and work boots.

I was about to remind Ted that being kind to Paddy was not optional when Paddy suddenly tripped, falling flat on his face. The box of nails fell into the river. I was on my feet, hurrying toward Paddy. I could see that his lip was bleeding. He began to cry.

"Look what you've done, you little moron," Ted snapped.

"Hey—" was all I got out before Ted said, "Get up and stop crying. Don't be such a baby."

For the first time since he *was* a baby, I saw Paddy get angry. He crawled to his feet and ran at Ted. "I'm not a baby or that other thing you said. You are mean and ugly and stupid!" Paddy screamed.

"Get this idiot away from me." Ted's voice was low and controlled.

I put my arms around Paddy. His body was tense, and he was crying and still screaming, "I hate you! I hate you!"

"All right, Paddy, that's enough." He turned toward me and buried his face in my jacket. "Darling boy. No more talking. *Tu ne vas pas avoir à parler à Ted nouveau.* Take your life jacket off, and go on up to the house. I will be right there in a minute to take care of that lip."

Paddy did as he was told, never once looking back at Ted.

I turned toward Ted. "Well, that was quite the adult display, Ted. Did it make you feel like a big shot to berate a little boy who has done nothing but try to be your friend this week?"

Ted's reply was merely a disgusted snort.

"I think we're done here. Go pack your stuff while I get your pay ready." I turned to go, then stopped. "And I am calling Libby."

"Tell good old Sparky goodbye for me." He sneered and thrust his hips forward in an obscene way.

I wanted to pick up the nearest tool and throttle him. My fists clenched, and I could feel myself losing control.

"Get out," I snarled and hurried to the house to check on Paddy.

I quickly figured hours and dollars and scribbled out a check, taped it to the kitchen door, locked the door, and ran upstairs to find Paddy. I found him sitting on his bed sobbing.

There were no words to comfort him now. I just held him and let him cry it out. I wondered what had triggered such a dramatic reaction. Paddy had learned long ago that some people treated him differently. He shook it off for the most part, but I didn't think anybody had ever been as vicious as Ted—used words like idiot and moron. I imagined it would only get worse as Paddy got older, when hormones kicked in, confusing him further. I needed help.

"Come on, Paddy. Let's get that lip cleaned up, and maybe a bubble bath would feel good. Yes?"

Paddy nodded and followed me into the bathroom. The cut on his lip was not deep but was already swelling, and there would be a bruise. I had just finished running a bath for Paddy when I heard Ted leave.

"It's ready. Have a nice long soak, and then we can watch *The Lone Ranger* together. I'll build a fire," I said as I hurried down the kitchen stairs.

Ted's truck was nearly out of sight. I unlocked the door and looked to see if he had taken the check. He had.

I reached for the phone, and for once, it was clear. I dialed Libby.

"Spark's Diner, Libby speaking."

Without preamble, I said, "I just fired Ted. He's pretty angry, and he's coming your way."

"He's not coming *my* way. He just flew past the diner at about a hundred miles an hour waving a middle finger. Yikes, girl. What happened?"

"Nothing terribly serious, but could you come stay the night?"

"I'll be there by eight o'clock. Sure you're okay?"

"Yes, I'm calling Danny next. Thanks, Libby. I'll see you later."

I dialed Danny's number, and Betty answered. "Oh, hi, Quil. You're still coming for Thanksgiving dinner, right?"

"Of course. What can I bring?"

"Pie. I love your pies. There will be eight of us."

"Betty, is Danny at home?"

"Napping on the couch just like every Saturday afternoon."

"May I speak to him, please?"

Danny came to the phone sounding sleepy. "What's up?"

"Can you come over right away? I have fired Ted, and Paddy is a bit freaked out."

"Why? What happened?"

"Just come, okay?"

"I am on the way."

Danny found us on the sofa. Paddy was in his pajamas watching *The Lone Ranger*.

"Hi, buddy boy."

"I've got a fat lip." Paddy lifted his face so Danny could see.

"You sure do. Let me have a look at that. Ouch. I bet that hurt. What does the other guy look like?"

"Like a moron."

"Paddy, never use that word again. Understand?" I was shocked he would repeat Ted's word. Thank goodness he didn't know what it meant. "It's a bad word that came from a bad man."

Paddy nodded and turned back to his television program.

Danny had me by the arm, steering me toward the den. He closed the door. "That jerk called Paddy a moron?"

"Sure did."

"Give me all the facts while they are fresh in your mind."

We sat down in the two plush armchairs near the window.

When I finished relating the story, Danny asked, "Did he do anything I can arrest him for? Did he touch either of you?"

"No."

"Did he threaten you?"

"No."

"Steal anything or damage any property?"

"I don't think so, but then, I haven't been out there to check."

"Let's do that now," Danny said, getting to his feet.

"I'll just check on Paddy and meet you outside."

Paddy was sound asleep on the sofa—completely spent. I covered him with a throw quilt.

Danny and I first checked cabin number five. It was messy but not damaged, and nothing seemed to be missing. Next, we looked through the shed and workbench for missing tools, and the boat shed for missing or damaged equipment. Everything looked fine.

"He really didn't have time to do much damage. He cleared out pretty fast," I said. "And if you value your hide, don't even think about throwing an I-told-you-so my way."

Danny opened his mouth as if to say just that but stopped. "I think you and Paddy should spend the rest of the weekend with us. I'm worried about that jackass coming back. Sounds like you made him pretty mad."

"Paddy is too freaked out to leave his home right now. Besides, Libby is coming to stay the night."

"Perfect. Let me just draw that picture in my head: one traumatized child, one blonde girlfriend with the IQ of a rock, although she *is* a very pretty rock, and then there is you, who doesn't have a lick of common sense. That sounds like a very safe scenario."

"Works for me."

"Maybe I should sleep over too."

"Actually, that sounds like a great idea."

"Well, then, I'll just dash home and get my jammies."

"Seriously, I think Paddy needs you."

"Do you need me?"

"Maybe."

CHAPTER 19

THE SLEEPOVER

Hackberry, Tennessee
November 11, 1961

D anny was back within the hour, stoked the fire, and settled in with Paddy while I cooked dinner. It wasn't long before I heard my brother giggling, and I breathed a silent thank you. Danny was the tonic for whatever ailed Paddy. He always had been.

I fried pork chops and put them in the oven. Grand-mère used to say that a pork chop wasn't cooked until it fell off the bone.

I made a macaroni and cheese casserole and put it in the oven with the chops.

"Green beans or peas?" I called from the kitchen.

"Green beans," two voices answered.

I smiled and realized it was the first time I had felt relaxed since breakfast—actually, if the truth were told, since Ted arrived. I hated it when Danny was right, and he was right a lot. Maybe I should consider listening to his advice. *No.*

I sliced tomatoes and sprinkled them with parsley and a little olive oil.

"What sounds good for dessert?" I called out again.

There was a pause while the conspirators made a decision.

"Dark chocolate brownies with walnuts and ice cream," came the two-voice reply, followed by loud laughter.

I gathered all the ingredients from the pantry, sifted the flour and sugar together, and got an egg from the refrigerator. As I was melting the chocolate, the phone rang.

"Tandy's, Quil speaking."

"Hey, girl, just wanted you to know that Turbo Ted came by a few minutes ago to collect some things he left behind. Says he's gone for good…can't wait to get away from this hellhole…blah, blah, blah…and he *did* drive away from town on 31A toward the mountains. You might want to tell Danny. Business at the diner is dead. Maybe I'll come over early. What's for supper?"

"Pork chops with macaroni and cheese."

"Oh, goody. Diet food."

"Don't forget your jammies."

Libby arrived in a flurry. The temperature had dropped, and the wind had picked up.

"Brr. I think winter is coming early," she said with a shiver.

"It's those woolly chestnuts' fault." I laughed, lifting the brownies from the oven and burning my thumb. "Ouch!" I said, running cold water over it.

Danny came in and took Libby aside. "You said Ted came back. Tell me he stole something or hurt you."

"Thanks, Danny-boy. Would you like it if he hurt me?"

"You know what I meant. I want to arrest him."

"Sorry. I don't have anything to tell you."

"Danny is in Good Daddy and Gigi's room, and you can have Grand-père and Grand-mère's," I told her.

"How fun. A pajama party with a sheriff!"

Dinner was lively—Libby was, as usual, a party starter. Paddy's lip was swollen and bruised, but he wore it like a badge. Libby and Danny exchanged friendly insults, and I simply watched, grateful for the comfort of friends.

"This is so delicious, Quil," Libby said as she stabbed another pork chop.

"You act like you haven't eaten in a week."

"I haven't."

"Vanity, vanity," Danny teased.

After dinner, we had dessert by the fire as usual, and then I took Paddy upstairs. He said his prayers, ending with, "Help Ted be a nice person." How like Paddy to be kind and forgiving.

I tucked him into bed and sat down next to him.

"Paddy, I have never seen you lose your temper before."

"I know."

"Do you get angry when you aren't at home?"

"No."

"Can you tell me what caused you to be so upset today? I mean, I know why, because Ted was being mean, and you hurt yourself. I would have been angry, too, but it was so unlike you."

"I'm sorry."

"Oh, honey. You don't have to be sorry. Ted was wrong, very wrong. It's just that when we lose self-control—that means getting so angry you just say or do anything you feel at the moment—then the other person has control. You don't want that, right?"

"Right."

"So what are you going to do the next time you feel as angry as you were at Ted today?"

"I'm not going to cry or scream. I'm going to punch him in the mouth."

I rolled my eyes and sighed. *"Bonne nuit, mon petit homme"*

"L'homme moyen"

"Yes, my *medium* man." I kissed him and told him I loved him.

When I got to the bottom of the stairs, I saw Libby and Danny facing each other from either side of the sofa. They were leaning in, looking serious.

"Are you two arguing or making out?"

"Discussing," Danny said without looking up. "I was just telling Miss Sparks here to not send any more men out here."

"I don't think you are the boss of me, Owens," Libby hissed.

"Okay, knock it off. I just had a conversation with Paddy about anger. Don't make me have one with the two of you," I said, flopping into an armchair by the fire.

"What did you tell him?" Libby reached for her tea and sat back. Danny did the same.

"I told him that discretion was the better part of valor." I tucked my feet under myself and buried my hands in my sweater.

"You did not," Libby said.

"Yes, in essence, I did. We talked about self-control and how getting so angry that you lose control makes you vulnerable."

"And what did he say?" Danny asked.

"He said he wouldn't cry or scream, just punch him in the mouth instead!"

Libby nearly snorted tea through her nose, and Danny roared with laughter.

"What am I going to do with him? I am completely ill-equipped to be a parent. Which is basically what I am now." I sank further into my chair and must have looked totally overwhelmed.

"Don't be so hard on yourself. You're great with him," Libby said, dabbing at spilled tea on her shirt.

"Yes, but he is growing up and must be *changing*, you know what I mean. How am I going to cope with *that*?"

"I'll help you," Danny said seriously.

"Thank you for that," I said, smiling at him. I swallowed the last of my tea, stood, and stretched. "Well, I will leave the fire and the kettle to you night owls. I'm going to bed." I patted Libby on the head and kissed Danny on the cheek. "See you in the a.m."

I had a bath, soaking the day away. *Honestly, Quil, when are you going to stop attracting bad men?*

I crawled into bed and fell asleep knowing my friends were there to protect me.

CHAPTER 20
THANKSGIVING

Hackberry Tennessee
Thanksgiving, November 23, 1961

Time flew by as I finished preparing for winter. The days grew shorter and colder. I started running in the afternoon, after chores and before Paddy got home from school.

Danny was spending more "guy" time with Paddy, and my brother responded positively. He seemed surer of himself and less defensive, and I didn't ask about the magic potion Danny was using. I was relieved rather than curious.

I was sleeping better and feeling less edgy. I wrote letters to colleges that offered master's degree programs in marine biology, especially those on the Florida coasts. I contacted a travel agent in Knoxville about winter rentals in Key West. *Danny is going to flip his wig when I tell him I'm taking Paddy out of school and becoming a snowbird.*

I didn't discuss my plans with anyone, not even Libby. I wanted it to be a surprise for Paddy, and to be honest, I didn't want anyone attempting to dissuade me.

I was making pies for Thanksgiving dinner at the Owens' and watching the leftover geese feeding at the river's edge as the winter sun evaporated behind the mountains into icy blue skies. Paddy would be home any minute. I checked the lamb shank in the oven and stirred the apple-sauce on the stove.

I rolled out pie dough with Mama's rolling pin on the pie board that was Grand-mère's, peeled and cored hard green apples, and set them to soak in saltwater. Headlights appeared in the distance, and I knew Paddy would be starving by the time he hit the back door. I poured a glass of milk and laid two cookies on the counter.

"I'm home!" he sang as he pushed the door open. Cold air rushed in behind him.

"Brr, fermez la porte, s'il vous plaît."

"Désolé." His arms were full of school stuff. He shoved the door shut with a foot. "I'm starving!"

I pointed to the milk and cookies. He dropped the school paraphernalia on the kitchen table and scooped up the snack.

"I have a report card," he said, reaching into his notebook.

"Do I want to see it?" I lifted a pie crust from the board and laid it gently in a pie pan.

Paddy didn't answer. He looked out the window, obviously avoiding the question.

"Let me have a look at that," I said, dusting my hands off on my apron.

I sat down at the kitchen table and opened the card. Predictably, his scores for academic achievement were low, but he had all A's for deportment, social skills, and initiative.

"Paddy, these scores are wonderful! *Bon travail!*"

Paddy smirked, a milk mustache thick on his lip.

"Good job," I repeated. "I am so very proud of you. Okay, run upstairs, change your clothes and get washed, and we will read everything your teacher said together."

"Can I have another cookie?"

"Nope. Take a bath, and don't forget to clean your ears. We are going to the Owens' for dinner tomorrow," I called after him.

I finished the apple pies and popped the pie birds that had been Gigi's into the center of each pie and swapped lamb for pies in the oven. Pumpkin filling would be next.

As I rolled out more dough, I saw and then felt a blue illumination fall across the kitchen wall. A huge full moon was creeping over the valley, shimmering on the river—so beautiful I abandoned my pie making, grabbed my coat, and walked out on the dock.

Down at the river I watched the giant orb climbing into the sky as if it were in a hurry. *Slow down, I want to enjoy you.*

The air felt cold and crisp, and I breathed it in like a tonic. I would miss this place if we moved away, but I knew that life and time move forward with abandon and so must I.

We arrived at the Owens' at around two o'clock the next day. Paddy carried the tray with the pumpkin pies, and I brought along the apple pies.

Libby's car was in the driveway, as was the Jacksons' and another I didn't recognize. Libby's parents were snowbirding in south Florida, and I was glad Betty and Warren had invited her. They must have gathered up another stray person as well.

Warren met me at the door and relieved me of the pies. Danny took my coat, and I followed him into the living room.

"Can I help you with anything?" I called into the kitchen.

"No thanks. I've got it."

"She's got it," Paddy said, reaching up as if catching a ball. It had become his signature move.

"Quil, since you know everyone here except Libby's friend, let me introduce you. Tranquil Tandy, meet James Turner," Danny said.

Where does she find these guys? "Pleased to meet you, James," I said, extending my hand.

He kissed it instead of shaking it. *"Enchanté mademoiselle."*

I was momentarily taken aback by his perfectly schooled French.

"Bienvenue Monsieur," I responded.

He was charming and handsome—dark hair and light eyes, well dressed, and obviously well educated. He had something else—electric charisma— the dangerous attraction that had caused so much trouble in my life.

I looked away just as Danny said, "Okay, you two show-offs, let's get some English back in the room."

"Dinner is ready," Betty called from the dining room. Warren placed a gigantic, perfectly roasted turkey on the table.

Danny and I were seated together, with Libby and James across from us.

Danny, the natural interrogator, asked Libby, "So tell us where you met this interesting fella."

"I was over in Knoxville, and I met him at a stoplight."

Knowing Libby as we all did—friendly and chirpy—nobody was surprised that she could, and did, meet a man while waiting through a red light.

"He asked me if I wanted to get a cup of coffee, and here we are."

I watched James as Libby chattered away about how coincidence could turn to happy events. He seemed attentive and comfortable with her.

"James, tell us about you. Where were you raised? What do you do for a living? You know, your whole life in five minutes," I asked.

James put down his fork, dabbed the corner of his mouth with his napkin. "I am Mississippi French. My father is in the oil business—a born and raised Mississippian. My mother is Parisian. They met before the war, married, and she became a US citizen. I studied architectural engineering in Paris and now work for my dad. And *you*." He directed the conversation my way.

"Well, let's see. I'm a native Tennessean. My grandparents on my dad's side were Louisiana Cajun, and my grandparents on my mom's side were Nova Scotia Acadian. Nothing special."

"Where did you go to school?"

"I have a bachelor's in marine biology from Tulane in New Orleans."

"And what do you do now?"

"I run Tandy's Hunting and Fishing Camp."

"That's interesting. Where is it?"

He was effortlessly sucking information out of me like a vacuum cleaner. My private side kicked in, and I changed the subject. "Betty, this sweet potato casserole is terrific. I definitely need the recipe."

Paddy couldn't leave a question unanswered. "We live up Deer Spring Road on the river. We have boats, but I can't swim."

Danny could see I was getting uncomfortable. "Paddy, tell everybody about learning to play football."

That's all Paddy needed, and the next fifteen minutes were filled with very funny descriptions about throwing and catching, falling and tackling.

"James, what brings you to Knoxville?" Dave Jackson asked.

"I'm on the way back to Biloxi from Detroit."

Conversation shifted to college football and the games on TV later. James did not seem to be interested, nor was I. We did a lot of looking at each other.

James leaned toward me and said, "That's a lovely necklace you're wearing. It looks like an exquisite antique."

"It was my mama's. I never take it off in memory of her."

After dinner, overstuffed people settled into overstuffed chairs, and Warren turned on the television while Dave Jackson adjusted the rabbit ears and Libby gave direction.

Danny caught me by the elbow and whispered, "How about we walk off dinner?"

"Deal."

We put on our coats and headed down the dirt road toward the barn. The fresh air felt exhilarating, but I had eaten too much, and I was moving slowly.

"Come on, granny. Pick up the pace," Danny teased.

"Don't push me, Owens. If I walk any faster, I might explode. There's an image for you."

At the barn, we sat down on some straw bales. We were quiet for a couple minutes, then Danny said, "Quil, I need to talk to you."

"Sounds serious. Is it Paddy?"

"No, you."

I gave him a confused look.

"I want you to tell me about what happened in New Orleans."

I was startled and did not recover well. "What do you mean?" I stood and turned away.

"You know what I'm talking about."

"Well, if you know so much, why don't you tell *me*?" I spun around and stared at him.

"Because I want to hear it from you. And I'm wondering why you felt like you couldn't trust me."

"Who the heck do you think you are snooping around in my past like some kind of hound dog?"

"Because it's not behind you, is it?"

"Mind your own business!" I shouted, turning toward the house, ready to run, but he grabbed my arm.

"When are you going to figure out that I still love you? I want you. I want us to be together again."

"You don't want me! I'm used, very used. You can do better! Find somebody else. Let go of my arm," I growled.

I tried to pull away, but he put his arms around me and held me close. I struggled, but he held tight.

"How did you find out, and why did you even look?" I felt trapped.

I was shaking with anger, but he held me upright. I was furious and comforted all at the same time.

"I hate you," I choked.

"No, you don't."

Minutes passed and I finally said, "All right, let me go, and I'll sit down and listen."

Danny hesitated. "Promise?"

"Promise."

"Super-pinky-promise?"

I couldn't stop the laughter that rolled up inside, right past my anger and frustration. Big Sheriff Owens reminding me of the childhood promises we used to make. He laughed too. We sat down together on a bale, and he wrapped an arm around me. I gave up.

"Look, Quil, you haven't been the same since you got home a year ago. It wasn't anything I could put a finger on at first, just small differences in attitude and behavior. You simply weren't yourself. Then the other night when you got all nervous and jerky over that New Orleans murder, I decided to do some digging."

"How much do you know?"

"Everything," he said. His voice was low and emotional, and he looked away.

"Then why do you still want me?"

"I'll always want you."

We sat in silence while I thought out my next move. I *did* love Danny, but there was not, nor would ever be, any fire. Being together would be comfortable and safe, but I was dragging along too much baggage. I was too damaged, and he deserved to have all the facts.

"Well, Danny, here's something I bet you don't know." I leaned away from him, turned so I could look him square in the face, took a breath, and said, "I had an abortion because of the rape and was so damaged by it I will never have children. Never. Still want me?"

He looked too stunned to answer.

"So I guess we're done here." I stood and looked at him, then headed back to the house alone. I wanted to cry, but I was way beyond tears.

"Thanks for dinner, Betty, it was all wonderful. I'm so full I can hardly stand."

"Where's Danny?" she asked.

"At the barn. He'll be up in a minute. Come on, Paddy, we need to get going."

"But it's only halftime, and we are playing a word game."

"What kind of game?" I was trying to be patient.

"We are trying to find out whose birthday is closest to the exact middle of the year," Libby explained. "Yours is in October, right?"

James was watching me.

"Yep, the twelfth, and Paddy's is June 3."

"I win! I win!" Paddy squealed.

Danny came through the door and saw me with my coat still on. "Leave him, Quil. I'll drop him off after the game is over."

At home, I crawled into bed with a book. The doors were locked, but Paddy and Danny both knew where the key was hidden, and I had left the back porch light on for them. Even if Danny was disappointed in me, he would make sure Paddy got home and into bed. I was sure of this.

I couldn't settle. I hated fighting with Danny, and the argument today had left me feeling as wobbly as a boneless chicken. I pulled my knees against my chest and groaned deep and long. It was almost keening, a sobbing without tears. A full palette of emotions bubbled up to the surface: pain, fear, shame, regret—they were all there. They had faces to go with their names: ugly faces.

I needed some comfort. *Pull yourself together, Quil. Don't be such a wimp,* I chastised myself on the way to the kitchen.

In the kitchen, I made a huge mug of chamomile and peppermint tea and splashed some brandy in for good measure. I was still full of Thanksgiving dinner, and I hoped the tea would work on both my digestion and my anxiety. If the tea didn't, the brandy would.

I crawled back into bed, pillows stacked up behind me, cradling my tea and thinking. This mental tussle with Danny was really the last straw. Over the last two months, I had had all the trauma that I could stand. Monday I was going to call the travel agent and tell her to book something—anything.

I got out of bed again, sat down at the desk, and started a to-do list. Monday: travel agent, call Frank Watson to winterize the house, pack for Paddy and myself, clean, store…the list got longer by the second. But I was on a mission, and nothing was going to stand in my way.

An hour later I had put together a fairly comprehensive list and figured we could be on the road by the second week in December. I wouldn't tell Paddy until the last minute; keeping a secret wasn't his strong suit. I would have Frank winterize the house the day we left. Frank knew how to gossip, so giving him a head start was not optimal.

I would call Libby and Danny from Florida.

I crawled back into bed. The tea and the brandy had done their job, and I fell into a deep, dreamless sleep.

CHAPTER 21

JAMES

Hackberry, Tennessee
November 24–25, 1961

Paddy and I had a quiet Friday together. The weather was cold, and an icy rain spit at the windows like tiny nails.

We spent most of the day by the fire playing games and looking at pictures. I read Paddy stories, and he told me all about the football game the day before.

"Paddy, what did you think of Libby's new friend, James?"

"Nothing."

I laughed. "What do you mean 'nothing'? You can't think nothing."

"He doesn't like football."

"Okay, that's something."

"He doesn't like Libby."

"Paddy, he wouldn't have come to dinner with her if he didn't like her."

Paddy shrugged and asked what was for supper.

We both went to bed early; it seemed like the past few weeks had taken their toll. Paddy went right to sleep while I curled up in bed with a book. Before I turned out the light for the night, I checked on my brother. The hall light cast a faint yellow glow on his sweet face.

I watched dreams flicker behind his eyelids, and I kissed him good night.

"*Bonne nuit,* my medium man."

The next morning broke clear and cold, but in contrast, a bright sun rose in warm shades of pink and violet.

I made a hearty breakfast of orange juice, scrambled eggs, hash brown potatoes, sausages, and rye toast.

"Come on, my medium man, let's go close up the boathouse and then run into town to the matinee. I think *The Absent-Minded Professor* is playing." I had purchased the tickets on Wednesday while I was in town, and I held them up for Paddy to see, then slipped them back in my jeans pocket.

"Yeah, let's go!"

Down at the boathouse Paddy finished wiping down the fishing gear and stowed it in the fishing locker.

I swept the last of the summer dirt into the water inside the boathouse. "Paddy, get the gas can, the one with the used gas in it, and put it by the truck. We'll get rid of it on our way to town."

"I need to use the bathroom."

"Okay, but hurry back. It's nearly noon, and the movie starts at one thirty."

I watched him take the can from the dock and head toward the house.

A few minutes later, while I was putting tools away, a shadow blocked the sunlight. Someone was standing in the doorway, and only their outline was discernable

"Dang it, Danny, you scared the living daylights out of me! But I'm glad you're here. I wanted to talk to you about Thursday."

Danny did not answer.

"*Non Danny ma douce.*"

"James, what are you doing out here? Is Libby with you?"

James stepped into the boat shed, and I could now see him clearly. His face was hard and cold, his gray eyes locked on mine.

"Libby won't be joining us." His voice was as cold as his eyes.

Still holding the broom, I froze in instinctual fear. He stepped toward me, and I attempted to dodge him. *Just get to the door.*

James grabbed my jacket, and I took a swing at him with the broom, but he neatly jerked it out of my hands and shoved me into the wall outside the boat shed. I screamed. His hands were suddenly on my throat.

"My name isn't James, it's Fletcher, and I am here because you are my stepsister, and I am going to kill you." His voice was completely without emotion, as if he were reading the phone book.

His fingers closed on my throat, thumbs pressing against my windpipe. His eyes narrowed, and his pupils widened. A flashback from my rape rocketed through my brain. I heard the screen door slam and knew Paddy was on his way back. I brought a knee up sharply into my attacker's groin. He let go of me and fell to his knees.

I wanted to scream for Paddy to hide, but I had no breath. I stepped past James, leaning forward to run, but he grabbed my boot, and I fell. He dragged me to my feet and slapped me hard.

"Would you like some of what I gave Libby?"

"Paddy, run!" I choked.

James slammed my head into the boathouse wall, and I reeled, falling to my hands and knees. I saw him draw a foot back to kick me. That's when I saw Paddy's feet running on the dock.

"Let go of my sister!" he shouted as he hurled himself at James and connected hard, but James knocked him flat with a single backhand. I watched Paddy fall to the dock, his bright orange life jacket shielding his face.

"Well, if it isn't the little idiot." James grabbed Paddy by the back of his life jacket and dragged him swiftly down the dock toward the river. His intent was obvious.

"No! Come on, you coward! It's me you want!" I cried.

He didn't even flinch. When he reached the end of the dock, I watched in absolute horror as my brother was shoved into the river.

"Boathouse! Get in the boathouse," I screamed at Paddy, scrambling to my feet. *Get help!* I ran for the house.

Running in boots felt like moving through gelatin, and I could hear James behind me. His rental car was parked next to the truck, and I glanced to see if the keys were in the ignition. They were not.

I staggered up the back porch steps, pushed through the door, and slammed it shut, locking it and reaching for the phone in one motion.

Mrs. Dawson and Mrs. Watson were on the line.

"This is Tranquil. We've been attacked by James," I shouted.

I glanced out the kitchen window as James rounded the front of my truck. He had the gas can in one hand and the ax from the woodpile in the other.

"Call for help. Hurry!" I screamed, dropping the receiver.

I pulled off my boots and slid into my sneakers. The kitchen door was beginning to splinter. I ran through the front door as I heard the door give way. *Run, Quil. Just run.*

On the footbridge, I shrugged off my jacket. Down to the meadow I ran, adrenaline-fueled running, fast and uncontrolled. Across the river, I could see Paddy still in the water holding on to the boathouse pier.

"Paddy! Boathouse! Boathouse!"

I heard a car engine ignite. My best bet was going to be through the woods and over the hill to the Owens'. My arms were pumping and legs pounding as I ran up the path. At the top of the hill, I smelled smoke and looked back. Flames were pouring out of the first-floor windows of my home, and James's car spit gravel behind it as it spun out of the driveway and over the bridge.

"Why? Why!" I ran along the ridge path. I could still see Paddy in the water. "Why!" *Don't think, run!*

Deer Spring Road wound around the ridge in a long, wide curve, then switched back before the final climb to County 31A. James would have more than two miles to travel and though I only had a half mile to the Owens', I would have to cross Deer Spring Road to get to their back meadow.

I thundered down the forest path, running hard on my heels to control my descent. I could hear the fire now, roaring and snapping in the distance, and I could hear James's car as it climbed.

At the base of the forest path, I tripped on an exposed root, falling onto Deer Spring Road. James's car slid around the bend a hundred yards behind me. I stumbled across the road and dove for the fence bordering the Owens' meadow. My shirt caught on barbed wire. I yanked it off. I could hear James's car slide to a stop on the gravel road. A moment later his hands were in my hair, yanking me backward. I kicked out hard behind me and connected. He yelped but did not loosen his grip.

I heard another car on the gravel and then Danny's voice. "Drop her! I would be quite happy to kill you!"

James let go, and I clambered through the ditch toward Danny.

"Hands on your head. Don't move. I have a very nervous trigger finger."

"Get in the cruiser," Danny told me.

I gasped for breath, choking, near vomiting. "Paddy is in the river, and the house is on fire!" I had James's car door open. "His name is not James, it's Fletcher, and I think he has hurt Libby!"

I pulled my exhausted body behind the wheel of James's car, spun the car into a U-turn, and floored it, barreling for home.

CHAPTER 22
THE AFTERMATH

Hackberry, Tennessee
Saturday Afternoon, November 25, 1961

The house was an angry pile of flaming destruction by the time I reached the driveway.

I could feel the intense heat at my back as I ran to the end of the dock and jumped into the water with Paddy. There was nothing I could do for him. His life jacket was caught on a nail, and my brother had been helpless to save himself. I could not free him without tearing the jacket and possibly losing him in the river's current.

I was in shock, holding Paddy's head above water from the dock when the ambulance and fire trucks arrived. Danny pried my fingers from my brother's jacket so the emergency personnel could pull him from the water and begin to treat him. He threw a blanket around me and carried me to the ambulance.

"Libby?" I asked Danny as he held me in the ambulance while the medics worked on Paddy.

"She's already on the way to the hospital."

I didn't remember much about the ride to the hospital, only the medic treating me for shock and me looking over at Paddy being treated for hypothermia. I heard someone say, "He's got a lot of water in his lungs."

At the hospital, I was taken one way and my brother the other. I was too weak and traumatized to protest.

The gash on my forehead near the hairline took nine stitches to close. I had a severe concussion, and I ached all over. My neck and face were bruised, but X-rays showed no permanent damage to my vocal cords, though my voice would sound strange for a few days. Once again, time would heal my wounds.

After being treated, I was wheeled into Paddy's room and listened while his doctor explained his condition.

"Patrick…" he began.

"Paddy. We call him Paddy."

The doctor scribbled this information onto the chart he was holding. "Yes, Paddy. Is there anything I should know about your brother? Is he allergic to anything? How profound is his Down syndrome?"

"No," I croaked in answer to his first and second question and, "Mild," in answer to his third.

"Good. Well, here's what we know. The hypothermia is being actively treated by obvious means, warmth, and he is responding well. His temperature has risen a full degree since admission. The problem is, Paddy swallowed a lot of river water, then aspirated it into his lungs. Why he didn't drown is beyond reason. We are doing all we can to suction the water from his lungs, but even this will not prevent infection. Pneumonia is our biggest fear. He has not regained consciousness, and that is troubling, though it may simply be the body's defense for healing." The doctor put down the chart and pulled up a chair in front of me. "Miss Tandy, you should be prepared for some brain damage to have occurred—maybe severe."

Danny appeared in the doorway. "I'll wheel her back to her room."

"I'm not going anywhere." I looked at the doctor. "Bring me a bed, please, and I'll stay here with Paddy."

Danny leaned in and whispered, "I need to talk to you." He pushed my wheelchair into the hall. "Libby is in pretty bad shape and is asking for you."

Danny wheeled me to the elevator, and we emerged on the intensive care ward.

Libby lay on her back, her face hardly recognizable, her neck braced.

She was conscious, but both eyes were swollen shut. Her leg was casted, and both arms lay flat at her sides, hands still a bit bloody and nails torn. She looked like a broken, brittle bird. A nurse was adjusting the IV running to Libby's arm.

"I just gave her a shot of morphine. She might be a little incoherent," she said.

"Libby, Quil is here." Danny spoke calmly, though I could see his emotions were just below the surface.

"Quil, I am so sorry I brought that monster into our lives." Tears slipped from the corners of Libby's eyes and dropped onto the sheet.

"Libby, you couldn't have known." I reached for her, not knowing where to touch that would not hurt her. I laid my hand on her arm and squeezed it gently.

"What about Paddy?"

"He's alive."

"Thank God," she breathed and then fell back to sleep, the pain medicine taking hold. *God is the last one I would thank,* was my thought.

Danny rolled me down to the cafeteria and bought two coffees.

"All right, here's what we know about your attacker," he began. "James Turner is really Fletcher Pickford, a resident of Miami. We have him booked on arson and three counts of attempted murder. We don't have a motive yet."

"He told me I was his stepsister and he was going to kill me." I strained to speak, my throat raw.

Danny shook his head. "What do you think he meant by that?"

"I have no idea."

Back in Paddy's room a bed was made for me, and I pushed it close and climbed in. I lay back in utter exhaustion. My head pounded, but I refused medication. I shouldn't sleep—the concussion was only ten hours old—but nevertheless, I fell asleep holding his hand.

CHAPTER 23

ALEX

Hackberry Tennessee
Monday, November 27, 1961

The phone rang in Danny's office.

"Sheriff Owens."

"Hey, Danny, it's Alex. Have a good Thanksgiving?"

"Marginal. What's up?"

"You asked me to look into Ted Fisher, and I finally found him. Actually, he is Larry Winkler with a rap sheet as long as my arm—all of it petty, nothing dangerous. He has since been arrested on an outstanding warrant and is doing sixty days in the Atlanta County Jail."

"Good."

"Here's something else. My daughter Liza has been working in the administration office at Mercy General in Baton Rouge, Louisiana. She was home for Thanksgiving and was babbling away at dinner about a guy looking for an employee who had a waiting inheritance. And get this, her next of kin was in Hackberry."

"You're kidding. Did she get his name?"

"Yep, as ditzy as she is, I was surprised, but she remembered it, Richard Blevins, and the date because it was three days before her birthday, November 2."

"I'm speechless."

"Wait, it gets better. The day before, a guy by the name of Richard Blevins was admitted into the morgue at the hospital, and Liza saw his name come across her desk for filing. So this morning I got on the horn and started checking. Richard Blevins, a private investigator, fell out of his office window and died the day before somebody with the same name talked to Liza."

"Fell?"

"Or jumped or was pushed. Nobody knows."

"Do you think it was Ted…or James?"

"It crossed my mind, but it couldn't have been him because according to you he was already in Hackberry."

Danny was quiet for a moment.

"Still there?" Alex asked.

"Yeah. Alex, I need some information on a guy by the name of Fletcher Pickford."

"Have I become your own personal agent?"

"Yes. You are going to want to be a part of this."

Danny laid out the entire story from Thanksgiving to the present, and Alex listened.

"I'd like to add a murder charge to this sordid scenario."

"Okay, I can get the agency involved now, and that vastly expands our resources."

"Thanks, Alex."

Danny drove over to the hospital and looked in on Libby, who was sleeping, and then headed for Quil and Paddy's room. Quil sat in a chair next to Paddy's bed, holding his hand as he slept.

"He has spiked a fever. It's pneumonia," she whispered.

"That's treatable, right?"

"Yes, but he is still unconscious, and they suspect serious brain damage."

The hospital officially released me around noon, and it felt good to put clothes back on. Betty had shopped and bought underwear, jeans, a long-sleeved T-shirt, and a fuzzy sweater.

Paddy's temperature continued to climb in spite of the IV antibiotics and fluids that were being pushed into him. By midafternoon, his doctor took me aside and told me it didn't look good.

"What? Nobody dies from pneumonia anymore," I snapped, incredulous.

"I don't think he's fighting. Even if there is brain damage, the drugs should be working."

"What do you mean not fighting?"

"My guess is that he has given up. Something in him has switched off, and he doesn't want to survive."

"I won't accept that."

"Good. My advice is for you to start talking to him. Encourage him to fight."

I pulled my chair next to the head of Paddy's bed and laid an arm over his chest and the other around his head. He felt hot and dry.

"Paddy, you have to want to get better. I'm telling you to fight! *S'il vous plaît Paddy, reviens, reviens à moi*. Please, come back to me," I begged.

I continued to speak to him, demand, plead, but there was no response.

The nurse bathed him with cool water, and we both rubbed his limbs, speaking his name.

Throughout the day, his temperature soared, and his breathing became shallow. By early evening, a distinct rattle could be heard in his breathing, and the doctor came back in. He checked all of Paddy's vitals.

The doctor sat down next to me. "I'm sorry to tell you that your brother's organs are shutting down and I think he is coming to the end of his journey. I am so very sorry, Miss Tandy."

"No. No! Don't give up on him!" I grabbed hold of my brother, pulling him close, begging him in both French and English not to go. Yet his breathing continued to slow, and I could feel him leaving.

"Do something!" I screamed at the nurse.

"I wish there was something to do," she said sadly.

"Paddy! Paddy!" I shouted into his face, but he went completely limp. His mouth fell open, and his breathing stopped.

Danny laid his hands on my shoulders, gently pulling me away. The nurse was joined by another and together checked for signs of life. There were none.

Paddy was gone.

Betty and Danny drove me to their home. The doctor had prescribed something for sleep and pain. Too stunned to resist, I let Betty put me to bed. I took the pills and fell asleep hoping I wouldn't wake.

The next morning the Owens broached the difficult subject of funeral arrangements.

"No funeral. Nothing. I will never go through that again, and Paddy doesn't care, does he? I'm going to have an immediate burial next to Mama and Daddy. No funeral, no embalming. It's all barbaric." I reached for the phone.

Betty looked horrified. "Who are you calling?"

"The cemetery and then the funeral home."

"Quil, don't," Betty begged.

"Don't what? Put an end to all this? Paddy is dead. They're all dead. I'm done."

I gathered my things, thanked Betty and Warren, and hugged them.

"Take this with you, darling girl." Betty pressed Gigi's pie bird into my palm.

I stared at it, realizing that this one little thing was all that was left of the life I had known.

"Thank you, Betty. You are my only mother now, and I love you." I could feel tears welling up behind my eyes.

She took me in her arms then and let me weep. "You are, and will always be, our girl, darling Quil."

I nodded but had no more words. I closed the kitchen door softly behind me.

I drove into town and made arrangements with the mortuary and the cemetery. My next stop was Danny's office.

"What do you know about my brother's murderer?" I demanded.

"Not much yet."

"Why not?"

"Calm down, Quil."

"I want to see that SOB. Let me see him!" I knew I was being irrational, but I couldn't stop. "Let me just shoot him. I could save you all the trouble of a trial." I reached for Danny's holster.

"That's enough, Quil." He blocked my hand. "Or you'll end up in a cell yourself."

"Enough? It's never going to be enough. I'm done." I realized I had said the same thing not more than an hour ago. Maybe I *was* done.

That afternoon I finalized the burial arrangements, signing the necessary documents. I had a message from Richard Ingles at the insurance office and stopped to see him.

"How are you doing, Quil?"

"Peachy." My voice was flat. I sat down in the chair across from his desk.

"Well, I called you because there are a lot of insurance issues to deal with. The house was not insured for replacement costs. It was too old and too costly to reconstruct, but your dad had it appraised last year, and that appraisal came in at around fifty thousand. I'm fairly certain the insurance carrier will pay that."

I sat quietly, looking out the window, watching people going about their lives as if nothing had happened.

Richard continued, "Your dad also had life insurance policies on both you and Paddy. Paddy's will pay out at one hundred and fifty thousand. I am authorized to issue that check today." He gently slid the check and a release form across the desk.

"I don't want it."

"Yes, you do. Sign the release, and I can deposit the check at the bank for you. It's what your dad wanted, Quil."

I looked up at him then. His kind face and his expression were encouraging. I picked up the pen and signed, choked out a thank you, and left the check on his desk.

The next day I buried Paddy alongside our parents in a plain cedar box. I did not look at him after the hospital. He was gone. My darling, loving, innocent brother was gone, and I wanted to remember him as he was before Fletcher what's-his-name had murdered him. I stood over the graves of my family for a long time. *The last little Indian.*

I went to the bank and got new checks and cash. Richard had deposited Paddy's insurance money as he had promised.

I drove to Knoxville to visit Libby. She was out of ICU and in her own room. The swelling in her face had subsided somewhat, and she could now see me, but she was in a lot of pain. Her nose had been broken and reset. Her jaw had been broken and reset, wired shut so talking seemed impossible. Her parents were, of course, rushing to be with her and would be home by tomorrow. I told her about Paddy and the house, about Fletcher and his claim that we were family. I told her I was going away for a week or so. "I'll be back before you know it. There is something I need to do." I kissed her goodbye as the nurse came in with pain medicine, and I waited until it took hold and she fell asleep.

Downtown Knoxville had everything I needed. I bought a suitcase and three changes of clothing, underwear, shoes, and toiletries. I filled my truck with fuel and headed south on I-75 toward Louisiana.

CHAPTER 24

MICHELLE

New Orleans, Louisiana
November 30, 1961

I parked the truck in the parking lot of the New Orleans County Jail. Inside I asked to visit Michelle Conners.

"Are you family?"

"A sister."

I was ushered into a room with a long row of double counter tops separated by glass. I waited on the bench next to the wall until a door on the opposite side of the glass opened and a young woman was led in. She had dark hair and dark eyes, a little thin, but I could see she had been lovely.

I stood and moved toward the glass, sat down as she sat down across from me, our mouths framed by the circle cut in the glass. The guard stepped to the side.

"Do I know you?" she asked.

"No, but we have everything in common. My name is Tranquil Tandy. You can call me Quil."

She looked confused.

"I dated Pruitt Penn about a year and a half ago."

I watched her connect the dots.

"He raped me, and the police let him get away with it. I'm betting I wasn't the first. You, of course, were the last. Thank you."

Her eyes welled with tears.

"I should have killed him, but I was a coward, and that left him to ruin your life. I want to help you. Who is your attorney?"

"Jackson Smith. He is court appointed. I couldn't afford to hire an attorney, and my parents couldn't either." She cried quietly.

"All right, Michelle, here is what is going to happen. In a few days, another attorney is going to contact you, and you are going to let him help you. Understand? Tell him everything."

"Yes," she said, wiping her face on her sleeve.

I leaned forward, made hard eye contact, and said, "See you in court."

I checked into a hotel in the French Quarter, ordered dinner—shrimp and cheese, grits, salad, and wine—and looked through the phone book for an attorney.

The next morning I dressed in a lightweight sea-blue dress and heels and walked into the offices of Lincoln, Stanley, and Aspen.

To the genteel-looking receptionist, I said, "My name is Tranquil Tandy, and I would like to speak with an attorney, please."

"Do you have a preference?" She smiled.

"Whoever is able to speak to me this morning."

"Just a moment, please. Do have a seat," she said, motioning to the comfortable-looking chairs in the waiting area.

I sat down to wait.

"This way, please. Mr. Lincoln will see you." The receptionist motioned for me to follow her.

She ushered me into a large corner office and introduced me to a tall man in his midfifties. "Mr. Lincoln, meet Tranquil Tandy."

"Pleased to meet you, Miss Tandy," he said, extending a hand.

"Call me Quil." I liked him instantly.

"What can I do for you?"

"I would like you to represent Michelle Conners. She is the woman who murdered Pruitt Penn."

He studied me for a moment and said, "Good for her."

"I agree."

"And what is your interest in Michelle Conners?"

"Like me, and probably others, she was raped by Penn. But unlike me, she had the courage to stop him. Her public defender is Jackson Smith. I have just come from a visit with her at the county jail. She knows someone like you will be contacting her, and she will cooperate fully. I realize your kind of representation does not come cheap." I smiled. "Here is a check for ten thousand dollars." I pushed a cashier's check across the desk, and he picked it up. "You can bill me for the rest of her defense if this is not enough," I handed him my post office box address in Hackberry.

"Are you willing to testify?"

"Yes, and I'd be willing to bet others will, too, once it's known that Michelle has a good attorney."

He smiled. "Here's my card. I will be in touch."

"Thank you, Mr. Lincoln. You are her only hope."

I arrived back in Hackberry four days later; I had been gone a total of eight, and Danny was furious.

"Where the blue bloody heck have you been?" he demanded. "We have all been worried sick. Richard Ingles said he saw you the day you buried Paddy and then you disappeared."

"I needed some space. I'm back now. I have rented a room from Lorraine Kimble."

"Why are you staying there when you could be staying with us?"

"Too close to home, Danny. I need to be away from Deer Spring Road if I am going to start rebuilding my life—what's left of it. How's Libby? What's happening with the case against Fletcher?"

"Libby is coming along well. Her parents brought her home yesterday. As for the case against Fletcher, I think you should hear it all from the district attorney in Knoxville. I can drive you over tomorrow if you like." He sounded cool.

"Thank you, Danny. What time tomorrow?"

"I'll swing by Lorraine's at eight o'clock."

The next morning Danny arrived promptly, as was I. We drove in silence. I figured he might be angry or maybe simply fed up.

At the courthouse in Knoxville, Danny put the cruiser in park, and I reached for the door handle.

"Wait, Quil." His voice sounded serious.

"What?" I was afraid to ask.

"The DA has a huge amount of information. It's a great, long, convoluted trail, and I just don't want you to be blindsided by it all."

"Are you coming in with me?"

"Do you want me to?"

"Yes, yes, would you? I have to admit to being on emotional overload. I may need a strong arm."

We walked into the district attorney's office, and Danny introduced us. "Tranquil Tandy, this is Philip Randall."

"Please sit down." Mr. Randall directed us to a pair of leather sofas facing each other with a broad glass table between. "Would you like something to drink? Coffee? Water?"

"Water, please," I answered.

"Loretta, bring us all some water, if you please," he said to his assistant.

Danny and I sat on one sofa and the DA on the other.

"Loretta is going to join us, if you don't mind. She will be making notes on our conversation today. I hope that is all right with you."

I nodded that it was.

On the table were three stacks of files.

"All right, then, let's begin at the beginning. Miss Tandy, are you aware that you are adopted?"

"I am not adopted." I gave him a have-you-lost-your-mind stare.

"I am afraid I have proof here that you are." Mr. Randall lifted a file off the first pile. "The FBI found a file among Mr. Pickford's belongings in his home in Miami."

He laid open the file in front of me and from it lifted a five by seven black-and-white photo and handed it to me. It was a picture of a blonde woman on a breezy beach sitting in a beach chair waving at the camera.

"Do you know this woman?" Randall asked.

"No."

"Look closer, please, at her necklace. What about that?"

I peered deeply into the photo and then gasped.

"That woman is wearing *my* necklace," I said breathlessly, lifting the necklace from under my shirt.

"Could you take it off, please, and lay it on the table? Loretta, let's take a photo of this. We will have to tag it into evidence."

"Sir, this necklace has not been off my neck since I was thirteen. I am not taking it off."

Danny put a hand on my arm and said, "It's evidence, and they can compel you to take it off. At the end of the trial, they will give it back, I promise."

I set my jaw and unclasped the necklace. "What the heck does that woman have to do with me anyway?"

"We think she is your biological mother."

"What? This is crazy!"

"Please try to stay calm, Miss Tandy. There is a lot of information you may find shocking. Staying calm and listening will be essential."

"Fine. Tell me everything." I crossed my arms tightly over my chest and leaned back.

"The woman's name was Clarice Pickford, at least that was her married name, and she was married to a wealthy businessman named Charles Pickford."

"Are you saying I'm related to the monster who murdered my brother?" I felt nauseous.

"No. Fletcher Pickford was the son of Charles and Jane Pickford. Fletcher was born on February 11, 1931, and Jane died of cancer in July of 1932. Charles married Clarice in January 1933."

"So how is it that if that woman in the picture *is* my mother, the monster and I aren't related?"

"Because Charles is not your father."

I rubbed my eyes. "Are you saying that my dad, Henry Tandy, had an affair with that woman?" I sounded shrill again.

"No. Clarice had an affair with someone else." He opened another file. "Were you born on October 12, 1936?"

"Yes."

He handed me the document that Charles and Clarice had signed on May 8, 1936.

"She sold me!"

"We don't think she had a choice. Charles Pickford was well connected and powerful. He was from old money. His family fortunes go back further than the Civil War. The only other thing we know about him to date is that he shot himself in 1951. Clarice died of breast cancer about eighteen months ago."

"I don't understand." My head was cradled in my hands. "Then if Charles Pickford isn't my dad, and my *dad* isn't my dad, who is?"

"We don't know. But here's what we do know," he said, lifting yet another document. "This is Clarice Pickford's will." He handed it to me. "Look at the date."

It was a simple two-page document dated October 20, 1936, about a week after my birth. I scanned the first page and then the second. There on the last paragraph I read, "...and to the daughter to whom I gave birth on October 12, 1936, I leave the entirety of my estate." The pages fluttered to the floor as I stood and walked over to the window.

"I can see how overwhelmed you are. Should we take a break?"

"No. No," I groaned. "Let's get this over with."

Danny stood, joined me at the window, and put his arms around me.

"Think about it, Quil," he whispered. "If Charles Pickford was dead and then Clarice died, willing you everything, then we have a clear motive."

"What?" My head swam with too much information.

"Fletcher had a good reason to kill you *and* Paddy," Danny continued. "If you were gone, then Paddy would be the only surviving heir."

"Heir to what?" I pushed away from him.

Mr. Randall spoke up. "Around four million, give or take a few hundred thousand."

I had reached my limit and slumped to the floor.

"Let's take a break," Danny said, lifting me into a chair. "We'll get some lunch and meet you back here around one o'clock. Work for you?"

"Works for me."

Danny put an arm tight around my waist and steadied me. Down in the cruiser, he waited for me to gather my thoughts.

"This is some sort of twisted joke, right? I mean, this reads like a script from a soap opera. Tell me it isn't true. Please."

"I wish I could."

I leaned my head against the window.

"Come on. Let's get you something to eat," Danny said.

"Something half raw, please."

After a lunch of steak and salad, with a glass of wine for me and a Coke for Danny, I was ready to take on the rest of the afternoon.

We settled into the familiar sofa.

"Ready?" Mr. Randall smiled at me encouragingly.

"Gosh, I hope so," I answered.

"All right, let's move on to Fletcher. We have had a forensic psychiatrist working on him, but he had access to a platoon of lawyers right from the first day, and so we haven't gotten much out of him. The one diagnosis we have been able to nail down is that Mr. Pickford is a complete sociopath bordering on psychosis."

"Not surprising."

"According to his personal secretary and flight, car rental, and hotel records, we have been able to patch together his attempt to find you. All this was needless because according to Florida law, where Clarice's will was filed, in seven years, if you, Miss Tandy, hadn't come forward to claim your inheritance, Fletcher would have been declared the legal heir." Randall shook his head in disbelief.

"I'm getting confused again."

"Sheriff Owens, tell Miss Tandy about your conversation with Alex Bennett at the FBI."

Danny told me about his friend and his friend's daughter and how the FBI got involved. The story came out about Dickie Blevins and how Clarice had been searching for me for years. How Dickie had died under suspicious circumstances and that Fletcher had been in Baton Rouge at the same time.

"Apparently, Mr. Blevins was trying to blackmail Fletcher, and it is our guess that it all went badly."

"You guess?"

"So far there is no proof, but sometime during Fletcher's visit to Baton Rouge, he managed to break into an archive storage unit of Henderson, Hathaway, and Jenkins." Randall produced yet another file. "Here are your actual adoption papers."

I took a deep breath as I reached for the file.

"As you can see, a woman by the name of Naomi Leblanc was the original adopting parent."

"Who is that?" I asked.

"As it turns out, she was the sister of your maternal grandmother. Naomi was also the attending maternity nurse at your birth. Again, we are guessing, since the entire delivery was elaborately hidden. Naomi then turned you over to Henry and Christmas."

"Glee. Her name was Glee."

Mr. Randall looked again at the file in front of him. "It says here Christmas."

"Christmas was her first name, but she always went by her middle name, Glee."

Mr. Randall scribbled Glee on the file.

"As for a great-aunt named Naomi, I am in the dark. I never heard her name, and I certainly had never met her."

"Naomi died in 1941, very young, only thirty, but it is our theory that the necklace in the photo was passed to Naomi by Clarice, Naomi to Glee, and finally Glee to you."

"So how did Fletcher actually find me?"

Danny filled in the blanks. "Fletcher got Hackberry, Tennessee, from

Liza Bennett, Alex Bennett's daughter at Mercy General, your birthdate from the will, and we think he knew about the necklace from the photo."

"But he showed up at Thanksgiving dinner as James."

"We think he had been watching you for a while and that his meeting Libby at that stoplight here in Knoxville was no coincidence."

My mind flew back to Thanksgiving and his comment about the necklace. The "birthday game" was the final clue.

"But why Libby? He nearly killed her."

"We think he did *that* for fun, and he probably thought he had killed her," Danny said. "He has a history of brutalizing women."

"Where do we go from here?"

"Well, if I were you, I'd get an attorney and accountant in Florida and get my hands on that inheritance. After that, we will need you to come in for depositions at the end of the week. In the meantime, write down everything you remember. No detail is too small. We will need your contact information and for you to stay close to home for a while. The trial is months away, probably spring, but for now, we need you to be available for questioning."

We all stood and shook hands, and then Mr. Randall said, "I can't begin to tell you how sorry I am about your brother."

"Me too," I whispered.

PART THREE

Go confidently in the direction of your dreams.
Live the life you have imagined.
—Henry David Thoreau

CHAPTER 25
GOING HOME

Hackberry, Tennessee
December 6, 1961

I provided all the information I knew about the attack in a single deposition. There really wasn't much to tell, since most of it the DA already knew and had dismissed until the trial—set for April 20 the coming spring. Fletcher had been denied bail, and for that, I was grateful. With all this completed, I was free to go. *Go where?*

After the deposition, I had asked District Attorney Philip Randall for a private meeting. I needed advice about what to do about the insanely huge inheritance that caused the killing of my brother and burning of my home. Mr. Randall was a compassionate man who had children about my age. He ushered me into a private conference room.

"Mr. Randall, thank you so much for taking time out of your busy schedule."

"It's fine," he said, giving my hand a fatherly pat.

"Well, let me get right to the point," I began. "I guess I need adult supervision."

Mr. Randall laughed. "About your inheritance?"

"Yes, exactly." I exhaled a long breath. "It can't be true. Is it?"

"Yes, in fact, I knew you might need some help, so I made copies of the will and investment portfolio." He pushed a button on the intercom on the table. "Loretta, would you please bring the file from my desk marked Miss Tandy?"

Now looking at me he continued, "You are going to need a good lawyer in Miami and an honest investment firm."

Before I could speak, Loretta arrived with the file.

"Here is everything you will need. I have enclosed the name and contact info of a wildly successful attorney—I attended law school with him and trust him. Bidwell Canfield III is his name, but don't let his pretentious handle scare you off. You'll like him, and he will connect you with an investment firm you can trust."

"Have you called him?" I asked.

"Yes, but only to introduce you. The rest is going to be up to you."

"What if I don't claim it?" My voice was only a whisper. "It feels like blood money."

"Then Fletcher is next in line. There is no Tennessee law that can prevent him from having it all even if he is jailed for the rest of his life. I know how raw you must feel, Tranquil, but I beg you, please do nothing rash. Give yourself some time. If you feel uncomfortable about keeping the money, think of some other options—like a charitable foundation, for instance"

I sat there for a minute. I did feel *raw* and irrational. *Give it some time. Donnez-lui quelque temps.*

"How can I ever thank you?"

"No need."

"Mr. Randall, you should know that I am leaving for the winter, but I'll call with my contact information."

On the way back from Knoxville to Hackberry, my old truck seemed to turn onto Deer Spring Road on its own. I knew it was time to begin facing my new life; whatever it was going to be, it needed to start here.

I parked on the far side of the car bridge with the river between me and the inevitable. Nearly two weeks after Paddy's death and the fire, I had finally gathered the courage to go home, but now I felt sick with loss and dread. *I'll never be able to recover from this. What's the point?*

The weather was misty and cold. I pulled the hood of my jacket over my head and jammed my hands into the pockets. Looking across the river felt unimaginably surreal.

I turned away and walked out onto the covered footbridge. At about the middle of the bridge, I found my discarded jacket sodden and nearly frozen. I picked it up and remembered the exact moment I had dropped it there—Paddy in the river, Fletcher chasing me, blood running in my eyes. In the jacket's pocket, I found the theater tickets for *The Absent-Minded Professor.* My broken heart cracked even further. I groaned and gripped the bridge railing as I wiped my nose on my sleeve. I wanted to scream and should have.

I knew I had a choice now—die or keep living, make a new life or end the old one. I looked down at the river rushing past cold and gray. My life expectancy would be about four minutes if I jumped. I would float away until hypothermia rendered me unconscious like Paddy, and I would drown. It seemed like a quick fix, morbidly comforting.

All the loss and pain and anger would die with me. I remembered Mr. Randall's advice, "I beg you to do nothing rash. Give yourself some time." At this moment, I was in too much pain to give myself some time.

How much more could I possibly lose? Would I ever get used to the realization of my secret adoption? Had my whole life been a lie? Why hadn't they told me? How was it that nobody knew? Not even Betty or Warren? I felt homeless and orphaned.

I placed a foot on the bottom rail of the bridge, still holding the jacket. I brought up the other foot, balancing at thigh height against the top railing, arms wide, one hand holding the jacket and the other the theater tickets. The railing was icy, and I could feel my feet inching apart. Maybe fate would decide for me.

I looked back at the house, now a pile of frozen ashes, and I thought I heard voices in the wind and music and laughter and the smell of food cooking. *You are hallucinating.* Then I felt Mama's voice, like words in a brisk gust, brush across my face, *"Don't leave us. You can't die yet."*

My left foot slipped through the railing, and I landed stomach first onto the top rail, knocking the breath out of me, teetering dangerously. Suddenly, all I wanted was to be alive, but I had tempted death, and I was in a very precarious position. I needed my hands. I let the jacket fall into the river; then the tickets fluttered into the wind. Pushing myself backward, I fell hard onto the bridge floor. I caught my breath as I watched my jacket float away until it finally sank. *You fool. That could have been you.*

Driving across the car bridge and up to the remains of my home felt so bizarre I couldn't completely comprehend the loss. The arson team that had finished the investigation said the fire had burned so hot that nothing was identifiable—not even metal remained. They were, however, able to identify the source of the fire—gasoline—and the origin— fuel thrown around the kitchen and woodpile.

The huge, ancient oak next to the house was nothing more than a charred, twisted stump. Yet everything else—the cabins, dock, and boat- house—were completely untouched, as if nothing had occurred.

I stood there. Should I rebuild? Restart the business? In the end, I could not imagine life alone here. I knew it was time to say goodbye to the Tandy legacy. And I knew what I was going to do.

═╬ ╬═

On the way back to town, my truck developed a cough. *Probably water in the fuel tank.*

I pulled into Frank Watson's Fix Anything Garage.

"Hi, Frank, I think my truck needs a checkup."

"I'll give her a look, but I won't have a chance until tomorrow."

"That's fine."

"Can I give you a ride to Kimble's?"

"No, thanks. I'll just run. See you tomorrow."

I ran through town, acknowledging people as I went. I was hungry and stopped at Maybelle's Soup and Pie Shop. I didn't need to see a menu.

"May I please have the biggest bowl of clam chowder possible, a cou- ple huge chunks of crusty bread, and strawberry-rhubarb pie with ice cream?"

"Lordy, Quil. How can you eat like that and look the way you do?"

"Daddy used to say I had the metabolism of a racehorse."

I ate in silence, paid the bill, and headed for the comfort of Kimble's Inn.

Lorraine Kimble had given me her best room, large and comfortable; a four-poster feather bed by the window, a desk in the corner, and a comfortable chair for relaxing and reading.

Included with the room was a hearty breakfast, but I was on my own for lunch and dinner.

I had a long, luxurious bath and thought hard about my future. I wanted to get away from Hackberry for a while. Maybe even until spring. There was Michelle Conners's trial to consider and the land and all that inheritance money. My mind was whirling. *Slow down. One thing at a time.*

I slipped into the comfy flannel pajamas and fuzzy slippers Betty had bought me, then sat down at the desk and made a list.

Pick up the truck; call: Richard Ingles about house insurance, Mr. Lincoln concerning Michelle's trial, Bidwell Canfield re: inheritance; check on Libby.

I was asleep by eight o'clock and dreamed about the jacket floating in the river.

CHAPTER 26

Loose Ends

Hackberry, Tennessee
December 7, 1961

"Good morning, Lorraine. Delicious breakfast. May I use your phone? I need to make some calls. Two will be long distance, but I'll get time and charges, and you can add it to my bill. Will that be okay?"

"Slow down, Quil. Relax. Sure, you can use the phone in my office. It's more private."

"Thanks. You're a peach."

I ran up to my room and collected the file from Philip Randall, the insurance folder, and Mr. Lincoln's contact info. Settling behind Lorraine's desk, I first called Libby. Her mother answered.

"Hi, Mrs. Sparks. It's Quil. I was checking up on Libby. How is she doing, and is she accepting visitors?"

"She would love to see you. Her cast will be on for another month, but the wires in her jaw come out next week."

"That's great. I'll swing by the diner around noon. I am ready for one of your triple cheeseburgers. And then I'll go on up for a visit."

Next I phoned Richard Ingles.

"Glad you called. The insurance on the house paid out, and I have a check here for fifty thousand."

"Thanks, Richard. I'll come by this morning."

163

Next on the list was Frank at the repair shop.

"Well. Quil, not good news. The old gal is wearing out. It's still good for around town, but without a lot of repair and money, I wouldn't tax her. She's got over one hundred thousand miles on her."

"Rats. All right, I'll be over to pick her up before lunchtime. Thanks for having a look."

The next call was to Mr. Lincoln, Michelle Conners's attorney. I dialed the long-distance operator.

"New Orleans, Louisiana, 636-4122. And I will need time and charges, please."

"Lincoln, Stanley, and Aspen," the receptionist chirped.

"This is Tranquil Tandy, and I am hoping to speak with Mr. Lincoln."

"I'll transfer you."

"Lincoln speaking."

"I'm just checking in."

"I'm so glad you called. I was just going to write you a letter. Michelle's trial has been moved up to December 28. The Penns are pushing to get her put away before the New Year, and you know how influential they are. They have hired a high-priced lawyer, and he is throwing his weight around."

"I *do* know about them."

"The good news is that I have pulled some strings at the police department and there are a lot of names connected to our boy Pit. He has quite a track record."

"I'm not surprised. Have you contacted any of them?"

"Disallowed."

"Can I contact them?"

"Nothing in the law says you can't. But you will have to hurry. The trial is in three weeks."

"I will get there as soon as I can. I'll call you tomorrow."

The last call on my list was to Bidwell Canfield III. I connected again to the long-distance operator.

"Miami, Florida. 891-7743. Time and charges, please."

"Canfield Law Offices." The receptionist's voice sounded smooth and professional.

"Yes, my name is Tranquil Tandy. I was given Mr. Canfield's name by Knoxville District Attorney Philip Randall. May I speak with Mr. Canfield?"

"One moment, please."

A few seconds later the receptionist came back on the line. "I'm sorry, Miss Tandy, but Mr. Canfield is in court today. May I have him call you?"

"Yes, I will be near a phone toward the end of the day tomorrow. Will four o'clock be a good time?"

"His schedule says it is. I'll tell him."

"Great. I can be reached at Hackberry, Tennessee, 435-9264."

I ran the two miles to Frank's and picked up the truck. I had formulated a plan for the old gal as I ran and then drove directly to the Owens' farm.

Betty met me at the door and wrapped her arms around me, holding me tight.

"Darling girl, it's so good to see you. Come in and tell us how you've been."

Warren sat at the kitchen table having coffee after feeding the cattle.

"Hi there, sweetheart. Coffee?"

"Yes, please, with cream."

I sat down at the kitchen table with Warren. Betty brought the coffee and then joined us.

"Tell us how you are." Betty rubbed my arm in a motherly way.

"I think I'm better—beginning to heal and make plans for the future. I am actually here today to make a deal with Warren."

"Me?"

"Yep," I said, sliding an envelope across the table. "This is the title to my truck. She's too old to travel anymore, but she'd be perfect for farmwork. I'm giving her to you with love." I smiled at him. "She got new oil, filters, spark plugs, and belts yesterday. Frank flushed the radiator and cleaned the fuel tank. She's all ready to go."

"I don't know what to say," Warren said, opening the envelope and taking out the title.

"Thank you would be enough. See where I've signed? All you have to do is take it to the courthouse for registration. Oh, and you will need a bill of sale. Betty, do you have a scrap of paper I can scribble on?"

"Does Danny know about this?" Warren asked.

"No, and he doesn't need to. It's none of his business."

I wrote out a bill of sale selling the truck to Warren for a dollar.

"It's going to cost you one thing, however. Obviously, I'm going to need some new wheels. Would you take me car shopping in Knoxville tomorrow?"

"With pleasure, but me and my new truck will have to do the feeding first." He was grinning from ear to ear.

"Pick me up at nine o'clock? I'm staying at Kimble's, you know."

"Yes, and we don't like it one bit," Betty chimed in. "You belong here with us."

"Too close to home, Betty. I'm not ready."

Warren offered to drive me to the diner, but I said I was planning on a cheeseburger and a shake, so I had better run.

I arrived at Spark's Diner just before noon, and I was ready to eat. I ordered a triple cheeseburger with fries and a chocolate shake.

"Gee, Quil. Slow down, girl," Mrs. Sparks said, sitting down across from me.

"I just ran three miles in under twenty minutes. I could eat this table!"

She talked while I ate. "Libby is getting stronger every day, and I know healing takes time, but she has lost her fizz. Her personality has gone flat, and I don't know what to do."

I finished lunch, then trotted up the stairs to Libby's room. She looked good. Her nose had healed, and all the bruising was gone. She smiled at me, but it wasn't the old Libby I saw in her eyes.

"Girl, you need some lipstick!" I said, picking up a tube and a hand mirror.

Libby expertly applied it.

"Now there's my old friend." I sat down on the bed. "How's the leg?"

Through wired teeth, she said, "Better."

"Your mom says the cast comes off in a month but the wires will come out of your mouth next week. Bet you're ready for that!"

"Yes."

I could see it hurt to talk.

"Yikes. Look at your nails! How about a manicure and pedicure while I tell you a story?"

"Pink."

"Pink it is."

I gently soaked and trimmed her cuticles, clipped and filed her nails, and applied two coats of pink polish and a clear topcoat as I told her all about Fletcher and the adoption. She cried about Paddy. But most of all I wanted her to know that bringing James/Fletcher into Hackberry was not her fault. As it turned out, he had been watching us for weeks and had chosen her as the vehicle into our lives.

I told her that I was getting out of Hackberry for the winter—going to Key West, and when she was completely healed, I would send a plane ticket for her to visit. But it all had to be our secret for now. "Promise?"

Her eyes sparkled and she nodded.

"There you are, my darling friend, toes and fingers perfectly polished and lipstick on. You're a girl again. Do you want me to brush your hair?"

"Yes, please." She pointed to the hairbrush on the bureau.

I brushed her beautiful blonde hair with long, even strokes, forward and back, deeply massaging her scalp. I was just tying her hair into a high ponytail when Danny appeared at the door. He seemed surprised to see me.

"How's our patient? Wow, doesn't she look all spruced up?" He looked at her and she at him, and I saw a glimmer of affection pass between them.

I leaned over and kissed Libby on the cheek and whispered, "Our secret, remember?"

She nodded.

I gave Danny a hug on my way out of Libby's room.

Downstairs Mrs. Sparks stopped me as I was reaching for the doorknob.

"Quil, I found this—actually, I was looking for it. I know you lost everything in the fire, even photos." She handed me a small black-and-white picture.

They were all there: Grand-mère and Grand-père, Good-daddy, Gigi, Mama, me, and Daddy holding Paddy. We were all in our swimsuits standing in the shallow water of the upper river on a hot summer day, painted by the shadows of a cottonwood. Paddy was about a year old, and I would have been seventeen. I stared deeply into the photo, remembering the moment that picture was taken, Mama pinching my bottom to make me smile.

I pressed the photo to my chest. I couldn't speak, just looked at Mrs. Sparks, hoping my gratitude would show.

"Keep it." Mrs. Sparks's eyes welled with tears. "And thank you so very much for helping Libby today."

I ran the two miles into town, arriving at Richard Ingles's at around four o'clock. He wasn't there but had left the check with his secretary.

The bank was two blocks down.

"I'd like to exchange this check for a cashier's check, please, and I would like to get ten thousand in one hundred-dollar bills from savings."

The bank manager came over to the teller window. "Hi, Quil. Are you sure you want to carry around this much cash?"

"I appreciate your concern, I really do, but I have plans for it all."

I gathered up the check and cash and trotted the six blocks to Kimble's. In my room, I pulled out my suitcase and packed, slipping the cash, check, and photo into the lining of the suitcase. I was planning on buying a car the next day and then leaving for New Orleans.

A hot bath for my tired legs felt wonderful. I soaked and thought about what I would say to all the other victims in New Orleans; we needed as many of them as possible to testify.

Some might say Michelle Conners was none of my business, but I knew better. I had to help her. I had to.

After breakfast the next day, I paid the bill for my lodging, hugged and thanked Lorraine for her incredible kindness, and told her I'd see her in the spring.

Warren was right on time, and we were in Knoxville by ten o'clock. Along the way, we had talked about the kind of car I wanted, but I really didn't know.

"Let's start at Billy Boston's Ford Store. Billy and I have been friends for years, and I trust him. He might even give us a good deal."

We asked for Billy, and he came out to the showroom floor, obviously happy to see his old friend.

"Billy, this is Tranquil Tandy, and she is in need of a car."

Billy walked us around the new car lot and then the used car lot, but I saw nothing that flipped my switch.

Then Billy snapped his fingers and said, "Wait a minute, I might have the perfect car for a young woman like you. Follow me."

As we walked toward the service center part of the dealership, Billy explained, "About four years ago, a guy came in with an old Cadillac to trade. His wife had died, and he had decided he wanted a convertible sports car. He ordered a brand-new Thunderbird, drove it for six months, had a stroke, and the car sat in his garage until he passed away a month ago. I guess none of his kids wanted it, and I bought it back as a courtesy to the family. It's being detailed now. It's in perfect condition and only has about a thousand miles on it."

We followed him into the service center, and there sat my car—a turquoise-blue Thunderbird convertible, whitewall tires, white-and-turquoise tuck and roll interior, and white convertible top. It was love at first sight.

"Let's take it for a drive." I was so excited I squealed like a teenager.

The deal was over before I even turned the key. Billy and Warren put their heads together over a calculator, and before I knew it, I was writing a check.

"Plus a full tank of gas," Warren said to Billy.

"Already done." Billy smiled, handing me the keys. "Enjoy your new wheels, Miss Tandy."

Out in the parking lot, I told Warren about my plans to leave for the rest of the winter, and he said he understood. I promised to stay in touch. We hugged, and I thanked him. Then I slid into my new car and turned south.

Driving a powerful sports car was both terrifying and exhilarating. I could feel people looking at me, but I liked it, a brand-new sensation for a private person like myself. But I wanted to share this new experience with somebody.

At the first gas stop, I retrieved the photo from my suitcase and pressed it into the upholstery on the passenger door. *Now that's better.*

I made it as far as Birmingham, Alabama, the first night and arrived in New Orleans late the next day.

CHAPTER 27

MICHELLE

New Orleans, Louisiana
December 9, 1961

I arrived at the same hotel as I had on my last visit, exhausted from traveling more than six hundred miles in two days. I put the family photo in the glove compartment, checked in, and dragged my suitcase to my room—asleep by eight p.m. and awake by five the next morning, making lists and writing a script to persuade Pit's victims to testify for Michelle.

I arrived at Mr. Lincoln's office promptly at nine o'clock. Though it was a Saturday, we had planned to meet since time was short; we only had eighteen days before the trial, and there was Christmas to consider.

"Could you hold on to this for me while I'm in New Orleans?" I said, handing him a thick package.

"In the safe, I assume."

I nodded.

"All right, Quil, let's get right to work. Here are the names and addresses of women who filed a complaint against Mr. Penn," he said, pushing a sheet of paper my way.

"Eleven!" I was horrified.

"Yes, he deserved killing."

"And none of them ever went to trial? Surely his parents were tired of being his alibi?"

"Well, that's the thing. While I was digging up complaints on Pruitt, I found some similar complaints on the dad, Edward Penn."

"You have got to be kidding. This is a family tradition?"

"Looks like it, so I can see where covering up for Pit was important."

"How is Michelle?"

"Not good. She looks worn and is emotionally fragile."

"Can we bail her out before the trial? Say for Christmas?"

"Bail is set at ten thousand."

"I can cover that."

"Quite a risk, Miss Tandy. What if she runs?"

"She won't, because you are going to explain, in great detail, what will happen to her if she is caught. Besides, she will be with her parents, and that will make her feel safe. How do I make out the check?"

Mr. Lincoln looked intensely at me. "Good Lord, what on earth did Pruitt Penn do to you?"

I looked down at the floor. "Everything."

That afternoon I dashed out to pick up something for Michelle to wear. Mr. Lincoln had told me that all her clothing had been submitted into evidence, since they were soaked in Pit's blood and possibly Michelle's. At a local clothing store, I bought underwear, a sundress, and a pair of flip-flops, guessing at the sizes.

Together Mr. Lincoln and I arrived at the county jail with all the proper paperwork to bail her out. As Mr. Lincoln opened the door for me, he said quietly, "Don't forget she is, or could be, a murderer."

Chills scampered down my spine. *Yes, but given the opportunity, I might have done what she did.*

It took nearly an hour before a dazed-looking Michelle stepped through the jailhouse door into the reception area in her new sundress and flip-flops. She recognized us, but before she could speak, we whisked her out the door and into Mr. Lincoln's car.

"How are you feeling, Michelle?" Mr. Lincoln asked.

"Confused," she said.

She truly did look confused. She and I sat in the back seat of Mr. Lincoln's Lincoln. He turned to face us.

To Michelle, he said, "Miss Tandy here has laid out a substantial amount of money to get you out of that hellhole, and once you recover from the shock of being on the outside, your natural instinct will be to run. Let me explain what will happen if you do. You will be caught and most likely convicted of murder by a jury who will feel no sympathy for you whatsoever. Do you understand?"

Michelle nodded. She looked like a frightened bunny.

Now it was my turn.

"I am going to take you to your parents' house, where you will not drive or go anywhere alone. I have hired a private detective, who is going to help you with this list."

I handed her a copy of the list of the other women.

"The goal is to get some, or all, of them to testify. You only have sixteen days. Do you understand? This is crucial."

She nodded again.

"All right, we are going to get in my car now."

"Okay," she whispered.

I nodded to Mr. Lincoln, and he said, "Good luck, ladies."

We drove without conversation except for directions to her parents' house.

"Why are you doing this?" she finally asked.

"You know why."

"Yes, but you are taking such a risk."

"Let me make something perfectly clear. If you decide to run, I will kill you myself."

She gave me a wide-eyed stare, then said, "This is their house on the left."

I knew Mr. Lincoln had planned to call the Conners so they would be ready for her. Michelle's mother dashed out onto the driveway, and Michelle fell into her arms, both of them sobbing.

When the two gained their composure, I said, "Mrs. Conners, my name is Tranquil Tandy, a friend of Michelle's. There is a lot to explain. May I come in?"

The next morning I met with Doug Pooler, a man in his late fifties—the private detective I had hired. We went over the list of names and locations of Pruitt Penn's victims. Out of the eleven, nine still lived in Louisiana: two in Baton Rouge, one in Alexandria, three in Lafayette, and three in New Orleans. I pulled out my calendar and began to lay out a game plan.

We talked about Michelle's fragile state, but Doug assured me having three daughters of his own had taught him how to read and communicate with young women.

I explained my plan to have him and Michelle speak to other victims and convince as many as possible to testify. It was Mr. Lincoln's hope that though Michelle was supposedly caught red handed and had admitted to the stabbing, extenuating circumstances were abundantly in her favor. Victim and expert testimony, and proving the police department to be negligent might soften the jury. Mr. Lincoln was even going to call Edward Penn to the stand and would, if need be, expose his sexual past.

CHAPTER 28

THE HUNT

New Orleans, Louisiana
Monday, December 11, 1961

On Monday morning, Michelle and I, along with Doug Pooler, met with Mr. Lincoln for a strategic planning meeting.

We were in the conference room, a yellow pad and pen in front of Michelle and me, and a huge white poster board on an easel set up on the other side of the table, where a list, organized by date, was written in bold black ink.

Mr. Lincoln was in his I-am-in-charge mode. "What you are looking at here is our timeline. There is a huge amount to do by the twenty-eighth, but I have faith we can get it done.

"Michelle, your job between now and the twenty-eighth is to get as healthy as possible. No junk food, lots of fruits and vegetables, lean protein, and exercise.

"Doug, you are on the hunt for our nine victims, and you will be taking Michelle with you. Arriving as a duo is safer and more convincing. Give it your best shot. In addition, Michelle, you are going to need appropriate attire for the trial. The guidelines are as follows: nothing too fashionable or bright or short. No suits or high heels. Tasteful makeup and hairstyle. No perfume. In a nutshell: attractive and modest.

"This week I will be in jury selection and court preparations. In jury selection, we will be looking for damaged women and men with daughters."

As callous as that sounded, I knew he had to lay everything out in plainspoken perspective. There was no time for careful conversation.

"Next week, the eighteenth through the twenty-third, the three of us and a witness consultant will be working on testimony delivery. Either of you ladies have an issue with explosive anger?"

I raised my hand. Michelle, the supposed murderer, did not. I believed her.

"Then there is Christmas Eve and Christmas Day. After that, we have two days to pull everything together. Any questions?"

None of us spoke.

"All right, then, let's set the world on fire."

CHAPTER 29
FACING THE PAST

New Orleans, Louisiana
Wednesday, December 13, 1961

I lay in bed, and my thoughts before sleep became troubling as the realization of what a trial would mean to me personally—the rape and possibly the abortion. While Michelle, Doug, and Mr. Lincoln worked on their assigned jobs, I knew what my job in New Orleans would be.

I had endured so much trauma in the past two years—trauma that needed to be addressed. If I had thought through my involvement with Michelle, it should have occurred to me that testifying in her trial would unearth my past—the past I had diligently attempted to neatly package and bury. Now all my dirty laundry might be paraded around a courtroom for all to see. I wondered how I would react. Would I lie? Would I fall apart? What would it take to be strong enough to face it, say it, own it?

Michelle might be on trial for her life, but my mind and heart were still so damaged I knew I had to face the pain before I faced a trial. I couldn't put it off any longer. I needed to begin letting go. It was now or never. *One step at a time*, I had once thought, but now those steps needed to get quicker.

I woke the next morning with a plan. First, a long, cleansing run before I tackled any of the big stuff. Jogging down Tchoupitoulas Street along the west side of the Mississippi—nearly eight miles from the

French Quarter to the Audubon Zoo—gave me time to think. I bought a ticket and spent the afternoon strolling along the pathways. It had been an unusually warm fall, and even days before Christmas the temperature felt comfortable. The trees still had most of their foliage, and the animals were active. I bought an ice-cream cone and sat on a park bench watching the birds of prey study the ground—naturally watching for edible targets.

As I ambled through the zoo, I couldn't help but be reminded of innocence imprisoned. Beautiful animals caged for life, most likely their only crime being in the wrong place at the wrong time. True for all species, even humans.

At around three o'clock, I got on the trolley and spent the next two hours meandering back toward downtown. I reluctantly got off at my alma mater, Tulane University. As I walked into the student center where I had first met Pruitt Penn, my chest clutched slightly. He had been so charming and delightfully funny. It was there he had asked me out on our first date. I took a seat in the corner and watched the usual goings-on of students during their daily routine while I got my breathing under control.

I walked to my old student housing apartment and stood outside. Bile inched up into my throat as old memories squirreled around in my brain. I turned away and crossed St. Charles to what used to be my favorite coffee shop/bookstore. I devoured a bagel with cream cheese and deviled crab meat, coffee with whipped cream, and a bowl of sliced mangos. I felt better.

Walking down Charles Street, I believed I had the courage to cross the park where Pit had attacked and maimed me. To my shock, a park bench now sat under the same willow tree where I was raped—like a commemoration of the event. It felt like a joke, as if God were mocking me, but as I looked around, I could see new park benches dotted around the park in the shady spots.

I paced back and forth under the willow, forcing myself to remember it all, dragging it to the surface, thinking I could crush the fear, the pain, the total violation from existence one at a time by sheer will. I imagined a coat of fresh paint over a tarnished old wall. *Remember it and release it, Quil.*

As I paced, I could hear my screams, begging him to stop; the smell of his sweat and my blood; the rage on his face, and the jagged edge of the broken wine bottle ripping into my skin; the sound my arm made as it snapped; and every blow to my face. I remembered running into the street bleeding, naked, screaming hysterically.

My fists clenched, and my jaws clamped tight; silent tears ran down my face. I began to shake and feel unsteady.

I shouted, "I'm glad you are dead, Pruitt Penn. May you *never* rest in peace! I hope you are getting everything you deserve. You are dead, and I am alive. I win. I win!" I sat down hard on the bench. "And guess what, dead Pruitt? Michelle is going to *win* too!" *Let him go, Quil. Let it be over.*

I blew out my breath fully, then, breathing in and out slowly, deeply, and actually felt like the first wisps of what might be relief. Saying it aloud had seemed to help.

Of course, shouting at dead Pruitt hadn't really changed anything. I heard my mama say, *Une âme déchirée ne peut être réparé par Dieu...* a torn soul can only be repaired by God. "No!" I said out loud. "I am not a victim to be fixed by a myth. I am angry, and I am going to get even!"

Unfortunately, my attempt at letting Pruitt go simply transferred and compounded my hatred toward Fletcher. Yes, I could let Pruitt be dead and gone, but my revulsion and rage-filled need for revenge seethed and simmered like a bomb set to explode—the burning of my home, the attacks on me and my best friend, and the murder of my little brother, even my misery here in New Orleans now belonged to Fletcher, and he was going to pay for it.

Michelle's trial? I would do whatever I needed to do to stay in control, no matter what happened. *I will not be broken.*

I turned onto Broadway and ran hard back to the hotel. Past the hospital that had repaired my body and, in the French Quarter, past the building where the abortionist ruined me and helped me murder an innocent child.

CHAPTER 30

DISCLOSURE

New Orleans, Louisiana
Friday, December 15, 1962

On Friday afternoon, the four of us—Doug, Michelle, Mr. Lincoln, and I—met for a progress meeting at Mr. Lincoln's office.

Doug began, "Well, I must say of all the cases I have worked on, this has been the most unbelievably interesting. Let me start with the list. Michelle, feel free to jump in if I miss anything. Here in New Orleans we found Elizabeth Beringer, who pretended she had no idea what we were talking about. Next, Kitty Durant admitted to the rape but works in the courthouse and was afraid for her job. And Abigail Thayer literally chased us off the porch with her broom.

"In Alexandria, we spoke with Jody Ellison, née Johnson. By accident, we got a glimpse of her scar, but she refused to get involved. She said her husband knew nothing, and she insisted we keep it that way.

"Lafayette is where we first hit pay dirt. Michelle recognized the name Kelly Tillman."

"I worked with her at the coffee shop on campus at Tulane," Michelle added.

"There were three on the list for Lafayette. Besides Kelly, there was Annie Willis and Lynn Abbott. We stopped to see Kelly first, hoping she would be more empathetic to Michelle's plight. Her mother came to the door and after a brief explanation on our part invited us in. She proceeded to tell us the most incredible story. First, Kelly had committed suicide the summer before—stepping in front of a train, no less. I was ready to strike Kelly's name from the list, but then Mrs. Tillman, Pauline Tillman—"

"Wait a minute." Mr. Lincoln pulled a file from his desk and quickly thumbed through it. Finding what he was looking for, he said, "There was a report filed against Edward Penn on October 3, 1937, by a Pauline Oakley. Does that check out?"

"Yes. Our Pauline's maiden name was Oakley, and she claims Edward Penn raped her *and* that Kelly was his child!"

"So Pruitt raped his own half sister?" Mr. Lincoln stood and faced the window. "These Penns are a real piece of work. What else?"

"As it turns out, according to Mrs. Tillman the other two girls won't be of any help. Lynn Abbott moved to Chicago, and Annie Willis hasn't spoken a single word to anyone since the rape."

"Is that it?" Mr. Lincoln asked.

"Just one more. Peggy White."

"Did you get anything from her?"

"Boy, did we ever. She was a lingerie model when Pruitt raped her, and the scar he left her ruined her career, and, Paul, she has a massive scar on her chest; her husband knows everything, and she is more than happy to testify. So is Pauline."

"What a bag of worms." Mr. Lincoln rubbed his forehead. He looked tired. "Let me fill you in on my progress. Jury selection has been completed, and here are the results," he said, handing us each a single sheet of paper listing each juror according to selection. "Jurors three, six, seven, nine, and twelve are women. All but one has children, are conservative, and attend church. Jurors one, two, four, five, eight, ten, and eleven are men. Three have daughters, three are white collar, one is a teacher at Tulane—I don't know what the DA was thinking letting that one through, and four and one are blue collar. One is a bartender. I especially liked him since he probably has seen the worst side of humanity. All in all, I think we have a fair combination of people who will listen to a reasonable defense.

"We have subpoenaed a barrel load of hostile witnesses," he continued.

"What do you mean by hostile?" Michelle wanted to know.

"I mean I will probably get drawn and quartered in the town square if this goes badly. Here is the list," he said, pushing papers our way.

"These are all police and detectives and *Edward Penn*?" I was shocked.

"Marilyn Penn too," he said. "Women usually aren't willing to lie as easily under oath, and in a murder trial, perjury can cost twenty years."

"This is hardball," Doug said. "How is the fallout so far?"

"Like a hailstorm, but to be honest, I am completely enjoying watching the NOPD squirm. At least a few of them are going down. I've got them by…never mind. I have also subpoenaed the emergency personnel and doctors who treated you both," he said, motioning to Michelle and me.

I wasn't prepared for this. The medical community could close ranks as fast as the police department, and I was worried about the doctor who gave me the illegal abortion. Well, not so much him, his neck and license would be on the line if exposed, but the nurse who knew I was pregnant and sent me his way might be a problem.

"I think I need to tell you something. Doug and Michelle, could you give us a moment?" I asked. I didn't want either of them knowing anything that they might be compelled to reveal.

Doug and Michelle closed the office door behind them, and I laid out the whole graphic tale of the pregnancy and abortion.

"Well, why the heck didn't you disclose this before?" Mr. Lincoln demanded.

"Because Michelle's on trial, not me!"

"True, but you are our star witness, and I don't want to be blindsided by anything. Is there more?"

"No."

CHAPTER 31
TAKING A BREATHER

New Orleans, Louisiana
Saturday, December 16, 1961

I picked up Michelle at her parents' and headed into town.
"What's up?" she asked.

"Let's go over to Maison Blanche. It's on Carrelton, right? We can have lunch, then get our hair trimmed and washed and then have a facial. Do they still have that high-dollar makeup counter?"

"Lancôme?"

"That's the one. I think now would be a good time to work on your makeup for the trial. Mine too. Manicures and pedicures too."

Being pampered was the tonic for our stressful week, and at the end, we both looked and felt fabulous.

Then we shopped for trial outfits—clothes with clean, dignified lines and complementary subdued colors. Soft silk blouses and smooth cashmere sweater sets with straight skirts cut to the knee; fine woolen dresses with matching jackets or cardigans. Shoes and jewelry—classy, not flashy.

On the way to the car, loaded with bags, Michelle said, "Listen, I've been watching you shell out money left and right for a week. My attorney, my bail, a private investigator, and now all this fanciness—what are you, some sort of heiress?"

"I have a printing press in my basement."

CHAPTER 32
THE FINAL PREPARATIONS

New Orleans, Louisiana
December 18–24, 1961

I slept in, then ordered breakfast from room service: eggs Benedict, fresh pineapple-orange juice, and espresso with heavy cream.

Leaving the hotel, I trotted down Chartres Street toward Crescent Park along the Mississippi River. It was a brisk day, and I set a strenuous pace. This became my usual schedule, killing time before Christmas and then the trial. I ran and ran, thinking all the while about my part in the trial and Fletcher's trial awaiting me in Tennessee. I hoped he was miserable locked away in the county jail and that Danny would be making certain Fletcher's incarceration would be memorable. I wanted Fletcher to be as weak and fragile as Michelle had been. I hoped he was in a cell without sunlight, that the days were long and the nights even longer. My feet pounded away mile after mile, day after day. I ate and ran and plotted.

The week before Christmas was a flurry of activity.

Monday: Michelle laid out all her trial outfits on the conference table for Mr. Lincoln's approval. She was prepped for trial with one expert and I with another.

Tuesday: Pauline Tillman and Peggy White came in and were prepped by separate consultants.

Wednesday: Our depositions and last-minute witnesses for the prosecution were discussed.

On Thursday, Mr. Lincoln buried himself in evidence and opening remarks, while Michelle rested and I ran.

Friday came, and Mr. Lincoln and Michelle spent the day privately, and then her parents took her home for Christmas.

When Michelle was gone, Mr. Lincoln and I collapsed in his office.

"What do you think her chances are?" I asked.

"To be honest, it's a crapshoot at this point," he began. "Jury trials are tricky, and though I think we have some great evidence and experts in her defense, it will boil down to what the jury perceives to be the truth. The DA, William Estes, is a formidable foe. He's experienced and can be ruthless, and his family and the Penns go way back. We have drawn Judge Ellen Parrish—and that would seem an advantage, but she has a reputation for ruling to the letter of the law, and Michelle's case, as you know, has some pretty big holes—he-said-she-said kind of evidence we hope will be admitted. That she didn't bring the weapon with her to the crime scene is in her favor, that she was the one who called the police is also a plus, and then there is Pruitt Penn's history with women, not to mention his father's. All this, if laid out flawlessly, may prove her innocence. She is firm on the self-defense plea, and here is something you should know: she is not willing to take a plea deal. It's going to be all or nothing."

I had nothing to add. We had done all we could for her. She was either going to walk free or, most likely, face death in the electric chair.

Mr. Lincoln had graciously invited me to join his family for a traditional Christmas, and I gratefully accepted.

On Christmas Eve, I walked up the front steps of their stately Southern home, lights burning brightly. I did my best to balance the gifts and flowers I had brought. Lisbeth Lincoln met me at the door.

"Good heavens, Tranquil, you needn't have brought all this, but the flowers are gorgeous. I just adore red roses—so Christmassy, aren't they? Lordy, look here, Paul, the girl has brought us three dozen roses."

Mr. Lincoln took my packages and welcomed me into his home.

I had a delightfully quiet Christmas with the Lincolns, my first without my family. The sting was less than I had expected and more cheerful than I had hoped.

On Tuesday morning, I picked up Michelle, explaining to her parents that we would see them in court promptly at nine o'clock Thursday morning. They said they had their whole church praying that the truth would come out. *Right, praying. What a waste of time.*

Michelle started to cry softly as we drove away. I pulled over and turned to look at her.

"Okay, listen, Michelle. You need to buck up, girl. We don't have time for any self-pity. How on earth did a timid little thing like you have the nerve to stab Pruitt Penn in the throat?"

"He told me that if I didn't back off, he was going to hurt my parents. I just went over to his place to tell him something important, but he got mad and came after me. I grabbed a steak knife off the kitchen counter, and when he lunged at me, I held up the knife—he ran into it."

"Are you saying he stabbed himself?" I was astonished. *There really was poetic justice.*

"Yes, and then I tried to stop the bleeding, but he died. I called the police, and it all went downhill from there."

"Does Mr. Lincoln know this?"

"Yes, I told him the whole story right from the start—the rape and then the fight—everything."

I was speechless.

After dinner, we settled in for the night at my hotel. I ordered chamomile tea and shortbread from room service, and we curled up on either end of the sofa to unwind before bed.

"Did Pit give you that?" I said, pointing at the scar peeking out of her pajama top.

She pulled her top closed and looked away.

I unbuttoned the first three buttons on my top and showed her my own gnarled disfigurement. "He used a broken wine bottle on me."

"Scissors. He used scissors." Her eyes welled.

I reached across the sofa and took her hand. "I know how traumatic it all was. Don't forget I went through it too. You can trust me."

She nodded.

"Don't you see, Michelle? He was tattooing us, claiming us, and if he did this terrible thing to *us*, then chances are he did it to the rest of them. Not just Peggy White or Kelly Tillman, all of them."

I watched as it sank in. She dried her tears, and for the first time, I saw hope in her eyes.

I excused myself for a bathroom break, and on the counter, partially sticking out of her makeup bag, I found a bottle of pills—pills I recognized instantly. I slipped them into my pajama pocket.

Back on the couch I poured more tea.

"So tomorrow is the big day. Do you have any more questions for me?"

"No, no more questions. I'm just scared to death, is all."

"Well, I have a question for you." I reached into my pocket and pulled out the pills. She looked exposed.

"What are you doing with those?"

"Keeping you lucid. I had needed these in the past, and I know how numb they made me. You can't afford to be numb."

"Listen, Quil, I am so grateful for your concern and all your hard work to protect me, but I can handle myself."

"We—you, me, and Mr. Lincoln—have a lot at stake. You can't take these."

"I think you are being incredibly unfair."

"I agree, but you can't have them."

She turned her back on me and said sharply, "I'm going to bed. That's all right, isn't it?"

"Take that attitude to court tomorrow," I muttered.

CHAPTER 33

THE TRIAL

New Orleans, Louisiana
December 28, 1961

The morning of the trial Mr. Lincoln had breakfast with us at the hotel at seven o'clock, and we discussed last-minute details.

We arrived at the courthouse at eight-thirty. Michelle trembled as we walked up the courthouse steps. Mr. Lincoln hooked a hand under her arm and said, "Courage. We're ready. Right?"

I took a seat three rows behind Michelle in the gallery and watched as others arrived. The DA and his assistants came in together. Edward and Marilyn Penn arrived conspicuously with their high-powered attorney and sat one row behind the prosecution. The gallery filled up quickly. Mr. and Mrs. Conners sat behind their daughter. I watched Michelle. She looked sweet and pretty in a plain dove-gray woolen dress and pearls. Her hair lay soft and glossy over her shoulders, and she appeared calm, but I knew better. My palms were sweating, and my jaw felt tight. If *I* was this nervous, I could only imagine what she must be feeling.

The trial came to order, and the usual court procedures took place. Mr. Lincoln and the DA presented their opening arguments, which were both convincing.

The trial trudged through its first day—minor witnesses and evidence from the prosecution. The obligatory objections, sustains, and overrules seemed endless.

Michelle and I returned to the hotel drained but not shaken. Mr. Lincoln had told us that the next day would ramp up as the prosecution began to seriously prove their case. Then there would be the agonizingly long New Year's weekend, perfectly timed to give the DA time to examine the trial's progress. Mr. Lincoln expected the prosecution to rest on Tuesday, and then we would begin to lay out a careful defense. Of course, the DA would be able to cross-examine our witnesses.

Michelle and I spent a tense weekend. We ran to relieve stress and watched television and read to relax. We polished each other's nails. We did not discuss the trial except for the passing comment, nor the medication I had taken from her.

On Tuesday, Mr. Lincoln again retrieved us from the hotel. Michelle was wearing a winter-white skirt with a navy sweater set and navy pumps, her hair pulled back in a graceful ponytail.

As expected, the prosecution rested. Mr. Lincoln called his hostile witnesses from the police department one at a time and laid out the damning evidence concerning investigations of all Pruitt Penn's alleged rape victims. Hostile was the perfect description for these witnesses. At one point, a detective on the stand shouted at Mr. Lincoln, but Judge Ellen Parrish gave him a stern warning from the bench, making him choke back his rage.

Through it all, Mr. Lincoln remained calm and low voiced. I watched him with deep admiration and gratitude. I couldn't help but wonder how Fletcher's trial would play out when I would be rooting for the other team.

By lunchtime, Mr. Lincoln had accused nearly half the NOPD of abundant offenses, and much to the DA's chagrin, they had come away looking like negligent fools.

We recessed for lunch.

When the court reconvened, Peggy White made a dramatic entrance escorted by her husband, wearing a sleek black-and-white checked boatneck dress and red heels. She was impeccably groomed, beautiful, calm, and confident—her scar shockingly visible.

She was sworn in, and Mr. Lincoln took his time asking the first question. Peggy did not fidget. I followed her eyes and realized she was looking directly at Edward Penn.

"Mrs. White, can you tell the court why you are here today?"

"On November second, 1959, I was raped and maimed by Pruitt Penn."

"Objection!" The DA was on his feet.

Mr. Lincoln said, "Your Honor, the defense has already established the gross negligence on the part of the police department to investigate and charge Pruitt Penn for more than a dozen charges of rape over a six-year period. As noted, Mrs. White, née Watkins, filed charges against Pruitt Penn in November 1959. I am establishing a pattern of incompetence."

"Overruled."

"Mrs. White, when you filed charges against Mr. Penn, what actions were taken?"

"None. His parents provided an alibi, and no further action was taken."

"Can you tell us about the scar on your chest?"

Peggy White looked directly at the jury and in graphic detail describe the mutilation she sustained at the hands of her rapist.

"Your Honor, at this time, I would like to submit hospital records to confirm the date and injuries to Mrs. White. No more questions. Thank you, Mrs. White."

Judge Parrish said, "Redirect?"

The DA stood and walked toward Peggy. "Mrs. White, what was your occupation before the alleged rape?"

"I was a lingerie model."

"Well, wouldn't you say such an occupation is provocative?"

"No. If you are implying that modeling lingerie for a well-established women's fashion store somehow gave Pruitt Penn the right to brutalize me, it would be like saying women, by their very definition, are fair game at all times. Is that what you are saying?"

"I'll ask the questions. You give the answers, Mrs. White."

Peggy calmly watched him.

"Mrs. White, when were you married?" The DA was looking through some papers.

"Robert White and I were married on October 19, 1959."

"So how was it that you came to be in the apartment of Pruitt Penn on November second less than two weeks after your wedding?"

I remembered Mr. Lincoln saying that a good lawyer never asked a question to which he didn't already know the answer. I could see Mr. Lincoln look down at his notes.

"I wasn't in *his* apartment. He was in *mine*. We lived in the same building."

It was such an obvious blunder that there was a collective gasp. Pruitt's apartment was number 302 and Peggy's was number 402.

"Nothing further."

Peggy was released but stayed for the rest of the day as a reminder to the prosecution that she could not be bullied.

I was next. My knees wobbled slightly as I stood. I was wearing a dark blue straight skirt, a white silk blouse, and a powder-blue cashmere cardigan. I could feel the jury's eyes on me.

Mr. Lincoln walked up to the witness stand and made eye contact. A silent courage passed between us.

"Miss Tandy, on what day were you raped by Pruitt Penn?"

"Your Honor!"

"Mr. Estes, you opened the door for these types of witnesses by allowing testimony from the NOPD. Overruled."

"I was raped by Pruitt Penn on June 12, 1960."

Mr. Lincoln produced corroborating evidence: the police report and the hospital records.

"Is there any physical evidence of the rape that you wish to disclose?"

"Yes," I said.

I hesitated, thought about how brave Peggy had been and how brutal the Penns were. I thought about the child I had murdered.

"Miss Tandy?" Judge Parrish reminded me where I was.

"Yes," I said again. I stood slowly and faced the jury, unbuttoned the top few buttons of my blouse, and exposed my scar. There was a rumble in the courtroom. The faces of the jurors spoke volumes.

I was allowed to describe my rape and the weapon that was used to scar me. At the end, Mr. Lincoln patted my hand and whispered, "Well done."

"Your witness, Mr. Estes," Judge Parrish directed.

As Mr. Estes stood, I glanced toward Marilyn Penn, Pit's mother. She looked pale.

"Miss Tandy," the DA began. "You were dating Mr. Penn at the time of the alleged rape. Is that correct?"

"Yes."

"And were you having sexual relations with him?"

"Objection," Mr. Lincoln said.

"Overruled." Judge Parrish was going to get to the bottom of this slimy pit.

"No. I was a virgin at the time of the rape."

"And who is Leona Jenkins?"

"I don't know."

"Let me help you remember. Leona Jenkins was the nurse who processed your pregnancy test. Do you have a child, Miss Tandy?"

"No."

There was a pause as Mr. Estes looked at me and I processed what he might know. *He's bluffing.* I could not believe that a doctor performing an illegal abortion would expose himself at any cost, and neither would a nurse offering abortion information. I made a desperate decision.

"I had a miscarriage."

"Are you certain of that testimony, Miss Tandy?"

"Mr. Estes, a miscarriage is not something a woman would be confused over," I said. I could hear the quaver in my voice.

"Do you have any medical records to confirm this?"

"Your Honor! Badgering the witness!" Mr. Lincoln was on his feet.

"Sustained."

I glared at the DA and said quietly, "I don't have to."

Another exhausting day was behind us. Mr. Lincoln met with us in our hotel suite to recap.

"All went well today, very well." Mr. Lincoln knew I had lied under oath but said nothing in front of Michelle.

"Tomorrow we will present our expert witness on the stab wound to Pit's neck. Then we will change course by dropping Pauline Tillman in the court's lap, then Edward Penn will be called. He, of course, will have the audacity to lie, but then we will call Marilyn Penn. It is anybody's guess what she will do. She seems very intimidated by Edward, but that might work in our favor. The DA has surely warned her about the penalty for perjury. It's anybody's guess.

"After that, we will have to decide if you, Michelle, will take the stand. Without your direct testimony to the events of the night Penn died, it will be up to the jury to believe or disbelieve the facts we have laid out in court briefs. The danger is that Mr. Estes will come after you with every bit of intimidation and ferocity at his vast disposal. He will try to confuse you or make you angry. It will be imperative that you stay calm and focused, and I promise you it will be like having a roaring lion a foot from your face."

CHAPTER 34

THE VERDICT

New Orleans, Louisiana
January 3, 1962

The next morning I helped Michelle with her hair, pulling it back in a soft chignon. She put on a pale pink silk blouse tucked into a black skirt and gray kitten heels that made her look young and vulnerable.

"This is it, Michelle. Testimony will probably complete today, and then it will all be in the hands of the jury." She was already unsteady, looking like a fragile fawn.

"I know," she said. Her eyes welled with tears, and she hugged me. I could feel her trembling. She was in no condition to face the most important day of her life.

"Courage comes in a good many ways," I said, reaching into my purse and producing the contraband medication. "But just one. Promise me you will take just one, and take it only if you have to." I pressed the pills into her hand. I could have given her only one pill, but at this point, she deserved to make the decision on her own.

She nodded.

The courtroom was packed, and visions of *To Kill a Mockingbird* danced in my head.

As planned, Mr. Lincoln called our expert witness first and asked him to explain the difference between damage done to the body from a thrusting force compared to an impaling force. He was excellent. His description was clear and concise and left little doubt that the injuries to Pruitt Penn's carotid artery were caused by a clean plunge as opposed to a stab-and-drag motion. He was amazing on cross-examination, and I could see Mr. Estes's agitation growing.

Next Pauline Tillman took the stand, cold as stone, and told her story with clear conviction. I watched Marilyn Penn as the testimony about her husband and Pauline's daughter was revealed and then the horrific irony of the daughter being raped by the son. She talked about her daughter's grisly suicide. She stayed the course, staring at Edward Penn the whole time. She was completely believable. All the dates and places and police records matched up.

She teared up during cross-examination and seemed so broken Mr. Estes didn't dare attack her.

Edward Penn took the stand and, as predicted, convincingly lied, denying all of Pauline's accusations and all other accusations against him. He swore under oath that he had never given false alibis for his son.

I watched the jury watch Edward. I couldn't judge how they were reacting to his testimony, but the evidence against the Penns was mounting.

Marilyn was called, and she looked surprisingly confident as she was sworn in.

"Mrs. Penn," Mr. Lincoln began. "Have you been advised of the penalty for perjury?"

"Yes."

"Then let me ask you a simple yes-or-no question. Have you ever lied to the police about the whereabouts of your son or your husband on any of the dates either one was accused of rape?"

We all held our breath. There was literally no sound in the courtroom. Marilyn looked at her husband sitting confidently in the gallery, then at Mr. Estes. She swallowed and looked at the jury and then the judge. She folded her hands in her lap, looked up at Mr. Lincoln, started to shake her head, but then in a clear voice said, "Yes."

Edward Penn jumped to his feet and called her a liar.

"No, *you* are the liar, and I am never going to lie for you again!" Marilyn shouted back. "You have ruined me and our son and God knows how many women!"

Mr. Lincoln stepped back, trying not to look shocked, and said, "Your witness."

"No questions." Mr. Estes looked miserable.

"Mr. Lincoln, call your next witness," Judge Parrish said.

I saw him lean into Michelle, and they spoke briefly. The case against the NOPD and Edward Penn had been made, but there was still a chance that the jury would find the evidence against Michelle compelling. We had hoped for reasonable doubt. Had that point been undeniably made? I knew it hadn't.

"Your Honor, at this time, I call Michelle Conners to the stand."

Mr. Estes smiled.

Michelle stood and smoothed her clothing, took a deep breath, and walked slowly to the witness stand.

"Michelle, in your own words, tell the jury about the night Pruitt Penn died."

She seemed amazingly calm, and I was pretty sure she must be medicated. She told the whole story in such a sweet and vulnerable way. I felt certain the jury must believe her. She did not talk about the rape, just the night she had gone to Pit's house to reason with him. She knew it was a foolish move, but she had to do it. When she was finished, Mr. Lincoln said, "Thank you, Michelle," and sat down.

Michelle looked Mr. Estes's way as he nearly charged the witness box. *A roaring lion.*

"Surely, Miss Conners, you cannot think that anyone in this court will believe that you didn't go to Pruitt Penn's house to kill him," Mr. Estes barked.

"I believe that they will see the truth."

"Oh, come on, Miss Conners. Mr. Penn *fell* on the knife you just happened to be holding?" His voice was mocking.

"Yes."

"Isn't it true that you hated Pruitt Penn and wanted him dead?"

"At first, I did, after he raped me and gave me this." Michelle pulled her blouse open. Popping buttons scattered to the floor, and the angry scar stared out at the gallery. "He used scissors! You would want him dead too! But then I forgave him. It was the only way to be free of him. I had to forgive him. I went there to tell him that, but he laughed at me and chased me into the kitchen. I held up the knife to protect myself." She dissolved into tears, pulling her blouse closed, sobbing until the judge called a recess.

When the court reconvened, Mr. Lincoln stood and said, "The defense rests." He waived his closing argument—Michelle had done it for him. None of us had seen this coming. She had never spoken of forgiveness to me, and I was fairly certain it was news to Mr. Lincoln.

Mr. Estes made a pitiful stab at convincing the jury of Michelle's manipulative defense. It was a short speech.

Judge Ellen Parrish gave the jury their instructions, and we were all dismissed. It was three o'clock. I had wrapped my jacket around Michelle and held her quivering body. "Wow, if I had known how much courage those pills would give you, you would have had them sooner," I whispered to her.

And she whispered back, "I didn't take them."

We helped Mr. Lincoln gather all the files and pack them away in his court briefcase. Michelle and her parents sat in the courtroom and comforted each other. They all knew that when the verdict came in, she would either be going home or back to jail.

"It will be awhile before the verdict comes in, I'm hoping a day or two, because a swift verdict is usually a very bad sign," Mr. Lincoln said.

We waited for Michelle in the hallway. Neither of us wanted to rush her. It was nearly an hour before she emerged. We talked with her parents for a few minutes, promising to call them the moment we knew anything.

We were descending the courthouse steps when the bailiff caught up with us.

"The jury is in."

Michelle was wearing my jacket over her torn blouse, standing next to Mr. Lincoln, facing straight ahead as the verdict was handed to the judge. The judge read the verdict silently, then nodded and handed the verdict to the bailiff, who opened it and read aloud.

Time stood still. All the air seemed to be sucked out of the court-room. I felt nauseous.

"On the single count of murder in the first degree, we the jury find Michelle Ross Conners not guilty."

Mrs. Conners wept openly. Michelle fell into Mr. Lincoln's arms. I dropped my head between my knees and tried not to vomit.

"Order," Judge Parrish called out. "Miss Conners, you are free to go, and, Bailiff, take Mr. Penn into custody for contempt and lying under oath. I presume Mr. Estes will be filing charges for perjury."

I looked over at Marilyn Penn, and I was sure I saw the shadow of a smile.

CHAPTER 35
THINKING IT OVER

New Orleans, Louisiana
January 4, 1962

B efore I checked out of the hotel, I made a call to Bidwell Canfield in Miami and confirmed an appointment for Monday, and he in turn made an appointment with a recommended financial advisor for the following day.

I was reticent about these meetings. After all, what did I know about managing a multi-million-dollar inheritance? It was almost frightening, and what to do with it all was confusing. That amount of money was more than I could spend in two lifetimes, but as the Knoxville DA, Philip Randall, had assured me, "That's why you hire professionals you can trust."

I called Michelle to check on her. We had, in the last three weeks, formed what would become a lifetime bond. I told her I was headed for Key West and that she should come for a visit while I was there. Fletcher's trial was set for the end of April in Knoxville, and I saw no reason to get back to Tennessee more than a week prior. Once I got to Key West and got settled, I would call Danny to give him contact information.

At Mr. Lincoln's offices, I reclaimed the package I had left with him, and he handed over the retrieved ten thousand dollars in bail.

"How did you get this released so fast?"

"I know people."

"Mr. Lincoln, do you have a Superman costume under that suit?"

He laughed and said, "So what is next for you? Back to Tennessee, I assume?"

"No, I've got some business in Miami, and then I'm off to Key West for the winter."

"You *are* an enigma. I haven't quite figured you out."

"Good." I smiled.

He studied me for a moment. "You took a heck of a risk in court this week by lying to the court. I don't approve," he said.

"Neither do I, but my private choices were none of the court's business, and by discrediting me, it would have hurt Michelle's case."

"Still, an oath is an oath with sturdy consequences, and I wouldn't suggest you ever do that again."

"Got it." I nearly raised my hand as if catching a ball. A gripping sadness turned over in my belly as I remembered my brother and his awful death and the man who had caused it. *His time is coming.*

Mr. Lincoln noticed my temporary mood change.

"Got something on your mind?"

"No, nothing really." I changed the subject. "So shall we tally up the bill? I am almost afraid to ask."

"We're even. There was a thousand dollars for miscellaneous expenses, but Michelle has insisted on making payments for that."

"That's going to be a hardship for her," I said.

"Probably, but she wants to contribute."

"Well, if she can't follow through, let me know."

"You are an amazing young woman, Miss Tandy. You aren't looking for a job, are you?"

"You can't afford me."

He hugged me, and I expressed my gratitude for his expertise and commitment. Not only had he saved Michelle's life, but he had unknowingly provided a vehicle for a partial healing of my past, not to mention valuable legal experience I might be able to use later.

I left his office, took my family photo from the glove compartment, secured it again to the passenger door of the T-Bird, and turned east on

I-10. Destination: Key West. Since it was nearly noon by the time I got on the road, I figured I would only make it as far as Tallahassee, Florida, by nightfall.

As I drove along the coast, my mind drifted back to Michelle's trial. There had been so many places where it could have all gone wrong. In fact, should have gone wrong. For an experienced DA like William Estes to make the mistakes he had was baffling—Peggy White's address at the time of the rape, juror choices, and the cross-examination of the NOPD all were avoidable missteps. Had he done this on purpose, or had it been a simple "God thing," as Michelle's parents insisted?

Michelle had kept saying, "The truth will come out." Her parents had said, "The whole church is praying." And then Michelle's shocking testimony, "I went there to forgive him…I had to forgive him, or I would never be free." The last part was confounding. Forgive him? I was fairly certain I would have gone there to kill him.

I drove all the way to Miami the next day. It was Saturday, and though my meeting with Bidwell Canfield wasn't until Monday, I wanted to be rested.

CHAPTER 36

THE MONEY

Miami, Florida
January 8, 1962

I had imagined Bidwell Canfield to be large and loud. He was neither.
Mr. Canfield was a stocky and well-tanned man in his fifties, like somebody who had lived near the sun all his life. He had a firm handshake,
which I appreciated, and a toothy smile.

"Miss Tandy, such a pleasure to meet you." His Southern accent was
smooth and polished.

"Thank you." I didn't want to appear nervous and inexperienced,
but I was both of those things, and I was sure he could tell.

"I have prepared some documents in advance of your arrival." He
laid out a copy of the will, account statements for the trust, and release
forms, carefully going over each document.

"As your attorney on this matter, it will be my job to protect your inter-
ests. As per your request, I have made an appointment for you tomorrow
with the Alder Wallace Financial Group. They are well established and
solid. You will be meeting with Ken Durkin, and I have supplied him with
the necessary information."

He put his elbows on his desk and smiled. "What questions do you
have for me?"

"I don't know. I'm feeling over my head and out of my league." I hated saying that.

"I want you to feel comfortable and confident with me," Mr. Canfield said. "You may not know what to ask right now, but you will. You can call me anytime."

He hesitated and looked down at his desk. He seemed to be deciding something.

"Miss Tandy, I know Fletcher Pickford and the rest of the Pickfords—they are, and have been, both famous and infamous," he began. "Your biological mother, Clarice Pickford, was a beautiful but cold woman. That she would provide for you in such a generous way is both astonishing and confounding. I would have never expected it of her. If I may say, Miss Tandy, being raised away from the Pickfords is your true windfall."

At that moment, I felt a genuine kinship with this stranger.

The next morning I met with Ken Durkin, my new financial advisor. He was younger than I expected—blond and bespectacled, a serious fellow who got right to the point.

"Miss Tandy, currently your trust is worth four point six million, of which you will pay approximately five hundred thousand in inheritance and income tax. So roughly four million will need to be converted into a profitable investment profile."

"Meaning?"

"Meaning that even at current bank interest rates of 4 percent, your money would be earning approximately one hundred sixty thousand dollars per year."

I closed my eyes and swallowed.

"Of course, your money will earn much more than that if invested wisely. It is the suggestion of the firm that we optimize the growth of your wealth through a variety of means."

"Meaning?"

"Stocks, bonds, T-bills, real estate, foreign investments…"

"Charity. I want some—half—to go to charity."

"Certainly, we can actually start a charitable fund to benefit whomever you wish, but half is extreme. Personal donations are deductible up to 10 percent of your annual income and corporate up to—

"Down syndrome education and research."

The meeting went along this way until I finally could absorb no more.

"Mr. Durkin, until last month I was the owner of a not-so-profitable fish camp in Tennessee. You are talking about facts and figures that I have no idea how to manage. Mr. Canfield has suggested that your firm manage the money willed to me, and for now, I have to trust you with it because I don't have the faintest idea how to do so on my own."

I handed him the paperwork Mr. Canfield had sent with me.

"I will be in touch with an address and phone number, and when I have questions, I will call you. Does that sound like a good plan?" I smiled.

He really looked at me then. His face softened, and he said, "Miss Tandy, you can indeed trust us."

I left Miami with my mind spinning. Down I-95 toward Key West I flew with the T-Bird's top down and the radio blaring. With each mile, I got farther from Hackberry and New Orleans and closer to anonymity. It seemed as though with every turn of the tires I felt freedom growing inside me.

The sun was making a fiery descent into the Gulf of Mexico as I crested the Seven Mile Bridge. I was less than forty miles from Key West.

PART FOUR

Longest way round is the shortest way home.
—James Joyce

CHAPTER 37

KEY WEST

Key West, Florida
Mid-January 1962

I arrived in Key West on Saturday evening, road weary and, as usual, hungry. Though beautiful, the drive from Miami was a hundred and sixty-five miles of two-lane, mostly ill-maintained road along Flagler's old railway line. I checked into The Weatherstation Inn on Front Sreet, a comfortable place with "welcome to Key West" written all over it.

Because Key West had the pluck to be an isolated community free of most governmental interference, I admired it. Strolling down Duval Street to find dinner was like stepping back in time. With each breath, I pulled in salt air and pushed out New Orleans.

Walking through the doors of Sloppy Joe's, I could almost hear the past humming in the walls. It smelled of old wood and varnish and sounded like a party.

This had been Hemingway's hangout. In the 1950s, Joe's had been almost exclusively a male haunt where Hemingway and his cohorts drank and gambled and sang bawdy songs. Though Hemingway had killed himself the summer before, he lingered in the air like a shape-shifter. As far as I was concerned, he might have been anyone in the room.

I ate fish tacos and cucumber salad at a table in the corner and watched the locals mill around, talking and laughing—the later the hour, the louder they got. Since this was not my usual choice of atmosphere, I was back at the Weatherstation and in bed by ten o'clock.

In the morning, my host served sumptuous crepes with fresh pineapple and strong Cuban coffee with thick cream. Too full to run, I went for a walk, turning right onto Emma Street. Two blocks down, a "for rent" sign was tacked to a low fence in front of three small houses, one larger than the other two, each painted in bright shades of pink, lavender, and sea blue with white trim.

I knocked on the front door of the middle house. No answer. I knocked on the door to my right, the largest of the three houses, and a handsome Latin-looking man came to the door. He had a huge black cat with bright green eyes stuffed under an arm. I must admit, for a moment, being in the presence of a strange man sent a warning chill scampering up my backbone. *Shake it off. There's nothing dangerous about him—the cat, maybe.*

"Meet Mick Jaguar," the man said. "I am Eduardo Canales."

"Greetings, Senor Jaguar," I said, giving Mick a friendly chin scratch. "And greetings to you as well, Eduardo. My name is Tranquil Tandy, Quil for short."

I shook Eduardo's hand, and he smiled a kind of sweet, childlike grin.

"I saw the notice on the fence," I said, pointing to the sign.

"It's the middle house. Do you want to have a look?"

He led me to the middle house. His less-than-discreet gold cross slipped from his shirt as he leaned forward to open the door.

The three houses were separate but linked by a common front porch and fence. Eduardo put the cat down in the doorway, and he immediately trotted through the house, jumped onto the bed, and out the bedroom window. He clearly had done this before. Fine with me. I liked cats.

The place was compact but just right for a single person like me. It had a bedroom with a connecting bathroom along the back of the house. In the bedroom, a tall window faced a garden area, also common with the two other houses. The kitchen and living areas lined up across the front. It had pine floors, lots of light, was close to the water, and completely furnished.

"I'm here for the winter—until mid-March or April. Would that work for you? What is the rent?"

"Ninety a month." He leaned against the porch railing.

This seemed a bit steep, but I liked the house and was ready to settle down. Michelle's trial had zapped the last of my energy. I just wanted to sit with my feet up and listen to the ocean for the entire winter.

"Okay, deal," I said. "Let me get my checkbook and my things. I'm down at the Weatherstation Inn."

"It will be a pleasure to have you as a neighbor." He smiled that cute little grin again.

I liked him *and* his beefy cat.

By noon, I had moved in, the T-Bird parked on the street, and groceries in the refrigerator. Eduardo put a chair on the porch by the door, and I planted myself in it, feet on the railing.

Javier, Eduardo's brother, brought me a frosty glass of ice-cold tea, and the two of them, plus the cat, joined me on the porch. Javier was wearing a gold cross too. Was this a Latin thing, or were they the type of Christians I usually tried to avoid?

At around four o'clock, a woman I guessed to be in her early forties opened the gate and stepped up onto the porch.

"Dorothy, meet our new neighbor. Quil, meet Dorothy Lee," Javier said. "Join us."

"I'll be right out," she said, heading for the third house, the one next to mine.

"Tea?" Eduardo called after her.

"Oh, yes," Dorothy replied.

She was pretty in an exotic sort of way: long black hair that brushed her waist as she walked. Her features were prominent, with a nose that might have been considered a little large had the rest of her features not been in balance with large eyes and full lips. She was not wearing a gold cross, for which I was relieved.

"She makes jewelry—has a shop on Duval—and also makes the most fabulous key lime pie," Javier said.

When Dorothy joined us, she said, "All right, new renter, tell us a story." She pulled up a chair and smoothed her hair back from her face as she sat down.

"A story?"

"Everybody in Key West has a story. Ask Hemingway." She smiled.

"You first." I smiled back.

"Okay, well, I moved here from Indiana after my husband ran off with his secretary—a tale as old as time. I've been here almost two years, and I love it. Your turn."

"I used to run a family business in eastern Tennessee, but now I'm footloose and fancy-free. I'm here until April. What about you two?" I raised my glass toward the boys, deflecting attention from myself.

"We owned a cocktail lounge in Havana until Castro took over nearly three years ago. Fortunately, Javier saw the writing on the wall before it all fell apart. We liquidated as much as possible and left Cuba for the US. I have a good-sized boat, and on a calm day, we motored the ninety miles to Key West," Eduardo explained.

"We bought these houses in 1960 after Hurricane Donna had done her best to destroy them, opened a Cuban restaurant on Duval, and that's our story," Javier added.

The sun was drifting into the sea, and we sat watching it as if it were the last one we would ever see—mesmerizing. Becoming contented in Key West was not going to be a problem.

"Dorothy…" I began.

"Call me Dot."

"Okay, Dot. Are you Cuban too?"

"No, I was born in Jordan. My parents immigrated in 1940, and I followed them. My birth name is Raghda Al Shawan, but I adopted the name Dorothy when I became a US citizen. *The Wizard of Oz* was the first American film I saw. I guess Dorothy and those red shoes spoke to me." She laughed.

And so it went into early evening, when a potluck in the garden was suggested. The boys grilled fish, and Dorothy brought veggie kebabs smothered in curry sauce. I offered up a fruit salad. We ate and talked into the night. The boys, who shared a ridiculous sense of humor, carried on as the restaurant stories got louder, wilder, and more animated.

Dot's humor, wry and ironic, interjected funny stories about her customers. I listened and laughed and thoroughly enjoyed myself. It felt so very
good to laugh, as though the disquiet I had internalized was releasing a
little with each breath.

I slipped between the sheets after midnight, wondering about my
new life here in Key West as I drifted off. The temperature was cool and
refreshing, and the bedroom window was wide open. I felt safe. The
smell of salty air and the sound of water lapping a block away lulled me
into a deep, dreamless sleep.

Sunlight flickering through my open bedroom window woke me
around eight o'clock the next morning, and I found that Mick Jaguar
had joined me at some point during the night. He was comfortably posi-
tioned at the foot of the bed, flat on his back, sound asleep.

"What are you doing in here?" A scratch on his belly produced a
long, luxurious stretch.

He followed me into the kitchen and had a teaspoon of cream while
I made coffee, then hopped back through the bedroom window, seeking
a sunny location in the garden.

I ate the leftover fruit salad spooned over shredded wheat for breakfast, then took my coffee to the pier and sat as the sun worked its way up
my back—a peaceful life without expectation. I was in love.

Around noon, I called Danny from Eduardo and Javier's restaurant.

It was Sunday, and I knew he would be at home. He answered on the
fourth ring, but when I said hello, his voice sounded hesitant with the
slightest chill.

"I wanted you to have my contact information," I said.

"Sure, give it to me."

"Are you mad at me?"

"Nope, not mad, just finally getting the message that you don't want
me in your life."

"That's not true!" I was surprised by his attitude.

"You treat me like somebody you need to protect yourself from, and
I don't like it very much," he said.

"I'm not secretive." I could hear the defensive edge in my voice.

"Really? Then where have you been for a month?"

"Give me a break, Danny. I don't know who I am anymore, and I've lost everything. I needed time to digest it all."

"So have you digested?"

"Who are you? And what have you done with my Danny?"

"I don't think I am *your* Danny."

"As in romantically, right?"

"You know how I feel."

"I don't want to be romantically involved with anybody right now, Danny, and you know why."

"Have it your way." There was a pause. "Anything else?"

The way he said that had a sound of release that rang like an echo. I felt it in my gut, like a door closing. I wanted to say something to put our friendship back the way it once was, but even over the phone, I felt it splinter like glass hitting hard tile. I changed the subject.

"How's Libby?"

"She's doing great. No more wires, and the cast is off. She looks like herself, but the attack has changed her, as you might expect. She's lost the bubbly girl we all knew and is more guarded. She actually reminds me of you in that way."

"So now you have two damaged women in your life."

"No, just one."

Later that afternoon I trotted down to the harbor near Mallory and bought as much shrimp as I could carry. When Dorothy got home, I invited her to join me for a peel-and-eat shrimp boil. She added corn on the cob and chopped salad. The boys were at the restaurant, but Mick Jaguar attended in their place.

We built a fire in the clay chiminea in the garden and pulled the picnic table close as the sun set. The fire's orange flames glowed invitingly. January, even in Key West, had chilly evenings.

I poured the boiled and drained shrimp onto a plastic tablecloth. Lime-seasoned cocktail sauce and a pitcher of iced tea completed our feast. We ate and talked and talked and ate; Dot told me about her life in British-occupied Jordan, the country's struggles with Israel, and finally her immigration. She talked about the Persian culture, holding me in rapt attention as she described food and traditions and her transition from east to west.

The cat curled onto my lap like he belonged there. He was such a big animal he had trouble finding a comfortable spot.

Dot did the talking and I did the listening for much of the evening. She spoke so eloquently that I could have listened forever. I was satiated by food and relaxed by Dot's voice. Then the conversation shifted.

"So, Miss Quil, tell me about your life. What is your heritage?"

I looked down at the cat in my lap and stroked his back. He turned his big face toward me, and I scratched his chin.

"Did I say something wrong?" she asked.

"No, not at all. It's that, well, there have been some big changes in my life recently."

"It doesn't sound like these changes were happy ones. Am I going to have to apologize for asking?"

"No. It's good for me to talk about it." Mick jumped down from my lap as if he were getting uncomfortable too. "Where to start? Until two months ago, I would have said I was Cajun and Acadian, but I found out that I was secretly adopted as an infant, and so I don't know what my heritage is."

"What did your adopted parents have to say about keeping this from you?"

"My family are all dead. My little brother was the last. He died of pneumonia in December."

"Oh, I am so very sorry, Quil." Dorothy reached across the table and cupped my hands in hers. "I could tell you were in pain when I first met you, but I could never have dreamed the extent of your loss."

She had seen my scar, as had the boys. I made no effort to hide it. I was done hiding. I told her everything—everything except about the money.

"Have you ever tried journaling?" Dot asked.

"No, I'm no writer."

"You don't have to be a 'writer,' silly. Journaling is writing for yourself. You can safely say *anything* in a journal. It's like a diary, but instead of a catalogue of daily events, it is a compilation of deeper thoughts. It's only for you."

"I suppose you are going to tell me you are also some sort of shrink."

"No, but my dad was."

"We have mangos!" The boys arriving home surprised us.

"Join us for shrimp and salad," Dorothy said, letting go of my hands.

CHAPTER 38
THE JOURNAL

Key West, Florida
January–February 1962

Falling into a comfortable routine was effortless. January and February slipped by like soft butter over warm bread, and I stopped keeping track of the days. My friendship with the boys and Dot grew, and it wasn't hard to embrace them as family. We were the perfect set of oddballs, easy and predictable. I could live here forever.

On Sunday mornings, Eduardo and Javier attended early Mass at St. Mary's Star of the Sea and then joined Dot and me for brunch. Sometimes Eduardo took us out in the boat for fishing or snorkeling. It was a happy, easy existence without all the wild personal upheavals of my former life—simple and safe.

My mind steadily healed in baby steps; a deep and lasting strength rebuilt my foundation a day at a time. Through many conversations around the chiminea, Dot helped me regain my authority over my life—not a victim but a victor. My experience with Michelle had proved it. If I could fight for a stranger, I should be able to fight for myself.

I bought a volume of bound blank paper and started a journal. Writing was, in the beginning, halting and slow. Yet soon I fell into a natural rhythm of writing more about how I felt than what I knew. I dug deep and gradually let myself remember most of what I had buried.

Some days my thoughts filled page after page; I wrote about Pit and Fletcher, Michelle, Paddy, my anger and my fear, the joy I hoped for. It escaped from me like liquid: words both sweet and sour, like a leak in a dam. Writing was the outlet I needed to cope with my past, and it was a cleansing exercise that I looked forward to each morning. Within two weeks, I had filled the first volume and bought two more.

Assimilating into the climate and community was smooth. There was no hurry, no deadlines, and most of all no danger. There were, of course, men who would not be good for me, but I had stopped being attracted to them. The alluring excitement of danger no longer mattered. I wrote about it all and wondered what had changed in me that I no longer sought or invited dangerous men into my life but came to no conclusions other than I was happy.

My diet consisted of mostly fresh food and fish, which aided in my physical and emotional well-being. As usual, I ran every day but without the driving urgency—running toward rather than away from something. My body grew hard and my mind clear. On an island that was only four miles long and a mile wide, running a crisscross course became the routine—up one street, down the next. Within a few weeks, I had covered every street on the south and west sides several times, and soon I was off to conquer the east side of the island.

One bright morning in late February, I put my swimsuit on under a T-shirt and shorts, laced up my sneakers, and ran east on Duval, then north on South Street, and east again on White all the way to the sea.

The weather was warm, and I was hot and sweaty by the time I ran out of road. The Atlantic, clean and sparkling, beckoned me. I stripped down to my swimsuit, then threw myself into the water, something the locals would never do this time of year, but I found the bracing water temperature refreshing. I floated while the current slowly pulled me north along the shallow coastline. Puffy clouds and blue sky drifted by—bliss.

The houses along Atlantic Boulevard were easily recognizable. Moderate in size, yet substantial and appealing, here the older, more expensive summer homes pushed up against the shoreline. Built of three-foot-square white limestone blocks, these structures were designed to withstand wind and water. They were the summer homes of the Southern rich long before much of the north realized Key West existed.

I was about to turn against the current and swim back to White Street when I saw a "for sale" sign on a post near the water's edge. I was intrigued and wanted to see more. Leaving the water near the sign, I stepped onto an oyster shell beach. The shells were hot, and some were sharp, and I hopped through the shells like a fire dancer.

The house was obviously unoccupied—shutters closed and locked. *Interesting place. I wouldn't mind having a peek inside.*

The Realtor was Miami based. I memorized the number and got back into the water, swimming hard against the current, back to my clothes and shoes.

On the run home, I stopped at Javier and Eduardo's restaurant for a late lunch. Javier greeted me.

"My *Dios, chica!* Where are your clothes?" He acted scandalized. "Eduardo, our renter is here, and she is naked!" he called into the storeroom.

"What?" Eduardo shouted back.

"I said Quil is naked."

"What?"

"He's as deaf as a post." Javier laughed.

"I'm not naked," I protested. "I'm wearing my swimsuit, for heaven's sake."

"Might as well be naked. *Your* body in that suit might as well be a birthday suit. Key West locals could think you are advertising." Javier cocked his head and rolled his eyes.

I laughed at the man who already felt like a brother.

"Well, I had been swimming and didn't want to put my soaking wet body back into dry clothes. That might have looked even more indecent, if you know what I mean?" I cocked my head and rolled my eyes.

About that time, Eduardo stepped out of the storeroom, took one look, and said, "My *Dios,* you're naked!"

Javier roared with laughter.

"All right, already." I pulled my T-shirt over my head. "What a pair of prudes."

"What is prude?" Eduardo asked.

"Magnificent," Javier answered.

"Yes, we are magnificent," Eduardo agreed.

Eduardo drew up a chair while Javier made lunch. Since they were between lunch and dinner rushes, he could sit and chat.

In a few minutes, a fabulous tropical fruit salad sprinkled with shredded coconut arrived. A generous tray of oysters on ice followed.

"You were swimming?" Eduardo seemed surprised. "The water is *muy frio*, foolish girl. And the current is very fast."

"Not so bad," I said, reaching for an oyster, splashing it with hot sauce and a squeeze of lemon before letting it slide into my mouth. It tasted salty and deliciously fresh. I picked up another and another. "Yum. Who knew something that looked like *that* could taste so good!"

"You eat like a local," Javier said, slurping down an oyster himself.

"Listen, while I was swimming, I saw one of those summer homes for sale. I think it is on Atlantic Boulevard. What do you two know?"

They looked at each other and shrugged.

"Okay, I'm going to have a drive out there and look around. It's listed with a Miami Realtor."

Eduardo rubbed a thumb and two fingers together and said, "Lots of dineros, chica."

Back at home I showered and changed, checked my mail, and fed the cat.

I put the top down on the T-Bird and drove toward the eastside of the island, the sun warm on my neck, hair flying loose. I turned north on Atlantic Boulevard, driving slowly, looking for a "for sale" sign. I didn't see one on the first pass, but driving the other direction on Atlantic, the sign was obvious. A lush jasmine bush had blocked it from view earlier. There was a permanent signpost with the "for sale" sign tacked to it, but I paid little attention as I pulled into the driveway.

The front of the house was even more compelling than the water side. Wide front steps led onto an even wider wraparound porch. The white limestone structure gave the house an unyielding feel. The landscaping was well manicured with lots of shade and flowering fragrant plants. Bugs buzzed and birds chirped in the foliage, while sunlight flickered through the palms.

I meandered through the garden and around to the back. The ocean sparkled like a million gems, so beautiful in the afternoon sun I felt breathless.

Why *couldn't* I live here? I had no other real ties. I could live anywhere I wanted. Why not Key West? I loved it here and felt more comfortable than I had in years and decided it was worth making a call to the Realtor. No harm in asking for a price.

On the way out of the driveway, I stopped, curious about the permanent sign. I unfastened the bottom of the for sale sign, lifted it, and recoiled as the name "Pickford" stared back at me.

Anger welled up in my throat. Even here at the farthest tip of the continental US, in a place that already felt like home, that name pursued me.

A long walk around the harbor helped me put everything into perspective—deliberating, weighing my emotions, and transforming knee-jerk reaction into useable thought. At first, all I wanted to do was run away, get away from the Pickfords again, but the longer I walked, the clearer my plan became.

If money was the most important thing to Fletcher Pickford, then using the money he was willing to kill for and taking his property might be perfectly poetic. I could let him begin to feel loss. I could erase part of his history like he had erased mine.

Dot's encouraging words about being a victor instead of a victim rang in my ears. *Stand up and fight.*

I trotted down to the boys' restaurant and asked to use the phone. When Bidwell Canfield picked up, I said, "Mr. Canfield, Tranquil Tandy, I'm calling from Key West."

After the usual pleasantries, I told him, "Ken Durkin, my new financial advisor, suggested that real estate was a good investment at present, and I have found a little place here in Key West that I would like to buy."

"I think Mr. Durkin meant large investments in real estate, not personal property, but if you have found something you want for yourself, there is nothing stopping you from buying it."

"I need you to negotiate it for me. It's the Pickford Cottage."

There was a pause while Mr. Canfield processed this.

"I see. Fletcher Pickford must be liquidating assets to pay for his defense."

"That's what I was thinking, and I would like nothing more than to buy up what he owns and cares about. Can you find out what else he is selling?"

"Yes, but I should remind you to think about the reason you want to buy. Please don't be hasty."

"Are you my attorney or my priest?" I laughed.

I gave him the Realtor information and a phone number where I could be reached.

"How much do you want to spend?"

"I have no idea. You decide."

I only had to wait a day. Eduardo came home with a message to call Mr. Canfield.

"Best cash price, thirty-four thousand two hundred dollars," Mr. Canfield said.

"Do you think it's worth that?"

"It's pricey, but I think it will be a good buy for you. The market is low at present, and the value will only grow with time, but you should have a walk through and get somebody local to inspect it for termites, et cetera. The Realtor says the keys for the cottage are in a lockbox under the front porch. I have the combination. Do you have a pen? Let me know your thoughts when you have had a look. Also, the Pickford family estate is for sale here in Miami. It's been on the market for a while, and I'm not sure why."

"Does Fletcher still own it?"

"No, *you* do." He said this as though I should have already known.

"If I own it, then why is it on the market?"

"He had it for sale before he found you. It was part of Clarice Pickford's estate, and technically he could sell it, but then you were discovered, so it automatically became yours. Do you *want* to sell it?"

I drummed my fingers on the edge of the bar. I wondered about a house that had been Fletcher's family home. Wondered if it were gone, would he feel the loss?

"Miss Tandy? Are you still there?"

"Yes, sorry. No, I don't want to sell it, but I would like a copy of the transfer deed listing it as mine."

"I'll get that done by the end of the week. Shall I hold it here or mail it to you?"

"Keep it, please, and thank you for being so kind to me."

"My pleasure."

The next morning I drove out to Pickford Cottage and retrieved the keys from under the porch. Inside, the house smelled close and pungent. I opened all the shutters and windows. It was midday, and light burst into each room. Dust motes scattered in the breeze as windows opened and fresh air replaced musky air.

The ceilings were vaulted, following the natural pitch of the roof: open beamed with wooden slats and painted robin's-egg blue, which gave the whole house a feeling of being a part of the sky. Plaster crown molding painted bright white separated the ceiling from stone walls, and the bedrooms and the living area each had huge chocolate-colored wicker ceiling fans. The floors were tiled with Italian stone and the furniture made using hardwood and wicker, with rich print fabric in a tropical design.

In the master bedroom, I ran my hand along the mahogany, pineapple-carved four-poster bed frame. The bed, smooth and rich looking, seemed perfectly sized to the room. Large windows flanked the bed, and a matching mahogany wardrobe with carved pineapples in relief monopolized the opposing wall, along with a huge matching chest of drawers.

The bathroom had a large claw-foot tub, the appointments in copper and the tub porcelain. The room, amply sized, had paned windows that faced the sea.

The kitchen was small, the custom of construction when this cottage had been built, but the entire waterside wall opened to the back porch through a huge sliding barnlike door. A large wood- and charcoal-fired grill sat just outside the door. I guessed most of the cooking would have been done here.

A total of three bedrooms and the single large bathroom. The floorplan was open and made for outdoor living, I figured about eighteen hundred square feet, huge by Key West standards.

Sitting on the back porch steps, I wondered if I could actually live in this house—I imagined Fletcher's poisonous presence everywhere. The Pickfords had owned this place for generations. Could I wipe that from my mind—their history and, most likely, sins? I wondered what had gone on in this place. Could I make a future in a place that had fostered the destruction of my past? The truth was that I did not have to live there to own it, but owning something gave me new roots.

The next day a local carpenter, recommended by the Realtor and contacted by Mr. Canfield, inspected the roof, porch, and foundation and declared it all sound. By the end of the day, Mr. Canfield was making a deal, and the next evening I had given my okay for the purchase. As soon as a check had been issued from my new corporation, Thunderbird, Inc., I drove out to the cottage with an ax and chopped down the Pickford sign.

CHAPTER 39
SAYING GOODBYE

Key West, Florida
Mid-March 1962

Word was all over town in a flash that some rich northerner had purchased the Pickford Cottage and chopped down the sign. Since I had asked about it earlier, my neighbors suspected me, but I admitted nothing. After all, if I were rich, why would I be living in a tiny house near the harbor? Soon enough, gossip died down, and I prepared to leave Key West. I hated to go, but I had business in Miami that might take a week or two, and I had to be back in Hackberry for Fletcher's trial preparations by mid-April. I had a plan, and I wanted to be ready.

The day before I was to leave, Eduardo and Javier took Dot and me out for a ride in the boat. It was a calm and sunny day, and the wind in my face felt exhilarating as we raced along. We headed west toward the Dry Tortugas. In the shallows of the old fort, we snorkeled and picnicked. We lounged in the sun, and I soaked it up as though it would be my last tropical opportunity.

That evening we had potluck in the garden. Fresh raw oysters and sautéed scallops were on the menu, along with stir-fry vegetables and Dot's famous key lime pie. After dinner, when the food had been cleared away, we lit a fire in the chiminea, and the boys brought out their record player.

"We are going to teach the chicas to cha-cha," Javier said. "Come on. Up on your feet."

"I'm too full," I groaned, but my objections were ignored.

Eduardo took my hand, and Javier pulled Dot from her chair.

"Okay, it's like this." Javier moved forward and back, then turned. "All you have to do is follow."

"Good luck making Quil follow anybody." Dot laughed.

Before long we had the hang of it and were dancing all along the porch and in the garden, laughing at our missteps.

"All right, Dot. It's your turn to teach us some exotic Jordanian moves," Eduardo said.

"Well, I'm certain you will not have any suitable music, so you three can do the rhythm. Like this, clap, clap, pause, clap. Not too fast, smooth and easy."

We did our best to stay together on the beat. Dot set her hair free from the scarf that held it tied. She kicked off her sandals. Her head moved right, then left, and her hips swayed to the beat. Feet gently stepping, she turned in slow, liquid circles. She raised her scarf above her head and let it float with the breeze—it seemed magical. I became so involved with her dance that I forgot to clap and got a nudge from Javier.

When she was done, the three of us applauded wildly.

"Dot, that was wonderful!" I hugged my friend. "Why didn't you show me that before now?"

"You didn't ask. Now, your turn."

"Me? Oh, well, I guess I could teach you to step dance."

"Good. Give us a beat to follow," Dot said, changing places with me. The three of them sat next to each other on the porch, like mischievous monkeys on a branch.

"I'll need a hard surface, so I'll join you up there. Okay, here's the beat. Just clap like this." I put my hands together in a steady rhythm. "Like a metronome. That's good, now a little faster."

I heard "Papa's Reel" in my head, closed my eyes, and tapped out the beat with a heel. I imagined Paddy and me learning to dance to this song. Bare feet on wood did not do this sort of dancing justice, but I hopped and stepped as my audience of three clapped and whooped.

All too soon the evening wound down. We were all worn from sun and wind, food and dancing. One by one we wandered off to bed. Mick Jaguar slept with me that night, as though he sensed my departure. I rubbed his furry face and told him I would miss him.

The next morning I packed my ever-growing belongings into the T-Bird and got ready to say goodbye to Dot and the boys.

"Wait, you can't go just yet," Dot said, reaching into her pocket and producing a lovely pair of hand-crafted earrings. They were made of simple spun gold spheres on delicate gold wires. I put them on there on the spot, so light they felt like nothing. The wires were short, and the little gold balls lay just barely below my earlobes.

"Perfect," Dot said, standing back to look at her handiwork.

"I love them," I said, touching one. I hugged her and called her sister. "*Soeur chérie,*" I whispered.

Eduardo said, "Javier and I have something for you too." He handed me a package and said, "Open it, chica."

It was a Polaroid camera.

To someone passing by on the street, he called, "Could you please take our picture?"

We stood together on the porch in front of my little house, arms around each other, faces smiling, Eduardo holding Mick Jaguar, who also seemed to be smiling. *Click.*

We all watched as the picture emerged. There we all were, each so different yet exactly the same. My little family. Emotion nearly overtook me, but as usual, I swallowed it. I hugged them all. Javier helped me put the top down on the T-Bird. I placed the new photo in the glove compartment next to the photo of my other family; then I got in the car, started it, and put it in gear. I didn't dare look back at them. If I had, I might not have gone. I drove away with my hand in the air and "I will be back" happy in my wake.

CHAPTER 40

MIAMI

Miami, Florida
March 26, 1962

"You look healthy and tanned," Mr. Canfield said as he ushered me into his office. "Coffee?"

"Please."

"Let's move into the conference room. More comfortable." He picked up a few files, and I followed him to a large room with windows overlooking Miami.

"Where do you want to start?"

"Real estate," I said as if I had an agenda.

"All right." He flipped open one of the files. "Here is the deed to the cottage in Key West." He slid a paper toward me. "And this is the deed and keys to the Miami house. The Pickford Investment Group building was owned by Fletcher, and he sold it for a song, presumably to finance a high-dollar defense. That's all the real estate I could find—a very small part of your portfolio."

"Thanks for doing this."

"You are so very welcome. What's next?"

"I want to talk about putting together a charitable foundation for Down syndrome children."

"Let me make some notes. First you will need to decide what percentage of your portfolio you will want to set aside."

"Half."

"Half of the current investment, or half of future investments?"

"I don't even know what that means."

"I'm sure this is confusing. Let's get Ken Durkin in here tomorrow to help put it all into perspective." Mr. Canfield buzzed his assistant. "Cathy, give Ken Durkin a call and see what time he can meet with us tomorrow, please."

I looked down at my hands. "Mr. Canfield…"

"Miss Tandy, I think we should start calling each other Quil and Bidwell."

I grinned. "Which one should I be?"

He sat back in his chair and smiled at me. "Key West was good for you."

"I was happy there, and I made friends that I will cherish forever."

"I'm so happy for you."

"Mr. Canfield…Bidwell…" I smiled at him. "There are some details you should know." I took a breath. "Fletcher Pickford murdered my brother and burned our home. My brother, Paddy, had Down's. He was innocent and sweet, and I adored him. Fletcher erased my history, and now I am going to have to build a new life." I rattled this off like a well-rehearsed speech: without emotion and under control.

"I am so very sorry. I knew Fletcher had been arrested, but I didn't realize his crimes were so catastrophic. You must feel devastated."

I nodded. "I want Fletcher to know that his wealth is gone and *where* it has gone."

"I understand, just as long as you know the difference between justice and revenge."

"There you go again, trying to be my priest." I smiled.

"Point taken, but I have seen people say and do things that they later deeply regret. I don't want you to be one of them."

"I will keep that in mind."

"What's next?"

"My whole life has been a kind of lie, and I don't know who I am. I think I need to know. Can you help me find out who my biological father was?"

Bidwell tapped the file in front of him with his pen. "We can, perhaps, trace Clarice's roots, but your biological father might not have a footprint."

I leaned forward. "There has to be a way to find out. I can't accept that he is invisible. He might still be *alive*."

"We can hire a private detective and see what happens. I know someone good. Shall I do that?"

"Yes."

"I should warn you that you may be setting yourself up for disappointment. It might be a Pandora's box better left undisturbed. Are you prepared for that?"

"Yes." I sounded sure of myself even though I was not.

"What's next?"

"Nothing I can think of this minute." This short meeting had covered a lot of ground.

"All right. As soon as we know when Ken Durkin can meet with us, I'll call you." Bidwell stacked the files he was keeping and handed over mine.

"Sounds good. Oh, and can you give me directions to the house here?" I looked down at the deed. "Six Sea Island Drive."

Driving up to the house took my breath away, not because of its size or beauty but because I could only imagine the lives lived there.

I unlocked the door and pushed it open. A wide, impressive staircase wound up from the foyer, and my eyes followed it to the second floor. To the right of the foyer, a large room sat empty except for a grand piano. To the left, huge wooden double doors opened into a dining room with a long, elegant dining table and eighteen chairs, one of them smashed to bits. A shudder scampered up my spine, and I instinctively backed away as if whoever had done this was still in the room.

Back in the foyer, I then moved on to the piano room, then the library stacked with empty floor-to-ceiling oak bookshelves, then into a smaller room that smelled of furniture wax and tobacco. This must have been a smoking room.

Double glass doors opened from this room onto a large, walled garden, which threaded through palms leading to a large swimming pool, dry with concrete beginning to crack along the bottom. More double doors led into the butler's pantry, then the kitchen and food pantry. At one end of the kitchen, I noticed a narrow staircase leading both up and down. Downstairs housed an empty wine cellar and laundry; upstairs climbed past the second floor to the third, where I found three small bedrooms, a bathroom, and a small sitting area. I assumed these rooms had been for servants.

On the second-floor landing, there was a door allowing access to the main part of the house. I opened it and found myself in a wide corridor. Six substantial bedrooms, three bathrooms, and another sitting room occupied this floor. There were no furnishings in any of the rooms except one: a bedroom that had been dismantled, ruined. It was a mess, with furniture overturned and framed pictures on the floor. I wondered if some sort of burglary had taken place, but that didn't make any sense. Everywhere else in the house was orderly except for one dining room chair. I made a mental note to speak with Bidwell about this.

I walked down the center staircase toward the front door, my hand sliding along a wide polished banister. I stood in the foyer and thought about the possibilities. Should I sell and be rid of it or keep it? Why would I want this gigantic place?

Had I not been adopted, I might have grown up here, and I wondered how it would have shaped my life. I wouldn't have wanted this. What I wanted was my old life back, before Pruitt and Fletcher. I wanted my family back. I wanted to be normal again—rewind to the year before I left for college, before Mama died, before my bad choices led to this downward spiral.

There was a message from Bidwell waiting for me at the hotel; I was to meet him at his office at ten o'clock the next morning.

Ken Durkin and I arrived at the same time and rode the elevator together to the ninth floor.

"How have you been, Miss Tandy?" Ken asked.

"I'm well, thank you."

"You must have spent the winter here in the south by the looks of you."

"I did. Winter in Key West could be addicting."

Bidwell was ready for us, and we got right to work.

"First on the agenda is a charitable foundation. I think Miss Tandy mentioned this at your initial meeting," Bidwell began. "Tell us about your vision." He motioned to me.

I wasn't prepared for him to pass the ball to me so quickly, but I gathered my thoughts, turned to Ken Durkin, and said, "Ken, I have decided to fund an education and research foundation for Down syndrome children, and it is my plan to use half of my inheritance to finance it. Beyond that, I have no idea how to make any of it happen, but I know the two of you do." I tossed the ball into their court.

My ultraconservative financial advisor looked pale, while my lawyer tried not to look amused.

"Are you sure, Miss Tandy? Half?"

"Yes, half. You should know that my inheritance was a complete windfall. I feel hoarding it would be next to immoral. Half still leaves more than two million, right?"

"Right."

Bidwell added, "Miss Tandy, your current portfolio balance is nearly five million as of yesterday. Is that correct, Ken?"

"Yes, that's correct."

"See, plenty of money." I smiled.

Over the next two hours, we discussed legal and financial plans and strategies. Having put together a plan to organize and fund a foundation, Ken said, "We will need a physical address here in Florida to finalize. When you decide on that, let me know."

"Actually, I have one already. Six Sea Island Drive. And I want it to be a live-in school."

I watched Ken absorb this information. I could see him picturing where the address was located, and the realization became evident on his face. "Miss Tandy, that area, well, it's very upscale, and a house in this location is worth, well, probably more than two hundred thousand."

"She owns it," Mr. Canfield said, looking pleased. "A real estate search revealed her ownership just a few weeks ago."

Ken looked dumbfounded. "I'm not going to ask you if you are sure," he said, writing down the address.

We parted with the understanding that Bidwell and Ken would work together on the formation of the foundation while I was in Tennessee.

Bidwell walked us to the elevator, whispering to me, "When you get to Tennessee, remember, there is a difference between justice and revenge."

CHAPTER 41
DANNY AND LIBBY

Hackberry, Tennessee
April 1, 1962

Driving into the Tennessee mountains filled me with both excitement at returning to where everything was familiar and dread thinking about Fletcher and his upcoming trial.

Though it was the first of April, the weather was still a bit chilly. At a gas stop, I took a jacket out of my bag and rubbed my hands together as I looked from the foothills to the highlands.

I arrived in Hackberry around noon and stopped at Spark's Diner for lunch. There were several locals having lunch. I greeted people as I passed, but they seemed surprised to see me. Libby was behind the counter.

"Hey, girl. You look wonderful," I said as I leaned over the counter for a hug. When she reached for me, I noticed she was wearing a ring on her left hand. "Wow, is that a diamond?" I grasped for her hand. "It *is* a—"

"Quil, let's go upstairs. I need to talk to you." She gently pulled her hand away.

"Are you engaged? You aren't back at your old 'men habits'? Tell me you're not," I whispered.

I followed her to the stairs and realized the diner had gotten quiet.

"I didn't know you would be home so early. What a surprise," she began.

"*You* are the surprise! Who's the guy?" I grabbed her hand again and stared at the ring. It looked distantly familiar.

"Quil, I…"

"What's the matter, Libby? You're acting weird. *Are* you engaged? Who's the guy?"

Libby turned away.

"Libby Sparks, who is the guy? If you are picking up worthless men again, I am going to strangle you."

There was a long pause before she said, "Not worthless."

"Who, then?" I demanded.

"Danny," she said quietly.

I stepped back and heard myself gasp.

"Oh, Quil. I am so sorry. It all happened so fast, and it took us both by surprise…falling in love…after all this time. I never knew what it was to actually be in love. We didn't want you to hear it over the phone. We planned to tell you together…when you got back. I thought you would write or call…let us know when you would be home…"

"Libby, you're babbling."

"Please don't be angry." Her eyes welled with tears.

"I'm not angry, just a little shocked. When?"

"When?"

"When is the wedding?"

She looked away again. "June."

I hugged her then, she tearful and me reassuring.

"Libby, I need to tell you a few things."

We sat in her bedroom, and I told her everything—the rape and the abortion, who Fletcher really was, everything. She sat in stunned silence, her mascara smeared.

"I could never marry Danny," I said. "Even though he *thought* he loved me, I could never marry him. He seems like a brother. I'm happy for the two of you…really, I am…I just need to let it sink in."

"How could you keep all this drama from me? I'm your best friend." She sniffled.

"I didn't tell anyone. Not even Daddy."

"Does Danny know?"

"Of course he knows. Nobody can keep a secret from Danny."

I drove into town and checked into the Kimble Inn. Lorraine looked surprised to see me. Did the entire town think I was never coming back?

"It's okay, Lorraine. I know all about Danny and Libby, and I'm happy for them."

"You do...you are?"

"I stopped by the diner on my way into town for lunch."

"Oh, does Danny know?" she asked.

"Know he's what...engaged?" I smiled at her.

Lorraine laughed, but I could tell this conversation was going to be one of many on the same topic. *Get used to it.* Maybe I should put a notice in the newspaper saying, "I'm happy for them, y'all."

Secretly, a part of me *was* sad—it felt like loss again. Why it felt like loss, I couldn't say. Maybe I really had loved Danny. Maybe I had made a terrible mistake. I needed to run.

I checked into my old room, changed into running clothes and sneakers, and ran down Main Street toward the police station. Certainly, Libby and a dozen others would have called to warn him by now.

He passed me driving the opposite direction on Main Street. I stopped. He stopped. He rolled down the window and said, "I was just coming to talk to you."

I glared at him, enjoying his discomfort. Then I smiled and said, "Congratulations."

"Get in," he said, pushing the passenger door open.

We drove in silence for several minutes, neither of us knowing what to say. Out away from town, to the south toward Knoxville, Danny finally pulled the cruiser over at a wide patch on the road. He didn't look at me.

"Danny Owens, if you tell me this is an April Fool's joke, I swear I will wring your neck like a chicken."

He looked at me then. "No joke. It's true."

I scooted across the seat and wrapped my arms around him. "You couldn't wait for me forever," I whispered. "And forever was what it would be. I could never love you as you deserve to be...the way Libby will."

I sat back, rubbing his arm in reassurance.

"Thanks, Quil. Mad at me?"

"Nope."

"Don't be mad at Libby. I pursued *her*, and she couldn't resist my handsome self." He laughed a little nervously.

"Mad at Libby? Are you kidding? Thanks for taking her off the market!" And then it dawned on me. "Is that Grandma Owens's wedding ring she's wearing?"

"Yep. Dad insisted. I think he always expected to see it on your hand."

I thought, *You are lucky to have Libby and not me. Everyone I love dies.*

On Monday, I phoned the Knoxville DA, Philip Randall, letting him know I was back in Tennessee and available. He asked me to come into the office the next morning.

It was a glorious spring day, and I was ready for a long, cleansing run. I trotted through town, smiling and acknowledging those I passed. In a small town, everybody knew everything about everyone, and I didn't want anybody thinking I was distressed about the engagement of my friends.

As I ran, the crisp mountain air invigorated me, and soon I found my stride, that sweet spot that I waited for. A pinch of pain bit at my chest as I turned down Deer Spring Road and then onto the Owens' driveway. I slowed to a trot for the last quarter mile to the farmhouse to let me catch my breath. Warren saw me coming and stepped out onto the porch.

Not wanting him to have a moment's discomfort at what could have been an awkward meeting, I called, "Is this the father of the groom?"

His relief was obvious, and he reached for me.

"Oh, Warren, don't hug me. I'm a sweaty mess!" I cried, but he paid no attention.

"How about some sweet tea?"

"Love some."

That night I crawled into bed with my journal to put thoughts into words. Seeing my reflections manifested into writing made me know the power of the written word. They were words of joy and sadness all mixed together. On one hand, I was happy for my friends' engagement, but on the other, I feared I had missed the opportunity for my own happiness. I felt strangely adrift, the odd one out, but as usual, journaling calmed me and put into perspective the ever-changing details of my life. I burrowed into the bed and turned off the light. My thoughts before sleep were peaceful.

The next morning I drove into Knoxville for my meeting with Mr. Randall. We chatted over coffee, making small talk until I brought up Fletcher and his trial.

"Just eighteen days to trial, right? Where are we?" I asked.

"Not where we hoped, I'm afraid."

"What does *that* mean?"

Over the next hour, Mr. Randall explained that Fletcher had, as expected, hired a host of high-dollar counsel who had buried the DA's office under a flurry of senseless, though legal, paper. They had petitioned the court to reduce the charges against Fletcher, citing no concrete evidence to support premeditated first-degree murder against Paddy, nor attempted murder against Libby and me, nor first-degree arson in the burning of my house. The court had thrown out the murder since Paddy had, technically, died of pneumonia. Libby's attempted murder charge stuck, but mine was reduced to assault. The arson charge was in question because nobody, not even me, had actually seen him set the fire. There was no evidence, not even the smell of gasoline on him when he was arrested.

I paced around the office as he spoke, unable to believe my ears. I was furious.

"How could this happen? Fletcher Pickford is a monster who planned to kill me for money! Are Paddy and Libby considered collateral damage? And my home—a hundred years of my heritage burned to the ground!" I groaned, feeling the familiar signals of panic seep in; my heart was pounding, and my breathing became rapid and shallow.

"You should sit down." Mr. Randall pulled me into a chair. He was alarmed and barked into the intercom, "Loretta, we need some water in here!"

I brushed him off and stood up. "If you can't kill him, I will!" I shouted as Loretta entered the room.

Danny arrived at Kimble's minutes after I did. I saw his car pull up outside and moments later heard him thunder up the stairs. I opened the door before he could knock. He grabbed my elbow and ushered me down the stairs and into his cruiser.

"Good grief, Owens. People are going to think I'm under arrest."

"I should lock you up to protect you from yourself. What kind of idiot stunt was that in Randall's office?"

"I see I have no secrets." I glared at him.

"Secrets? You threatened to kill Fletcher in the DA's office *in front* of his assistant."

"Not technically. I didn't use Fletcher's name."

"I don't think you have room for smugness, Quil. Randall is worried about your ability to testify."

"What?"

"If you lose your grip on the witness stand, like you did this morning, you could throw the entire case in the can. You *are* the only witness to Paddy's murder."

I glared at him then. "Haven't you heard? Fletcher isn't being tried for murder." I got out of the cruiser and walked back inside.

CHAPTER 42

THE PROSECUTION

Hackberry, Tennessee
April 23, 1962

The trial began on Monday the twenty-third, and, like Michelle's, this trial would be tense and angry. Unlike hers, I was working for the other side, and I was ready. This trial would be personal in a different way. One way or another, Fletcher would be punished.

Two weeks of legal preparation by the prosecution, and a promise to control myself, preceded Fletcher's trial. The charges were as followed: one count of first-degree assault for my attack; one count of attempted murder for Libby; and one count of first-degree arson. As expected, there was no mention of charges for my brother's murder.

Danny, Libby, and I entered the courtroom early and sat one row behind the prosecution's table. The gallery began to fill, and the defense team arrived: three dark suits with determined faces. My stomach lurched when Fletcher was led in. I had expected him to be dressed in prison garb and look worn and pale like Michelle, but that was not the case. He was impeccably groomed in a gray suit and a white starched dress shirt with an expensive blue striped tie that made him look handsome and secure. The dark dye was gone from his hair. It was now a sandy blond, which appeared to be natural. His gray eyes, cold and intimidating, were the same. He carried himself with authority and confidence; he looked our way, and his eyes narrowed. Libby looked away, but Danny and I stared back at him. If eyes could kill, we would all be dead.

The first day was all about opening arguments and the logging of evidence. I watched Fletcher, who looked straight ahead, calm and controlled, as if he were unconcerned and bored.

The second day had a little more meat to it. Mr. Randall called his first witnesses: people from the emergency rescue, hospital staff, and Danny, who testified to part of my attack as he came upon the scene.

There was no objection from the defense, but the lead lawyer chose to cross-examine Danny.

"Sheriff Owens, what is your relationship to Tranquil Tandy?"

"We are childhood friends."

"Isn't it true that you are more than Miss Tandy's friend? Were you two planning to marry?"

"No, I'm engaged to Libby Sparks."

"But wouldn't you say that you were very close to the Tandy family?"

"We were neighbors and friends."

"But being close to Tranquil Tandy and her family might make you less than objective?"

Mr. Randall spoke up. "Objection, leading the witness."

"I'm a law enforcement officer. I get paid to be objective." Danny spoke with calm authority.

Mr. Randall's next witness was the state's lead arson investigator, who testified to the origin of the fire and the accelerant used. He was knowledgeable and believable. He left no doubt that a fire of this heat and speed could have not occurred any other way than by arson.

The state's forensic psychiatrist, Dr. Lawrence Peterson, took the stand and spoke articulately, thoroughly explaining his diagnosis of Fletcher Pickford following six one-hour sessions.

"I would diagnose him as a sociopath with strong evidence of personality disorders leaning toward psychosis. I have not eliminated the possibility of schizophrenia."

"Would you call him dangerous?"

"Yes, very."

"Would you say he knows the difference between right and wrong?"

"Definitely."

"Your witness." Mr. Randall sat down.

"The defense reserves the right to recall the witness," the lead counsel said matter-of-factly without looking up.

After lunch, Mr. Randall called Libby, and she testified to the attack with as much composure as possible in the face of horrific memories.

"Miss Sparks, during this attack, did you fear for your life?"

"Yes. He said he was going to kill me and enjoy doing it."

"By *he*, do you mean the defendant, Fletcher Pickford?"

"Yes, him." She pointed at Fletcher, and he pretended to be shocked.

On cross-examination, Libby's less-than-chaste past was exposed, and her relationship with Fletcher, including how she had met him, was discussed. She held up well. I could see her distancing herself from the reality of the attorney's questions and her answers in order to stay calm.

I watched Fletcher and thought I saw him suppress a tight smile. Familiar hatred for him welled up in my throat like acid. My heartbeat stepped up, and I fought to control my breathing.

Libby sat down between Danny and me, and I hoped I wasn't going to be the next witness.

Mr. Randall said, "At this time, the state calls Miss Emily Wallace."

A woman about my age stood in the back of the gallery and walked toward the witness stand. She did not look at Fletcher, and I wondered if she, too, had once been attacked by him. While she was sworn in, he stared at her.

"Your Honor, the state considers Miss Wallace a hostile witness."

I felt confused. Who *was* this woman? I only had to wait a moment for the answer.

"Miss Wallace, before we begin, let me remind you of the penalty for perjury. Please tell the court if you have been advised of this."

"I have."

"Miss Wallace, what is your relationship to the defendant?"

"I was his assistant at Pickford Financial Group," she replied, not looking at Fletcher.

"I only have a couple of questions for you. First, are you aware of a history of brutalized women at the hands of Fletcher Pickford?"

"Objection. The witness cannot know what her employer did or did not do while not in her presence," Fletcher's lawyer barked.

"Sustained."

"Well, let me ask you this. Did you write corporation checks to women not employed by Pickford Financial Group?"

"Yes."

"How many?"

"I can't remember."

"Your Honor, at this time, the state would like to present financial records from Pickford Financial Group that clearly show checks written in the amount of more than five hundred thousand dollars over eight years."

He showed the documents to the judge, then to Emily Wallace, who confirmed she had written these checks by direction of her employer, Fletcher Pickford.

"Were these payments considered hush money?"

"Objection!" Fletcher's lawyer jumped to his feet.

"Sustained. Mr. Randall, get to the point," the judge warned.

"Let me rephrase. Miss Wallace, did you either know or were you told that these checks were being written to women for the purpose of keeping them quiet?"

"Yes."

"Your witness," Mr. Randall said.

"I have no further questions," Fletcher's lawyer responded.

It was my turn. I stood and walked toward the witness stand. I did not hurry. I concentrated on my breathing and unclenched my fists. Mr.

Randall fussed with papers at the prosecution table to give me time to completely compose myself. He asked me about the day of the fire and my attack. He asked me about what happened to Paddy. He asked me about what I saw Fletcher do and what I heard him say.

"Miss Tandy, who is James Turner?"

"The defendant, Fletcher Pickford. I met him on Thanksgiving Day at the Owens' house. He was introduced to me as James Turner."

"Why do you think Fletcher Pickford, also known as James Turner, attacked you?"

"Because I am the beneficiary of a huge estate left to me by my biological mother, who was Fletcher Pickford's stepmother. If I was dead and my brother was dead, then he would be the beneficiary. My brother, Paddy, being my only living relative, would of course have been my heir."

There was a collective gasp in the gallery. I stole a glance at the jury. They were awake.

"Did Mr. Pickford threaten to kill you?"

"Yes."

"Did you believe he would kill you?"

"Yes."

"Did he burn your house?"

I looked over at the jury and said, "Yes."

"Objection, Your Honor!"

"Your witness," Mr. Randall said and winked at me.

"Miss Tandy, do you hate men?" Fletcher's counsel began.

"Objection!"

"Withdrawn. Miss Tandy, you had a traumatic event happen to you in New Orleans two years ago. Is that right?"

"Your Honor!" Mr. Randall leapt to his feet.

"I'll allow it, but I'm warning you to make your point and move on." The judge was annoyed and impatient.

"Miss Tandy, were you brutally raped?"

I swallowed hard, looked down at my hands, and said, "Yes."

Murmurs rolled through the gallery like a slow-moving wave, and I glanced at Fletcher, who narrowed his eyes. I wondered what he was imagining, and I shuddered.

"Miss Tandy, did you see Mr. Pickford throw gasoline into your house and light it?"

"No, but I saw him running toward the house with a gas can I knew was full and—"

"No more questions."

"And I watched him break down my kitchen door with an ax!"

"That's enough, Miss Tandy," the judge barked.

I was excused.

"The state calls Dolores Watson."

I turned as my neighbor stood. Jill Dawson was sitting next to her, and it dawned on me what Mr. Randall was after. *Impressive.*

"Mrs. Watson, did Tranquil Tandy call you for help on the day she was attacked by Fletcher Pickford?"

"No. Jill Dawson and I were on the phone talking with each other."

"Your telephone system is a rural party line, correct?"

"Correct."

"When Miss Tandy picked up her phone, she heard the two of you talking and asked for help, correct?"

"Yes."

"Tell the court what she said."

"She said that James attacked her and for us to get help."

"Did she hang up the phone then?"

"No, it sounded like she dropped the receiver."

"What happened then?"

"Well, with a phone off the hook, neither Jill nor I could call anyone, so Jill drove into town to get help, while I stayed on the line."

"Could you hear anything?"

"Yes, I heard crashing and breaking sounds and then a man cursing and yelling."

"Could you understand what he was saying?"

"Clearly. He was shouting that he was going to kill Tranquil an inch at a time and burn the house to the ground."

Fletcher's mouth fell slightly agape. It was obvious he did not expect this. His lawyers would have seen Mrs. Dawson's and Mrs. Watson's names on the witness list, and it would have been easy to find out who they were but impossible to know what they knew. He hadn't seen this coming. I smiled at Fletcher, and he glared at me. I looked toward the aisle. The jury could see his face but not mine.

"Thank you, Mrs. Watson. Your witness."

"No questions at this time."

"The prosecution recalls Sheriff Daniel Owens."

"Objection."

"Overruled."

After a reminder from the judge that he was still under oath, Danny settled into the witness chair.

"Sheriff Owens, who is James Turner?"

"The defendant."

"When did you first meet him?"

"He was a guest in my parents' home for Thanksgiving last year and introduced himself as James Turner."

"So everyone at dinner that day would have known him, Fletcher Pickford, as James, correct?"

"Yes."

"Objection, hearsay."

"Your Honor, should I recall all the state's witnesses to confirm the identification?"

"Sustained." It was four thirty, and I guessed the judge did not want to go through most of Mr. Randall's witness list again. "Call one to confirm."

He recalled me to the stand, and I confirmed Danny's identification and connection between James and Fletcher.

We adjourned for the day.

I was exhausted, but I needed a run to blow off the day. I ran south of town a few miles and then back to Maybelle's Soup and Pie for dinner.

Back at Kimble's, I shed my sweaty clothes and slid into a hot bath full of bubbles. After a long soak, finally the stress of the day melted away. I imagined the emotional toxins pulling out through my skin, and I left them behind as the water drained.

That night I wrote in my journal.

I think it all went well today. It was hard to watch Libby suffer, and I didn't like it happening to me either, but in the end, Fletcher looked very guilty. I recognized the looks on the jurors' faces. The charges of assault, attempted murder, and arson will hopefully stick, though Randall says the defense might seek a plea deal if the evidence becomes damning. That he won't be prosecuted for Paddy's murder is devastating, and it means he will not die for his crimes...at least not in the electric chair.

CHAPTER 43

THE DEFENSE

Knoxville, Tennessee
April 25, 1962

On the third day, Fletcher arrived still confident, and anyone watching his entrance could not look away. He was beautiful and dangerous and moved like a sleek predator. He looked my way and leveled a menacing glare. I glared back, refusing to be intimidated.

Fletcher sat between his lawyers calmly. He reminded me of a spider in the center of a web: controlled, motionless, waiting for prey.

The prosecution rested by noon, and we broke for lunch. I did not join my friends. I had an errand to run. I was back in the courtroom before anyone else. It was completely empty, and I laid an envelope on Fletcher's chair at the defense table.

The court reconvened, and as usual, Fletcher made a powerful entrance. I watched as he pulled out his chair and picked up the envelope. He drew no attention to this discovery. While the attorneys at his table unpacked files and discussed what I imagined were secrets among themselves, Fletcher opened the envelope and removed the contents. I waited as he looked at Polaroid photos of the Key West cottage and the mansion on Sea Island Drive. On the latter, I had printed *Paddy's House*.

Fletcher discreetly slipped the photos back into the envelope and slid it into the inside pocket of his suit coat.

His jaw was set, and I savored every moment as the realization of what had happened to his property dawned on him—it was written on his face. His head slowly turned toward me, the hatred evident in his eyes.

I narrowed my eyes and smirked, mocking him, goading him as if to say, "Come after me again, I dare you." He turned away, but I saw his fists clench.

The court came to order. The defense called their first witnesses: an expert to challenge our arson expert and business character witnesses from Miami.

Emily Watson was recalled, who spoke about Fletcher in a well-rehearsed yet apprehensive way. I wondered if she had been threatened.

The defense could not deny Fletcher's presence in Hackberry, nor the attacks, so they made remarks about his lack of criminal record and pressed witnesses to drone on about Fletcher as a successful businessman.

After lunch, Fletcher's lead counsel asked to approach the bench, and the judge beckoned him and Mr. Randall to come forward.

In a low voice, Fletcher's attorney explained that an unexpected witness had come forward and he wished to call her to the stand. Mr. Randall reluctantly agreed.

"The defense calls LilaJune Walker."

Fletcher did not react as a black woman I guessed to be in her late sixties came into the courtroom and was sworn in. Fletcher looked at her then, but I didn't see recognition in his eyes, even though she smiled softly his way. It was almost a motherly smile.

"Miss Walker, is it true you contacted Fletcher Pickford's defense team this morning?"

"Yes, I did."

"And why not before?"

"Because I read about his case in the news, and I have been traveling by bus ever since to get here. I'm from Savannah, Georgia."

"What is your relationship to the defendant?"

"I was his nanny."

At this, recognition, anger, then pain swept across Fletcher's face like a series of changing colors. He scribbled something on a legal pad and shoved it at the lawyer sitting beside him. I saw the lawyer shake his head and Fletcher push back his chair as though to stand. The lawyer grabbed his wrist and whispered something. Their body language suggested a struggle might occur. It did not, but the jury focused on them.

"Miss Walker, what is it you wanted the court to know?"

LilaJune Walker told a tale of the horrible physical and emotional abuse Fletcher had suffered at the hands of his father, Charles, in such a compelling way that even *I* was momentarily moved. Some of the female jurors quietly cried.

She then told the court about Clarice and her cold, indifferent treatment of her stepson, how Fletcher had been a sweet, innocent child brutalized by his parents.

LilaJune described in detail about the day she was fired and Fletcher's head injury that had been left untreated for more than twelve hours. Finally, she described how she had prayed for Fletcher every day for the past twenty-four years and how she was here today to beg the court to consider his abuse in connection with his behavior.

Fletcher looked uncomfortably shaken, which only added punctuation to LilaJune's speech. It was as if he was hearing it all for the first time. His hand shot to the scar on his forehead. The jury watched him.

"Yes, sweet boy, just there," LilaJune said to Fletcher.

"Miss Walker, you will not speak to the defendant," the judge warned. "Do you understand?"

"Yes, sir." Her cringe appeared involuntary.

I was certain that a black woman being reprimanded by a white man, let alone a judge, would have threatened her. In fact, simply being in a courtroom was extraordinary for a woman of color, and I wondered what had truly fueled her bravery. Would the jury find a black woman credible? I did, but would my Southern peers? It was anyone's guess.

"Your witness."

Mr. Randall stood and asked in a kind voice, "Miss Walker, were you compelled to testify today?"

At that moment, I realized that Mr. Randall had made a fatal mistake, remembering Michelle's attorney, Mr. Lincoln, saying, "Never ask a question to which you don't already know the answer." Now *I* cringed.

LilaJune straightened and looked Mr. Randall in the eye. "I was compelled only by my conscience."

I felt ill. This could be the deal breaker where the jury was concerned. Would they feel such sympathy for the abused Fletcher as a child that their judgement might be skewed? The defense had done a better job, and we all knew it. I did not believe for one second that LilaJune had simply shown up. She had been saved as an ace in the hole, but I believed she had no idea she had been used. How the defense team had manipulated this was beyond me.

"The defense recalls Dr. Lawrence Peterson."

Dr. Peterson took the stand.

"Would it be your expert opinion that a person brutalized for years as a child could be turned into a sociopath?"

"Well…" Dr. Peterson began.

"It's late, Dr. Peterson. Yes or no?"

"That's really not a yes-or-no question."

"Yes or no, please," Fletcher's attorney pressed.

"Yes."

"Or a psychopath?"

"Yes."

"The defense rests."

The judge called for closing arguments the next morning. And we were adjourned.

I sat stunned as the jury filed out. In the last hour, the defense had established both doubt and sympathy in the jury's minds; it was written all over them. I couldn't believe what had just happened. Surely the jury would see through the defense and come to reasonable conclusions. I wanted to embrace this but knew we were in trouble.

We all met for dinner in Knoxville. Danny, Libby, Mr. Randall, and I settled in at a table at Louie's Steakhouse.

"How do you think it will go?" It was the question on everyone's lips.

"I think he is a goner for Libby and Quil, but the arson may not fly." Mr. Randall rubbed his face. "There isn't any concrete evidence. And LilaJune Walker put a nail in the heart of our case. When he is convicted, and he will be, the defense will surely ask for psychiatric commitment instead of prison."

"What? This can't be happening. How could you let this happen?" I was incredulous.

"Quil, don't." Danny reached for my arm, but I shrugged it off.

I was not prepared for Mr. Randall's admission of defeat even before a verdict. With an attitude like this, closing arguments would be transparent and ineffective. I was suddenly furious.

"You were expertly manipulated by an expensive set of suits!" I pushed my chair back and stood.

"That's not fair," Libby said. "Everybody did their best."

"Did Paddy do his best?"

No one spoke.

"I'm done." I threw down my napkin and headed for the door. Danny was hot on my heels.

He caught up to me in the parking lot. "Quil, settle down. You're acting like a hysterical female."

I slapped him. "Wake up, Danny! The law doesn't protect those without money."

I jerked my car door open and got in. "See you tomorrow."

It was after dark before I parked the T-Bird in front of Kimble's, but that didn't stop me from tying on my running shoes. The moon was nearly full, and I ran through a town closed for the night but illuminated by moonlight.

I thundered down 31A and onto Deer Spring Road, fueled by anger and disappointment. My chest was burning and my legs throbbed as I came to a halt in front of the ruins of my old home, heaving and gasping, bent at the waist. I vomited.

I had run hard and long, but my anger had followed me. It reared up before me like a hideous behemoth, and I screamed at it, my voice so shrill it hurt my ears. I felt myself losing control. I smashed my fists against the boathouse wall, the same place where Fletcher had smashed my head. I heard Paddy screaming for help, me screaming for help. I cried then, tight, squeezed tears, hot and silent—something I hadn't done since the rape.

The defense attorney's voice rang in my ears: "Miss Tandy, are you a man-hater?" *Was* I a man-hater? I tried to remember the last man who had not betrayed me. Danny? I knew my anger at Danny was temporary. No, not Danny.

I paced up and down the dock in the moonlight. The river rushed by, and the night birds called out. It was true that I hated Pruitt and Fletcher. Were there more? I began a list in my head of men I trusted: Daddy, Good-daddy, Grand-père, Warren Owens, Mr. Lincoln, Mr. Canfield, Javier, Eduardo…all men who didn't challenge or threaten me. *All men who didn't challenge or threaten me.* The realization made me feel vulnerable and weak, and I didn't like it. Would I ever be able to trust a man romantically? Could I love a man and trust him unconditionally? I had no answers, and maybe I had no future. Tears still ran down my face as I trotted for home.

It was more than five miles back to Kimble's, and I had time to think and come to a decision.

I loaded the snub-nose .38 I had purchased the morning before and slipped it into my purse, turned out the light, and lay awake until dawn.

CHAPTER 44
THE VERDICT

Knoxville, Tennessee
April 27, 1962

At breakfast the next morning, Lorraine brought me a legal-sized manila envelope with my name typed on the front.

"What's this?"

"I don't know. It was on the counter this morning," she said, hurrying off.

I put down my coffee and released the envelope's closure. Inside were photos of me: several eight by ten black-and-white photos of me shopping, running, eating breakfast in this very room, talking to Danny in the cruiser. It was unnerving, but I tried not to react. I stilled my hands and did not look around, putting the photos back into the envelope, casually pushing it aside as my breakfast arrived. I forced myself to eat slowly and calmly and had a third cup of coffee before slipping into my jacket and stuffing the envelope under my arm.

In the T-Bird, I tossed the envelope over my shoulder into the cubby behind the seat. If someone was watching, I hoped they had taken a picture of *that*.

At the courthouse, I waited in the foyer for Mr. Randall to arrive. He was not happy to see me, but I was prepared to eat a plateful of my words.

"I am so very sorry for my outburst last night. It was inexcusable, and I hope you will be able to forgive me."

"You were right, you know. I did blow it."

"No. No, you absolutely did not. You were outgunned by money and outmaneuvered by deceit. It is all going to be made right in time."

"That's pretty philosophical for somebody whose life has been shattered."

"Not philosophical, just pragmatic. I have to get through this, and it starts today."

He looked at me then with a questioning expression, but I turned away before he could ask me anything more. I took a seat on the aisle in the row we—Libby, Danny, and I—had occupied all week. I laid my hand on the gun in my jacket pocket and waited.

Danny and Libby arrived together, and Danny slid in next to me.

"I understand you ate some crow this morning with Randall. Do you want to eat some with *me?*"

"Sorry," I said curtly. I didn't look at him.

"That's not very convincing."

"Sorry a lot."

He touched my jacket pocket and the gun. "Come with me, Quil." He slipped a hand under my elbow.

"No."

"Yes, or I'll arrest you for carrying a concealed weapon in a courthouse."

"What?"

"Stand up, or so help me you are going to jail."

I stood, and we walked down the center aisle and out of the court-house doors.

On the steps, I turned to him and smiled. "We are being photographed."

"What did you say?"

"Don't take the gun here. Let's go to my car, and I'll hand it over—besides, I have something to show you."

I looked at my watch. It was seventeen minutes before nine o'clock. We walked calmly to my car and got in. I put the gun in the glove compartment. Danny took the car keys out of my hand, locked the box, and put them in his pocket.

"Hey! Don't treat me like a child, Owens!"

"Then stop acting like one."

"How did you know about the gun anyway?"

"You are borderline nuts, know that? Do you think you can buy a gun without me knowing about it? I suspected you might do something crazy when you came unglued last night. Then when Randall told me about your conversation with him, the red flags were obvious. You make a terrible criminal."

"There is a manila envelope on the floor behind my seat. Don't make a big deal about retrieving it."

Danny, still looking at me, slid a hand to the floor and brought the envelope onto his lap.

"Open it."

He flipped through the photos.

"When did you get these?"

"This morning at breakfast. I'm scared, and guess what, Owens? The criminal who is really good at it is going to get off."

"He can't. There is too much evidence against him."

"For a smart cop, you can be incredibly naive. Money can make anything happen, and it's happening to me!"

The clock in the courthouse tower chimed nine times while we stared at each other.

"Got any more weapons? No switchblades or grenades in your purse? You won't look good in stripes." He smirked.

"Let's go in. And, Owens, heads up. Libby isn't safe either."

Closing arguments were already underway as we slipped into our seats. Mr. Randall looked our way, and Danny nodded to him. I was angry and relieved at the same time. I hated their smugness but was relieved to have been saved from myself, even if I would never admit it.

The jury looked diligently at their notes; some watched Fletcher, who was the picture of composure, while others looked alternately from Mr. Randall to the defense counsel.

As expected, the prosecution said nothing in his closing remarks to make a stronger case against Fletcher.

Fletcher's lead counsel approached the jury for his summation. He smiled at them and encouraged them to look only at the evidence presented. He talked about Fletcher's abused childhood and the effects on Fletcher the adult. He was thorough and believable.

The judge gave the jury their instructions, and we were adjourned.

It was Friday, and the jury would have the weekend or the next week to discuss Fletcher's fate. Or they might simply take a vote and return in an hour, as the jury had done in Michelle's case.

I felt angry and frustrated. Was it possible that they would find him innocent of all charges and set him free? No, that could not happen— surely not. I felt anxious and needed to run. I hurried down the court-house steps toward the T-Bird, searching for my keys, then realized that Danny had them. My eyes searched the crowd.

"Looking for these?" He stood behind me dangling my keys.

"Listen, Owens, I am not going to put up with you trailing me like a hound dog. Back off."

"Okay, I can do that, but you don't really want me to. Give me that envelope with the photos. Make a show of it so our secret photographer sees us. I will run them for prints. Anything other than yours and mine, and we will have them."

I unlocked the car and handed the envelope to Danny.

"I want them back," I said.

"Come spend the weekend with Mom and Dad. They miss you, and you could use some family time. Just a suggestion. And Randall wanted me to give you this."

Danny handed me my necklace, the one I had worn for years and had been used in evidence at the trial. It glittered in the sunlight. My necklace? No, Clarice's necklace. Another part of the lie. I folded my hand around it and dropped it into my purse.

The weekend moved along slowly. Monday passed without word from the court, but on Tuesday morning, we were told the jury was in.

We all gathered in the courtroom and fell silent when the judge came in. The bailiff brought the verdict to the judge, and he read it.

"Will the defendant please rise?

Fletcher and his lawyers stood.

"The verdict is as follows. On the charge of assault, the jury finds the defendant guilty." I exhaled and reached for Libby's hand.

"On the charge of attempted murder, the jury finds the defendant guilty."

Libby breathed in sharply, and Danny put an arm around her. I clenched my fists and waited.

"On the charge of arson, the jury finds the defendant not guilty."

I put my face in my hands.

"In addition, the jury recommends commitment to the Tennessee State Psychiatric Hospital in Nashville rather than incarceration in the Tennessee State Penitentiary."

"No," I whispered.

"The court is prepared to pass sentence. Fletcher Pickford, you are hereby sentenced to twenty-five years for your crimes. However, it is the opinion of this court that the first five years of your sentence be served in treatment at the Tennessee State Psychiatric Hospital in Nashville. If after three years you do not show proven successful rehabilitation, you will be transferred to the Tennessee State Penitentiary to serve the remainder of your sentence. Bailiff, take the prisoner into custody."

I wished I had my gun.

That night I paced in my room. Even a long run had not relieved my shock at Fletcher's sentence.

I packed my belongings. All I wanted was to be gone.

A letter arrived the next morning before I checked out. It had no return address.

The single piece of paper read:

You are as good as dead.
There is nowhere you can go to hide from me.
All you can do is wait for it to happen.
And it will.

The note had been typed, and I was fairly sure no fingerprints would be found. I refolded the paper, slipped it into its envelope, and pushed it into my jacket pocket.

On my way out of town, I stopped by the police station to speak with Danny, but he was not there. The envelope with the photos was on his desk, and I picked it up.

I left a note:

Danny, I'm going back to Key West for a while. I can't be here, but I will be back in plenty of time for the wedding at the end of June. I've taken the photos. Don't be mad. You can reach me at the same number in Key West. Quil

CHAPTER 45
ROOTS

Hackberry, Tennessee
May 3, 1962

I drove out of Hackberry and farther into the mountains toward Asheville, North Carolina—no chance of running into Danny up here. At Greenville, South Carolina, I called Eduardo and Javier.

"Have you rented my house yet?"

"Chica? Is it you?" Eduardo said to me and then over his shoulder called, "It's the chica! Javier, it's Quil!"

I laughed.

"No, we have not rented it. Come home at once!"

"It would only be for a month or so, but I'm on my way, and I can't wait to get there. I should be in by Friday."

"Prude!" Eduardo replied.

"Prude?" I shook my head in confusion.

"Yes, prude. Marvelous, *si?*"

"Yes, Eduardo, marvelous."

My next call was to Bidwell Canfield. I told him all about the disastrous trial. He was, of course, empathetic, though, like me, was helpless to change the facts.

"What now?" he asked.

"Key West, I guess, or maybe…I'm not sure."

"Quil, the private investigator we hired has results."

"Really? What kind of results?"

"Do you want to talk over the phone or come here?"

"I'm actually already on my way. I'm in Greenville, South Carolina." I looked at my watch. It was only ten o'clock. "I'll be at the hotel late, but can we meet early tomorrow?"

"I have a breakfast meeting. I can see you at nine thirty. Will that work?"

"Perfect, see you then."

I drove hard to Miami, taking a minimal number of breaks, and by midnight, I was at the hotel.

It was good to see Bidwell's welcoming smile the next morning.

"How was your trip?" he asked.

"I'm pretty tired but anxious to hear what you have to say."

We took our coffee into his office and sat on either end of the red leather couch. He flipped open a file.

"All right, Clarice first?"

I nodded.

"Her maiden name was Jensen, a Danish surname, and she was raised in Bemidji, Minnesota, by Danish immigrant parents who were grain farmers. She had two brothers, both killed in the war, one in France and one at sea. Both parents have also passed away."

"Any other relatives?"

"None that we found. Clarice left home at seventeen and went first to New York City, where we think she met Charles Pickford, but there is no concrete evidence of that. They married in 1933. Fletcher would have been two. His mother died of cancer."

"So I'm half Danish. I would have never dreamed. I resembled my dad, Henry, dark haired and all. What about my biological father?"

"Again there was nothing concrete except for one of Clarice's friends—a May Nelson, who told us she knew Clarice was seeing a professor of Middle Eastern Studies at the University of Florida. She did not know how they met or his name, but we found records to support this information at the university. There *was* a professor teaching there in 1934 by the name of Ahmed Jassim. He was from Qatar, a tiny country on the Persian Gulf. His visa ran out in late 1936, the year you were born, and he returned to Qatar. We have nothing more on him."

I dropped my face into my hands. "Danish and Persian. Are you kidding? And all this time I thought I was French. Guess I learned the wrong languages."

My head reeled.

"What next?"

"Quil, there is no next. We have gone as far as we can go."

I stood then and walked to the window, arms crossed like a hug. We said nothing for a long while.

"At least I know *what* I am even if I still don't know *who* I am."

"Listen, you are the woman your parents, Glee and Henry Tandy, raised. You are a part of *their* heritage. Parenthood has little to do with blood. You were lucky to be raised by them. If you hadn't, you might have ended up like Fletcher. Have you thought of that?"

I looked at him and could see the sincerity in his eyes. He was more than my attorney—he had become a trusted friend.

We discussed the foundation, then ordered lunch to be delivered. We ate quietly for a while.

"What's on your mind? I can tell when you are thinking hard about something."

"Bidwell, I have decided to disappear."

"What?"

"I want to change my identity and citizenship and disappear, because I will never get away from Fletcher." I pulled the photos and the letter from my bag.

"Good grief! I had no idea what kind of trouble you were in. Have you talked to the authorities?"

"Of course I have, but there are no fingerprints on anything and no way to trace any of this back to Fletcher. Somehow he has money we did not know about—lots of it, and he has eyes and ears everywhere. It's just a matter of time before I have a tragic accident or a fake suicide. Don't you see? I have to become someone they can't find. Can you help me?"

"Let me think." He stood and walked toward the window. "I am not willing to do anything illegal, but I do have connections, and I do know people who know people, if you get my meaning. What is it exactly you need to do?"

"I thought about disappearing in France—Paris maybe. My Parisian French is good, then I considered Nova Scotia. My maternal grand-parents were from there, and I could adapt to accents in both English and French. I had a great-grandmother by the name of Desiree Renée long dead and buried near Halifax. Her last name was d'Moss, origin unknown, but the family thinks she married a Spanish or Portuguese sailor. My grandmother was born in 1895, so I'm guessing Desiree was born sometime in the 1870s. The thing is, I could become her. There would be Canadian paperwork, right? There must be a way for me to become her."

"I assume she is dead."

"Of course, but wouldn't it be easy to resurrect her identity—easier than starting from scratch, right?"

"I wouldn't know, and why would *you?*" Bidwell rubbed his face. "Instead of all this cloak-and-dagger business, why aren't you contacting the authorities? Your life has been threatened!"

"The authorities are an inept bunch of idiots. I can't trust them. I have to do this my way. Only you can help me."

I could see I had nearly stepped over an ethical line and said no more about illegal activity. I had to assume he would get it done without incriminating either of us.

"You have really thought this through." Bidwell looked resigned. "Then what?"

"Well, I would have to assimilate, of course, and I would need time to find where to live and what to do."

"What about the money?" he asked.

"I have no idea how to make that happen, and I certainly don't need to disappear with millions. You will be the only one who knows where and who I am. I will keep the Key West place, and the house on Sea Island Drive will become a fabulous school for kids like my brother. I want to call it Paddy's House. Use as much money as you need for renovations, staff, operations, insurance…everything. Be sure to pay yourself…a lot," I babbled.

"Whoa, slow down. When are you planning to make this happen?"

"I have dear friends marrying on June 30, and I must be there. I was thinking July 4 would be a good day. Holiday traffic will be heavy, and I could slip through customs with less trouble than on a day when officials have more leisure time. Besides, I think Independence Day is perfect, don't you?"

"Quil, this is a huge decision, and you are talking about it like you are making a grocery list. Think! You will be effectively dead. Everyone you know now, including me, will be dead to you. Are you prepared for that?"

"You and I may be dead to each other, but Desiree d'Moss won't be. You will know who I really am, and we will communicate somehow. It's not illegal for me to change my name or open bank accounts in Canada, right?"

"Not technically, but you want it done secretly."

I could see the wheels turning in him. He would have less than two months to make everything happen.

"I am going to need a durable power of attorney, which gives me the right to anything in your name. How much do you trust me?"

I laughed.

"Seriously, Quil. You would be trusting me with everything you own or will own. Ready for *that*?"

"Yes."

He raked his fingers through his hair. "I don't like this, not one bit, but if you are set on this course, then I would rather help you than have you try it on your own. Lay low. Don't do anything that draws attention to yourself. Don't ask me questions that will incriminate me. Let me think this through."

"Thank you, thank you."

"I will set it all in motion right away. I can do the money transfer to a bank in Halifax when you get a new passport, but that is all I will do directly, the rest will be up to…to whomever. I don't want to know, and you won't know anything until you actually get on the plane to Halifax. How you prepare for that is all on your shoulders, I am afraid. A bit like jumping off a cliff, blindfolded, trusting someone will break your fall."

On the drive to Key West, I thought about everything Bidwell had said. It *was* going to be a nerve-racking process over which I would have no control, but I knew it was the right choice and that I *would* follow through.

CHAPTER 46

PULLING IT TOGETHER

Key West, Florida
May 5, 1962

I pulled up to the curb in front of my old house shortly before six p.m. Dot was waiting on the porch. She threw her arms around me as I got out of the car.

"Hungry?"

"Always."

"I'm so glad you are back."

"It feels wonderful to be back. It feels like home to me now."

Mick Jaguar trotted out to say hello and rubbed my legs with his face and back.

"Well, hi, you handsome boy," I said, picking him up and throwing his hulking body over a shoulder.

"He's missed you too. We all have. To be honest, I wasn't expecting to see you back so soon."

"Plans change."

"Let's eat. I made Jordanian food."

We feasted on curried lamb kebabs, sautéed vegetables over rice, flatbread, and hummus topped with sour yogurt and sweet cucumber sauce.

"So tell me about the trial," she said as we flopped down on lawn chairs in the garden.

"It was a disaster."

I told her everything, including the shocking sentence. Mick Jaguar crawled onto my lap and got comfortable.

"So now what?"

"Well, here's some news I just got yesterday. I hired a private investigator to track down my biological parents."

"Really, you are full of surprises."

"You haven't heard the half of it. As it turns out, my mother was Danish and my dad was most likely Qatari."

"No kidding! So you are Danish and…"

"Persian."

Mick Jaguar and I were cuddled in bed and asleep by the time the boys got home. Once again, the past month had gotten the best of me, and I was ready for undisturbed sleep. It felt so good to be back.

The next day I had lunch with Eduardo and Javier at the restaurant.

"You look stressed, chica," Eduardo said, rubbing my hand.

"It's been a rough month."

"Do you want to talk about it?"

"Not right now, but thanks for being so sweet. I'm going for a run and a swim."

"Always running, chica." Eduardo shook his head.

"See you tonight," I called over my shoulder as I trotted out the door.

I ran down Duval and zigzagged my way to Atlantic Boulevard. At the cottage, I shed my clothes on the back porch and tiptoed through the shell beach to the water. The bright midday sunlight flooded over my naked body, warm and penetrating. The sea embraced me, and I floated peacefully, face to the sky. The tide was changing, and for these few minutes, the Atlantic seemed to be suspended, as if holding its breath. Soon I felt the tug of the current and knew I should get closer to shore. Eventually, I became chilled and left the water for the warmth of the porch.

I lay naked in the sun. No one could see me here. It was one of the beauties of this cottage, completely private, almost an island unto itself.

I wondered if I could dare live here in defiance of Fletcher's threats. A part of me wanted to dare him, to lure him, to ambush him. I could be as stealthy as him, but I knew I could not be as cruel. Even if I did entrap him, I would hesitate, and he would not. What was the old saying, "She who hesitates…"

An hour later I dressed and headed for home.

I spent six luxuriously restful weeks in the company of my friends. I wrote in my journal, swam and sunned, ran and feasted, and most of all laughed. The boys polished my cha-cha, and Dot even got me to try a Jordanian dance called Al-Hashi. I felt clumsy next to my expert friend, but it was all in good fun.

I ran to the cottage nearly every day, swam naked, sunned naked. The days grew warmer: summer was coming, the heat reliable. My skin browned, and my hair sun streaked. I was happy.

Then one day reality slapped me in the face when I found a manila envelope taped to my door. Though there were no distinguishing marks, I knew what I was holding. I laid the envelope on the kitchen counter, poured a glass of tea, and stirred in a tablespoon of sugar. I tapped the envelope with the spoon and drank my tea, not wanting to open it. Finally, I broke the seal, and four glossy photos slipped out. One of me running down Duval. One of me sitting on the front porch with Dot and the boys. One of me swimming, and one of me lying in the sun naked. My hands trembled as I tore the photos into tiny pieces and threw them in the trash.

Time had run out, and any foolish ideas I had been entertaining about challenging Fletcher or living here in Key West evaporated. I had, after all, been the one who had shown him the photos of the cottage, stupidly played my hand, tempted fate. Now not only was I in danger, but I had also put Dot and the boys in jeopardy if I stayed in Key West; Danny and Libby if I was in Hackberry. I hoped Mr. Canfield had done his job.

I would return to Hackberry for the wedding, but while Danny and Libby were on their honeymoon, I would disappear.

On June 25, I once again loaded my car and said goodbye. I took a picture of my friends and the cat on the porch waving at the camera. As the picture developed, the reality that I might never see them or this magical place again nipped at me like a cold wind at my back.

In Miami, I signed over my financial life to Mr. Canfield.

"Well, I guess this is it." Emotion tugged at my chest.

"Yes, this is it, but, Quil, we *can* figure out a way for you to come home should your situation change."

I hugged him, thanked him, and said goodbye. Before we parted, he handed me an envelope and whispered to open it only in private.

Dressed in clothes not common to my style and my dark hair piled under a straw hat and sunglasses even too big for a fashion goddess, I spent the rest of the day shopping. I bought two good-quality wigs—one blond, the other red, both in nondescript shades intended to deflect attention. I chose clothing, makeup, and shoes again not normally my style. I packed it all in the T-Bird and headed north.

The night before the wedding, Hackberry
June 29, 1962

Sitting quietly at the desk in my room at Kimble's, sipping chamomile tea with milk, I began to write.

> *Dear Danny and Libby,*
> *By the time you read this, you will hopefully have had a glorious honeymoon and will have returned rested and ready for your new life together. I miss you already.*
> *As you can see, enclosed is the deed to the Tandy land along with water rights and applicable licenses and titles for the boats and fishing equipment. The Thunderbird (key enclosed)*

*is for Libby (every girl should have a convertible) and is in
long-term parking at the Nashville airport. The title is in the
glove compartment along with the extra keys.*

*Also, a check in the amount of fifty thousand dollars is
waiting for you both at the bank in Hackberry for the building of a home for your future. It was the fire insurance money.
This is actually a gift from Paddy. If he were here, he would be
so happy that the two people he loved as much as he loved me
would begin a new life in the ruins of ours. Build a house, and
raise a litter of kids with our blessing.*

I stopped and thought about what to say next.

*This is goodbye, my dear friends. Don't look for me. You will
not find me. Because I will never outrun Fletcher as Tranquil
Tandy, I have become someone else and vanished. You may see
me again someday, who knows. If I outlive Fletcher, it might be
possible, but until then, you can't know me; it's not safe.
Be good to each other. I love you both so much. Remember me.
Tranquil*

CHAPTER 47

GETTING MARRIED

Hackberry, Tennessee
June 30, 1962

Libby was nervous and fidgety. So was I.

"Come on, Libby. Pull it together. You're getting married in two hours."

"I can't...no, I can't. Let's drive somewhere...Key West...yes, let's go there. Danny will understand."

"No, he won't! Now sit down and let your mother fix your hair."

She teared up.

"No, no, no, Libby. Don't cry. Red eyes on a bride are completely unattractive."

"I don't deserve him."

"I said that once, and look where I am." I shook her and hugged her. "Danny loves you. He has always loved you. He thought he was *supposed* to love me, but he didn't really. He loved you all along. Can't you see that? *I* can, and so can everyone else. He lights up around you." I handed her a tissue. "Libby, let him love you and you love him and have a dozen little Owens." I held her close.

"Are you mad at me?"

"Oh, for the love of Pete, Libby! You will be my best friend forever. Now get dressed! It's almost eleven o'clock!"

I left her to dress, and I went back to Kimble's to do the same. As I was the maid of honor, it was my job to wear the ugliest dress I had ever seen.

"Do you think she could have picked a brighter shade of pink?" I said to the mirror.

I pulled my hair up into a gentle chignon and slipped into dress-matching hot pink heels. At the church, I found Danny pacing around in the garden where the ceremony would be held.

"How are you holding up?" I asked.

"Good. Good. Really good. Wish I could say the same for you. Good grief, that dress is some kind of ugly."

We both laughed hard, just like we had as kids. It felt like the old days, warm and carefree.

"How is she?"

"Fabulous."

Warren walked up then. "What's so funny?"

"Look at her dress!" Danny snickered.

"Yikes, that's really ugly," Warren agreed.

We both dissolved into laughter again, and Warren joined us.

"Stand next to your son," I said. "I want a picture." I motioned them together.

My Polaroid snapped, and the familiar whir produced the picture. We stood there waiting for it to develop.

"Now you two." Warren took the camera from me.

"Me in my ugly dress immortalized." I groaned.

Danny and I stood together, arms around each other's waists—click, whir. Warren handed me the photo. There we were, Danny and I, older versions of our childhood selves, laughing as the photo developed. I would cherish this.

Guests began to arrive and arrive and arrive some more. It looked like the entire town was attending. All the chairs filled, and people were standing in the shade of the garden oaks.

I took Warren aside and handed him a packet.

"I'm giving them a honeymoon for a wedding present, but don't say anything just yet. They are going to the Bahamas for two weeks, and their plane leaves tomorrow from Nashville."

"That's so generous, Quil. Danny will say it's too much."

"For a change, I am calling the shots." I smiled. "And this is for them when they get back. Promise you won't give it to them before," I said, handing him another fat envelope.

"Promise."

Libby arrived in her parents' car, and I hurried up the back stairs of the church and stepped into the sanctuary. Libby was standing at the far end near the door, silhouetted in the filtered light of stained glass and sunshine. She looked unbelievably beautiful in her mother's dress and her grandmother's veil, her blonde curls loose around her shoulders.

I came toward her, and her eyes welled.

"Don't you dare, Sparks! Pull it together, or I *will* give you something to cry about." My voice was stern.

"Okay," she breathed.

We stood inside the church while the last of the guests arrived and the mothers were seated. Warren was best man, and of course Libby's dad would be walking her down the aisle.

"You look pretty," she said to me.

"Oh, thank you, almost-Mrs.-Owens." I curtsied. "Libby, in case I don't get a chance to say it later, I want you to know that I love you and want nothing more than your happiness," I said, handing her a bouquet of pink baby roses from Betty's garden.

"Wow, that sounds like a goodbye. I'm only going to be gone for two days. We're going to Nashville."

Her dad came in. "Ready, ladies?"

"Ready," we said.

"See you down there." I lowered her veil and walked into the garden ahead of Libby.

I watched Danny's face and knew without looking back when he saw her.

The strains of Wagner's famous "Bridal Chorus" wafted into the garden from the piano through the sanctuary's open windows. Guests who were sitting stood, and everyone turned to look at Libby.

She moved slowly down the bricked path on her father's arm looking radiant, smiling at her groom.

Danny touched an eye with a knuckle. Fearing if he shed a tear Libby would dissolve, I hissed, "Buck up, Owens!"

My two darling friends recited their vows in such a loving way I was unexpectedly moved. Now it was my turn to well up. A single tear fell onto my ugly satin dress before I choked the rest back.

Danny and Libby would have the life I had denied myself. They would live a peaceful, average life. They would be happy and safe together.

Late that night, after the reception and the newly wed Owens had left for Nashville, I put on my running shoes and jogged down Deer Spring Road. I stood on the covered footbridge and said goodbye to my ghosts, my childhood, and my history.

I cried a little and paced a lot. Mama and Daddy seemed to be there with me, or at least I imagined they were. I thanked them for saving me from a childhood raised by monsters and forgave them for keeping secrets. I told Paddy I was sorry for not protecting him and my grandparents for not becoming the woman they had hoped for. I asked them all to forgive me for not being a Christian, loving God, and trusting him blindly.

Strangely, for the first time, there was the absolute knowledge that they, my entire family, were together—wherever they were. Together, I knew, beyond a shadow of a doubt, I knew it. What did this mean? *Did* I believe there was a heaven?

The sun was rising, glowing pink and purple over the river, as I started back to town. I didn't look back. I just ran.

It was three o'clock that afternoon before I woke, groggy and unbelievably hungry. Sunday afternoon in Hackberry was not a good time to find a meal. I knew nothing was open, so I wandered downstairs to beg dinner from Lorraine, who was happy to invite me into the family quarters. As she opened a can of tomato soup and sliced bread for grilled cheese sandwiches, we talked about the wedding and how happy Danny and Libby had seemed.

"How are you, really?" Lorraine asked, dishing soup into a deep bowl. "Do you want chips? Pickles?" she interrupted my answer.

"Good, and yes," I said. "I am truly happy for them. They are perfect for each other. Libby knows how to manage him, and Danny will cherish her."

I bit into the thick, crusty bread filled with gooey cheese and groaned. "Yum, thank you so much, Lorraine."

"Tea? A brownie?"

"Yes and yes," I said with my mouth full.

Lorraine busied herself with the kettle. "Do you want to know a secret?" She turned toward me. "You know that Libby and I are cousins and we are very close?"

"I do."

"I want you to know that Libby was not the flirt she wanted everyone to think she was. It was mostly an act."

"Why?" I asked, drinking the last of my soup.

"I think she felt isolated and left out here in Hackberry and just wanted attention. You were off to college, and Danny was in Korea. She was young and foolish and made mistakes, but I don't think she actually was 'loose.' If you ask me, I think she was waiting for you and Danny to make up your minds."

I was shocked. "What about that creep, Ted?"

"I think he tried to have her, but according to Libby, it never went any further than making out."

"But why would she want everyone to think she was—you know?"

"It was all a ruse, as though she wanted everyone to think she was worldly, *and* it sure kept the locals from chasing her."

"What about Fletcher? That sure seemed like more than flirting." I took a giant bite of rich, warm brownie.

"Now, Fletcher was a true attraction. She fell hard for him, and given enough time, he might have seduced her. He was handsome and sophisticated, and I think Libby thought he might offer a way out of Tennessee."

"But he raped her in the attack, right?" I stirred milk into my tea.

"I thought he had, but she said he wasn't interested in sex, just violence."

"If this is true, Libby is lucky to be alive. All those men she pretended to be involved with were all dangerous, very dangerous. Fletcher really did mean to kill her."

"I know."

"Why are you telling me all this, Lorraine?"

"Because you didn't really know her, and I want you to."

Even after sleeping all day, I was tired and slept through the night. When I awoke, it was July 2—time to go.

Bidwell's envelope had contained a bus ticket in the name of Deborah Thomas on the night bus from Nashville to Atlanta. Instructions were as followed:

> *Drive to Nashville airport; park in long term. Abandon it.*
> *Change clothing and appearance in ladies' room at airport.*
> *Take a taxi to bus station and board #2391 to Atlanta at 10:31 p.m.*
> *Allow enough but not too much time for all of the above. Neither rush nor loiter. Be inconspicuous.*
> *In Atlanta:*
> *Take a taxi from bus station to the Sinclair Hotel and pick up a package there. Do not leave the hotel for any reason until one hour before flight time on the fourth.*
> *Take a taxi to the Atlanta airport. Change appearance in ladies' room.*
> *Board Eastern Airlines Flight #3180 to Halifax.*

Mr. Canfield was right. It felt exactly like jumping off a cliff.

CHAPTER 48

ESCAPING

Atlanta, Georgia
July 2, 1962

I looked back at the room—the bridesmaid dress and shoes, along with a note to Lorraine to pass these to Libby, were the only things left of me.

I had breakfast and paid the bill.

"Where to now, Quil?" Lorraine asked.

"I think I'm going to spend the rest of the summer traveling and then who knows."

I followed Bidwell's directions exactly, arriving at the bus station in Nashville at 10:15 p.m.

July 3, 1962

In Atlanta, I checked into the Sinclair Hotel at around two p.m. as Lorraine Fisher and picked up the package waiting for me.

In my room, I systematically cut all that remained of my old life into tiny bits and flushed them down the toilet, but buried in the lining of my suitcase were the photos I kept. I knew it was a risk, but in the end, they were the things I could not leave behind.

I ordered a filet mignon with all the trimmings, apple pie, and a glass of red wine from room service, then headed for the shower.

I scrubbed the makeup from my face and washed my hair. I had worn the red wig all night on the bus from Nashville, and it felt wonderful to be free of it.

I pressed my hands against the tile and let the water stream over me like a comforting caress. I had lost everything and knew nothing would ever be the same. I was giving it all up: my history, my identity, even my citizenship would all be gone because of greed and deceit.

"Don't feel sorry for yourself, Quil," I told myself. "Get tough and stay alive."

Inside me, emotional brittleness was turning hard as stone.

Room service brought my dinner, and I devoured it. I hadn't had a substantial meal since I left Kimble's the day before, and with my appetite, that was too long.

Hair still wrapped in a towel, body wrapped in a bathrobe, I curled up on the bed and lifted the manila envelope from my bag. I ran a finger along the seal, then pressed it to my chest as though it were something precious—as if holding it close would protect me. Slowly emptying the contents onto the bed, I found an airline ticket to Halifax; a Canadian passport and driver's license; an American Express card; a Maritime Bank checkbook; fourteen thousand dollars in Canadian currency, all in large bills; and finally a Halifax phone number with the name *Candice* scribbled next to it, and below a three-word message: *Will meet you.*

Independence Day 1962

At the airport the next day, as instructed, I changed clothes and put on the blond wig in the ladies' room. I was relieved it was empty. I got in line for my flight at the Eastern Airlines counter.

As I waited, a thin rivulet of perspiration tiptoed down my spine and pooled momentarily at the small of my back. It was hot in the terminal, which added to my discomfort, and I picked at my white cotton shirt in an attempt to manufacture a breeze. My mouth felt dry, and my hand trembled slightly as I smoothed the airline ticket I had unconsciously clenched into a crumpled twist. *Don't look around. Stay calm. Don't be obvious.*

The line crept forward, people shuffling luggage along with their feet, preoccupied, reading a book or staring, bored and vacant.

"ID, please." The ticket agent smiled.

"Yes, of course," I said, forcing a grin, handing over my passport and ticket.

"Traveling alone this evening, Miss d'Moss?"

The agent looked down, busy with luggage tags and boarding passes. I hesitated. *D'Moss, yes, d'Moss, that's me.*

"Miss d'Moss?"

"Yes…no…sorry, I was distracted. What did you say?"

The harried agent made eye contact with me, and I wondered if he sensed my nervousness. He opened my passport, looked at the picture again, the name, signature, and resident address. "Afraid of flying, Miss d'Moss?"

"No…heights…I'm afraid of heights." I smiled. *What a ridiculous thing to say. Don't draw attention to yourself. Stay calm. You're almost there.*

"I asked you if you were traveling alone."

"No. Nobody with me." *That's right, nobody. I am nobody. There is nobody.*

I watched him glance over my shoulder at the long line of ticket holders behind me. "Enjoy your flight to Halifax." The agent handed back my ticket and passport. "Gate 23-C."

I boarded the plane and found my seat two rows behind the wing. No one seated next to me, and I was grateful. I had never been on an airplane before, clenching and unclenching my fists as the plane rumbled down the runway and lifted effortlessly into the air.

Moonlight inched along the wing like a slow, shallow tide as the jet banked left, climbing in a gentle turn to the northeast. The night was clear and cool in a hundred shades of blue, leaving behind the summer heat of Atlanta.

I took another long look—a last look—at the quickly disappearing lights of the city and took my passport out of my bag. The face inside the passport was mine but the name Desiree Renée d'Moss was not. I whispered the name over and over, trying to own it. I had to become this person—my life might depend on it.

With a ragged sigh, I melted into the seat, my gaze focusing now upon the iridescent trail exhaust. Then I closed my eyes and tried to remember the last time I felt safe.

PART FIVE

Let a joy keep you. Reach out your hands and take it when it runs by.
—Carl Sandburg

CHAPTER 49

HALIFAX

Halifax, Nova Scotia
July 4, 1962

The luggage carousel growled as passengers stood shoulder to shoulder, expectantly waiting for bags. Tired and hungry, I wondered what the next move would be. My wig itched, and I was feeling a little irritable. The instructions said, "Candice will meet you." There was a lot of noise: people talking and the sounds of doors opening and cars running outside.

"Desiree." The voice sounded even as if the person might be speaking to someone she knew.

I heard this near me but was so distracted I neither recognized my new name nor reacted.

"Desiree."

The voice seemed closer as I was reaching for my bag.

"Desiree."

I had picked up my bag and turned to move away from the carousel. There was a blonde woman standing right behind me.

"Desiree," she said, smiling. "Calmly follow me, please."

I hoped she was Candice. We walked out of the terminal and into the parking garage. She stopped at a dark green Volvo, opened the trunk, and put my luggage inside.

"Get in the car, please."

I did this. When she got behind the wheel and before she turned the key in the ignition, she said, "I'm Candice."

"I'm so relieved."

She smiled. I smiled. We drove into Halifax without saying much, then north onto Highway Two toward Bedford and the harbor area. Candice looked in the rearview mirror often, though discreetly.

"Welcome to Nova Scotia," she finally said. *"Bienvenue à la Nouvelle-Écosse"*

"Merci. Il est merveilleux de se sentir en sécurité. So good to feel safe. "

"Well, we are definitely going to have to work on your French." She gave my arm a pat.

It was late for a small town, and we saw no car lights behind us as we turned off Highway Two and onto a side street along Bedford Harbor, finally turning into the driveway of a modest brick home and into the garage: number 21 Wyatt Road.

"Hungry?" Candice asked, putting the car in park and turning off the ignition.

"Starving," I said, pulling off my wig and setting my dark hair free.

It was ten o'clock Atlantic time. I was exhausted but wired.

"Let's start with a pot of tea and some shortbread, shall we?"

"Wonderful." I sighed.

"Dessert first, eh?"

"Yum."

Over tea and warm shortbread, we talked; she knew everything about me, and I knew nothing about her. This should have made me feel uncomfortable, but Candice was so warm and confident that I quickly relaxed.

Homemade chicken vegetable soup with oatcakes followed. We talked about my future in general terms.

"Tomorrow we will get down to business and start sorting things out." Candice patted my hand. "But for now, I imagine bath and bed sound best. Yes?"

"Yes. Nothing would be better."

Candice ushered me into a kind of private area in the back of the house: a bathroom, sitting room, and bedroom.

She showed me where to find towels and toiletries.

"Welcome to Nova Scotia, my dear." She hugged me tenderly and said good night.

The sitting room had a comfortable chair and desk, the bathroom a deep tub, and the bedroom a luxurious double bed with a feather tick mattress and down duvet. All three rooms were tastefully decorated in shades of sunny yellow and cool blue.

I set my one small suitcase on the chair with my few photos tucked inside and took out my journal. Unpacking took only minutes; clothes were folded and put in drawers. I took my pajamas, toothbrush, and hairbrush into the bathroom and ran a bath, noticing that Candice had thought to place a bottle of lavender-scented bubble bath near the tub.

Sinking into the steaming tub with a groan, I slid beneath the water, letting my hair soak away the feeling of wigs and my skin the feeling of stress.

My hair wrapped in a towel and my body clad in clean flannel pajamas, I flopped onto the bed. Though it was July, the weather was much cooler here in Nova Scotia. Nevertheless, I opened the bedroom window and let the smell of the Atlantic waft in, heavy with the familiar scent of salt. It smelled, of course, completely different from Key West. This salty air was not laced with the sweet fragrance of tropical flowers but with the hint of pine trees, cool and crisp on the breeze.

Feeling safe but tired, I pulled the down duvet over me and slept long and hard.

It was nearly noon by the time I woke, opening my eyes to an enormous fuzzy cat staring at me from the top shelf of the bookcase. He meowed loudly and leapt heavily onto the bed, strolled casually up my body, and flopped down on my chest. He had a purr that seemed as loud and throaty as a muffled lawn mower. His big gold eyes fixed on mine. His gray tabby back, white face, and belly were soft as cashmere. His gray and black tabby mustache looked as if he had dipped his muzzle in color. His face only inches from mine, he closed his eyes and stretched out, a soft and friendly paw on my cheek.

"Listen, big boy, you might be ready for a nap, but I am ready to get up." I rolled onto my side, and, unfazed, he slid off my belly and flopped onto his back. I got up. He stayed flat on his back with all four white paws bent at the wrists, gold eyes watching me.

There was a quiet knock on the door.

"Come in," I called.

"I see you have met Big Beef."

"He's a bed hog. So huge. What is he anyway?"

"Maine Coon. They are very common here. I'll fill you in on their history sometime. Breakfast or lunch? What are you hungry for?"

"Pancakes and eggs. I can cook," I offered.

"Now there's a deal."

I dressed in jeans and a long-sleeved shirt, rolled at the cuffs, and followed her into the kitchen, where I homed in on the coffee pot. Candice handed me a mug.

"Cream? Sugar?"

"Cream, please."

While I drank my coffee, Candice gave me a tour of the kitchen and pantry, and we began pulling breakfast ingredients as we went.

"There is a cast-iron griddle in the drawer under the stove. Perfect for pancakes."

We ate buttermilk pancakes smothered with butter and real Canadian maple syrup over easy eggs and ice-cold orange juice. After the dishes were done, we took another cup of coffee out into the sunroom, which faced the water.

Candice handed me a notebook and a pen. She had the same.

"All right, Desiree, let's get to work. First let me tell you who *I* am and what I have been asked to accomplish. My name is not Candice, but you will know me as this to keep us both safe. This house is rented, and when you and I have completed our goals, we will not see each other again. The only thing real is Big Beef, and he goes where I go. Questions?"

"Yes. Do you do this for a living? When you are through with me, will you move on to someone else?"

"Yes, on all counts, but you shouldn't think of all this in a callous way. I do this for a reason, and I am doing this for *you* because you matter. Do not think that I will abandon you. Look at it this way: if I were teaching you to swim, you would not need me when you could swim on your own. Understand?"

"Yes." I took a sip of coffee. "Do you know people I know?"

"If I do, you will never know it, and please don't ask. Understood?"

I nodded.

"Second, know your name. Over the next month, I will speak to you using the name of Desiree in various situations from a variety of distances and will expect you to react as if this has always been your name. Also, know your full name: Desiree Renée d'Moss. Say it over and over again until it rolls off your tongue in such a natural way no one will suspect you have ever been anyone else."

I nodded.

"Third, when we are here at home, we will speak only in Acadian French until both the accent and the vernacular become natural. In addition, you should decide what kind of English you will choose to embrace: Canadian or British. Losing your Tennessee accent will be the hardest part of all this, but you must do it. That accent will be a dead giveaway and will draw unwanted attention. Canada, like England, has a dozen regional dialects. When we choose your 'history,' your dialect will have to match."

"My history?"

"You and I will build a bulletproof past. Nothing tricky, just hard facts that you will know forward and backward without missing a beat."

I wrote a list as she spoke to mentally reinforce her words.

"Fourth, though you do not need income, you will need to have a visible means of support."

"Like?"

"Well, like working at a library or owning a little business. Think about it. When you decide where you will actually settle, your means of support will become self-evident. Tomorrow we will begin a series of day trips to look at areas the right size for beginning a new life."

"The right size?"

"Not so big you get swallowed or become discouraged and homesick. Not too small where you will stick out like a sore thumb."

"I feel overloaded," I said.

"Understandable, but our conversation today is only an overview. It will all fall into place as we go along. You'll see."

"Running?"

"You may run only at dawn or dusk, and only along a specified route, and only monitored."

"What do you mean monitored?"

"Meaning, while you are running, I will be in the car watching from a distance. I will be discreet. Questions?"

"Not for now."

"All right, from this moment forward, only French. You will listen to me and my accent and try to mimic me. This will happen naturally, and I will not correct you unless something is obviously incorrect. *Oui?*"

"Oui." I smiled at her. Her matter-of-fact manner was not off putting but rather reassuring. She knew what she was doing, and all I had to do was follow her lead.

CHAPTER 50
FINDING MY WAY

Halifax, Nova Scotia
July 1962

The next morning I went for a run at the first signs of gray light and was back inside by the time the sun was rising pink over the harbor. Candice followed me by car at a discreet distance along a route we had predetermined the afternoon before.

Over the next few days, we established a pattern: run, eat, explore, and sleep. We moved at an incredible pace. Our day trips from Bedford included Lunenburg, Truro, Antigonish, and Yarmouth, each with attractive aspects for relocation, but none seemed a good fit for me.

We also drove to Maitland and to the Shubenacadie River, where the tidal bore of the Bay of Fundy was most visible. Standing on the bridge at the moment the tide changed was shocking as the sea over ran the river at incredible speed, rushing in with a twelve-foot wall of water. Candice explained that this happened every twelve hours. It was an unbelievable experience.

At the end of the first week, Candice decided, "I think we should take a break from exploration and concentrate on history and occupation.

Don't forget, my knowing where you choose to live is not a good thing. When you decide, you must keep it to yourself. My job is to *prepare* you, not *land* you."

"I understand."

It was Friday afternoon. Candice asked me to cook something I had learned from my Acadian grand-mère. I chose chicken and pork pot pie with baked beans.

Candice watched me cook: making the pie filling of cooked, chopped pork and chicken, diced onions, and carrots in a thick cream sauce, then rolling out the dough and filling the pie. The beans had been cooking in the oven for two hours when the pie joined them for baking. Brown sugar and molasses would be added to the beans at the table.

We sat down to dine by seven o'clock, and I watched Candice take her first bites of pot pie. She seemed to savor each bite.

"This is delicious and completely typical of Acadian cooking. You could serve this to any Nova Scotian, and it would be deemed authentic. I'm impressed!"

"I think food and making it have always been a big part of my life. I love it—instantly gratifying." I took a bite of pie and a second helping of beans sprinkled with brown sugar and a drizzle of molasses. "Candice, I wonder if opening a small café or bakery would be an occupation I could embrace. Definitely something small and not too flashy."

"Well, if this meal is typical of your abilities, I think you are on the right track. Have you thought this through? Should we work toward this end?"

"Yes. When I think of everything I would most love to do, cooking would be it. Of course, my real love is marine science, but I know that would be too transparent."

"It would."

"So then, yes, I'm sure."

"Good, Desiree, good. That's a big step."

We did the dishes and made a pot of tea. Big Beef joined us on the sofa. He snuggled in and began to purr, once again flat on his back, fluffy tail wagging slowly. He reminded me of Mick Jaguar when he did this, and my mind floated off to Key West and my friends. I remembered floating naked in the sea. I remembered the photos and the danger and why I was here in Halifax. I looked up and realized Candice was studying me.

"*Où avez-vous été, Desiree?*"

"I was remembering."

"Let it go. For your sake, you must. Concentrate on new memories."

"All right! All right! I hear you," I snapped.

A long, pregnant silence followed. Candice did not react, and I felt incredibly foolish.

"I am so sorry. Really. You didn't deserve that."

"I was wondering when that would happen. It's good to see the back-bone I've been looking for. Good job. Let's make a new history, shall we?"

Through the course of the evening, Candice and I approved and rejected a plethora of details that would eventually form my history, finally deciding I would be from Alberta, all my family dead in a fire, grandparents from Halifax, and I came here to start over. Details close enough to the truth to avoid a slipup. We worked on my French and English, the latter now becoming Midwestern rather than Southern.

As we wandered off to bed, Candice said, "Let's go shopping for a vehicle for you tomorrow."

I wrote in my journal into the wee hours. Writing the new details of my life, recording my progress and setbacks, my thankfulness for Candice and her expertise, her patience. I flipped back to the beginning of the journal and tore out all the pages before my escape and committed once and for all to a new life.

The next day Candice and I shopped for a car but ended up with a four-wheel drive truck. My dark blue 1958 Chevy Fleetside rode like a bulldozer—a truck ready for the legendary maritime winters.

That night after a sumptuous lobster feast, we settled in with our usual pot of tea.

"Why do you do this?" I asked.

Candice hesitated, and I wondered if she was weighing the facts.

"I had a daughter once," she began. "She married a terrible man, ran off with him, and for a year, I didn't know where she was. Then one day she showed up at the door, bruised and broken. Of course, we did all the right things: filed for divorce, got a restraining order, et cetera. He found her. I tried to hide her by sending her to my sister in Cleveland, but he found her there too. He was drunk and pushed past my sister. He had a baseball bat. He beat my daughter to death right there in my sister's house."

Her voice was weak then. It was the first sign of weakness I had seen in the month we had been together. I leaned forward and touched her arm.

"This is why I do this. I couldn't do anything to save my daughter, but I *will* be able to save others. You have been one of many."

"Have been? That sounds like goodbye." I laughed anxiously.

"It is, Desiree. Tomorrow we will tie together the loose ends and part on Monday."

"But I'm not ready!"

"You're ready. As ready as you will ever be. Find a place, and start a life. Use that backbone of yours and be resourceful. I am certain that within a month you will have found your new home and begun to settle in. After all, it was never optional, was it?"

"No, I'm *not* ready. You can't just *leave* me like this!"

"You're ready." She was firm.

"I'm going for a run."

"I think that is a good idea."

I stomped out of the room and returned in running clothes and shoes. I slammed the kitchen door as I left and ran down the street along the familiar route. I was running hard in the darkness, the occasional streetlamp my only light.

At the far end of the regular route, I turned left instead of right. Then right and left and straight and left again. It wasn't long before I was lost in the darkness. I turned around and started back, but I couldn't remember how I had gotten here. I had a moment of panic. *Get a grip, Quil...Desiree. Think it through.* I looked down the road toward a streetlight and ran toward it. I had been here. Right or left? I was sweating, and my throat was dry. I looked up at the street sign. It was not one I recognized, but I turned right and ran to the next street and then the next.

It was late. The moon had traveled as far as I had. Finally, a street inter-sected with Highway Two, and I knew where I was. Three streets to the right was Wyatt Road. I was exhausted by the time I reached the house. The kitchen light was on, the rest of the house dark. It was 2:30 a.m. By the time I had bathed and snacked, it was almost dawn. I fell into bed and threw the covers over my head.

I slept until noon. My body ached from overexertion, and I felt com-pletely dehydrated. After two huge glasses of water, I wandered into the kitchen for coffee and breakfast. Candice had left a note on the counter.

It read: *Desiree, I'm out running errands and will be back around 3:00. I'm bringing dinner. Candice*

It was Sunday, and Candice had said Monday was departure day. After breakfast, with Big Beef helping, I packed. I now had three suit-cases. Shopping with Candice had produced a down jacket, anorak coat, warm waterproof boots, gloves and scarves, three sweaters, two pairs of warm pants, a bathrobe and fuzzy slippers, and two more sets of paja-mas, along with several sets of necessaries like underwear and socks. In addition, I bought an extra pair of shoes for running, sweatpants, and a hooded sweatshirt. I opened all three suitcases on the bed. Big Beef lay in each of them, making sure I was taking an adequate amount of cat hair with me. I finished packing both of the large cases and set them by the door. Big Beef crawled into the last case, stretched, and fell asleep. I was inspired and lay down for a nap as well.

The next thing I knew Candice gently shook me.

"Dinner is ready. Want a glass of wine? Oh, and don't think you are packing my cat. He stays with *me*."

"That's pretty narrow minded." I stretched and followed her into the kitchen, where the aroma of garlic and onions greeted me. "Yum. What *is* that?"

"Roast beef, mashed potatoes with gravy, corn on the cob, steamed broccoli, and apple pie."

"When did you have time to make all this?"

"I didn't. Charmaine's on Front Street did."

"I'm starving. Can we eat now?"

"Fine for me."

She was hungry too. We piled our plates with food and ate, making satisfied groaning noises. No talking, just eating.

Candice poured a glass of red wine for each of us and lifted her glass. "Here's to a new life."

"New life," I repeated.

We sat back in our chairs and drank our wine, our bellies full.

I said, "Are you really going to throw me to the wolves tomorrow?"

"Yes, but I'm completely confident you will do fine. You look like a fierce wolf killer to me. Come on. Let's clear the table. I have some things to show you."

Candice spread a large map of Nova Scotia on the dining room table and walked me through it carefully, pointing to all the places we had been and the ones left to explore. "You might have a look at Cape Breton—Sydney has some attractive aspects—or go west along the Bay of Fundy toward Annapolis Royal."

She handed me a Nova Scotian driver's license, proof of auto insurance on my new truck, and an Albertan birth certificate. She gave me some books on Canadian and Nova Scotian history, recent maritime laws, a copy of Longfellow's *Evangeline,* and a list of hotels along the main routes of Nova Scotia.

We folded the map and packed the books in a box. I put the driver's license in my wallet, the insurance documents and birth certificate in my suitcase.

"Ready for pie?"

"I'm always ready for pie. I'll put on the kettle."

As usual, we ended the evening on the sofa, the cat between us.

We worked on language accents, and Candice gave me a complex personal history quiz.

"Here is some additional information. If you do indeed open an eatery, you will need a local attorney to help you with licenses, et cetera. You will need an attorney to represent you if you should decide to buy a house or a building. Real estate laws can be very tricky. Also, be sure to hire an accountant to guide you through the maze of Canadian tax structures."

"I don't mind telling you. I'm a bit scared."

"Good. Being scared keeps you on your toes. Just think before you speak or act, and you will be fine."

"Promise?"

"Promise."

After a long bath, I spread the map out on the bed and studied it in earnest, deciding to drive up to the northern coast in the morning.

I took the copy of *Evangeline* to bed and fell asleep reading.

CHAPTER 51

GRAND-PRÉ

Grand-Pré, Nova Scotia
Monday, July 30, 1962

On Monday morning, Candice and I each loaded our belongings into our vehicles. I said goodbye to Big Beef and hugged Candice.

"There aren't words to thank you," I whispered.

"My thanks come in knowing you will survive and thrive," she whispered back.

We drove away in different directions. I headed north on Highway 101. I was truly on my own now.

At Avonport, I impulsively left Highway 101, turned toward Grand-Pré on Highway 1, and checked into Durand Acadie Inn. I booked a week's stay.

Marie Durand checked me in. "*Bienvenue.* Shall we speak in English or French?"

"Either is fine. *Soit est très bien.*"

"Your French is very Acadian. *Très bien.* Where are you from?"

"Alberta, but my Grand-père and Grand-mère were Nova Scotian."

Marie turned the ledger my way and said, "Your name, *s'il vous plaît.*"

I had a moment of panic. It was the first time I had been asked to actually sign my name. I printed Desiree d'Moss, then signed, surprised by what I saw. My new name written on the page looked back at me like a stranger.

"D'Moss. *Nom intéressant.* What is the origin?"

Here was a detail I had not planned for. I heard Candice say, "Use your wits."

"The rumor is there was a Spanish or Portuguese sailor in the wood-pile. Or maybe Cajun. My father's side. Generations back."

"So you are Acadian for generations. You are aware of the Acadian Expulsion?"

"Not really."

"Grand-Pré was the origin of this. There is information at the Acadian Heritage Center." She smiled, warm and friendly. "Here is your key. Breakfast is served at eight-thirty and supper at seven. Do you have food preferences?"

"No, I will eat anything that doesn't eat me first. *Imported quoi.*"

At this, Marie laughed hard. *"Vous avez une bonne humeur."*

The room she assigned me had wide windows that overlooked a meadow of wildflowers with large mounds of dirt at the distant edges.

I put on shorts and a white men's undershirt I had started to use for running. I laced up my sneakers and went out to explore Grand-Pré. The day was warm, about seventy degrees Fahrenheit—twenty-one Celsius. I reminded myself to think in Celsius and metric. The sea breeze was behind me, and I felt as light as air. I ran toward the long mounds of dirt and as I got closer realized they were some sort of dyke structures. Were these built to hold the water in or out? Tomorrow might be a good day to do some research on the area.

I wrote in my journal that night:

> *I miss the security Candice provided, the little house on the bay in Bedford, and Big Beef. My tether has been cut, and I am drifting like a balloon in the breeze. I know I have to be brave and smart, and I will be, but right now, this minute, I feel nervous and afraid. I'm living a lie, one that is also my truth. Black is white and white is black…I need a nice even gray to cloak me, smooth and invisible like a still and cloudy day.*

Grand-Pré is quaint and filled with Acadian history, and I can't wait to dig deeper. Marie Durand is charming and kind. I may have met my first friend. Why she feels like hope is beyond me.

After a breakfast of perfectly poached eggs, oatcakes, steamed apples, and rich coffee, I was off to the Acadian Heritage Center to learn about three hundred years of Acadian culture.

"How far is it?" I asked Marie.

"*Pas trop loin.* Two or three kilometers. No problem for walking."

"*Merci*, Marie. What's for dinner?"

"Seafood chowder, yeast rolls, steamed greens, and egg custard with fruit compote."

"Sounds fabulous! I will be home early! *Je serai à la maison tôt!*"

Marie smiled and said, "You may join me for tea at four thirty if you are back early."

"It's a date."

"You Albertans have the funniest sayings. *Dictons impair.*"

At the heritage center, I looked through the displays and read about the Acadian Expulsion of thousands of Acadian French settlers who had farmed this area for generations. Then, from 1755 to 1764, Acadians were captured and deported by the English without regard to family structure: men sent to one destination and women and children sent to another. Their villages were burned and belongings destroyed. Hundreds were sent to France, a country they had never seen, and the rest were dumped along the coasts of New England and the Carolinas. Many ended up in Louisiana near current-day New Orleans. Hundreds died from exposure and starvation.

I was taken aback at the realization that my father's family were ancestors of these deported Acadians-turned-Cajun, hearing for the first time the similarity in names.

I wondered how my Acadian grandparents' ancestors had faired. My great-grandmother's surname, now mine, d'Moss, was a mystery. I searched the Acadian records for the name but did not find it. The name was not Acadian, yet she was a part of the Acadian community.

After a walk through the historic Catholic church and a leisurely stroll through the gardens on the site of the old Acadie village, I lay down in the grass near a pond in the shade of a giant oak, the grasses fragrant and the flowers sweet. Bees buzzed in the oak. I lay there a long time, relaxing. It was all good.

Around four o'clock, I arrived back at the inn, washed and changed, and found Marie alone in the dining room with a pot of tea and a plate of warm oatcakes. I joined her.

A sip of black tea with milk and a bite of oatcake. "Marie, I love these," I said, holding up a cake. "You have to teach me how to make them."

"So very easy, a staple of Acadian life. My great-great-grandmother made these over an open flame when they first returned to Acadie."

"Tell me about the dykes." I pointed out toward the meadow.

"Acadians built them by hand, *imaginez l'effort.* They used nutrient-rich seawater to fertilize the soil they farmed, letting water in and blocking it out as was needed. Rainwater nurtured the crops, but it was the seawater that fed them."

"Amazing."

We drank our tea in silence for a few minutes.

"My young guest, why are you here? All alone and sadness all around you?"

I tried not to act shocked. *Use your wits.*

"I lost my entire family in a fire, and I couldn't stay in Alberta. It hurt too much. I am actually wanting to relocate, and I am looking for a place."

"*Mon cher,* I am so sorry." Marie's voice was soft and sympathetic.

"Life goes on whether we like it or not. I'm ready to start over."

"What is it you are wanting to do?" she asked.

"Actually, I thought I might buy a house and open a café or bakery somewhere."

Marie studied my face, and I could see the wheels turning in her head.

"What are you thinking?" I asked.

"Thinking?"

"I can see it all over your face."

"My sister Leoni lives in Annapolis Royal. She has a handicapped child, and her husband has died in a fishing accident. She has a house on St. Charles across from Fort Anne she would like to sell, must sell."

"What would she do if she sold?" I was concerned for this stranger, though I wasn't sure why.

"We have a big family, and she would have to move in with one of us."

"So she would lose all independence—*autonomie*."

"Yes, but she would be cradled by her family."

"So you are telling me this because you think I might buy her house?"

"To be frank, yes."

"I would like to have a look." I smiled.

CHAPTER 52
FLETCHER/LILAJUNE

Nashville, Tennessee
Monday, July 30, 1962

Fletcher had been in the Tennessee State Psychiatric Hospital for three months, and though he was being given mood-controlling meds, most days he managed to avoid swallowing them. He saw a resident psychiatrist daily, Derek Mead, a young, sharp, not easily fooled doctor who was onto Fletcher in a flash. But, day by day, Fletcher found ways to manipulate his therapist, and he was gaining ground.

Dr. Mead spoke to him about LilaJune Walker's trial testimony and took it apart bit by bit to judge its validity. What did Fletcher remember? How did her testimony make him feel? He asked about Charles Pickford and Clarice Pickford. On most topics, Fletcher claimed to remember nothing, but Dr. Mead picked away at the scab that covered what he knew must be a deep, festering wound.

Fletcher admitted to his hatred where his father and stepmother were concerned, though never revealed details. His hatreds were his own, and no two-bit doctor was going to drag it into the light.

Every day he thought about Tranquil Tandy and what she had stolen from him. His loathing of her sustained him. It grew like mold on his spirit, fostered and nurtured. Lies about her became truths, and reality distorted. That he had brought all this trouble on himself was not anything he would willingly admit, not to anyone, even himself. In fact, with time, he deemed himself completely blameless. She had done this to him, and she would pay. He lay in bed most nights thinking of the things he would do to her when he found her. She would suffer long and painfully before she died.

His lawyer told him that the private investigator he had hired had lost track of Tranquil; she seemed to have evaporated into thin air.

"The last sighting was in Nashville on July 3," Fletcher's attorney had said.

"Well, find her!" Fletcher nipped sharply.

⥱╫╫⥲

On Monday, July 30, a visitor arrived at the hospital, and Fletcher was ushered into the visiting area. As far as the hospital staff knew, Fletcher was adequately medicated and therefore not dangerous.

He sat across the table from LilaJune Walker.

"How have you been, dear boy?"

"Don't call me that. Why are you here, anyway? It was *your* testimony that put me here."

"No. It was your behavior that put you here."

"What do you want? I don't even know you."

"You were an innocent child once. And I have come all this way to remind you of that."

Fletcher looked away.

"Your head is sick because of what Charles and Clarice did to you. You weren't born with this sickness. They made you," LilaJune said. "Please understand, I had no choice but to desert you. Will you forgive me?"

"Forgive you? You are nothing to me."

LilaJune waited for him to look at her again.

"You know, Fletcher, forgiveness comes from in here." She patted her heart. "When you forgive somebody, it heals this." She patted her heart again. "Sometimes forgiveness ain't about the person who hurt you as much as it is the hurt in *you*." She reached out to him, but he pulled away.

"You're the crazy person. Maybe they can give you a room here," he snarled.

"You can't push me away. Your father tried twenty-five years ago, and I had to leave then, but I never stopped praying for you, and now I'm here to stay."

"Praying. What a joke!" Fletcher jeered. "Praying to what?"

"God…Jesus."

"There is no God, you old fool." Fletcher stood.

"Please, let's you and me be friends. You need friends," LilaJune quietly pleaded. "I'm going to leave you this Bible. It's the one I gave you as a little boy. I took it with me when I left."

"That's the key word. You *left*."

Fletcher turned toward the door. Dr. Mead stood against the jamb, watching and listening.

"Get out of the way," Fletcher snapped.

"Careful, somebody might think you're not taking your medication." Dr. Mead's tone was even; he made eye contact with his patient and stepped aside to let Fletcher pass.

LilaJune looked after the blond boy, now man, she still loved.

"Hello," Dr. Mead said as he moved toward her. "My name is Dr. Derek Mead, and I treat Fletcher Pickford here at the hospital." He extended a hand, and LilaJune cautiously took it.

"My name is LilaJune Walker. I was his nanny once upon a time. Can you make sure Fletcher gets this?" She handed the Bible to Dr. Mead.

"It's a pleasure. Would you like some coffee? I just brewed a fresh pot in my office. It's just down the hall. I would really like to talk to you about Fletcher."

CHAPTER 53
ANNAPOLIS ROYAL

Annapolis Royal, Nova Scotia
August 1962

On Friday morning, I headed west on Route #1 toward Annapolis Royal. My appointment with Leoni wasn't until three o'clock, but I wanted to look at all the little places along the way. I had lunch in Bridgetown: the best grilled salmon I had ever tasted.

Arriving in Annapolis Royal at around one-thirty, I drove past Leoni's house and parked at the Fort Anne Historical Site. I sat in the grass on the mound at the top of the fort and looked over the house and property, which were located across the street. It was probably a quarter-acre lot, rectangular but narrow in the front and wide toward the back. There seemed to be a smaller building in the back. The house itself was charming, well cared for, and painted in bright colors: periwinkle blue, white, and deep violet. It had a wide front porch and paned windows with a small balcony on the second floor in the center, over the front door.

As I sat there, a car pulled up to the curb in front of the house. A dark-haired woman with a young child got out and walked through the low gate and into the house. There was something familiar about the little girl, but I couldn't put my finger on it. I looked at my watch; it was three o'clock, but I decided to wait a minute or two before approaching, giving them a moment to settle.

When I knocked on the front door, the little girl answered.

"Hi, my name is Margaux, but you can call me Maggie. What's your name? Mommy will be here. She said I should answer the door."

Maggie was about eight years old with lush strawberry-blonde curly hair and a face that was unmistakably Down's. I felt my breath suck in, and my eyes threatened to well up. I squatted to eye level, looked deeply into her sapphire blue eyes, and said, "You are the prettiest little girl I have ever seen."

"Hello, you must be Desiree. I'm Leoni. I see you have met my daughter." Her eyes searched my face for signs of intolerance. She found none because there was none. She gave me a relieved smile. "Please come in. My sister Marie says you are looking to relocate to this area."

"That's right. Your house is lovely."

"I will miss it."

The three of us walked through every room: a living room, dining room, and kitchen took up the first floor. Three bedrooms and a bath comprised the second. It was as well cared for inside as out.

"What is the building in the backyard?"

"Fifty years ago it was a small carriage house, but now it is only storage. It is in good condition structurally, I am told."

"May I look?"

"Of course."

"I can lead the way," Maggie chimed in, skipping out the kitchen door into the backyard.

The carriage house did indeed seem solid, and I loved the backyard. A big oak shaded the carriage house, but the rest of the yard had full sun. Flower beds trimmed the fence, and a vegetable garden flourished between the main house and the carriage house. It all felt warm and welcoming. I was sold.

"You will miss this place."

"That's true, but I'm sure my sister has told you I must sell."

"What are you asking?"

"I would like to get twenty-one thousand. There is a mortgage. The truth is, if I don't sell soon, the bank will take it, so I can take less if I have to."

"Tell you what. Let me sleep on it. We can talk again tomorrow. How would that be?"

"Fine, very fine."

"What time is good?"

"Maggie gets out of school at two thirty, and I can be home by three o'clock."

"Three o'clock it is. And, Leoni," I added, "I love this house."

I checked into a little inn on Chapel Street, found dinner nearby at a local eatery, and feasted on crab cakes, salad, and berry cobbler.

Back in my room I put pen to paper, scribbling ideas and crunching numbers. By midnight, I was satisfied and ready to make a decision.

I wrote in my journal:

> *Seeing Maggie today tore a fresh hole in my heart. All I could see on her face was Paddy. Turning them out of their home is not acceptable. I simply cannot do it.*

I slept until nearly ten o'clock, put on my running shoes, and ran to find breakfast along a three hundred-year-old waterfront. The harbor was empty of boats at this hour. I figured they were all out fishing on this gloriously calm and sunny morning.

I found a little café serving hotcakes with melted butter and pure maple syrup—Paddy's favorite. I ordered coffee, a big glass of milk, and a small orange juice.

People in the café, having long since had breakfast and were now on coffee breaks, looked at me curiously. Newcomers were noticed. I ate in silence, avoiding inquiring eyes aimed at me, though when I made eye contact, I smiled and nodded.

After breakfast, I drove across the bridge and turned left toward Port Royal and another Acadian village long since destroyed by the English. The history of this small place was rich with intrigue and deception yet filled with the closeness of family and cultures. Acadians and Huguenots,

French, English, New Englanders, and Mi'kmaq Indians all took a part in shaping its history and boundaries. Fort Anne was a prime example of the political tug-of-war: first Scottish, then French, and finally the English, who expelled all who would not bow to the king's dominance.

═╬ ╬═

Promptly at three o'clock, I pulled up in front of Leoni's house and was greeted by a smiling Maggie, who threw her arms around me, then took my hand and led me inside.

"Tea?" Leoni asked.

"Love some."

"Milk?"

"Please."

"Maggie, would you please go play in your room for a little while. Be a good girl." Leoni smiled at her daughter. "You can take a cookie with you and offer some to our guest."

Maggie made a great show of serving cookies to us at the kitchen table, then took a cookie to her room.

"She is an adorable child. How old is she?"

"Maggie will be nine on March 4."

"What a coincidence. That is my birthday as well."

"You seem drawn to her. Why is that? Most people are repulsed by her abnormality."

"I had a brother with Down's. He died of pneumonia last year."

"I'm so very sorry for your loss."

We drank our tea and ate cookies.

"These are delicious. What do you call them?"

"They are cardamom and cinnamon sugar cookies. A local favorite."

After a second cup of tea, Leoni asked, "Well, Desiree, what do you think?"

I hesitated, gathering my thoughts.

"I think that I can in no way turn you and your daughter out of your house."

"Then it is no." Leoni looked crestfallen.

"Leoni, I definitely want to buy your house, but I have an idea that might be good for the three of us."

"What?" She looked confused.

I pulled a notebook from my purse and showed her my scribbling.

"Would you be amenable to working out a business deal? I will pay you your asking price of twenty-one thousand and let you live here as well. Here are my thoughts: you and Maggie can keep the upstairs, maybe use one of the bedrooms as a sitting room. We could renovate the downstairs to make a bakery a *patisserie, oui*. There doesn't seem to be one in town. Right?"

"That's true."

"We can make a commercial kitchen by combining the current kitchen and dining room. The living area could become a place for customers to eat pastries and drink tea and coffee by the fireplace. We would have to add a small bathroom on this floor, of course."

I could see the wheels turning as all this began to sink in.

"This is a blur. But where would *you* live?"

"I would renovate the carriage house. I don't need much room, and I'd be quite happy out there. In addition, I could hire you to help in the bakery. We could work it together. A bakery means early start hours, but we could close by two thirty in time for you to pick up Maggie."

"My head is spinning," Leoni said. "Are you an angel? Did God send you?"

"Hardly."

"Well, you should know that Maggie and I have been praying for a miracle, and I think you are our miracle."

I pressed on. "We will need a good contractor to do the renovations quickly before winter."

"I have a brother who needs work, and he is very good."

"All right. Do we have a deal, Leoni?"

"We do indeed."

We shook hands and hugged. This was a bold move. I had just made a business deal with a woman I hardly knew, yet it *was* the right move. I knew it.

What followed was a flurry of legal documents for the purchase of the house, licenses for the bakery, and contracts to protect Maggie and Leoni should I die, and me should they.

Uncle Gus, as Maggie called him, arrived with three brothers, who flew into action like a swarm of ants.

Leoni and Maggie moved upstairs, arranging the upper floor in a fashion that would be useful and comfortable. They would share the large bedroom with the balcony, and the other two would become a sitting room and small kitchen. They both seemed happy.

I made three trips to Halifax for building materials and to order the ovens, equipment, and serving ware for the bakery. Gus was definitely in charge: making lists for me and steering his brothers in their tasks. I liked him: stocky and well muscled with thick, wavy auburn hair tied back to keep it out of his face. His skin was the slightest bit weathered, but he was kind and handsome in a rugged way. I guessed him to be about thirty. He had the same sapphire-blue eyes as Maggie.

The work on the carriage house happened in an organized squall of energy, everyone working in concert to clear and clean, save useable items and discard others. Within two weeks, it was nearly livable. A bathroom, sitting room/kitchen, and bedroom had been framed, wired, plumbed, and insulated. Plasterboard went up in a single afternoon, and I agreed to paint inside while a small covered deck was installed. Wood floors were laid and varnished by Gus, while the brothers, Albert, Robert, and Louis, began work in the house.

A wall came down between the dining room and the kitchen, and one went up between the new kitchen and the front counter area. The equipment began to arrive and was installed. Leoni and I unpacked and washed dishes, cutlery, and utensils. The glass display case was the last to arrive with, unfortunately, a cracked panel that had to be replaced. I dashed off to Halifax for a substitution and while there bought five wooden rockers, one for my little dollhouse and four for the bakery's front porch.

Gus installed a small coal-burning stove for heat in my cottage, and I moved in.

The sign for the front gate arrived. It read "Pâtisseries Margeaux."

CHAPTER 54

LILAJUNE LETTERS

Nashville, Tennessee
August–December, 1962

The first of many letters arrived the week after LilaJune's visit.

> *Dear Boy,*
> *I know you are angry at me and everybody else that left you or hurt you, but I hope you will find a way to forgive. Whether you like it or not, Jesus loves you and wants you to believe that he can heal your life. Please believe that. All you have to do is ask him for help, and he will give it to you. Ask to know the truth.*
> *My address is on the envelope, and you can write to me.*
> *I love you, LilaJune*

Fletcher read the letter, wadded it into a ball, and basketball tossed it into the trash can on the other side of his room. But the letter got him thinking. Maybe he could use her words to convince Dr. Idiot Mead into thinking he was "healing." As if he were searching for something. A "higher power."

And so it went. LilaJune's letters arrived like clockwork every week, and Fletcher gleaned from them key words and phrases about love and forgiveness, truth and acceptance. He opened the little blue Bible she had left him and began to read it, looking for more manipulative information.

LilaJune had put in a few old photos of his childhood, of the rare happy days: one of him at a birthday party, a young LilaJune cutting cake for him, both of them smiling at the camera. There was a photo of him at about age three sitting on her lap reading a book. One of him in the swimming pool laughing. Fletcher was sure LilaJune had meant for this last photo to be a happy memory, but all Fletcher remembered of that afternoon was Charles pushing him into the deep end of the pool, shouting, "Swim, you little sissy!"

He had a flash of memory: sinking under the water, gulping water instead of air, terror gripping him like a vice, and then a hand jerking him to the surface and pushing him onto the grass. He had choked and vomited, but only LilaJune had helped him.

Fletcher tore the pictures to shreds and screamed at the walls of his room until a nurse and two orderlies arrived and forced a shot into his arm. His sight became fuzzy then, and he fell, weak, onto his bed.

Dear Boy,

When I think of the torment you suffered as a child, I cry. I know you didn't cry. You learned to bury it deep, let it be like a pocket of pus in your gut. And that is just what it is now, a pocket of pus poisoning you. You are letting those horrible parents of yours rule you from the grave. I beg you to let it go. Give it to Jesus.

Just say this…Jesus, take my pain. I forgive them like you forgive me.

Love always, LilaJune

CHAPTER 55

THE KITCHEN PARTY

Annapolis Royal, Nova Scotia
September 1, 1962

On Saturday September 1, the renovations were finally finished, the pantry was filled, and the counter polished; we were ready to open the bakery. Everything was ready. I wrote out the final checks for the LeBlanc brothers and thanked them.

"You are the stars of this show. Without you, this could not have been done. Thank you, thank you, and thank you again."

I hugged them all. Albert and Louis each gave me a platonic embrace, but Robert hugged me like he meant it, and I recognized the red flags of dangerous desire. As I pulled away, I could see he was looking for my reaction. I hugged Gus, and he hugged me back tenderly, whispering, "Be careful of Robert."

The warning gripped my gut. Here was yet another man, dangerous perhaps, but certainly like every other man I was naturally attracted to.

"Well, good night to you all, and thank you once again. Monday is opening day! It's so exciting."

"No good night for you," Gus said. "Tonight is Saturday, and that means kitchen party."

"A what?"

"It's sort of an end-of-workweek tradition in Acadian homes. Soup and bread supper and then music and dancing," Leoni said.

"Join us," Robert said. Albert and Louis agreed.

"Yes, dancing!" Maggie added.

I showered and dressed and followed Leoni to her parents' home, where I met the rest of the family: two more sisters, Rachel and Aimee. Marie and her husband were there too. The brothers Albert and Louis brought their spouses and children. Leoni's mother, Annabelle, and father, Theodore, welcomed me as though I were family.

We gathered around the big kitchen table and ate lobster soup over thick slices of buttermilk bread. Everyone had wine, and though I was not much of a drinker, I was polite and had a glass.

After food, the dishes were whisked away and the table moved into the living room. Only the chairs remained. Theodore reached into a cabinet above the pantry and retrieved a squeeze-box-style accordion. Annabelle picked up the guitar. Aimee and Rachel were prepared to set the beat with double spoons against their thighs. Albert had his harmonica, as did Marie. Robert and Gus had fiddles.

"For our guest, Mademoiselle Desiree, here are the rules," Theodore said. "The children will start the dancing, then they will choose someone to join in, then each will replace a player, and the player will dance."

"But I—"

"Come now, don't be shy." Robert smiled slyly at me.

The music began, sweet and familiar, a reel as simple and recognizable as my name used to be. The children rushed forward and began to step dance. I was instantly lost in it, clapping and laughing along when Maggie came forward and offered her hand. I stood and walked forward a little self-consciously, but in just a moment, the beat had me, and my feet joined in.

"Look! She *can* dance!" Marie cried.

One by one each child chose a partner, and then the partners were required to replace an instrument. I took Robert's fiddle, and he stepped forward to dance. Though I had not held a fiddle for nearly a year, musical muscle memory kicked in, and I played and played. Gus and Leoni looked at me as though I had been a fraud all this time.

When everyone had had a turn, we took a breather for cold refreshment. I took a glass of something that reminded me of fruit punch and stepped outside. Gus followed me.

"Since when do they play fiddle and step dance in Alberta?"

"My grandparents were Acadian."

"Were?"

"My whole family died in a house fire." I said this without emotion.

"My gosh, Desiree. I am so sorry." Gus was looking at me as if wondering how I could speak so casually about catastrophic loss.

"Thanks, but we all die sooner or later."

"That sounded cynical. Not like the Desiree I have come to know."

"Maybe I *am* cynical. I've lost a lot. And I'm very tired. I think I'll call it a night."

"Mass is at ten thirty."

"I'm not Catholic."

"Oh, a Huguenot, are you?"

"I don't go to church."

He looked at me but said nothing more.

"I'll just go in and say good night to everyone."

Inside I thanked Theodore and Annabelle for including me and for the delicious dinner. "I had more fun than I've had in ages. You have a wonderful family."

Annabelle took my hands and looked me in the eyes. "Thank you for all you have done for Maggie and Leoni. You are indeed a gift from God."

The next day, Sunday, I rested. I slept late and then had a short run toward the National Historic Gardens, where the flowers and foliage were still wildly in bloom even as fall approached. In a week or so, the first nighttime frost would nip the most delicate of buds, but for today, they were glorious. Though the gate and gift shop were closed on Sundays, locals knew that the gardens were open for walking and reflection, and so I took the opportunity to do the same.

My life was still whirling like a top, yet instead of fearful stress, it was now productive—moving forward at an incredible speed. My mama would have said it was meant to be, *prédestiné*. Maybe she was right—good and bad, right and wrong, all happening for a reason, shaping me for a purpose. It wasn't that I believed in her God. How could God allow such horrors to happen in my life? But perhaps there was something in the universe that allowed life to occur in a certain way. Karma? What goes around comes around?

I crossed a small wooden footbridge and leaned on the railing, watching water trickle under the bridge, then over a tiny waterfall. Flower petals pooled in the swirl at the base of the falls, moving slowly round and round in the eddy without urgency.

That's what I wanted for my life: simple peace without urgency.

I sat on a bench in the midst of roses, fragrant, dewy petals that begged to be touched. I closed my eyes and let them fill me, soothe me, be me.

"I thought I might find you here," Gus said, and I jumped.

"You scared the bejeebees out of me! Out of church or Mass or whatever you do already?"

He laughed. "Church. My family is Catholic, but I am an Acadian Huguenot—Protestant."

"That seems odd. You were raised Catholic, right?"

"Yes, but five years ago, I went away to New Brunswick to work on a construction job with a man named William Frost. He and I became close."

"Close? What does *that* mean?"

"Not what you are thinking, you wicked girl. Friends. We had a lot in common, big Acadian Catholic families, fishing, and woodcrafting. We talked a lot about life and faith and what we wanted faith to mean. In the end, I realized that though my Catholic roots are deep and would always be there, I was ready for a more personal relationship with God. I wanted a one on one. I started attending church with William. By the time I came back to Annapolis Royal six months later, I had made a decision. I was Protestant. My family, especially my parents, took it hard—my father did not speak to me for a month, but eventually they accepted my decision. What about you?"

"Well, I was raised in a small Baptist church in Ten…Tensley, Alberta, but I never connected. I just couldn't buy it all—God and Jesus and all.

Then when my family all died, I couldn't believe that a *loving* God would kill everybody I loved and leave me to live with it."

"They say everything happens for a reason."

"And what is *that* supposed to mean!"

He touched my arm, sapphire eyes apologetic. "Just a saying, nothing personal meant, truly. Come on. Let's walk."

We followed a path to the edge of the gardens, where water pooled in a small marsh. Cattails, pampas grass, and pond lilies grew thick, and frogs croaked. Gus imitated them, and I laughed so hard at his croaking antics I finally begged him to stop.

We walked and talked and laughed for more than an hour, then sat on a bench near a clear pond surrounded by wildflowers. The sun was warm on our backs.

"What is Gus short for?"

"I'm not saying."

"How fun. A secret to crack. Let's see. Gustav?"

"No."

"Gunther?"

"No."

"Guido?"

"Not even close."

"Goliath?"

"Goliath? Enough. All right, I will tell you. Then you can have a great laugh, and we will be done with the nonsense."

"I'm waiting."

"Cheshire."

"What? Why?"

"Because my father said I had a grin like a big Cheshire cat when I was born."

I fell forward at the waist and laughed hard. Gus laughed too.

When I caught my breath, I asked, "But how did they get 'Gus' out of Cheshire?"

"My father chose my first name and my mother the second."

"Which is?"

"Augustus, after her father."

"Cheshire Augustus LeBlanc. Sounds quite regal. You aren't a secret prince, are you?"

His reply: "Ribbit, ribbit."

I howled with laughter again. "Well, Mr. Froggy, don't think I am going to kiss you to find out!"

"Horrors!"

We walked toward the front part of the garden along a path that led around the front gate.

"So let's see. Your turn. What is your middle name?"

"Renée."

"And d'Moss?"

"I really don't know the origin."

"I would guess Portuguese," he offered.

"No. Really? What makes you think so?"

"I studied the history of language in college, and names beginning with a small D were either of Moorish origin, early history—or Portuguese, after the fifteenth century. Do you have any Portuguese heritage?"

"Not that I know of, but then, my dad's side of the family were a bunch of Cajun mutts."

"Not very nice talk for a lady."

"Who said I was a lady?"

We were in the parking lot by then.

"Give you a lift home?"

"No thanks. I'm going to run down to Lequille and buy a fishing pole and bait."

"Desiree, my friend. Nothing is open for business on a Sunday. But I have an extra pole and bait and would be happy to take you fishing this afternoon."

"Deal."

He dropped me off in the alley behind the bakery with a promise to pick me up in an hour. I had lunch and changed into woolen pants and boots, a T-shirt, and sweater, then went out to the front porch to wait for Gus. *Cheshire Augustus LeBlanc. That's quite a name.*

Gus's red truck arrived at the curb at one thirty, and we drove east along St. Charles, crossing over the bridge to Granville Ferry, then left onto Granville Road to a rocky outcropping. We sat on the big boulders there, strung our lines, and baited our hooks.

"These lures are huge. What are we fishing for, whales?" I asked.

"Salmon. They're beginning their run upriver."

"How fun. I've never caught a salmon."

"Who says you will?"

I jabbed him in the ribs, and he laughed.

Like all good fishermen, we fished mostly in silence until finally something tugged hard at my line.

"Pull up firm but don't jerk," Gus said.

I did so and felt the hook set. The fight was on.

"You've got a big one there, Desiree. You'll have to tire it out some before we can bring it in. Just keep the line tight and let him fight, then slowly reel him toward us. I'll get the net."

Gus reached for the net and stood at the ready. "Now there, did you feel him slow down some? Start reeling in—even and steady. We don't want him to spit out the hook at the end of the battle."

It took another ten minutes before the salmon surfaced, a large, tired eye looking up at us.

"Now steady while I slip the net under him."

Gus expertly netted my fish and pulled him up onto the boulder with us. It flopped and fought in the net.

"Look away," Gus said.

"I've seen fish knocked senseless before."

"All right, then." He took out a small wooden bat-like club and smacked the fish hard on the head. It lay still. "Good job, Rae. He's a whopper. I'm guessing a thirty pounder!"

We laid the salmon in the cooler.

"Okay, now your turn," I said. "Start without me. I need to find a bush."

I walked across the road and into the trees to relieve myself. On the way back to our fishing spot, I heard a wee little yip, weak and dry. I listened again, searching. I heard it again, and then I saw him, a tiny puppy barely a month old, shivering and crying. I picked him up and cradled him in my sweater.

"Gus, look what I found in the rocks. I think he is almost dead."

"Let's give him some water and then we can take him back to Mom. She has saved lots of orphans."

I held the puppy as Gus dripped water into his open, searching mouth. We gathered our gear and set out for the LeBlanc homeplace.

"Mom, we have a huge salmon and a starving puppy," Gus called as we came through the kitchen door.

"Oh, Lordy. Here, Theodore, you keep it warm while I get the water bottle from the bathroom and fill it with hot water. Gus, you get some canned milk from the pantry and some vegetable oil. Desiree, separate an egg, please."

We all hurried to accomplish our assigned tasks. Annabelle gently mixed the egg yolk with a teaspoon of vegetable oil, then added a half cup of canned milk, stirring gently as to not form froth. She wrapped the squeaking pup in a heavy towel and laid him on the water bottle. Then, with an eye dropper from the kitchen junk drawer, she began to gently feed.

"Gus, you hold the bowl, and I will feed this wee squirrel of a baby."

The pup gulped down dropper after dropper of formula until, finally satiated, he fell asleep.

"I'm thinking he's a Russel terrier, wouldn't you say, Mother?" Theodore offered.

"That would be my guess."

"How old do you suppose?"

"About three weeks to a month. He will be eating on his own in a week. So, Miss Desiree, it looks like you have a dog."

"Me! No, I don't need a dog!"

"Looks as though he chose you and not the other way of it." Theodore laughed.

"But I have never had a dog, and I wouldn't know how to care for him."

"Well, my sweet miss, you just saw how to do it. Gus, get a small box from the shed and some old, clean towels."

"No, *really*. I can't take him," I protested.

Gus laughed as Robert came through the door.

"Wow, what a whopper of a salmon!" he exclaimed. "And what the heck is that?" He pointed at the puppy in his mother's arms.

"It's Desiree's new dog."

Gus laughed harder now.

"It's not funny, *Cheshire!*"

It was Robert's turn to laugh. "I see you two are on a first-name basis. Come on, *Cheshire,* let's clean this fish before it starts to smell."

"Shut your trap, Robert." Gus slugged his brother in the arm as they took the fish to the backyard for cleaning.

"Annabelle, please. Can't you keep the puppy? The bakery is opening tomorrow, and I am up to my eyeballs in alligators."

"What's an alligator?"

I put my face in my hands.

"You'll do fine. Leoni and Maggie will help you. Look how sweet he sleeps."

I looked at his angelic face, realizing there was no getting out of this mess I had been pulled into.

"All right, but only if the girls will help me."

"Good. He will be awake in an hour, and you can practice feeding some before you take him home."

"Argh. What have I done?"

Annabelle smiled at me. "Stay for supper. We're having salmon."

CHAPTER 56
THE GRAND OPENING

Annapolis Royal, Nova Scotia
September 3, 1962

My alarm rang loud and shrill at four a.m., waking the puppy. I had been up most of the night, either too anxious to sleep or feeding the puppy. Today was the bakery's opening. I packed the puppy in a basket, along with all the appropriate puppy accoutrements, and hurried to the main house, where I found Leoni already hard at work.

Maggie was still asleep, and Leoni was baking apricot turnovers and rolling out puff pastry for a mixed berry version.

"Good morning, what's in the basket?"

"A puppy."

"You aren't going to bake it, are you?" She giggled.

"I might."

"What's its name?"

"Nothing yet."

"That's a very funny name." She giggled again.

"How can you be so calm? We open in two hours."

"An hour and a half, actually. *Pret ou pas.*"

"Ready or not, that's right. What's first?"

"Feed that squalling puppy."

We worked steadily, baking the pastries and sweet yeast breads first: turnovers, bear claws, cheese Danish, and cinnamon rolls.

Promptly at five thirty, I turned over the sign on the door from closed to open, turned on the lights, and unlocked the door. Within minutes, local fishermen began to arrive. Leoni took their orders, and I filled their thermoses with coffee or tea.

By six o'clock, the first wave was over. Maggie wandered in at six fifteen, and we all had our breakfast.

Leoni got Maggie ready for school while I fed the puppy again, who looked at me as if I were his whole world.

Maggie wanted to hold the puppy.

"What's his name?"

"I haven't named him yet."

"Where did you find him?"

"In the rocks by the river."

"Let's call him Rocky."

"Sounds good to me. Rocky it is."

Maggie held Rocky while Leoni and I began making shortbread and oatcakes, then cookie dough and pie filling.

At seven thirty, Leoni left with Maggie, taking her to school. They had no sooner driven away when the early morning breakfast crowd arrived. I stopped baking and started serving. By the time Leoni returned, we were down to a single cup of coffee and the kettle was screaming on the stove. Our inventory had shrunk to one turnover, three cinnamon rolls, six oatcakes, and four shortbread squares.

"Here I come to save the day!" Leoni said as she flew into action.

She did not see my expression change as I once again remembered Paddy in his Mighty Mouse costume sliding down the banister, dissolving into laughter. *How long will this pain haunt me?*

By the time the morning rush had passed, we were more or less recovered. We took a break before tackling the baking of cookies, scones, and a couple apple pies for teatime.

A few fishermen came back in at one thirty, and some came by for pie, which they ate out on the front porch. They stank of fish, and I was glad to have them eat outside. Leoni traded pie for lobster from a lobsterman.

A few ladies wandered in to buy scones and pie or a bag of cookies, and then the day was done. At two thirty, Leoni left to pick up Maggie from school while I cleaned up.

Later Maggie played with Rocky while Leoni and I counted out the cashbox. I would do the accounting later, but I planned to pay Leoni each day. I knew she needed the ready cash.

"All right, my friend and hard worker, here is your money for the day." I counted out twenty dollars in small bills.

Leoni stared at the money. "No, no. This is too much. We live here for free, and the bakery is your investment. Twenty dollars is twice the going rate of pay. I cannot accept. *Absolument pas.*"

"*Absolument, oui.* You earned every penny, and I am happy to pay you this. Don't forget tomorrow is another day." I stood and stretched. "I will get better at all this, I promise. But now I am taking my pooch home, having a hot bath, and collapsing. See you in the morning." I hugged her and thanked her, picked up my hungry puppy, and walked to my cottage, exhausted.

Rocky and I had dinner. He drank canned milk and egg yolk, and I made myself a fat, juicy hamburger and a green salad and ate a leftover piece of pie from the bakery. I bathed and collapsed into bed with my journal. I was asleep by eight o'clock.

The next day was easier, and the day after that was even easier. By Friday, we were in the swing of it. Rocky took his first bites of soft food and had turned round and robust in just a week. Walking turned to stumbling and sliding and playing with Maggie.

Saturday was a half day; we closed at ten thirty in the morning. That night I was once again invited to the kitchen party at the LeBlancs'. I brought Rocky along, and the children were delighted.

Annabelle served a delicious chicken stew with crusty rye bread. We ate and laughed, danced and played music until we were all spent. Robert, Gus, and Marie sang a French song about a woman waiting for a long-lost love. I thought I saw Leoni look troubled, and knowing her husband had died, I wondered why her siblings would sing such a sad song.

Outside, while I was walking to my truck, Robert stopped me.

"No need to rush off," he said, touching my arm.

"I'm not rushing off. It has been a strenuous week, and I am really tired."

"I could bring a bottle of wine over to help you relax."

I looked at him and remembered Gus saying, "Be careful of Robert." Robert had all the characteristics of men whom I had been attracted to in the past. Past: that was the key word, the past, and it would never be the future—not ever again.

"Robert, let's put something straight. I am not attracted to you in that way."

"Oh, I think you are." He reached out and put his hands on my shoulders, but I backed away.

"No." My voice was low and firm.

"What's going on out here, Robert?" Gus wanted to know.

"Just conversation. What's it to you, brother?"

"Desiree?"

"It was nothing. I'm tired. Good night."

"Fishing tomorrow?" Gus asked.

"Thank you, no, Gus. I need to have a long, hard run."

At home, I curled up on the sofa with Rocky. For the first time, I closed the curtains. I felt uneasy, not afraid but edgy. I wrote in my journal:

Here is a fact: even in my new life, I will find men who are dishonorable. Is that the word I mean? Or would a better word be aggressive where women are concerned? As if they were entitled to women...so sure of themselves...so self-involved. One thing is for sure: I recognize them now, and I don't want what they offer. Surely this is progress. Good job! Bon travail, Quil!

The next morning I ate a big breakfast of eggs and toast, fruit, and coffee, then laced up my sneakers. I took Rocky outside to potty, then put him in the bathroom with some newspapers, food and water, his bed, and a chew toy. I would only be gone and hour or so, but I wanted him to be comfortable.

I ran over the bridge to Granville Ferry and turned right onto Route 1. There were no obvious shoulders, but I ran facing oncoming traffic, preparing to dodge a vehicle if need be. I relaxed into my runner's sweet spot, my breathing even and my pace rhythmic. I ran and ran. I felt exhilarated. After an hour, I turned for home. By the time I reached the bridge, my legs were feeling it. I hadn't had a long run for a week, and my body reflected the neglect. By the time I reached the cottage, I was used up.

I showered and took Rocky out into the garden for some exercise. I lay in the grass with Rocky running a crisscross course over my body, barking, his little voice more like a shrill yapping than a real bark. I was growing attached to him, his sweet face and the way he snuggled with me in the evenings. He always seemed happy to see me, and I liked that most of all.

I fell asleep in the sun and woke to Maggie staring at me. She sat down next to me in the grass.

"Look what I found on the road by the church."

I rolled onto my side. Maggie was holding a young calico kitten maybe three months old.

"Mommy is 'lergic to cats, so I'm giving her to you!"

She set the kitten on my chest and skipped away.

"Maggie, no. I can't!" I called after her.

"Yes, you can. Her name is Priscilla. I'll come and see her all the time."

I looked up at the kitchen window and saw Leoni laughing, laughing so hard she had to dry her eyes on her apron. "Very funny," I mouthed.

Priscilla and Rocky were already on a tear around the yard. I stuffed the kitten under one arm and Rocky under the other. "Great, this is just great," I muttered.

Later I begged some kitten food from the neighbor four houses down who I knew had cats. I set a small dish of water and the dry food mixed with canned milk out for Priscilla, and puppy food and water for

Rocky. They ate each other's food. I found a box, lined it with newspaper, and added some sand from the alley. Priscilla knew just what to do.

"See there, Rocky. Take a lesson." He barked to go outside.

I made a note to ask Gus to build a pet door for my brood.

CHAPTER 57

FLETCHER'S PLOT

Nashville, Tennessee
October 1962

LilaJune's letters were relentless. Week after week they arrived filled with detailed instruction on forgiveness and salvation. It felt like Jesus was being shoved down his throat. Though some of her wisdom began to make sense, Fletcher still trashed the letters and would not talk about her with Dr. Mead.

Late one night, as he lay awake looking at the ceiling, a plot began to formulate in his devious mind. By morning, he knew how it would all play out.

Any inmate mail coming into or going out of the hospital was read before being delivered. Fletcher assumed this since all LilaJune's had been opened. His new plan would take time, but he had nothing but time.

After lunch, he sat down to write LilaJune a letter. He needed to set a pattern of correspondence to his former nanny. He could manipulate her, he was certain. Slowly but surely, he would write the words both she and Dr. Mead wanted to read.

> *Dear LilaJune,*
> *I wanted to thank you for your continued interest in me. There*
> *must have been something in me as a child that makes you care.*

I have been looking at the Bible you left me and can see the
places you underlined. For now, I cannot believe in the Jesus
you and the Bible describe, but maybe with time I can change.

Fletcher folded the short note and slipped it into an envelope, leaving it unsealed as the rules required, and put it in the inmate out-box.

Later in the day Dr. Mead picked up the letter and read it. "What is he up to?" he muttered.

At Fletcher's next session, Dr. Mead brought up the letter. "You know, Fletcher, if you fake it long enough, that plan can turn on you."

"I have no idea what you mean." Fletcher's tone was without emotion.

"Meaning that when you start saying things or writing them, you may think you are faking it, but your brain starts to believe them."

"I have no idea what you mean." Fletcher's tone was again without emotion.

"I think you are using that old woman."

"Oh, really? Are you going to start preaching about Jesus now?" He curled a lip and rolled his eyes.

Two days later Fletcher penned another letter to LilaJune, and then another, and another, until their back-and-forth correspondence became as regular as sunrise and sunset. By spring, he was sure she would be ready to take the bait.

Dr. Mead was wary, but Fletcher had done nothing to incriminate himself. When Dr. Mead wrote his biannual report, he was obliged to show emotional progress based on Fletcher's letter writing and relationship building. It galled him. He knew Fletcher was using LilaJune, but for what purpose, he could not imagine.

CHAPTER 58

A NORTHERN WINTER

Annapolis Royal, Nova Scotia
October–December 1962

Life moved along as winter approached. The bakery settled down after the first month—we were no longer a curiosity, which was fine with me. We still earned plenty to be profitable and keep us busy, but most days either Leoni or I were able to handle the shop alone. We still got up early to do the initial baking together, though by the time Maggie left for school, we were able to do other things—important things like reading with our feet on the hearth.

Rocky had become my best friend and went everywhere with me. We ran and shopped and slept together. He tormented Priscilla, but a couple well-landed, claws-out swats and he learned to respect her space. She also began snuggling into bed with me as the weather changed from crisp fall days to shorter, colder ones. I had a full house and a full bed.

Gus and I grew closer. Closer by baby steps. In many ways, he reminded me of Danny—his kindness and strength, quiet presence and intellect. But unlike Danny, I felt a certain allure: those blue eyes drew me in like tropical water.

We were a good match on every level, and though I could not say I was *in* love, I had certainly learned to love him. He taught me to fish for the big salmon in the river, to dig for clams on the beaches, and to play chess. Theodore and the brothers took me shrimping before the weather got too cold. I felt safe and happy.

I taught Gus to sharpen his fiddling skills. He taught me to play the guitar. I taught him to cook, and he taught me to feel vulnerable without reservation. I never thought I would learn to say such a thing—me, the man-hater. It wasn't a romantically heated kind of love. It was comfort and joy and a longing to see him. I made his favorite cake for his birthday, October 12—my old birthday. What a coincidence. Now I shared a birthday with Gus and one with Maggie, March 4.

By December, the snow came in and stayed. Annabelle told me, "We won't see the ground until spring." I burrowed in for the long haul.

On December 7, Leoni asked if I could keep an eye on Maggie for the day. She needed a day to drive into Halifax.

When she got home, she looked tired, but then, she had been looking a little tired for a week or so.

"Are you okay?" I asked.

"No. Let me put Maggie to bed and we can talk."

I lit a fire and put the kettle on. By the time she came downstairs, I had put a pot of tea, mugs, and a plate of cookies on the side table between two comfy chairs.

We stared at the fire and drank our tea in silence for a while before Leoni spoke.

"I have cancer," she said softly before the tears came.

I was stunned. "What? When? How?" I stammered.

"It's breast cancer—advanced. The doctor said he could do surgery, remove both my breasts, but I have lumps in my armpits as well. The cancer has spread to my cervix too."

"So how do we fight this?"

"We don't."

"You have to fight. What about Maggie?"

"My family will take care of her. The doctor thinks I can last until after Christmas, but nothing is written in stone. When the pain gets too bad, they will keep me doped up until…"

"Leoni, it can't be that cut and dried Let me send you to the Mayo Clinic in Minneapolis. Better yet, I will take you. We can close the bakery until after Christmas. Maggie can stay with your parents. We'll leave tomorrow."

"Don't tell anybody about the cancer yet."

"Well, you have to tell your parents."

"I can't."

"You have to do so, Leoni. Why will they think you are going to Minneapolis?"

"How am I going to pay for treatment in America? This is crazy!"

"You let me worry about that. I have money put away."

"But—"

"No more arguing. Let's get packed. I'll call Gus, and he can be there when we tell your parents."

"I'm too exhausted to pack."

She went to bed, and I called Gus.

The next morning I phoned a travel agent in Halifax and booked a flight to Minneapolis for five p.m. Then I called the Mayo Clinic and made arrangements for Leoni to be seen the following day.

"No, she is not an American citizen, and she has no insurance, but I will be paying the bill in full," I explained.

Leoni and I packed for an extended trip, then drove out to her parents' home to speak with Annabelle and Theodore. Gus was waiting for us in the driveway. He hugged his sister and whispered words of encouragement.

Of course, Theodore and Annabelle knew something was terribly wrong. Though they took the news well, I recognized the stiff-upper-lip attitude for which their generation was famous.

I hurried Leoni away before she could liquefy into tears. Nevertheless, she was crying by the time we got to the car.

"I'm going to take good care of Maggie. Don't worry." Gus hugged his sister and then he hugged me. "And you take good care of *her.*" He kissed me on the cheek.

We were in Halifax by four p.m. and in the air promptly by five, Boston by six, and Minneapolis by nine.

Being back on American soil felt comforting and frightening all at the same time. I looked at my passport as we waited in line at immigration, and Leoni noticed my hesitation.

"What's wrong?" she whispered.

"Oh, nothing. A little stressed."

We fell into bed at the hotel after a hasty supper and woke in time for breakfast and a taxi ride to the clinic for our nine o'clock appointment.

The day was spent with tests and X-rays and more scheduled for the next two days. She was admitted to the hospital and was so exhausted I left her to rest, returning to the hotel alone.

It was nearly four, and I hurried to get a call into Bidwell before he left the office for the day.

"It's good to hear from you, of course, but you're taking quite a chance calling."

"I'm in Minneapolis."

"Have you lost your mind?" His voice was laced with both shock and irritation.

"Probably, but it was an emergency. I'm at the Mayo Clinic."

"Good Lord. Are you ill?"

"No, a friend is. Listen, Bidwell, I don't have much time. I will be sending you a bill from Minneapolis—from the clinic. Promise me that no matter what the figure is, you will pay it. Check with Ken Durkin and see how it should be done. Promise?"

"Certainly. How are you? I've been worried."

"Life is good. I'll add a letter with the bill. Just don't keep it. Miss you too, Bidwell. Goodbye, my friend."

"Goodbye."

I called to check on Leoni after breakfast but was told she was spent and would be for the next few days. Nobody was willing to speak to me about test results. I left a message for Leoni that I would see her in a couple of days.

I called Theodore and Annabelle and told them what I knew, which was absolutely nothing, but assured them that more tests may equal more hope.

I waited alone in the hotel, anxious and fidgety, wanting to do something to help.

Being in Minnesota sparked something in me. I remembered Bidwell saying how Clarice had been raised in Bemidji, and I wondered if by chance there was family there that had not been discovered in the initial search.

On a whim, I packed a small bag and took a taxi to the airport, then bought a ticket on the 1:15 p.m. flight to Bemidji. I was there by 2:30 and found a hotel on Main Street.

In the lobby, I asked the desk clerk, "I am here visiting, looking for family members that may still live here."

"How interesting. What would their names be?" she asked.

"Jensen. Laurence and Mildred Jensen. I believe they have passed away, but they had two sons and a daughter."

The clerk looked up then and surveyed my face—like I might be joking. "Jimmy, Arthur, and Clarice."

I was surprised. "Then you knew them."

"I was married to Jimmy, but he was killed in France. Marlene Eriksen was married to Arthur. He never came home either, presumed lost at sea. And Clarice ran off, left her parents to grieve on their own and fend for themselves as they aged. They never saw the wretched thing again. Did you know her?"

I looked away. "No. My mother did. I just thought I would ask while I was here. Are there any other family relations I might speak to?"

"No. All gone."

"I'll just be staying one night. Thank you for the information."

I went for a run along icy, salted roads. It was cold and damp, and I picked up the pace to stay warm. Running through town, eventually passing the city cemetery, I looked over the fence at the headstones as I raced by. *Was my biological past buried in there?*

On the way back, I impulsively turned in at the gate and slowed to a walk out of respect for those buried. It took about thirty minutes to find my biological grandparents' graves.

There they were side by side. Laurence and Mildred Jensen had died within three months of each other—he of a failed heart, the head-stone read, and she of a broken one, I guessed. I didn't know why it felt so emotional to see them there. Perhaps it was actually my biological mother that had made me feel so sad and ashamed. I had no real reason to be ashamed, but she had given birth to me, and I was a part of her. Was I like her in a small way? Was I cold and hard like her—even a little? What had I inherited besides her money? I didn't want to be like her, but deep inside I knew I had grown hard and brittle. *I don't want to be like her.*

I backed away from the graves and hurried to the street. My hot, steamy body was now chilled. I ran hard back to the hotel, straight past the desk clerk and to my room. I showered and went out for dinner, finding a little restaurant serving hearty Midwestern food. I ate like it was my first meal since breakfast. Roast chicken, mashed potatoes and gravy, corn, peas, and chocolate cake.

It was cold and dark as I walked back to the hotel, but the skies were crystal clear, the stars bright and twinkling. Why had I come here, really? What was I looking for? Curiosity? Some sort of connection? Whatever my reason for coming here, it had been fruitless, and my heart felt as chilled as the winter cold.

The next morning I returned to the airport and flew back to Minneapolis, taking a taxi directly from the airport to the hospital.

Leoni was in her room, sitting up, with her untouched lunch on a side table. She looked glassy eyed and numb.

"Leoni." I pulled a chair up next to her bed. "What have they told you?"

"Nothing, but the doctor will be by to talk to me around three."

I looked at my watch; it was 2:45. "How are you feeling?"

"Foggy. I have had a lot of pain, and they are pumping me with who knows what."

I rubbed her arm and made a feeble attempt at light conversation. The doctor arrived at 3:20.

"Hello, Mrs. Arsenault. I'm Dr. Peterson, and I am here to speak with you about the tests we have been running. May we speak privately?"

"No need for that. This is my sister Desiree, and she should hear it all."

"All right, then. I am afraid I don't have good news."

Dr. Peterson ran through a litany of test results and diagnoses. He was kind and sensitive, but the news was devastating.

Leoni did indeed have cancer. It was in her breasts and had metastasized to the lymph nodes, her uterus, and cervix as well as her lungs. It was a death sentence.

"Here's what we can do. If we remove your breasts and give you a complete hysterectomy, then do intense radiation on the lungs, I think we can extend your life by about three months. Without these measures, I'm afraid you might not make it to Christmas. If you opt for treatment, I would suggest we do so immediately."

"I want to go home. If I can't be cured and my life is over, I just want to go home."

"What about the pain?" I asked.

"It will be bad, especially toward the end," Dr. Peterson said. "We can prescribe as much morphine as she needs, but she will need a nurse who can administer and manage the drug. It can be very dangerous. Also, she will need oxygen and someone to be with her around the clock."

"We wouldn't want the drugs to kill me before the cancer." Leoni's sarcasm was spiked with pain.

"Maybe we could give her something now. She is obviously in pain. And I can hire a private nurse when I get her home. Thank you for trying, and even though you couldn't give us hope, you have given us clarity." I shook his hand, and he wished us safe travels. Once he was out in the hall, I heard him instruct the nurse to administer what was needed to keep Leoni comfortable for traveling.

"Well, are you ready to get out of here?"

"I can't tell you how much."

I slept there that night and in the morning signed all the paperwork for release and payment. While Leoni was bathed and dressed and made ready to travel, I went back to the hotel for a quick shower. I packed our bags and took a taxi back to the hospital.

We were on the 10:30 a.m. flight home, this time through Toronto, the fastest route. We landed in Halifax at 2:00. I was grateful no new snow had fallen and the roads were dry. Leoni was in pain and exhausted by the time we arrived home. I put her to bed.

I was horrified at how fast she had gone downhill in just a few days. *She has given up.*

"Gus, we are home. The news is very bad, and we are going to need a full-time nurse. Who do you know?"

"I'll call somebody in Halifax and see what I can find out."

"Thank you, Mr. Wonderful. I want her to be well taken care of. Cost is not an issue." My voice cracked.

"I'm coming over," Gus said and hung up.

He was at the house in minutes, and I fell into his arms sobbing. I was tired, so very tired, emotionally and physically.

"What is it? Tell me?" He held me close and stroked my hair.

"It's terminal cancer—no hope, and it's moving fast, ravaging her body even as she sleeps."

"There is always hope. She worships a God of miracles, don't forget."

I pushed away from him. "Your God—her God! The only God I know is one who takes and gives nothing back. Do you really think that this God of yours will heal Leoni? Trust me, he won't. I'm tired. Let's call it a night."

"Why are you so angry, Rae?" He looked shocked and hurt.

"Sorry. I just know firsthand how *God* doesn't come through when you need him."

"Have you ever asked for his help?"

"If God is omnipotent, all knowing, and loving, then how did my entire family perish while he watched and did nothing? It's easy to believe in God when you have never experienced catastrophic loss! Go ahead, hope and pray, but I promise you, Gus, you will be disappointed."

He studied me, his brow furrowed, eyes empathetic. "What in heaven's name happened to you?"

"Everything."

"Tell me."

"No."

CHAPTER 59

THE VISIT

Nashville, Tennessee
December 1962

On December 16, LilaJune Walker arrived at the Nashville Psychiatric Hospital with a Christmas present for Fletcher. When he was led into the visiting area and saw the package, he thought, *I hope there is a metal file and a set of key molds in there.*

"Hello, sweet boy," LilaJune greeted him. "I brought you a Christmas present."

"You shouldn't have." Fletcher forced a grin.

"Oh, it's nothing much. Just something I knitted."

"I'm sure I will love it." Another patient grin.

"How are you keeping?" she asked.

"Confined and restless."

"Are you still reading your Bible? You know Jesus can forgive you, and though you are going to have to pay the price for your sins here on earth, he will keep you for himself and erase all your sins. The Bible says God will forget your sins ever happened. All you have to do is ask for forgiveness. If you aren't sure what to believe, just ask to know the truth. Just ask to know the truth, and you will be given it."

Fletcher could see Dr. Mead standing near the door watching.

Fletcher smiled and said, "I'm still reading the Bible, and thank you for the photos I found inside."

Fletcher took the package from LilaJune and discreetly looked it over for signs of tampering. There were none, and he was astonished that it had not been inspected. But then he had overheard the guards complaining about the volumes of packages arriving daily and all the extra work involved. It appeared in all their rushing his package had been missed. *Maybe there is a God,* was his sarcastic thought.

The two chatted for another half hour about life in Savannah and LilaJune's church—Fletcher avoiding any pointed questions about his beliefs.

"Before I go, I want to pray with you," Lila June said, reaching for Fletcher's hands.

Fletcher groaned inwardly but lowered his head as LilaJune took his hands in hers and began to pray.

"Lord, you know this boy. Let him remember the God of his childhood. Never let him go. Show him the truth."

Fletcher picked up his package and said goodbye to LilaJune, then smirked at Dr. Mead as they passed in the doorway.

In his room, Fletcher opened the package to find a blue afghan with two large knitting needles pushed through her knitting. Fletcher wondered if she had done this on purpose, but nevertheless there they were. He removed the needles and tucked them under his mattress.

Christmas passed, as did New Year's. Fletcher used the time to think and rethink his plan. He made friends with a pretty young nurse by the name of Kelly Walsh, who was happy to play cards or visit. He carefully manipulated her. Under the guise of charm, he learned security information, the grounds' layout, schedules, and routines.

On January 2, Fletcher phoned his lawyer and arranged for a visit. Wilson Planter arrived the next day, and the two took a corner table in the lounge.

"Where is she?" Fletcher pressed.

"We aren't sure yet, but we did ferret out the lawyer who represented her in the purchasing of the Key West house."

"Well, what are you waiting for? Get someone in there. There must be files. He knows where she is. She can't hide forever."

"I'm not doing anything *that* illegal."

"No? But you have connections. Use them, and do it now, or when I get out of here, you will be sorry you ever met me."

"I already am."

"Oh, aren't you the brave one with me locked up. Good for you. I like hired help with a spine."

CHAPTER 60

CHRISTMAS

Annapolis Royal, Nova Scotia
Christmas, 1962

Lisa Conroy arrived late the next day. She had just graduated from nursing school, and this was her first real job, but we were glad to have her on such short notice. The problem was she had grown up in Alberta, and I feared she would expose my lack of Albertan knowledge if she found out I claimed to be from there. If I spoke mostly French around her, that might throw her off. Besides, she would be busy with Leoni.

Lisa was kind and gentle and attentive to Leoni, managing her pain like an old hand, but Leoni was going downhill fast. On December 17, Lisa ordered an oxygen tank, and from then on, Leoni wore a nasal breathing tube constantly.

I set up a bed in the sitting room for Lisa, and we took turns being with Leoni. One evening just days before Christmas, Leoni wanted to talk. I pulled a chair close to her bed.

"How is Maggie?" Leoni asked.

"Confused and missing you."

"I need to talk to her."

"Yes, you do," I agreed.

Talking was hard for Leoni now. She became breathless quickly.

"Leoni, I need to tell you something, but you have to promise to never repeat what I am about to say."

"I think it will be a short promise, don't you? But yes, I promise. You're not a murderer or bank robber, are you?"

"No, but I am not who you think I am." I turned my chair so she could see my face. "I am rich. Very rich. Multimillionaire kind of rich, and I am not Albertan. I'm from Tennessee."

Over the next hour, I told her every single detail of my old life, and she understood why I was now who I pretended to be.

"I want you to know that you should not worry about Maggie. I will make sure she has everything—she will want for nothing." I looked at her squarely in the eye. "I want to adopt her."

There was a great, long pause while Leoni thought.

"Would you keep her near her family? I want her to know who she is."

"Absolutely. I am going nowhere."

"Will she be safe with you? What about your past?"

I had to think about that. She would be safe as long as I stayed hidden, and I *would* stay hidden—I had to.

"Yes, I will make sure she is safe."

"Desiree, you think you're not, but you *are* a gift from God. *Un grand cadeau de Dieu.* An angel here on earth. Thank you for all you have done. Surely, God sent you."

I couldn't tell her that I didn't believe in God.

Maggie continued on at her grandparents' house, confused about the reasons she couldn't go home. Though Gus had tried to explain, she became more and more insistent until finally Gus brought her for a visit. We left Leoni and Maggie alone. I knew Leoni would find the right words, and though Maggie would not, could not, comprehend death, I was certain she would eventually adjust. No one could ever replace her mother, but she would learn to love and trust the person Leoni chose to raise her.

As for me, my motives were transparent: I loved Maggie. I wanted her to always feel wanted and special, not just passed on to family. Adopting her was my chance to have a child, one I loved the way I had loved Paddy. I wondered what the family would think. What would Gus think? Was I being selfish? Would this adoption be best for Maggie or for me?

On December 26, Lisa knew it was the end, and I called Leoni's family. She had been barely conscious all day, and at around six in the evening, she breathed her last. Her parents were, of course, inconsolably shattered.

There could not be anything more unnatural than a parent outliving a child. Leoni was gone, their firstborn, the child of their youth, the only time they would have the luxury of a single baby. They would never say they loved her more, but there had to have been a special bond, one unique to this first child. Their pain was palpable.

The funeral Mass was held at Saint Louis Catholic Church, where generations of LeBlancs had worshipped, been baptized, confirmed, and married. It held all their history, and Leoni's death was registered into church records next to the notification of her birth and marriage.

Two days later I met with her family to discuss Leoni's will. I now owned the bakery completely, as we had contracted when I purchased her house, and Maggie was left Leoni's belongings and bank accounts in trust.

The topic of Maggie's future and Leoni's wishes became open for discussion at last.

"Leoni has designated you as custodian of her daughter, and we understand you wish to adopt her," Theodore said.

"Yes. Leoni and I talked about this at length, and I promised to never remove her from her extended family."

"But you are a single woman, and Maggie needs a father. Wouldn't it be better for her to join Albert or Louis or Marie, who have families already?" Annabelle said.

"Maybe, but I do love Maggie, and if she were with me, she could stay in her own home. Please don't think I am taking her from you. I want her to have a good education and life experiences that will enrich her. I will be devoted to her, but I will not fight you for custody. My relationship with this family trumps everything else. Maggie is your blood."

"To be honest," Robert began, "though we all truly like you, until four months ago, we had never heard of you, and then you ride in like a white knight on a north wind. You had only known her a day when you bought Leoni's house and gave her permanent shelter. You paid her medical bills. Who does that?"

"Robert! That's a bit harsh." Annabelle hushed her son.

"We don't really know anything about you," Albert added. "Your history and family—forgive any of us for bringing this up, but you are asking to adopt our niece, and we should know you better." Albert smiled at me, and I knew it was hard for him to ask tough questions.

"What about her religious training?" Theodore asked. "Gus has told us you do not go to church."

"I would make sure that Maggie continued attending Saint Louis, and if necessary, I would go with her."

"But going to church on Sunday isn't really enough, is it? Faith is reinforced at home in everyday living. Surely you can understand that," Marie added.

I had no defense. Looking at it from their eyes, I was indeed a virtual stranger. In their world, relationships were built on experiences and trust. I *had* rushed in from nowhere. They *didn't* know me. *Couldn't* know me. To them, I was an impetuous young woman with an unknown history and unknown resources. I had to admit I was all those things. So anxious to belong, I had charged in and unconsciously pushed my way into their family and reality. Were my reasons for wanting Maggie just a selfish desire to be needed? Was I thinking of her welfare or mine? I suddenly saw myself as they must, and I didn't like it. I felt exposed and vulnerable.

Gus came then and sat close to me.

"I'll tell you what I see," he began. "Desiree had lost everything and came here to make a new life in Nova Scotia. You all want to burden her with our grief when the facts are she saved Leoni and Maggie when the wolf was at the door. Her motives were pure, yet we are punishing her for them. She loves Maggie and loved Leoni. And…" He paused and took my hand. "And I love *her.*"

There was a collective gasp for no other reason than this sort of declaration rarely occurred in their culture. I gasped too.

"I didn't say she loves *me*. I am only saying that my feelings for her are on the table, and if you bully her, I will defend her."

The room was silent. I could hear the kitchen clock ticking. Finally, Theodore broke the stillness.

"We all admire her for her kindness," Theodore said. "I'm so sorry if we were unkind. Did you say you loved her?" He cocked his head and smiled at his son.

Gus smiled.

In the end, we all decided that Maggie should live at home with me and I would be her guardian, as Leoni had wished, but the adoption should wait a year. This way we could all move forward with clear heads not clouded by grief.

Maggie came home with me, sad and baffled by her mother's absence. Death was a concept for adults, not a Down syndrome child. She looked for her mother everywhere.

"Is she hiding?"

"No, darling girl. Mommy is with us in our hearts, but her body is gone. You can still talk to her, but you can't see her."

"When I die, will I see her then? Grandma says I will."

"I think you should believe her."

After I tucked Maggie into bed, Priscilla curled her calico body into the hollow behind Maggie's knees and settled in for the night.

I stoked the fire in the sitting room, made a cup of tea, and Rocky and I snuggled before the flames in Leoni's chair. A bottomless sadness flickered in the fire, as if the only warmth to be had were the flames. I felt cold and empty. The pain of all those I had lost before had been laced with anger, but this loss was purely pain. Would I never learn to distance myself and shield my heart fully?

Gus's declaration at the Leblancs' earlier had stirred a cluster of emotions at the time: shock, embarrassment, humor, gratefulness, and something else. Was it love I felt? Could it be, or was I just feeling picked on and he had come to my rescue? One thing was for certain, I loved how safe he made me feel.

I finished my tea and started a letter to Bidwell:

> *Dear Bidwell,*
>
> *It was so very good to hear your voice when we spoke last. I miss you and your strong presence in my new life.*
>
> *Thank you for settling the bill from the Mayo Clinic. I'm sure it was a whopper. I understand they sent it to you directly (probably didn't want to take a chance on a Canadian check). It was for a friend who was suffering from, and has since died of, cancer...a tragic loss, and I miss her.*
>
> *Of course, I can't tell you where I am, but know I am happy and maybe even in love. Imagine me—angry, vengeful me—in love.*
>
> *I am hoping to come home one day.*
> *Regards, Quil*
> *PS...don't forget to destroy this letter.*

PART SIX

And right from the start I knew you were the one,
You make it easier to walk these days than run.
—"Waterbound" by The Fretless

CHAPTER 61

LOOKING FOR SPRING

Annapolis Royal, Nova Scotia
March 1963

As the winter passed, Gus and I spent most evenings together with Maggie and the pets.

I decided to keep the bakery closed for the winter, the truth being I couldn't face "business as usual." Without Leoni, the heart of the business had gone, and I began to think of alternatives.

With Gus's help, I closed up the carriage house and moved into the house with Maggie, turning the upstairs sitting room back into a bedroom.

Evenings were spent before the fire doing homework or playing board games, and Gus had dinner with us most nights after work. We were beginning to look and feel like a family, and I wasn't sure how that felt—on one hand comforting and the other premature.

When Maggie and the cat went into bed, Gus and I got to know each other. An inch at a time, we asked each other questions, and slowly the answers came out, at least answers about beliefs and personal preferences. All my big truths stayed as secret as stone.

I was falling in love with Gus, and Gus fell more deeply in love with me. When he kissed me, I felt a surge of longing for something I had never experienced—something I never knew existed. I was twenty-seven, and though I had loved, I had never fallen head over heels in love until now. It should have felt natural, but I was still hiding.

Being in love was going to complicate my life in ways I hadn't planned on. I couldn't move on to the inevitable, take the next step, get married, without coming clean about who I really was and what had happened to me, what I had done. Why I couldn't have children haunted me. How had I let our relationship come this far without telling him *that? Oh, and by the way, I was raped and had an abortion that left me sterile.*

By the time the first signs of spring appeared, I knew I was going to have to tell him the truth and nothing but the truth—so help me God— or something.

Maggie insisted she wanted to see "the big tide" she had heard about in school, so on the Saturday before her birthday, we drove up to Aunt Marie's for lunch and then over to Wolfville to watch the tidal bore roll in. It wasn't quite as ferocious as the tide's impact on the Shubenacadie River farther into the Bay of Fundy, but it was still a shocking event.

I looked at my watch and then the tide timetable I had picked up at the tackle shop. "Just about four minutes and you are going to see something really special."

The words were hardly out of my mouth when a low rumbling sounded from the west.

"What's that?" Maggie leaned into me.

"I think it's the tidal bore coming. Excited?"

"No. Why is it growling at us?"

"It's not growling, honey. It's just water moving really fast."

At that moment, the wave came into view in the distance. "Look, Maggie, here it comes!"

Instead of her being fascinated, the rushing water terrified her. For a moment, she froze as the wave approached, and then she ran toward the truck screaming.

I chased after her. "Maggie, don't be afraid!"

Before I reached her, she was in the truck and had locked the doors.

Begging her to unlock a door did no good. She looked straight ahead, eyes wide, still screaming.

I could see the keys dangling in the ignition. All I could do was wait for her to calm down.

I begged and cajoled, my face close to the passenger window, but she wouldn't budge. Not wanting to reward her behavior with bribery, I waited nearly an hour before giving in, long after the wave had passed and the bay was full but settled.

Finally, I threw my hands in the air. "I'm going to Aunt Marie's to have ice cream. See you later," I called over my shoulder.

I hadn't walked more than twenty feet when the truck door opened and she got out.

"I want ice cream too."

"Good, but it's a long way. We better drive."

"Okay."

Inside the truck, I said, "Maggie, why did that scare you so badly?"

"It just did. I didn't like it. It's a monster that growls and eats people."

"Oh, honey, it doesn't eat people. Why do you think that?"

She didn't answer.

"It's all right that you didn't like it, but the next time you get scared, give me the keys before you lock the doors, okay?"

"Okay."

On March 4, we celebrated Maggie's tenth birthday and my twenty-eighth. The LeBlanc clan put on the usual potluck feed, and I made dessert. As per Maggie's instruction, I made a rich dark chocolate sheet cake with blue buttercream frosting. "Happy Birthday to Us" written in pink finished our creation.

Everyone was there: all the aunts and uncles, their spouses and children. Theodore and the boys hand cranked vanilla ice cream while Annabelle and the girls laid out the feast: roast pork with roasted potatoes, candied carrots, butter beans, corn bread with molasses, home-canned peaches and pears, cucumbers, and cabbage slaw. We ate like polite hogs at a trough.

As the evening came on, there was cake with ice cream, music, and dancing. It had been a wonderful day. Even if it wasn't truly my birthday, I enjoyed it like it was.

Maggie stayed the night with her grandparents. Gus drove me home, and I put on the kettle for tea. I brought in the tray. Gus and Rocky were sitting on the sofa, and I joined them. I reached for the teapot.

"Wait," Gus said.

"Why?"

"Because I have something to ask you." He took a small box from his jeans pocket.

No. No. No, my brain screamed. *You can't ask me because I'm not me.*

He opened the box and said, "Marry me?"

There it was, a lovely filigree ring with a single diamond set inside. I stared at it and swallowed.

"Gus, before I say yes, and I really want to say yes, I need to tell you a long story." I felt nauseous. *Would he still want me?*

"What is it, Desiree? You're pale."

I sat back and gathered my thoughts. *Get it over with and let him go.*

"First of all, my name is not Desiree."

I watched his face as the whole story tumbled out in layer after shocking layer. When I came to the part about the rape, the abortion, and my sterility, I began to cry and so did he. He pulled me close, and we held each other for a long time.

I showed him my well-hidden scar, and he laid a hand over it. "I am sorry your life has been so hard. You had to carry this secret all alone, but, Rae, none of it affects how I feel about you."

"You might want to think it over, Gus. We won't be able to have children, and I am a murderer." I buried my face in my hands. Rocky pushed up against my hip and whined. "It's okay, buddy. It will be okay." I pulled Rocky into my lap and stroked his head.

"Desiree, look at me."

I looked up.

"You are everything I've ever wanted. We can dig through your past together a little at a time. As for children, well, we have Maggie, and if you wanted, we could adopt."

"How can you be so logical about all this? I think you're in shock and tomorrow you will come to your senses."

"No, I won't."

"Oh, and by the way, we share the same birthday. The real date is October 12."

"Now that's a serious problem. I don't know if sharing my birthday is something I am willing to do."

I slugged him in the arm, and Rocky growled.

"So now what? The reason I'm Desiree and not Quil is that hideous man who is looking for me. If I tell all to your family—oh my Lord, your *family!*" I started to cry again. "If he finds me, he will kill me," I blubbered. "And all of you will be in danger."

"Why does anyone else have to know? You can still be Desiree, and nobody has to know anything else." He took my hand and slipped the ring on my finger.

"There is one more thing," I said. "I'm rich. Really rich."

CHAPTER 62
THE BURGLAR

Miami, Florida
January 1963

On January 21, Bidwell Canfield took off his suit coat and hung it over the back of his desk chair.

"Cathy, messages?"

"Yes, I'll be right in."

He noticed there was unopened mail on his desk and reached for it as Loretta came in.

"Here are your messages," she said, handing him a small stack of yellow while-you-were-out slips of paper. "Shall we go over your appointments for the day?"

"Please." Bidwell flipped through his mail while she spoke.

"Ten o'clock is Lawson Smith, then lunch with the Linton Corporation board members. Two o'clock is Roberta Jones…"

"I don't think I can face her on a Monday."

"Shall I reschedule?"

"No. Might as well get it over with."

"Three thirty is Thomas Walton, five o'clock is cocktails with Chuck Lewis."

"Is that all for today?"

"That's it."

"Good. I'm not feeling well. I think I am coming down with a cold."

Loretta headed for the door. "Oh, and security called earlier and mentioned that the alarms were sprung sometime during the night, but there was no evidence of a break-in. They figure it must have been a power outage."

"I don't like the sound of that. Let's stay on top of it for a day or two."

"Anything else?"

"Not for now. Thank you."

In the stack of mail was a letter postmarked Halifax, Nova Scotia. It was from Quil. He scanned the page, then put it back into its envelope and slipped it into his suit coat to read at home. His throat felt scratchy, and he was getting a headache.

In the file marked client checks, he removed the bill from the Mayo Clinic with a copy of the Thunderbird, Inc. check stapled to it. Bidwell folded this and put it inside his suit coat next to the letter.

He sneezed and felt warm. He loosened his tie and unfastened his collar button. He began to sweat.

"Loretta, do we have any aspirin?"

"I don't think so. Shall I go out and get some?"

"No, I think you should cancel my appointments for today at least. I feel like a wreck. I think I should go home."

"All right, but let me get you to sign a few documents before you go."

"I'll come out."

"You look terrible. That sure came on fast."

"We had company for the weekend, and the little boy was sick. I suspect I got this from him."

"Okay, just sign these three letters and initial these two documents."

He was feeling worse by the minute, sweating, his head pounding.

"I really need to go." He turned toward the elevator.

"Call when you get home," Loretta called after him.

Bidwell raised a hand in acknowledgment. He was home in bed before he realized he had left without his suit coat.

"Cathy," he croaked into the phone. "I left my suit coat behind. Could you please put it in the closet in my office and lock the door?"

"Attached to it, are you?"

"Very funny. I'll call you in a couple days."

That night the building alarm went off at 1:30 a.m. and again at 2:45. Both were investigated by security and the Miami Police.

"You better get this system serviced," a policeman told the security guard on duty.

"Will do. What a pain in the neck."

After the police left, the security guard pulled the fuse on the alarm system and made a note for the day shift to have it repaired.

At 4:00 a.m., a man wearing dark clothing and gloves removed the lock blocker he had placed in a side door at the 2:45 alarm failure. The guard was reading a newspaper when the burglar silently slipped past.

He took the stairs to the fourteenth floor and jimmied the lock on the Canfield and Associates glass doors. Once inside, he worked swiftly and neatly, looking through desks and thumbing through file cabinets, looking for clues.

In Bidwell Canfield's office, he paid particular attention to the unopened mail on his desk, popping the desk locks and rifling through the desk, being careful to return everything to its place.

The file cabinet gave up nothing. There was an innocuous file with Tranquil Tandy's name on it, but it contained no useful information.

The man scanned the room, and his eyes fell on the closet, and he found it locked. To his way of thinking, locked doors were locked for a reason. Inside he found a raincoat, three fresh dress shirts, and a suit coat. Just to be thorough, he checked the pockets of the raincoat and closed the door, but instinct told him to check the suit coat as well. And there was the prize.

CHAPTER 63

ON THE RUN

Nashville, Tennessee
January 1963

At the end of January, Fletcher met with his consistently semicorrupt lawyer, who gave him an accounting of the investigation of Tranquil Tandy.

"We think she is in Nova Scotia. Our contact found a letter and an enormous medical bill from the Mayo Clinic paid by Thunderbird, Inc. We are not sure if the two are connected, but they *were* found together. The letter was posted from Halifax."

"Send me somebody who can help me get out of here."

"I told you I wasn't doing anything illegal that is going to include big prison time."

"Send me somebody who can."

The following week a man posing as an attorney arrived to visit Fletcher.

"I need a passport—my face, different name."

"What name?"

"I don't care, and I will need matching ID, like a driver's license, a

plane ticket to Halifax for the date I will give you, and a ride to the airport in Nashville. It should be a night flight."

"I can do all that, but money first."

"Bill my attorney for services like money management or estate planning, something legitimate sounding. He knows to pay it. Then get on
with it. I want out of here," Fletcher growled. "How long will it take?"

"A month at least. I'll come back in two weeks, and you better be
ready with all the final details."

Bidwell Canfield was out of the office for a week. He had the flu and felt
too miserable to work. But on the following Monday he returned to the
office and unlocked the closet where he had hidden Quil's information.
To his horror, he found Quil's letter and the clinic bill gone.

He paced around the office, desperate to understand what had happened. He spoke to security and heard the story of the alarm system
malfunction. He called in an expert to examine all the locks, who found
expert tampering. He had the police check for fingerprints, but they
found none other than those that should be there.

Bidwell felt certain that the break-in, done by a professional, had
to be Fletcher's doing. He had no way of warning Quil. Though there
had been no return address on Quil's letter, the postal stamp had been
from Halifax. All he could do was hope she had not mailed it from the
town where she lived. She was in terrible danger, and he could do nothing to help her. Even hiring a private investigator was traceable and too
dangerous.

Fletcher laid out the escape plan in careful detail and ran it over and
over in his mind like a continuous loop film.

He had noticed that the shift change seemed a little loose on the
first and fifteenth of each month—paydays. Just enough distraction that

details might be overlooked. Paydays in March both fell on Friday, which was a perfect day to disappear. The airports would be busy, and he could dissolve into the crowds.

Fletcher chose March 15.

As planned, his fake attorney arrived after two weeks, ready for dates and times.

The man got his instructions and Fletcher got his.

"The person who picks you up outside the south gate will have all your documents. Goodbye, and good luck."

Fletcher had chosen the south gate because it would be shadowed from the yard lights. Now all he had to do was be calm and change nothing about his habits and conversation.

On the morning of March 15, when the door in Fletcher's room automatically unlocked for the day, he discreetly slid the knitting needle heads he had painstakingly fashioned to fit into the notch in the doorjamb where the dead bolt was designed to slide. The needle heads were not exactly the same color as the jamb, but Fletcher hoped nobody would take notice.

That evening Fletcher had dinner in the dining room as usual. He played cards with other patients as usual. He took his meds as usual, and he spit them out as usual. He went to bed at ten o'clock like everyone else. The door closed, and the locking mechanism clicked, but the dead bolt failed to engage. Lights out happened automatically at 10:15, and a guard passed by, looking in the window at Fletcher's prostrate body lying peacefully in bed.

At 10:45, Fletcher got up and dressed, then fashioned a lumpy imitation of himself in the bed with all his extra clothing.

At 10:50, shift change began by floor. Fletcher's room was on the second floor. At 10:55, Fletcher quietly opened the door to his room and quietly closed it, silently walked to the stairs, and descended. He pushed the stairwell door open on the first floor and slowly inched along the wall toward a side door he had jammed with knitting needle points earlier in the day. No alarm sounded as the door opened because no dead bolt had been compromised after lockdown. Outside, Fletcher followed the shadows to the south gate and slithered under it. The car was waiting, and he got in. The driver did not speak, just pushed a bundle his way. Fletcher changed clothes in the car as they drove to the airport.

At the airport, the driver pulled up to the appropriate gate. Fletcher got out, and the car drove away. He looked at his watch. It was 11:35, and his flight was leaving at midnight. He calmly walked into the men's room and into a stall, where he opened the bundle.

There was a wallet with a Georgia driver's license and two thousand Canadian dollars. His new passport had the same photo as his last with the name of John Smith.

"You have to be kidding. John Smith?" Fletcher muttered.

Fletcher put the wallet in a hip pocket, slipped the plane ticket inside his passport, and headed to the flight gate.

The plane lifted off on time. It was all going unbelievably well. When the plane landed in Halifax, the last hurdle would be customs. If he made it through, he was free. John Smith and Fletcher Pickford would evaporate into freedom and a delicious quest for revenge.

CHAPTER 64
THE ENGAGEMENT

Annapolis Royal, Nova Scotia
April 1963

The LeBlancs took the news of the engagement with their usual exuberance, though Theodore worried about my lack of religious commitment.

To Gus, his father said quietly, "I don't approve of you marrying Desiree with no agreed-upon faith. It's not a good start."

"Dad, have a little *faith*. God is working on her, and I believe with all my heart she will come around."

"Maybe she will come around to the Catholic side." Theodore smirked.

Theodore drew me aside next. "At least go to church with Gus. If you are going to marry him, don't be one of those families where one spouse goes alone."

I agreed to do as he asked. I knew that my beliefs, or lack of, were troubling to Gus. If I was going to be his wife, the very least I could do would be to pretend to believe as he did.

Gus attended the Hillsburn United Baptist Church in Granville Ferry. I asked to go with him the next Sunday, and he seemed pleasantly surprised. He was proud to walk his new fiancée into the little church. I had been raised in a church just like this one, and I felt comfortable with the service, though not the message, one on forgiveness. I bet Pastor Lawson found forgiveness easy, and I bet he didn't have much to forgive in his life. Forgiving wasn't anything I was going to do any time soon.

In fact, during the service my thoughts wandered Fletcher's way. I savored the idea of Fletcher drugged and miserable, incarcerated in a mental hospital. I imagined the smooth, sleek predator reduced to a simpering, fragile victim of the system.

Yes, they would let him go eventually, but would he be so damaged he wouldn't even care about me anymore? That was my hope, but I wasn't going to bet my life on it. One thing for sure, I would never forgive him.

After church and all the welcoming, hand shaking, and congratulations, we stopped for lunch: thick clam chowder and crusty bread.

Gus reached across the table and took my hand. He turned my engagement ring slowly with his thumb.

"I love you," he whispered. "And I thank you for coming to church with me."

"I love you too. I didn't want you to be going to church alone any longer."

"Does this mean you are changing your thinking about God?"

"Maybe. God *did* finally give me something good." I kissed him. "*However*, that message on forgiveness is still garbage."

"Sure of that, are you?"

"It's just church mumbo jumbo for 'let's sweep it all under the rug and pretend it never happened.'"

"You know, for a smart woman, you can say some incredibly dumb things."

"Really? Then explain it to me, Your Wiseness."

"Okay, well, here is my definition of forgiveness. When we forgive someone who, as in your case, has done unspeakable damage, we do two things. First, the pain and anger in ourselves is released. God removes it so far away you can never see it again. Then, in pain and anger's place, God puts seeds of peace and hope that grow into lush versions of themselves over time. Does that make sense?"

"Maybe. Go on." I stirred my tea.

"Secondly, when you forgive, the huge sin brought on by the offender is released, and God begins a new work in that person—a need to ask God for forgiveness as well as the person victimized."

"And I suppose you have proof of this amazing sermon."

"I do. I can drag my Bible out to show you, or I can just tell you."

"I'll take your word for it."

"All through the gospels of the New Testament, during Jesus's three years in ministry, he performed inconceivable miracles. He healed the blind, the crippled, the chronically sick, and he did so in the same way each time."

"Which was?"

"First Jesus told them that if they believed, he could heal them. Then he forgave their sins. And *then* he healed them."

"So how does this apply to me?"

"You believe that Jesus can heal you. You forgive your offender, and then *you* are healed."

"Interesting. Something to chew on," I said, taking an exaggerated bite of crusty bread. "So why didn't this God of yours heal your sister who believed in him? Or my brother who believed? Or my mom and dad who believed and died so young? What about that?"

"I don't have answers for any of that. God does things we can't possibly understand for reasons only he knows. What *I* know is that everything that happens to us in this carnal life, both good and bad, happens for our eventual benefit and growth."

"You can't possibly believe that."

"I do. Let's look at your life path. Don't you think it's possible that God was hanging on to you by the single thread you allowed Him in order to reel you in? You were raised in the church but walked away. You had parents and grandparents praying that you would come back. But you got a stiff neck and refused, right?"

"Right," I had to admit.

"God kept knocking on your heart's door. Your mom died—knock, knock. Your grandparents died—knock, knock. The rape—knock,

knock. Your dad died—knock, knock. Then your brother's murder and this terrible Fletcher character who drove you to Canada and to me. Can't you see that everything happens for a reason?"

I drank my tea in silence, thinking. "Are you saying that God let everyone I love die to get my attention? I rest my case. God is a jerk."

"I did not say that. The people you loved and the events that occurred happened at their appointed times, but God used it all to draw you toward him—in a sense break you, make you need Him."

"You *really* believe that?" I was feeling a bit irritated now.

"I do. Events in life, both good and bad, have a ripple effect—like a stone thrown into calm water. The initial entry of the stone into the water is a single blip, but the chain reaction moves water far out from the source. Little waves moving everything near them."

"Interesting. You are so poetic. Let's talk about something else. I've been thinking," I said.

"Don't hurt yourself." Gus laughed.

"Oh, ha ha. So very funny." I sipped my tea. "I have decided to hire somebody to run the bakery. I have no heart for it now. Or maybe sell it and buy something else—together—you and I."

"That's something to consider."

"Here is the thing. If I hire somebody to just run the bakery, I might have to do some sort of tricky employee/employer arrangement. Live-in would be ideal, but then Maggie and I would be back in my tiny cottage—not a good plan. It was perfect for one person but not two. At any rate, I have to do something. I can't just turn a blind eye and ignore the investment," I explained.

"I see what you're saying. What do you really want to do?"

"If I had to say right now, I'd say sell. What's your opinion?" I asked.

"I can't say. It's your place and investment, and whatever you decide is what I think is best."

"What a wimp."

"Thank you." He smiled.

CHAPTER 65

HIDING OUT

Halifax, Nova Scotia
March–June 1963

F letcher found a quiet place to live where he could be invisible, unremarkable, while the search for him died down. For the first few weeks, he relished his freedom and spent long hours relaxing into his new life.

He laughed at how the police would question poor old LilaJune when they found the bits of knitting needle jammed in every door that had stood in his way between imprisonment and freedom. Foolish woman. Did she actually think that she could undo the terror of his childhood by talking about Jesus?

His plan was simple. Assimilate, search, and destroy. When he found her, he would do all the things he had been dreaming of. Her body would never be found, and he would never be seen. Then he would disappear in Canada for as many years as it took to be a closed case. He still had lots of money, which was being moved to various banks in Canada. He could hide out forever.

He had left no clues. Now as John Smith, he became one of many. He cut and colored his hair, gained a few pounds, and changed how he dressed. Jeans and casual shirts were now his normal attire, which made him appear more like a local. Of course, he had a telltale Southern accent, and his French, though perfect, was unmistakably well-schooled

Parisian. For this reason, he rarely spoke to anyone. He watched and listened, his eyes and ears like antenna, alert for any woman who sounded different or appeared familiar.

An account at the Maritime Bank in Halifax had been opened in his new name with a balance of fifty thousand dollars.

He bought a nondescript used car. Having no experience in dealing with used car salesmen, he unfortunately ended up with a lemon.

The car locked without warning when any door was opened, then closed. Fletcher learned quickly to never leave the car without the keys in hand. Also, the transmission had issues, the biggest problem being the car would slip out of park unexpectedly. He discovered on the first day to set the parking brake when the car was stopped. It was as if the car was possessed, and Fletcher took it personally, often kicking and swearing at it.

Fletcher sat in public places and worked on his accent. His smooth Southern voice had to go. He spoke in public places as little as possible, all the while listening to the local dialect.

Months passed as Fletcher moved, quietly searching for his prey, looking at records of sale: real estate, automobiles, businesses, utilities. He spent hours at the library poring over anything that might point to her. Certainly, she would have changed her name, maybe even her appearance. If he was now John Smith, Tranquil Tandy could be anybody.

It became a frustrating and unfulfilling game. If she was indeed in Halifax, then spotting her would be the only way. After all, he was stuck here until he found her, but all this searching was giving him purpose.

Fletcher staked out the main grocery stores and gas stations. Nothing. Restaurants and clothing stores. Still nothing.

After two months, he felt safe enough to expand his search, driving all along the coastal towns west and east of Halifax. By now, he had masked his Southern accent and began asking questions about the woman he was searching for.

He headed north to Antigonish and Truro, where a waitress told him about the tidal bore. He drove to the bridge over the Shubenacadie River and stood with a dozen strangers as the tide roared in, more than twelve feet tall, roiling and swallowing everything in the riverbed. He was awestruck. The absolute power of the water moved deeply inside him. He closed his eyes and faced the sky as a silent roar filled his chest.

Back in Halifax, Fletcher researched the tidal phenomenon, and he studied its effects at different points along the Bay of Fundy.

After a few days, he headed out again, this time north on Highway 101, stopping at Wolfville for lunch. The tidal bore, due in an hour, inspired him to stay to watch it. The impact, not as ferocious as it had been before, was still very impressive. Fletcher stood on a bluff above the bay as the water rushed in barely a foot below him; the power of it sparked again a long-lost stimulation.

On the way home, Fletcher stopped at a local bar where, after a drink or two, became friendly with a woman sitting near him. He could feel the old need to dominate churn inside his chest. The woman was inebriated and loose, and Fletcher knew if he left the bar with her how it would all end. *Too expensive.* He threw back his drink and left the bar, but he felt angry and agitated. Halifax was turning into a dead end.

The next morning he drove back to Wolfville to watch the tidal bore again and after took a room at a little inn at Grand-Pré. He removed the keys but forgot the parking brake. The car began to roll, and Fletcher had to scramble to unlock the door, slide inside, and stuff a foot on the brake. *That's it. I'm getting rid of this car.*

Inside the inn a friendly woman greeted him. "Welcome. *Bienvenue.* Shall we speak English or French?" Marie Arsenault said to her new guest.

CHAPTER 66

THE NEW HOUSE

Annapolis Royal, Nova Scotia
June 1963

The date for the wedding was set for June 29, almost a year to the day when Danny and Libby had tied the knot. I felt a stab of regret at the thought, wondering if I would ever see them again.

I had decided to sell the bakery, and Gus agreed with me. It was only on the market for a month when a young couple from Truro made a reasonable offer. We would close the deal by June 1, and we—Maggie, Gus, and I—began to look for another home in earnest, finally deciding on a larger, four-bedroom Cape Cod in Grandville Ferry. Set back from the road, it had a beautiful front garden and a large backyard. But best of all it had a terrific view of Annapolis Royal and was close to the river. The house, painted a pale lemony yellow with creamy white trim, seemed warm and welcoming. I imagined it to be a bright ray of sunshine on gray winter days. We bought it on the spot.

At our usual Saturday kitchen party, Annabelle took me aside.

"I want to show you something," she said, taking my hand and leading me down the hall to her bedroom.

Lying across the bed was a wedding dress.

"Don't think that I am pushing it on you, but if you like it, I would love for you to wear it. It was my mother's. I was too tall to wear it, and the girls aren't interested. Grand-mère was about your height and shape. I just thought…"

"Like it? I love it! How like you to be so generous, Annabelle."

"Wonderful." She smiled. "Come by tomorrow, and you can try it on when Gus isn't around."

The next day I stopped by the LeBlancs' for lunch. Annabelle was hanging delicate white sheers in the living room windows.

"Are those new?"

"I ordered them from Quebec, and Theodore has been grumbling all morning about what I spent."

"Wasteful, if you ask me."

Annabelle rolled her eyes, and I giggled.

"They really are lovely, Annabelle." I ran a hand over them admiringly. "What's for lunch?"

"Jam sandwiches." Theodore said this as if he were being denied choices more delicious.

"Yum! My favorite," I said, patting Theodore on the cheek.

After lunch, Annabelle and I took a stab at fitting me into the wedding dress. It was a little tight, but Annabelle was sure she could alter it just enough to fit me.

I looked at myself in the full-length mirror, admiring the lace and workmanship of both the design and detail. The dress, a creamy ivory, had long sleeves. The sleeves were made in a sheer lace design with a bodice of lined matching lace and a sheer peplum waist. Hundreds of tiny seed pearls were sewn into the pattern. The neckline was high, perfect for hiding my scar, and a small cameo decorated the center of the sheer collar. The skirt was made of smooth ivory satin with lace along the hem. The dress had a matching chapel-length, lace-trimmed tulle veil. I looked beautiful and feminine in the delicate veil, and I unexpectedly teared up. Annabelle did too.

"The dress and veil were made in Paris. A family friend sent it to Mother for her wedding. In its day, this dress was a grand luxury."

"It still is. Thank you, Annabelle. It's perfect."

She measured me for alterations and said she would have it ready in a week. It was June 8.

"But why me? You have four daughters."

"My girls are built like their parents, tall and strong. None of them would fit into this dress, but it is perfect for you, my darling Desiree."

Gus and I began painting inside the new house on the following Monday. Maggie, of course, wanted pink for her bedroom, and Gus wanted a warm, rich, mossy green for ours.

Gus brought the brothers in and completely remodeled the kitchen—new cabinets, countertops, and flooring. I chose a color scheme to match the one that Daddy and I had used to redo the kitchen in Tennessee—blue tile counters, buttercream yellow walls, and white cabinets.

It was ready for move in by June 21. Once again, the brothers kicked into high gear and moved our belongings from Gus's house and mine. Gus moved himself into his parents' house until the wedding, and Maggie and I moved into our new home.

It was all too perfect.

On June 23, I tried on my newly altered wedding dress. Perfect.

I was getting married. Actually getting married to a man who truly loved me and I him. A year ago I couldn't have imagined any of this. A year ago I was a victim, lost and afraid, but now on top of the world.

It was all too perfect.

CHAPTER 67
THE FIND

Annapolis Royal, Nova Scotia
June 1963

"Good morning," Marie sang out as she served Fletcher his breakfast. Of course, *she* knew him as John Smith.

As was her nature to be friendly and each time she brought more food or filled his coffee cup, she asked questions. "John, are you an American?"

"No, Canadian."

"Really? Western Canada, correct?"

"Yes."

"How odd."

"Why?"

"Because my brother is marrying a young woman who moved here last year from Alberta."

Fletcher was suddenly interested. "What is her name? Perhaps I know her?"

"Desiree d'Moss...soon to be LeBlanc."

"No. I don't know a Desiree."

"Where are you heading today?"

"Yarmouth."

"Well, on your way, you simply must stop in Annapolis Royal. There

385

is a bakery there that serves the freshest of treats. It would be worth a stop." Marie smiled.

Fletcher left Grand-Pré and continued along the northern shore. At Annapolis Royal, he planned to stop for lunch and then move on to Yarmouth for a few days.

"The best pastries in all of Nova Scotia," Marie had said.

Following Route 1, Fletcher drove through all the little towns, into Grandville Ferry, and over the bridge to Annapolis Royal. He parked across from the bakery.

"Hello," a young woman greeted him.

"Someone in Grand-Pré said you made the best pastries in all of Nova Scotia. Is that true?"

"Well, I would like to think so, but we are just getting started. We bought this place two weeks ago from a young woman who is getting married," the young woman rattled on as she filled Fletcher's order. "She has a Down syndrome child."

"How sad."

"Doesn't appear to be. She adopted her."

"Sounds like someone I used to know. What does she look like?"

"Dark hair and very fit. She is a runner. Her name is Desiree d'Moss."

The hair on Fletcher's neck rose, and an excited shiver rolled up his spine. He tried not to seem interested, but she had his attention. Could this really be? Surely not. Tranquil Tandy was *minus* an idiot, not *plus* one. *Maybe she collects them.*

"Is she still local?"

"Oh, yes. In fact, she and her fiancé just bought a house in Grandville Ferry. It's the yellow one on the right. Here you go…ham and cheese on sourdough, sugar cookie, and coffee."

I hung my wedding dress on the closet door, admired it for a long moment, and looked at the clock. Maggie would be home from school in an hour. I trotted downstairs to start supper and noticed a car I hadn't seen before parked across the road. I shivered and wondered why, but while I was thinking, the phone rang.

"Hi, Desiree, the school bus has broken down again. You'll have to pick Maggie up," Miss Foster, Maggie's teacher, said.

"That's not a problem. I'll be by at two thirty. Thanks for letting me know."

I went back to the window, but the car was gone. I put a chicken in the oven and chopped vegetables for salad, peeled apples, and rolled out pastry dough for pie crust. Gus was coming for dinner, and he liked apple pie.

At around two fifteen, I drove into town to pick up Maggie and made a quick stop by the bakery for bread.

"Hi, Desiree. There was a man in here just about an hour ago who thought he might know you."

My knees felt weak, and instinctive fear swept through me. I tried to sound calm. "Oh, really, did he leave a name?"

"No, but he seemed very nice. He didn't recognize *your* name."

"What did he look like?"

"Dark hair, not real tall, a little fleshy. Said he was just passing through."

Fear instantly threw a red flag up whenever anyone asked about me, but I was so completely happy with my present life, I dismissed the stranger. He didn't sound like anyone I knew.

I picked up Maggie, and we headed home, her chattering away about school and I looking at every passing car. I saw only the usual vehicles and people. *Shake it off.*

At home, I put the pie in the oven and took the chicken out to rest while Maggie and Rocky played in the backyard. Priscilla came through, giving my leg a friendly rub on the way to her dish. *See, everything as usual.*

Gus arrived promptly at six o'clock and, as usual, said grace before dinner. *Relax, nothing has changed.*

In Gus's presence, I was safe. Soon we would be married, and he would be here always. Maggie and I would be safe always.

The next day Maggie left for school and I started painting in the living room. An elegant blue-gray color slid over the old paint as smooth as cream over custard. *Maybe I should order a set of Annabelle's window sheers for this room.*

I liked painting—instant gratification—and I worked hard to get it finished before supper. By two o'clock, I had finished the first coat and trotted upstairs to wash up. *Meatloaf and mashed potatoes for dinner and peas. Don't forget peas. Maggie loves peas.*

I stopped to admire my gorgeous wedding dress, imagining myself in it and Gus looking at me. With hands on hips, I swayed side to side and hummed.

When the bedroom door slammed shut, I spun around. A very different-looking Fletcher stood there with his back against the door, dark and fleshy, but the cold gray eyes were the same. I made a dash for the bedroom window, but he tripped me.

He dropped what he was holding and lunged at me. His thumbs on my throat pressed hard against my windpipe. I kicked and clawed at him, but he didn't flinch; he just pressed harder. The room swam, and I knew I was losing consciousness.

I came to, my wrists duct-taped together and hung over the bathroom door. My ankles were taped together, too, the tips of my toes barely touching the floor. My throat ached, and hanging this way made it hard to breathe.

Fletcher had a long, thin knife in his hand, and he eyed me like a butcher preparing to carve a beef.

"Oh, good, you're awake. I didn't want to start without you."

"Please, don't let it all end this way," I begged. "Run. Disappear. I won't tell anyone you were here."

"You are such a stupid woman. Do you think I would give up this time with you? I've dreamed of it."

Fletcher walked over to my wedding dress hanging on the closet door.

"You won't be needing this." He smiled at me and flashed the blade toward the dress.

"Don't, please don't!" I cried.

"Say it again. I like to hear you beg."

"Please, I am begging you."

With a wicked grin, he took hold of the skirt, stuck in the knife, and ripped a great, long gash through the satin. He threw the dress on the floor and laughed at my horrified face.

"So, Miss Tandy, how did that make you feel?"

Hot tears ran down my cheeks as I faced what I assumed would be the inevitable.

Fletcher walked slowly toward me, waving the blade back and forth, never taking his eyes off mine. Now his face was close, and he licked a tear from my cheek. I could do nothing to repel him. He grabbed my shirt and ripped it open.

"Well, look here. Someone has already been at you." He traced my scar with the knife. "Perhaps we should add one to the other side?"

The knife blade touched my other collarbone. "Shall we?"

I closed my eyes and waited to die. I could feel the blade push into my flesh and drag along my chest. It didn't feel like a deep cut, but I could smell blood.

I heard the front door open and slam shut.

"I'm home!" Maggie hollered.

I heard her feet on the stairs. Fletcher smiled and turned toward the bedroom door as it opened.

"Well, if it isn't your replacement idiot."

Maggie froze in the doorway, not understanding what she saw.

"Run, Maggie! Run away!"

She turned and started down the stairs, but Fletcher was on her in a flash, grabbing her by the hair, pushing her toward the first floor.

I could hear her screaming. Then I was screaming. "Help! Somebody, help! Maggie, I'm with you! Be brave!"

Suddenly, she stopped screaming, and I was petrified he had killed her—like he had killed Paddy.

I heard him on the stairs then. He dragged Maggie into the room by her hair. Her mouth was taped closed, her wrists were taped together, but other than terrified, she seemed unhurt.

"The idiot and I are going to take a little drive, and then I'll be back to finish what we started. Don't go anywhere." He smiled, pressing tape over my mouth, then dragging Maggie back down the stairs and out the front door. I heard it lock.

Fletcher stuffed Maggie into the passenger seat and slammed the door. He heard it lock, but for the first time, that sound felt advantageous.

He drove away from Grandville Ferry toward Wolfville, being careful not to speed or call attention to his driving.

In the beginning, Maggie cried and struggled, but each time she did so, Fletcher yelled at her and showed her the knife until finally she slumped into the seat, overcome with fear.

At Wolfville, Fletcher parked the car near the bluff where he had watched the tidal bore. What he could not know was that it was the same place where Maggie had become so frightened by the tide a few months before. She recognized it and screamed, her voice muffled by the duct tape gag.

It had taken longer than Fletcher had planned to get to this spot, but no bother, the tide wouldn't be in until 9:30 p.m., plenty of time to kill the idiot and hide her body underneath the bluff, then go back for Tranquil or Desiree or whatever her name was. By the time they were found, if they were found, he would be long gone.

Killing Maggie had no other motive than extreme emotional pain for Tranquil. Kill the idiot and then tell Tranquil all the details before he tortured her to death. Maybe he might bring a souvenir to her, say a finger or an eyeball.

I watched the clock. I had been hanging helplessly on the bathroom door for more than three hours. It was five fifteen. I couldn't feel my arms, and my throat was raw. Fletcher had cut me, but it felt more like a tease than a slash. He was going to make my misery last, that much I guessed. I could see blood on my shirt, but I wasn't bleeding much now. My arms pulled up this way had put a little pressure on the wound, and for that, I was grateful.

I hung there, powerless, in a silent house that smelled of fresh paint and once was safe but now reeked of evil, knowing that I would probably die at Fletcher's hands. That Maggie would die. Everyone I loved died. Maybe he was planning on killing Gus too. I felt myself giving up.

I was tired of running and being afraid. I couldn't do it anymore. I didn't want to do it anymore. Maybe it *was* time for me to die.

At that moment, my spirit cracked, and I finally broke. Like a ruined clay jar filled with water, I spilled out, weeping. I couldn't hold it in, and I couldn't change anything. I was trapped and defenseless, and yet another child would die because of me.

I reached out to the one who, until this moment, I had believed did not exist—the God of my youth. I prayed:

"Jesus, if you are real, I am begging you to save Maggie. Don't punish her for my stubbornness." Tears rolled down my cheeks; my body shook with anxiety and fatigue. "I am so very sorry for it—all the things I've said and done. Forgive me."

Strangely, I could feel a presence. Something peaceful and safe. I remembered my conversation with Gus about forgiveness and healing. I remembered Daddy saying that by just asking, Jesus removed our sins and remembered them no more. I heard Mama telling me that a relationship with Jesus was the most wonderful sensation when we released all to Him.

God, I have hated you for so long, I don't know how to trust you. How can you trust me? I heard Gus's voice at lunch that Sunday after church. "Jesus asked them to believe, then he forgave their sins, and then he healed them." I didn't know how to say what I felt or how to begin. *Just start,* my inner voice urged.

"Jesus, take my hatred and vengeful anger. I don't want it anymore, and I can't carry it. Do you want me to forgive Pruitt? Fletcher? I deserve to die for my sins. If that's what it takes for you to heal me, then I forgive them, even though Fletcher may kill me. I forgive him."

I thought about Michelle and her willingness to forgive Pit. She had said, "I had to forgive him, or I would never be free."

"I want to be free. God, help Maggie, and help me." Tears rolled down my face, my sobs silent.

A peace came then. Very slowly at first, but it was palpable, warm and soothing. It grew all around me like a comforting hug, a healing hand over my broken heart.

I stopped crying and listened. Someone was on the front porch, trying the locked door. Was Fletcher coming back for me? Then I heard the back gate squeak, Rocky barking, and Gus's voice greeting my dog.

I attempted a muffled scream but knew Gus would never hear me over Rocky. I dug deep, bending my knees and raising my legs. The pain was excruciating, but I kicked against the doorjamb again and again, creating what I hoped would be enough racket to attract Gus's attention.

I heard the kitchen door open. I screamed and kicked, and then I heard his feet thundering up the stairs.

CHAPTER 68

MAGGIE

Wolfville, Nova Scotia
June 23, 1963

Fletcher put the car in park, opened and closed his door. It, of course, locked. He unlocked Maggie's door and reached for her. She was hysterical now. Fletcher liked her fear, but again he could not know she wasn't afraid of *him*, she was afraid of the memory of the tidal bore.

As soon as the door was opened, Maggie threw herself out of the car and onto the ground, surprising Fletcher, who dropped the car keys as he tried to grab her. But she was having none of it.

As Fletcher reached for her, he braced his left hand on the car door post. He grabbed her hair, but Maggie kicked at him and, with all her might, kicked the car door. There was a sickening crunch as the door slammed shut so hard it completely crushed Fletcher's hand across all four knuckles. The door locked.

The pain was unbelievable. He reached into his pocket with his right hand for the keys, but to his horror, they were lying in the grass out of reach.

Maggie was crying and running for the road, the sun beginning to set.

Fletcher, his hand crushed and locked in the door, struggled frantically. It was at this moment he noticed that he had failed to engage the parking brake.

He heard the transmission click and grind, and then the car began to inch forward.

"No, no, no…" Fletcher dug in his heels, and for a second, the car stopped moving, but the slope, though gradual, was still enough to pull the car toward the edge of the bluff not more than twenty feet away.

"Help! Somebody help me!" he screamed, but the car was moving faster, dragging Fletcher along with it.

Fletcher yanked at his trapped hand, the pain not greater than his fear, but though he was willing to rip his own hand off to be free, he could not.

The car picked up speed, and Fletcher had to run along with it to keep from being dragged under the wheels. The car left the bluff, arching momentarily before crashing upright on the sandy, dry flood basin.

Fletcher was in agony, but even the fifteen-foot fall had not freed his hand, though it had broken his arm and probably his legs.

"Help! My God, somebody help me!" But there was no help. Anyone who might have heard him had long since gone home to their supper.

The sun set, and the moon did not replace it; darkness fell over Fletcher and the bay.

Maggie stumbled onto the road, where a concerned driver stopped to help her. He peeled the tape off her mouth and cut her hands free. She threw her arms around the man and sobbed.

"What are you doing out here? What happened? What is your name?" He pummeled her with questions, but Maggie was far too traumatized to speak. In fact, she couldn't speak at all.

He drove her directly to the hospital, and the hospital called the police.

Gus burst through the bedroom door and found the woman he loved hanging by her wrists, shirt ripped open, and bleeding slowly from a neat slice under her collarbone.

He peeled the tape from her mouth and cut the tape holding her on the door. She collapsed in his arms.

"Call the police! He's got Maggie!" she croaked.

"Who has Maggie?"

"Fletcher has her. Call the police!"

He left her then and ran downstairs.

"Send a police officer to fifty-four Route 1. Hurry, it's an emergency! We need an ambulance too. The front door is open," he said as he flung the front door open.

Taking the stairs two at a time, he knelt next to her on the bedroom floor. The cut on her chest had begun to bleed in earnest, and he pressed a hand over it, cutting the tape off her feet with the other.

He could hear the sirens.

"Where has he taken Maggie?"

"I don't know. I don't know," she sobbed.

The police and ambulance arrived, and Desiree was rushed off to the hospital.

"My niece, Maggie Arsenault, has been abducted by the same man who did that to Desiree," he said, pointing at the ambulance.

The officer was on the radio in a flash.

"We need an all-points bulletin. Child abduction. Maggie Arsenault. Kidnapped at around two o'clock in Grandville Ferry."

It was dark and late, and Fletcher knew it would only be a matter of an hour or so before the tidal bore would be on him. He had never experienced this kind of fear. Even as a child he knew he would survive the beatings and abuse, but this was most likely the end. The realization was paralyzing. Always in control, always the one manipulating or demanding or deceiving, he was now the one facing certain death. He could almost feel death lurking in the shadows, happily waiting to take him. He had watched fear as it devoured others and had relished it, but now it was he who was afraid: acutely, utterly afraid. Weak with it.

He thought about LilaJune and her relentless faith. Her shoving it down his throat. He remembered Dr. Mead saying, "Careful, Fletcher, fake it too far, and it can turn on you…when you start saying things or writing them, you may think you are faking it, but your brain starts to believe it all."

He remembered LilaJune telling him to ask for the truth. "You will have to pay for your sins here on earth, but no matter what you have done, God will forgive you if you ask. Just ask to know the truth."

He was weak and suffering, kneeling in the sand, no longer able to stand. "Truth," he whispered. He remembered faint childhood memories of LilaJune telling him about Jesus. "Please, if there is truth, show it to me."

He felt something then, like the earth rumbling, and figured it wasn't God. It was the tidal bore. In the darkness, Fletcher could not see it, but he could feel it coming.

"Truth," he said louder. "Tell me the truth. If you are real. Tell me! I beg you!"

If he had ever had the chance to tell his story, he would have said, "It was like a light switched on, and I knew absolutely that there was a God and he cared about me. Everything I had ever done was held up before me, and I begged for forgiveness—so deeply sorry. I felt like dirty rags, but then I felt Jesus standing with me as the wave bore down."

But Fletcher would never tell this story. Alone in the darkness, the water crashed into him like a freight train. The car tumbled like a leaf in a gale. Fletcher's body, like his sin, perished.

At around midnight, the Wolfville Police Department reported that there was a child at the hospital that matched Maggie's description, and Gus was notified at the hospital in Annapolis Royal.

He phoned Marie in Grand-Pré, and she rushed to the hospital, picked up Maggie, and took her home to the inn.

By morning, I had been stitched and rehydrated. Miraculously, I had escaped any further physical damage other than a multitude of bruises. The doctor who stitched the wound on my chest said, "Nice clean slice. In a month or two, you won't even have a scar."

Maggie still hadn't spoken a word, and that was alarming. What had she seen and lived through? What should we do? Gus left me at the hospital and went to retrieve her.

In Grand-Pré, Maggie fell into Gus's arms and held on for dear life.

"Maggie, honey, you're safe. No more bad men." He scooped her up onto his lap and cradled her. She said nothing, just held on.

"Has she eaten?" Gus asked his sister.

"Not a bite."

"Water?"

"Not a sip."

"I'm going to take her to the hospital at home in Annapolis Royal."

"I think that's best. My gosh, what happened to her?" Marie asked.

"We don't know. She was kidnapped from the house in Grandville Ferry and, as you know, is not talking."

"Did they catch the man?"

"I hope so, but we don't know for sure."

When Maggie saw me at the hospital, she crawled right into the bed with me. I held her close and spoke to her in French.

"Mon cher, tout est bien. Vous êtes en sécurité maintenant. It's all right. You are safe."

She had a drink of water, then fell asleep in my arms.

We were both released from the hospital the next day, and I worried she would never go into our new house again. She *did* hesitate on the porch, but Gus took her hand, and she walked in on her own. Together, we checked every room, every closet, every corner. Rocky and Priscilla greeted her like she had been gone a month. The three of them slept with me that night and the next. By the end of the week, she still had not spoken.

Fletcher's body, minus his left hand, was found half buried in the sand near Port Williams, and I was asked to identify him. I hoped it was him, that the terror his life had caused had ended.

At the morgue, the attendant said, "He still had his wallet on him, and his driver's license showed his name as John Smith."

"Perfect. That would be just like him."

"Well, he's in here, but I warn you he's a mess."

"I just need to see his face."

We walked into the cold room where the bodies were held. There was only one visible, covered by a sheet.

"Ready?"

I nodded.

It was Fletcher. Even though his face was cut and blue, his body drained of blood, I knew it was him. The gray eyes that had once petrified me were now cloudy and vacant. He was gone, totally gone.

I thought I would want to spit on the man who had terrified me and my family—brutalizer, murderer—but I had been changed. Instead, I felt a deep pity for him, his tortured life and horrendous death. There was such irony attached to him. If he hadn't found me and terrorized me, I would not be here in Nova Scotia nor have the money to do so. If he hadn't chased me, I would not now be free—free to say who I really was. I wouldn't have Gus or Maggie or family. I wouldn't have faith in a God I had long denied.

I paid for his burial. Though the marker read John Smith, I knew who he really was and where he was. To this day, I still go by his grave. I don't leave flowers or grieve for him. I thank God for my life.

CHAPTER 69
RECOVERY

Annapolis Royal, Nova Scotia
June 1963

We set the wedding back a month. July 27 would give us time for physical wounds to heal and, I hoped, long enough for Maggie to heal emotionally.

When she finally spoke, her first word was "safe," and before long she was chattering away like a magpie. Her resiliency was nothing short of amazing. There was nothing to be done or said about her kidnapping, especially since she seemed to no longer remember it.

I didn't know how this could be except for the remarkable way I thought the mind of a Down syndrome child worked. It was as though they were born with a "forgiveness gene," and this was what I think she did to survive. She forgave him.

Maggie said nothing and I asked nothing about her abduction, fearing questioning her would cause her to shut down again. I had to accept that we might never know what happened to her or Fletcher.

We called a family meeting to break the news about my identity. It was a difficult conversation, but Gus helped me explain. We did not discuss my wealth or the rape, but everything else was laid on the table. I cried when I told them about Paddy and the burning of my home.

"So what do we call you now?" Robert said. I took note of his thinly veiled sarcasm.

"My name is Tranquil Tandy *and* Desiree d'Moss. I'd like to go by Quil. In a month, you can call me Quil Tandy LeBlanc."

I called Bidwell to tell him about Fletcher and that I was safe. He told me about the break-in and how worried he had been.

"I'm getting married on July 27, please come. I need a few people sitting on the bride's side of the aisle."

"Married!"

"I will explain all later."

He said he would be there.

Then I called the boys' restaurant in Key West.

"I'm in Nova Scotia, and I'm getting married! On July 27. Please come and bring Dot. There will be plane tickets waiting for you in Miami. Say yes. Please say yes."

Michelle was next on the list.

"You disappeared! Where are you?" Michelle said, surprise and demand heavy in her voice.

"I have such a long story to tell you. Come to my wedding, and I will spill it all."

"Your wedding? Where are you?"

"Nova Scotia. The wedding is on July 27. I will send a plane ticket. Coming?"

"Of course."

I hesitated to phone Danny and Libby but realized I couldn't do this without them. I longed to see them. I called the sheriff's office and asked for Danny.

"Danny, it's Quil."

Such a long pause followed that I thought we might have been disconnected.

"Thank God it's you. Libby and I have been so worried. You

disappeared off the face of the earth, and we thought you might be dead. We figured it even possible that you had killed yourself—giving everything away like you did."

"I'm sorry I frightened you, but you were safer if you didn't know me. Fletcher is dead, I'm free, and I'm getting married. I want you and Libby to come. I'll send you tickets."

"Did you kill him?" The cop in Danny needed facts.

"No, but it's a long story. The wedding?"

"Of course we'll come. I won't even have to ask Libby. Oh, and we have a baby."

"That was fast!" I laughed into the phone.

"He's a handsome boy, Quil. We named him Daniel."

"That figures—you're so vain. Bring him, please bring him."

There was nothing to be done for the damaged wedding dress, though Annabelle tried her best. The scar across the satin skirt could be mended but not camouflaged. I knew she was as devastated as I, even though she did her best to hide it.

I didn't know what to do. I spent two days in Halifax shopping for a replacement but found nothing that spoke to me. I did find a fluffy pink dress for Maggie and bought it. *At least she will be wearing a dress.*

A week before the wedding, Annabelle called and insisted I come right over.

When I got there, Annabelle met me at the door, grinning from ear to ear. She hugged me and said, "Close your eyes, and no peeking."

She led me through what I guessed was the kitchen and into the living room, positioning me.

"All right, my daughter, open your eyes."

There hanging over the door was a wedding dress, but not just any dress, it was mine. The damaged skirt was still there but draped with two layers of fabric that made the scar invisible. Soft, sheer, elegant fabric. It was so beautiful I gasped. It was then I realized that Annabelle's new window sheers were gone.

"You didn't!"

"I did."

"It's so beautiful!"

"Let's try it on."

Two days before the wedding I drove into Halifax to meet my friends. Eduardo, Javier, and Dot arrived first.

"Chica, it's you!" the boys sang out in unison.

"Hello, my Persian princess." Dot hugged me.

Bidwell and his wife happened to be on the same flight.

"You are the most amazing woman I have ever met," Bidwell said as he hugged me. "Other than my wife, of course. Quil, meet Janine."

"It is so good to finally meet you," she said, extending a hand. "Bid told me the whole story on the flight from Miami. You should write a book."

We settled in at the airport restaurant and had lunch while we waited for Danny and Libby. An hour later my darling friends walked off the plane carrying nine-month-old Daniel. I ran to meet them.

I housed the Canfields, Michelle, and the Key West gang at the little bed-and-breakfast I had stayed at on my first night in Annapolis Royal. Danny, Libby, and little Daniel came home with me. Maggie was delighted, and Gus was a delightful host.

At the rehearsal dinner the next night, I introduced my friends to my new extended family. We laughed and toasted, played music and danced. When I crawled into bed that night, the last night as a single woman, I thanked God for my life. Though my past would always be a part of my memory, it now had no hatred or pain attached. I wasn't carrying it, Jesus was.

CHAPTER 70
THE WEDDING

Grandville Ferry, Nova Scotia
July 27, 1963

The wedding would be held in the garden behind the little church in Grandville Ferry, where a giant oak sheltered all those attending. The day, warm by Nova Scotian standards, made the shade welcome. Red maple trees lined the garden along with rose bushes, lots of them: white, pink, red, and lavender rose blooms everywhere around the garden. We would stand before three large white rose bushes to say our vows.

Gus's family was in charge of all the decorations and music. I wanted to be uninvolved and completely surprised.

Annabelle helped me dress, and Theodore would be walking me down the aisle. As with Danny and Libby's garden wedding, half the town attended, but the LeBlancs had planned for this with extra chairs.

The hour was upon me. Annabelle and Theodore drove me to the church. Annabelle was ushered to her seat, and soon after Maggie made her entrance—with Rocky, she in her fluffy pink dress and he with a collar decorated with flowers, which he ate as they walked down an aisle of flower petals. I heard the laughter and peeked around the corner of the church. Rocky barked, so pleased with himself, and Gus held out his hand. Obediently, Rocky sat down next to Gus. Maggie, as instructed, stepped to the bride's side. I was happy to see our cat, Priscilla, had opted out.

Dozens of white and gold ribbons tied to all the trees waved leisurely in the breeze, and the fragrance of roses wafted in the air. Magical.

I carried no flowers, I couldn't trump this garden of beauty, though Maggie insisted on a small ring of woven field daisies in her hair. She looked so sweet standing there, her strawberry-blonde curls like a halo all around her.

Marie, Rachel, and Aimee performed music I had never heard them play before. They were playing their fiddles in a way that sounded more like violins, and the music seemed to keep time with the breeze and ribbons rustling through the maples.

"Are you sure you are ready to be a LeBlanc?" Theodore asked me.

"I've never been more certain of anything in my life."

"You look very beautiful, my dear." Theodore offered his arm, and I slipped my hand into the crook of it.

As we stepped around the corner of the church, everyone stood and looked our way. Rocky whimpered twice and howled once, and even I had to laugh a little.

I felt beautiful and so filled with happiness that I thought I might burst. Gus looked at me as though he had never seen anything so lovely. His eyes beckoned me.

The luxurious sheer overlayer on my skirt fluttered around me as I walked, and Theodore did his best not to step on it. The chapel-length veil lifted lightly in the breeze, and I thought the only thing missing was fairy dust.

"Who gives this bride to be wed?" the minister asked.

"Her new family," Theodore said.

And all my friends said in unison, "And so do we!"

More laughter, but I wasn't laughing now. I was lost in Gus's gaze. He offered his hand; I laid mine in it.

"Do you…" The wedding vows began, and we repeated them, never losing eye contact with each other, oblivious of our guests. Then he kissed me, and I kissed him, and he held me for a moment. We were married.

"I give you Mr. and Mrs. Cheshire LeBlanc," the minister said, and everyone stood and applauded.

As I looked at my friends and family, I realized that in less than a month I had come light-years away from my past. I had a life without fear, hatred, and revenge. Jesus had lain his healing hand across my heart like a soothing balm. I was free.

Epilogue

Because I had kept my Tandy identity—birth certificate, driver's license, and passport—secure in Bidwell Canfield's safe, losing Desiree and finding Tranquil was simple. I filed for dual citizenship as Tranquil Tandy-LeBlanc.

On November 25, 1963, two days before my American Thanksgiving, I was beyond astonished when the doctor told me I was pregnant. How could it be that I would be given a second chance? Gus wept, as did I.

Six months later we welcomed a baby boy whom we named Henry Theodore Leblanc. Two years later Henry was joined by a brother, Patrick Cheshire LeBlanc. We adopted Maggie with the blessing of all the LeBlancs—even Robert.

We are happy—so very happy. We winter in Key West at Tandy Cottage while Maggie attends school at the Paddy House. She is seventeen and blossoming into a charming young woman. She loves school and wants to work there someday.

Eduardo, Javier, and Dot have become a part of our extended family, as have Libby and Danny and their six children: Daniel, Kristen, David, Philip, Suzanna and the baby, Quil. They have reopened the fish camp and still call it Tandy's out of respect for my family. The house they built there is large and perfect for a growing family. They are building a new history with my blessing.

Libby gave the T-Bird back to me—not a good choice for the mother of six—and it lives in Key West with Dot and the boys.

Michelle finished her education and is now a women's trauma doctor. She visits us in both Grandville Ferry and Key West. My children call her Auntie Mimi.

Bidwell Canfield is still my lawyer and friend. He and his wife adopted two little girls, sisters ages four and six, who had been orphaned in a failed escape from Castro's Cuba. Being a father has softened the edges on my dear friend. The girls, Leya and Sabine, are charming little girls, and it makes me smile to watch the girls and Bidwell adore each other.

In 1964, I contacted LilaJune Walker to tell her about Fletcher's death, my salvation, and the hope that in the end her prayers for Fletcher had been answered. It seems surreal that both Fletcher and I might have come to know Christ as Savior on the same day, but it's possible. Though we can't know for certain, LilaJune and I choose to believe it happened that way.

Paddy's House is thriving, educating and housing twenty-eight Down syndrome children per school year. Another school is planned to open next year in Tampa and yet another near Jacksonville.

Gus and I never talk about the money that has grown to nearly thirty-three million dollars in the past fifteen years. We live like any average couple, because in the end, money never matters unless you use it to make a difference, and we do.

My faith grows daily, and I thank God for second chances. Do I think about the baby I aborted? Yes. I grieve for that child, but I must believe I will see him or her someday—in the same way I will see Paddy and all the rest of my family.

Jesus is, after all, the God of grace, many chances, and endless forgiveness, for which I am deeply grateful.